The Christmas Eve Letter

Elyse Douglas

COPYRIGHT

The Christmas Eve Letter
Copyright © 2016/2021 by Elyse Douglas
All rights reserved.

"The only reason for time is so that everything doesn't happen at once."
—Albert Einstein

"Time is but the stream I go a-fishing in."
—Henry David Thoreau

"You must remember this A kiss is just a kiss, a sigh is just a sigh. The fundamental things apply As time goes by. And when two lovers woo They still say, "I love you," On that you can rely. No matter what the future brings As time goes by."
—Herman Hupfeld

For Eleonore, who often dreams of The Gilded Age.

The Christmas Eve Letter

CHAPTER 1

Eve Sharland had *Googled* and plotted her course to *The Time Past Antique Shop* the night before, while stretched out on a luxurious four-poster bed at Amy's Bed & Breakfast, fifty miles north of Philadelphia. She left early the next morning and drove under a crystal blue mid-October sky along a quiet, two-lane Pennsylvania road that threaded its way past flaming autumn trees, splashing streams and graceful farmland, spotted with the occasional tractor, red barn and silver silo.

As she approached a roadside farm stand, she slowed down, her eyes widening in wonder, like a kid's. There were giant pumpkins, bushels of colorful apples, jugs of apple cider, and a charming display of apple pies, candied apples, and plain and sugar donuts. Unable to resist temptation, she pulled over and parked. Eve loved all things apples, especially apple pie and apple cider. She mingled with gleeful, reaching children and anxious parents, finally choosing a plain donut, an apple pie, a bag of apples and a quart jug of cider. She poured some cider into a paper cup and drank it while eating the donut, enchanted by the sparkling Sunday morning, the last day of her three-day vacation.

Fifteen minutes later, Eve was back on the road, still sipping cider, excited by the prospect of browsing the antique store just ahead, one of her favorite things to do.

She turned off the road onto a wooden bridge that covered a rocky, gurgling stream, listening to her tires rattle across the old beams. She glanced left as she drove down a low road that led to open farmland and a small town that was visible in the hazy distance.

Minutes later she entered the town of Combs End. She immediately spotted the eccentric little antique shop, nestled under majestic elms and maples, with quiet homes partially hidden behind it.

She turned into the empty parking lot, her tires popping along the gravel, and parked near the front door. She climbed out into a snappy autumn wind and chucked her car door shut. Glancing around, she zipped up her brown leather jacket, pocketed her hands, and then stood back, studying the shop.

On the tiled roof, the battered *The Time Past Antique Shop* sign sat perched precariously, as if the next burst of wind would send it tumbling. The shop itself definitely looked like something out of the past, perhaps circa 1920s or 1930s. It was a small, quaint shop that seemed to lean a bit to the right, as if it were tired and just wanted to take a long nap. The red paint had faded into the old wood and the open window shutters were a sun-bleached blue. Eve stepped over to the filmy, twelve-pane vintage farmhouse windows and peered inside. She saw mantel clocks, vases, watches, a brass spittoon, and an ornate Victorian lamp, its opal, glass ball lampshade hand-painted with roses.

None of it looked particularly inspiring, but the shop was definitely a one-of-a-kind place. The lawn was yellow, the weeds high and rambling, and a flower garden lay wilted and neglected. The weathervane on the roof turned and creaked in the wind like a confused and drunken man. The poor little shop would be lucky to survive the next winter.

Eve removed her cell phone from her jacket pocket and took several photos, thinking she'd post them on *Pinterest* or *Facebook*.

With an ungloved hand, she reached for the cold doorknob and turned it gently. A bell over the pale blue door "dinged" twice as the door screeched open. She entered a dimly lit room that smelled of old wood, dust and a hint of mold. That excited her. These were authentic scents, not artificial sprays, candles or potpourris. This kind of shop was hard to find in our "modern antique" age.

She closed the door and allowed her eyes to adjust from bright sunlight to a place of shadows, where things were hidden, shy of light and waiting to be discovered again. It was so quiet, her ears rang.

"Hello," she said, in a modest voice. "Hello. Anybody here?"

When no one appeared, Eve browsed the rickety-looking shelves and narrow display tables, taking in the vintage jewelry, the shoes, the purses, a candlestick telephone, the baseball cards from 1910, old political campaign buttons, a top hat and, of all things, a corset. *Wouldn't want to have to fit into that,* she thought.

She turned in place and saw an old rocking chair, a wood-burning stove and, hanging on the wall, a large, over-the-mantel Victorian mirror with a subtle green, ornate plaster frame. The glass was slightly scratched, and it needed cleaning, but it was a beautiful piece all the same. Eve moved toward it, seeing herself reflected back, remembering what her ex, Blake, had once said of her: "Pretty but tentative." Why did she remember that? And why hadn't she asked him exactly what he'd meant? All she remembered now was that she'd felt criticized.

Eve would turn thirty on December 17th, and this long weekend getaway was a kind of birthday present to herself. Yes, it was two-months early, but she could never get away in December, the weather was often bad, and her birthday was so close to Christmas that many of her family and friends grouped her birthday together with Christmas. So, she let her friends have a good laugh at her peculiarity, wished herself an early happy birthday and set off on her journey. And, any-way, it was a good excuse to escape from New York and spend some time alone.

Her friends thought she'd get lonely traveling alone, but Eve seldom got lonely when she traveled and ex-plored. In many ways, she preferred it. It allowed her the freedom to follow her whims and fancies, lingering in old book stores and antique shops, when her friends would have been bored, scrolling through their phones or glancing impatiently at their watches.

Eve drifted closer to the mirror and examined her-self. She had a heart-shaped face, a broad forehead, strong cheekbones, and a small chin. Her straight, hon-ey-blonde hair fell loosely around her shoulders. When she was at work, she usually tied it into a ponytail or wrapped it in a bun, but not today. Today, she wanted to feel free. She shook her head and glanced again at the mirror. Her lips were small but full, and her eyes were blueberry blue. When she looked deeply into them, she had to admit she saw a hint of sadness. But she also saw curiosity. Yes, well, she'd always been curious about things.

She stood back and studied her figure. She was 5'6" tall, looking quite slim in her fitted jeans and tight, cream-colored sweater. Her two inch boots added height. The vintage brown leather jacket and dangling, 1960s, red-and-orange hoop earrings added a bit of whimsy. The merlot lipstick was new, something she was trying out. It might be too dark for her coloring.

Eve heard the wooden floor creak. She turned toward the sound.

A slender, elderly woman, wearing a print dress, a long white sweater, Benjamin Franklin spectacles, and white hair piled in a bun on top of her head, squinted a look at Eve. Her face was pale, with a map of lines. She smiled thinly.

"Can I help you?" the woman asked, in a small, shaky voice.

Eve swung the strap of her purse from her left shoulder to her right. "Oh, I was just looking around."

"Well, just keep on looking. My name's Granny Gilbert and I own the place, such as it is."

"It's very unusual," Eve said. "I've never seen one quite like it."

Granny Gilbert pulled a balled-up handkerchief from her sweater pocket and wiped her nose. "Well... it's old, just like me. We don't get many people coming in anymore. We're off the main road and with all this internet business…"

Her voice trailed off as she looked about. She continued. "We'll be closing the shop in a month or so."

"Oh, really?" Eve asked. "Before winter?"

"Yes. My sons don't want it. My daughter has no interest and neither one of my sons' wives care about it, so it's time to let it go."

"How long has the shop been here?"

Granny Gilbert went into a frown of concentration. She adjusted her glasses, calculated, and then looked at Eve from over the rim. "I should know that right off, but I forget sometimes. Age, I guess. Anyway, it's been in the family since 1921, I think. My grandfather opened it."

Eve looked about the place with new respect. "That's a long time. I bet you've had some nice pieces over the years."

"Oh yes…"

Granny Gilbert stood up a little straighter with sudden pride. She lifted her quivering chin and blinked slowly. "We once sold a gold watch to Harry Truman."

Eve's eyes widened. "President Harry Truman?"

"One and the same," Granny Gilbert said, and then her face wrenched in distaste. "My father didn't vote for him, you know, but he sold the President that gold watch. He was a businessman first, despite his political beliefs. Well, anyway, Truman said his grandfather had had a watch just like it. It was all the talk of the county back then. Me, my father, and the President himself, we all had our pictures in the Sunday paper."

Granny Gilbert searched the walls. "It's around here someplace, framed on some wall, but I don't know where. Maybe I gave it away. Maybe it's tucked away in some box."

"Do you live nearby?" Eve asked.

Granny Gilbert pointed right. "I live with my daughter just up a spell from here. I just happened to see your car parked in the lot, so I came down. You look around and see if there's anything you want. It'll all be gone in a couple of months. I'll give you a good price."

"Thank you. I won't be long."

With a deep sigh, Granny Gilbert eased down in a rocker. "Take all the time you want. I've got nothing but time, and not much to do with it except to wait on it, while it waits on me; one old buzzard staring down another old buzzard."

Eve gave a half smile, thinking Granny was rather poetic. Eve wandered, looking at jewelry and lamps, picking through a rack of sweaters and blouses.

"You all alone?" Granny Gilbert asked.

"Yes... alone."

"Not married, a pretty girl like you?"

"I was."

"Didn't take?"

Eve didn't look at the woman. "No... it didn't take."

"How long were you married?"

Eve inhaled a little breath. Granny Gilbert was certainly nosey. But then, as she'd just said, she had nothing but time.

"We were married a little over two years."

The woman rocked and made a tsk-tsk sound. "Well, that is just too bad. It seems that kids today don't stay married all that long. Me and Pappy, my deceased husband, were married over fifty years. He ran this place for a long time. Do you have any children?"

"No. We were going to wait."

"Wait for what? What was there to wait for? The clock just keeps on ticking."

Eve moved to the back of the room, drawn by an art deco-style side table. "This is nice," Eve said, hoping to distract the woman from her one hundred questions.

"Yep, that is nice. You can have it for a good price."

Eve found a chest of drawers. She opened the top drawer and gently rummaged through old newspapers and a stack of *Look Magazines* from the 1950s.

"Where are you from?" Granny Gilbert continued, her voice louder, as Eve searched the rear of the shop.

"New York. I live in Manhattan."

"Lord have mercy, that's a big place, with so many people. I was there once or twice, but it was just too busy, with too many people going every which way. It just made my head spin."

"Yes, it's busy all right."

"Do you work?"

"Yes. I'm a Nurse Practitioner."

"Oh, a nurse."

Eve turned so she could be heard. "A Nurse Practitioner is a little different from a nurse."

"What's the difference?"

"It takes more education."

Granny cleared her throat. "Do you have to have some kind of big degree?"

Eve breathed in her impatience. "Yes, a master's degree and advanced training in diagnosing and treating disease."

"My word! Do you work in a hospital?"

"No, I work part time in a doctor's office and part-time at a women's clinic."

Eve paused to look at a row of pocket watches. One caught her eye. Her grandfather had always dressed so smartly, and he always carried a pocket watch. Eve picked it up and examined it. She held it up to her ear to see if it was running. It wasn't, of course, but before she could study it further, her eyes settled on a lady's gold, heart-shaped pendant watch with gold filigree and pearls on the front. She'd never owned a pendant watch. It might be fun. She opened it gently and took the manual wind between two fingers, wondering if the watch was in working order.

"Granny Gilbert, does this watch work?"

Granny Gilbert looked up over her glasses. "Bring it here and let me see."

Eve did so.

Granny narrowed her eyes on it. "Yes, I think so, and it's a beautiful piece of jewelry. We got this watch from an estate auction about six months ago. It's of 1880 or 1890 vintage, and it's solid 14K gold. It's attractive, isn't it? I know all this because I almost sold it to a dealer a month or so ago. But he didn't want to pay the price."

Granny paused, studying it in greater detail. "Look at the intricate filigree design, and the pearls. And there are no dents in it, and the hinged covers are tight. My daughter did some research on this watch. The heart shape is rare."

Eve ran her fingers along the edge. It was a beautiful watch. She'd never seen anything like it. "How much?" Eve asked.

Granny Gilbert's eyes shifted in calculation. She pursed up her lips in thought. "Give me four hundred bucks and it's yours. Now that's a bargain. I'm selling it cheap because I think you'd appreciate it. Now that's three hundred dollars less than I proposed to that dealer."

Eve stared at the watch. She turned it over. That was a lot of money, and Eve didn't really know anything about watches. But it spoke to her somehow. It seemed special. Eve wasn't rich, but she wasn't poor either.

"I'll think about it," Eve said.

Granny frowned. "All right, you can have it for three hundred."

"I'll take it," Eve said.

"You got it for a steal," Granny Gilbert said, with some irritation.

Minutes later, Eve drifted deeper into the rear of the shop, exploring the shadows, moving wicker chairs and a 1950s style end table, stepping over a pile of old magazines. She sneezed, wiped her nose with a tissue, and then noticed the faint outline of something on a nearby shelf.

She stepped gingerly toward it. Standing next to an old typewriter was a lantern. Why Eve was drawn to it, she didn't know. She angled toward it, reached, grabbed the ring handle and lifted it, surprised by its weight. She stepped back and blew off a layer of dust, holding the lantern away from her as she examined it. It was twelve inches high and made of iron, with a tarnished green/brown patina. It had four glass windowpanes with wire guards, and an anchor design on each side of the roof.

Eve stared in rapt fascination. She liked the sturdy feel of it, and she liked the design. It was elegant and old—wonderfully old. Where had it come from? Who had owned it? How did it get to Granny Gilbert's little broken-down shop?

Eve decided to try to slide one of the panes open to look inside. With a gentle push up, a panel opened. Eve spotted something inside, blocking the wick. She moved back toward the light to get a better look. To her utter surprise, she saw what looked like an envelope wedged behind the pane. Intrigued, she lifted the lantern, peered in and tugged at the edge of the envelope. With a little effort, it slid out. It was a cream-colored envelope, glazed with dust and soot.

Eve found a tissue and wiped the dust away. But why would an envelope be wedged into an old lantern? Excited, she turned the envelope over to see the addressee. When she read the name and address, she gasped. It was impossible! She narrowed her eyes and read again, but the letters seemed to swim around on the page. Eve drew back and dropped the envelope.

"Everything all right?" Granny Gilbert called.

Eve stood in shadow, frozen, staring down at the letter, now illumined by a stray shaft of morning sun. The minutes ticked by. Reluctantly, slowly, carefully, as if it might bite her, Eve leaned over and picked up the envelope and straightened. With a pained expression, she read the address again. It was hand addressed, written in a beautiful calligraphy script, to Evelyn Sharland in New York City.

That was Eve's name. Sharland was her maiden name—she'd never taken Blake's last name. The letter was addressed to her!

A shiver ran up her spine. She swallowed hard. She saw a 2 cent stamp with a profile of George Washington she'd never seen before. To her complete astonishment, she also saw that the postmark circle read,

**New York, New York Main Post Office,
December 24, 1885, 3 p.m.**

CHAPTER 2

Eve lowered herself into a wicker chair, her eyes fixed on the unopened 6 x 8 envelope, her heart racing, her hand trembling. She stared at nothing for a time, and then her eyes traveled to the lantern that lay on the floor beside her, and then back to the envelope she held in her hand.

Coincidence? Of course it was. What else could it be? But Sharland was not a common last name. Shaken, she took a minute to gather herself. Gradually, her pulse slowed, and her thoughts began to clear. Of course the letter wasn't addressed to *her*. It was addressed to someone with her name.

An electric thrill ran through Eve's body as she pictured actually opening the letter and reading its contents. What could it possibly say?

"Are you okay?" Granny Gilbert called.

Eve turned her head. "Yes… Yes, okay," she said, distractedly.

Should Eve show Granny the letter? Yes, of course she should. She had found it in her shop. Granny might have some idea where it came from and how it got there. But what if Granny didn't want to sell the letter? What if she wanted it for herself? Eve pondered this, focused again on the name and address: Evelyn Sharland, 232 East 9th Street, New York, New York.

As Eve held the envelope, it seemed to burn her fingers. She had the sharp impulse to open it right then and there. But she didn't. She lifted herself from the chair, picked up the lantern and walked over to Granny Gilbert, who was still in her rocker, reading an article in an old magazine. Eve couldn't see the cover, just the yellowed pages and the black and white photos.

"See anything you like?" Granny asked, looking up, noticing the lantern at Eve's side.

Eve hesitated. "Actually, I did find a couple of things. Little things," and Eve stressed the word *little*.

"Where did you get that lantern?" Granny asked, her eyes falling on it with shiny interest.

Eve pointed. "Back there, behind some things. It's quaint, isn't it?"

Granny scratched the end of her nose. "I don't remember ever seeing it, and I thought I knew everything in this place."

"How much?" Eve asked.

Granny reached for it. Reluctantly, Eve handed it over.

"Good weight," Granny said. "Looks in good shape. I suppose it's about a hundred years old. Maybe older."

"It uses kerosene, I guess," Eve said.

"Yes, I'm sure it does."

Granny scrutinized it. "It's a good piece. I like it. I could hang it on my back porch. It would be comforting out there."

Eve took in a sharp breath. "I would like to buy it," Eve said, more forcefully than she'd intended.

Granny glanced up at her. "You would?" Granny adjusted her glasses, speculating. "Well, you did find it, after all."

Granny looked first at the lantern and then back at Eve. "I'll just have to rummage around back there and see if I can find another one like it."

Eve had the letter in her right hand, behind her back. She was still fighting with herself whether she should show it to Granny.

"Anything else?" Granny asked.

Eve made a vague gesture toward the rear of the shop. Her gaze was direct for a moment and then drifted away. With a little sigh, she presented the letter.

"I also found this. It's just an old letter."

Eve was not about to tell her she found the letter in the lantern, and that the lantern and the letter went together. She just couldn't bring herself to be that forthcoming.

Granny's face brightened again. "An old letter? Oh, let me see," she said, with girlish excitement.

Grudgingly, Eve handed it over.

It was obvious that Granny Gilbert loved old things. Her thin and peering face lost years as she brought the smudged envelope up to her eyes for close examination. Her voice took on strength and emotion. "Well, my stars, won't you look at this? It's postmarked December 24, 1885. I wonder where on Earth it came from? I have never seen it. No, not ever."

"Probably just a laundry list of things to do or some boring business thing," Eve said, already reaching for the envelope.

Granny raised her eyes. "No, I don't think so. It's addressed to a woman, a Miss Evelyn Sharland in New York, New York. Well, how about that? And look who it's from: John Allister Harringshaw II, on Fifth Avenue. He sounds important, doesn't he?"

The room was quiet for a time. Eve heard a distant lawnmower and a dog barking. The envelope claimed Granny's complete attention for a good minute, as she turned it over and over, her eyes softening on it. Eve saw a delicious gleam of curiosity forming in Granny's eyes.

Eve had to act fast or Granny would never sell Eve the letter.

"So how much for the lantern and the letter, Granny Gilbert?"

Granny lifted her eyes, staring at Eve's outstretched hand.

Eve swallowed away a dry throat.

Granny's attention left the letter and began to travel around the shop.

"I will miss this shop, you know. It's been in my life for nearly eighty-five years. I played here when I was a girl. I have so many good memories about this place. So many. Did you know that I kissed my first boy in this shop? That was about 1938. I was seven years old and Billy Tyler was nine. The place was so much nicer then. Clean and cared for, not so dusty and rickety as it is now. I was hoping I wouldn't be the last. I was hoping I wouldn't have to close it and sell off all the items to somebody I don't know. But life goes on and old things, like me and all the items in this shop, must go, mustn't they? It's the way of things, I suppose."

Eve liked Granny Gilbert, and part of her would have loved to sit and listen to her many stories about the shop; but the larger part of Eve wanted that letter, and she was worried that Granny wasn't going to sell it to her.

Granny bantered on. "All the items in this shop have so many stories to tell, you know. People owned these things and put them in their homes and their pockets and passed them on to their wives and lovers and children. Then, bang. Life happens. The world changes, somebody dies or gets divorced; someone loses all their money and their house, or their watch and their wedding ring and all their jewelry. And then guess what? Some of those items wind up here. Right here in my little shop. Isn't that something? All the energy—the love and the hope—gets stored up in these items and, if one could read the code locked inside them, well, what great epic stories they would tell."

Granny's eyes were staring off into distant worlds. She took off her glasses, reached for a wrinkled handkerchief from her sweater pocket and wiped them absently. "Yes... what great stories they could tell." She put her glasses back on.

Eve nodded. "Yes, I'd love to hear those stories. I love the feel of old things, and the smells. I love the mystery and I love to speculate about the lives that owned a watch or a ring or a lantern or an old unopened letter."

Granny looked down at the letter again. "I would love to know what is in this letter, young lady. Yes, indeed I would."

Eve's eyes came to the letter.

"Maybe we should open it now?" Granny said, conspiratorially. "Maybe we should read it together?"

Eve nibbled on her lower lip. She slowly shook her head. "I don't think so." Eve struggled for words. "It seems personal somehow. I'd like to buy it and then open it alone. Would you mind?"

Resigned, Granny bowed her head. "All right then. You found it and you want to buy it. So you shall have it."

Eve sighed, audibly. "Thank you, Granny. How much?"

Granny laughed a little. "Give me thirty dollars for the lantern. The letter I'll give you free, on one condition. You must promise to call and tell me what's in it. Will you do that?"

Eve nodded. "Of course. Yes, of course I will."

Granny pointed a stern finger at her. "Be sure you do. I want to hear everything and anything you might learn about these people, because I am sure you will try to find out who they were. I think I can read that much in you."

Eve reached for one of the shop's business cards. She smiled. "I promise I'll let you know everything."

"All right then. I suppose you'll be paying by credit card?"

"Yes." Eve fumbled in her purse for her wallet.

Granny Gilbert gave the envelope one last, longing look and then handed it back to Eve.

"Did you see any other letters back there?" Granny asked, her voice filled with hope.

"No, just this one."

Granny took off her glasses and gently wiped her eyes. "I wonder where it came from and how long it's been here. I should know that. I should have known it was here. Well, I am time grown old and that's what happens."

Granny pushed herself up. "Okay, let me run your card."

GRANNY STOOD IN THE DOORWAY and waved as Eve drove away in the bright autumn sunshine. After Eve's car had drifted away under the distant red and yellow leaves, Granny Gilbert strolled out into the parking lot, turned, placed her hands behind her back and took in *The Time Past Antique Shop*. Her eyes misted as she recalled old conversations, old transactions and old memories. It would be gone soon, just like she would.

That young lady had taken a piece of the shop with her, and that was a good thing. She knew Eve appreciated the items and would make good use of them. Perhaps the items she'd purchased, the heart-shape pendant watch, the lantern and the letter, would live on for many more years. Perhaps that mysterious letter would even wind up in a museum someday. Who knows?

Granny Gilbert turned to face the empty road. She hoped the young woman would call and tell her what was in the letter. Granny laughed. She felt girlish again. Maybe it was a love letter?

Then something struck Granny. Something that had been gnawing away at her for several minutes. What was it? When the realization struck, Granny stood bolt erect. She arched an eyebrow, feeling her breath catch in her throat.

"It was the name," she mumbled to herself in astonishment. "The name on the credit card. Evelyn Sharland, the same name as the name on the old envelope. Evelyn Sharland."

Granny shivered. It had taken her old brain too long to realize the coincidence, and now the woman was gone forever. No wonder Eve had felt so strongly about owning that letter and opening the envelope in secret.

Granny turned back to face the shop and focused on it, as if she'd awakened from a nap.

"Imagine that," she said into the cool autumn wind. "The same name. How could that be? My word, what a wonder this world is."

CHAPTER 3

Eve arrived back in New York a little before 6 p.m., seeing the great city rise up in glass, steel and stone. After returning the car to the rental drop-off garage, she started for home, which was only two blocks away. She propped a bag with her purchases on top of her brown leather overnight case, whose wheels growled across the sidewalk, and walked briskly, anxious to get home to open the letter and read its contents. All day long, she'd stopped herself from tearing the thing open and reading it, wrestling with curiosity and apprehension as she drove the back roads of Pennsylvania and then onto the highway. She constantly threw darting glances at the letter that lay on the seat next to her, like it was a living, breathing thing. But she'd disciplined herself. She had waited—even as she ate a late lunch at a pancake house—and it had been pure agony.

Eve pressed ahead, dodging families and dogs and people leaving restaurants. She felt feverish with expectation as she marched toward her apartment, the envelope pushed deeply into her purse.

As soon as she'd driven away from Granny's shop, Eve had decided she wanted to have a kind of ceremonial letter opening. Some kind of ritual, although she wasn't sure why. It was just a feeling. After all, the letter was a hundred and thirty-one years old. It might have historical significance. All the more reason to open the envelope carefully. She had an antique letter opener that she loved, a birthday gift from her mother. That would be the perfect tool. Eve would patiently and lovingly open the letter with it.

Eve arrived home and swung through the heavy, wrought-iron gate that led up the six steps to the heavy oak front door. The twenty-foot wide brownstone, built in 1895, was on West 107th Street, a quiet, tree-lined street. Eve's second floor, one-bedroom apartment had polished wood floors, a modern kitchen, a large bedroom, a small dining-room and bay windows that looked out on 107th Street through lacey yellow curtains.

Once inside, Eve parked the lantern and her suitcase in the living room near the marble fireplace, swung out of her jacket and tossed it on the burgundy leather, winged chair. She made a call to her friend Joni and left a message.

"Hey, Joni, I'm home. You can bring Georgy over whenever. See you soon."

Georgy was her half-beagle, half-springer spaniel, but he looked more like a Dalmatian, with white hair and black spots on his coat, paws and face.

At the oak dining table, Eve paused, reached into her purse and drew out the letter. She stared at it with new wonder and speculation playing across her face. What a find. What a treasure.

The letter had obviously never been opened. But it was postmarked, so John Allister Harringshaw had mailed it. Did Evelyn Sharland ever receive it? Perhaps she had, but why had she decided not to open it? Perhaps the letter was kept from her. By whom and, again, why? Maybe Evelyn never even knew that Mr. Harringshaw had sent it. Again, why?

On the other hand, maybe the letter had simply been misplaced. But how did it wind up in an old lantern? That made no sense at all, unless someone wanted to hide it. The glass panes were smudgy. Perhaps that would have been the perfect place to hide it.

Maybe Evelyn had received the letter but was forced to hide it in the lantern and then, for some reason, she never had the chance to retrieve it. So how did that lantern wind up at *The Time Past Antique Shop*?

So many questions. So many wonderful possibilities.

Eve glanced down at her phone and frowned. She had many texts she hadn't answered; a lot of emails she hadn't responded to. No doubt, most were from work. Even though her clinic calls had been forwarded to a colleague, there were always questions only she could answer. With a deep sigh, she laid the letter aside on the table and reached for her phone.

A half hour later, Joni, a perky, coppery redhead who reminded many people of a young Liza Minnelli, arrived with a barking Georgy, straining on his leash. Joni released him and he charged into Eve's open arms. She kissed his head and hugged him to her chest while he whimpered and licked her face, happy to be home with his best friend.

As Eve fed Georgy, she briefly summarized her trip for Joni, not mentioning the letter because she knew Joni would get intrigued and insist on seeing the contents. She wasn't ready to share it with anyone else just yet. Joni quickly told her about the two Broadway auditions she'd had, but didn't get cast for, and then dashed away to meet her boyfriend at the movies.

When Georgy was finally settled in his checkered bed near the fireplace, Eve reached for her cell phone and called her mother. She described the B&B she'd stayed in, told her about the heart-shaped pendant watch, and then shifted the conversation in a new direction.

"Mom, has there ever been another Evelyn Sharland in the family?"

"I don't know. Your father was into all that when he did our family tree a couple years ago. And I'm still pushing him to see if my side of the family is related to Jane Austen. You remember my great grandmother was an Austen?"

"Yes, Mom, of course I remember."

"Well, I wish your father would finish his search, but then you know your father. I don't know how he ever got to be an FBI agent. He never finishes anything. He still hasn't finished painting the second-floor bathroom that he started two months ago. We got into this big argument about it the other day and he told me he was going to disappear and go into the witness protection program if I didn't stop nagging him about it."

Eve tried to break in, but her mother kept ongoing.

"But, anyway, I'm sure we're related to the Austens. I just feel it. I'm reading *Mansfield Park* again. You read that one, didn't you?"

"Yeah, probably three times. Mom, is Dad there? Can I talk to him?"

"He's watching football, Eve, and you know he doesn't like it when I disturb him during a game."

"Please, Mom. Tell him I need to talk to him. It's important."

Eve's mother heard the tension in Eve's voice. "Are you all right? You sound stressed."

"I'm fine. Please, Mom, just ask Dad to come to the phone."

Eve heard her mother sigh into the phone. "All right… Just a minute."

Moments later, Eve's father was on the phone, his voice sounding impatient.

"Eve, how are you? What's so important? I've got the game on, the Steelers and Raiders. It's a helluva game. What do you need to know?"

"Dad, when you were doing our family tree research, did you find another Evelyn Sharland?"

There was a pause. Eve could hear the TV in the background and her mother's Pug dog, Jasper, barking his head off, and her mother yelling at him to shut up.

"Yeah, there was an Evelyn Sharland. Don't you remember? I told you about her. If I remember right, she was your great grandfather's younger sister, but then I could be wrong about that. I think there was a brother in there somewhere too."

Eve felt goose bumps on the back of her neck. "Is that who I'm named after?"

"No, we didn't know about her when you were born. Your mother just liked the name Eve. I wanted to name you Sally or Karen or Efrem Zimbalist, Jr," he said with a chuckle.

"Who?"

"You know, the actor who was in the FBI television series back in the 60s and 70s. You gave me the DVDs for Christmas two years ago. Remember?"

"Yeah, yeah," Eve said, dismissively. "How long ago did Eve Sharland live? What year?"

"Oh, I don't remember that. Why are you so interested in this all of a sudden?"

Eve wasn't ready to say. And as much as she loved her parents, her mother was an Olympic gossiper.

"I'm just curious. Can you look it up?"

"Now!?" her father, exclaimed. "Eve, the game's on, for crying out loud."

"Okay, okay. Did she get married? Have kids?"

"I don't remember, Eve. It was over a year ago. I'll look it up in the next couple of days and call you back."

Disappointed, Eve agreed.

AS EVENING DREW ON and darkness filled the room, Eve still hesitated to open the letter. Opening it would be like opening a present at Christmas. Once the present has been opened, the magic is gone. To Eve, the joy of Christmas had always been the anticipation, the waiting, the speculation and the surprise. This letter was even more than that. It was a vast, mysterious window into the past—perhaps even into her own past.

She glanced over at Georgy, whose one attentive brown eye was watching her.

"What do you think, Georgy?"

He shut both eyes, sighed, and buried his head deep into the curve of his bed.

"Thanks, buddy. I know, I know. Don't bother me."

Eve took a shower, wrapped herself in a white terry robe, and ordered seafood pasta from a restaurant nearby. While waiting for it to be delivered, she set the scene for her ritual. She washed the four glass panes on the lantern and placed it on the emerald green enameled hearth of her non-working fireplace. She set it in front of a wrought iron candelabra that held ten large candles. After she lit them, she noticed that the lantern looked strangely mysterious and bewitchingly beautiful in candlelight.

She opened a bottle of Sauvignon Blanc, poured a glass, and placed it on the end table near a winged chair that she had placed in front of the fireplace. She placed the letter next to the glass. After her dinner arrived, she settled in the chair, tucking her legs beneath her and eating slowly, savoring the flavors and the wine, contemplating this odd day. It had been just the kind of day she loved, filled with adventure, unpredictability and mystery. And now there was this bizarre experience, this letter addressed to someone with her own name from a previous century. She hoped she wouldn't be disappointed; that the envelope didn't contain just an invoice.

What else should the letter ceremony include? she thought, smiling at herself for creating such a dramatic scene. Wine, candlelight… ah, she must have music.

It was 9:30 when Eve finally got up, powered up her laptop and found the music she thought appropriate for the ceremony: Baroque music, Handel. She chose cello, piano and violins—those seemed right. She lowered the volume and turned toward her chair. The room seemed deliciously quiet and private, bathed in a soft, mellow, candlelight glow.

She returned to the chair and reached for the glass of wine. She lifted her glass in a toast to the lantern and then to the letter. She took another sip before reaching for the mother-of-pearl handle on her antique, sterling silver letter opener.

She set her wine glass aside and haltingly picked up the envelope, looking at it with an entranced expression. The music was soft and elegant; the room cast in a soft trembling glow; Eve's pulse was strong in her ears.

With the greatest of care, Eve inserted the tip of the letter opener under the seam of the flap. Gently, she nudged at it. Surprisingly, after all the years, it did not release easily. It seemed to resist, as if not wanting to give up its old secrets.

She looked at Georgy. He was sound asleep. Joni had probably taken him jogging with her. He'd be out for hours.

Eve inhaled a breath and again tried to open the letter by releasing the flap. She did not want to open it from the top. That might damage it. In any case, if it had historical significance, it seemed better to open the flap. Slowly, carefully, and persistently she worked, and the seam gradually began to release. When she was halfway across, she paused. She felt sweat beads on her under lip, felt her heart kicking in her chest. Her hand trembled and the palm of her hand was clammy.

Finally, with a gentle flick of her hand, the flap released and Eve saw the yellow ribbon of glue that had kept it sealed for all those years.

Her eyes widened and excitement bloomed in her, a kind of exhilaration she'd never felt before. Eve replaced the letter opener on the side table and, with a certain reluctance, she touched the open flap with her index finger. It was as if she were opening an Egyptian tomb or a sealed jar that contained *The Dead Sea Scrolls*.

She lifted the flap and drew in a sharp breath. Two fingers felt for the edge of the letter. Now, all she had to do was lift the letter from the envelope and read.

Eve paused as hundreds of thoughts played in her head. One hundred "what ifs" and one hundred possibilities.

With great care, Eve drew out the letter. It was six pages, written on a rich, cream-colored stationery bond. Amazingly, the paper wasn't tarnished by age. It appeared as if the letter had been written a week ago and not in 1885. Eve laid the envelope aside and turned her full attention to the letter. It had been folded once. She ran her finger along the crease and opened it.

She lowered her eyes to the page and shivered as she began to read. The hand that wrote the letter had taken great care to make each word legible. It was elegantly penned with swooping capital letters, dots directly over the i's, the t's perfectly crossed. But it was the letter itself that drew Eve's complete and focused attention. It seemed to radiate with life, and energy, and an ineffable vitality that drew Eve into its old, mesmerizing world.

Harringshaw House
644 Fifth Avenue
New York
24 December 1885

My Dearest Evelyn,

Your recent letter has opened my eyes to the tragic wrong course of action I pursued, believing that propriety and good conscience demanded it. I now regret it with all my heart. All night and most of the day I have been pacing my floor, fully engaged in an agonizing struggle that has filled me with self-loathing, and left me stunned with grief and longing.

I will not attempt to excuse myself, for I do not deserve your forgiveness or your gentle love. I will only say that I was myself deceived by my own feelings, believing that I could never offer you marriage because of my station in life, as well as my duty to my family and my business.

But now I clearly see that my failure to propose marriage arose from my own weakness of character, from an immature notion of courage, and from pure and simple ignorance. I had mistakenly believed that no matter how congenial we were together, I could not turn my back on society and my family's wishes and, therefore, we could not marry and have the happiness we both so richly wished for.

Our closer intimacy should have proved my error, but my dearest girl, I am afraid I was blinded by fear, by society and by my ambition. I was unable to imagine all the extravagant possibilities of the life we could have had together. Mine was an imperfect love. May

God forgive me, dear Evelyn. You say you never coveted a life of luxury and you would be content to live in poverty, so long as you and I could remain together, always happy and in love. Forgive me, dearest Evelyn, for I lacked your strength, courage and fortitude. I lacked your good and true love, and your good and compassionate heart, and for that I shall never forgive myself.

If I could but turn back the clock to live again those most cherished hours, I would surely do so without a moment's hesitation. But, alas, time moves on at its relentless pace and what is done is done.

Now you lie on your deathbed and there is nothing I can do to change all the misery of my selfish mistakes. Please, dear girl, know that I tried to come to you, and hired the best doctor in Manhattan to attend you at your bedside, but your mother rejected all my attempts with anger and frankness of word. She threatened to call the police and expose my family to scandal. When I told her I didn't care what she did to me or to my family, and then further made strong demands to see you, she told me you did not want to see me. She told me that you hated me and that you did not ever want to see my face again, either in this world or the next.

That, of course, shattered my heart and broke my spirit. She said you and I were finished and that you no longer loved me. I beseeched her, repeatedly, to forgive me and to let me see you, or at least to let my doctor see you, but she declined all my pleadings.

Your brother blocked my way with his two friends, cursing me and threatening bodily harm. That did not frighten me in the least. At that point, I did not care what happened to me. But I saw that it was futile. I could not break past them to get to you, and so I took some well-deserved blows from them and then was knocked to the ground. And so I have finally failed you once again, but for the last time.

How will I bear your leaving this Earth, dear Evelyn? Damn this illness, this consumptive fever that has overcome you. How will I bear your leaving this troubled world? How will I bear facing all my transgressions once you have left this Earth? What will I do with this full and loving heart that beats love and desire for you when you are gone?

Again, I simply and humbly ask your forgiveness and I tell you, with a true and full heart, that I love you and will love you for all eternity, whether that love is returned or not; for you, Dear Evelyn, have shown me that love is not only possible and real, but that love is always the final and only choice in this life.

So as a last resort, I have sent you this letter, trusting in merciful God that you will receive it and read its contents. I pray that you pass from this world into the next knowing in full measure that I love you and I always will. I pray to that most merciful God that your mother will have the kind-heartedness to deliver this letter to you.

You told me in your last letter that you still have the lantern. How that touched me, Evelyn. How that moved me to tears. If health permits, please light the lantern once more, the lantern that first revealed your angelic face to me on that wretched snowy night, and then read this letter again, and think of me kindly. Remember the good and pleasant times we had together;

recall the sequestered timeless minutes when I held you in my arms and recollect the tender kisses. Evelyn, pray to God that he will allow us to be together again, either in this world or the next, and that our good and true love will then be blessed and come to full flower.

The light from the lantern will forever symbolize our eternal and unceasing love. Please, dear Evelyn, please light the lantern and remember me with forgiveness, and with compassion and love in your heart.

And know this, Dear Evelyn. One day I will find you in that other, more just, perfect and loving world, and then we will live together in that most beautiful and gentle abode. I know it. I believe it, because love will somehow bring us back together again and make all wrongs right.

Until then, I am, ever your servant, your friend and your own true love,

John Allister Harringshaw II

Eve lifted her eyes from the page and stared ahead, at nothing. The letter's impact had moved her to tears.

The sentiment and the prose were flowery and emotionally embellished, but the letter was, after all, written in the language and style of 1885. But the impact was the same. The man was emotionally distressed at losing the love of his life, and Eve felt it in every agonized and flowery word.

Eve looked down at the lantern—the lantern that probably hadn't been lit since 1885.

Evelyn had almost certainly never received John's letter, so she had never lit the lantern. Perhaps she was too sick by that point. Perhaps she had even passed away and the letter and the lantern were lost until Eve found them in Granny Gilbert's antique shop.

Evelyn Sharland most surely died not knowing how sorry John Harringshaw was or how much he loved her. How sad, Eve thought. How very sad.

CHAPTER 4

M onday was a blur of activity. Eve saw patients every twenty minutes, performed annual physicals, e-mailed prescriptions, studied blood work and EKG reports, listened to the familiar complaints of regular patients and, at the end of the day, she took a throat culture on a 6-year-old boy who screamed and fought her all the way.

Eve struggled to stay on schedule and not keep patients waiting more than five or ten minutes. In other words, it was a typical crazy, busy Monday. Before meeting two college friends for a late birthday dinner, she called Joni to make sure she took Georgy Boy for his afternoon romp in the park.

At their favorite bistro on the Upper West Side, Eve and her friends sipped red wine while eating French onion soup and burgers. Eve recounted the highlights of her 3-day trip and her experience with Granny Gilbert at the antiques shop. She proudly showed off the heart-shaped pendant watch and told her friends about the lantern, but she didn't tell them about the letter. She sensed that discussing it would diminish its impact on her, and she wanted to savor the experience by herself for a while, until she had learned more about Harringshaw and had made a decision as to what she was going to do with it. Since neither of her friends was really interested in antiques, the conversation swiftly moved on to other topics.

Back home, Eve fed Georgy Boy, showered, slipped into a robe and slippers, and powered up her laptop. She lit the candles in the fireplace and sat in her usual chair, laptop poised and ready. Georgy Boy came over and dropped down by her feet, laying his chin on her right foot, something he'd done ever since she'd found him at the animal shelter two years before.

Eve's first search was for Evelyn Sharland, Census 1885. It was a long shot, but why not? She found a Rose Sharland 1873 to 1946. Relative? Not that Eve was aware of.

Eve scrolled down. The only census Eve found was for 1940. No help. Okay, Eve would call her father a little later and remind him to check his research.

Next Eve keyed in John Allister Harringshaw II and waited impatiently while her computer searched. When the page refreshed with the results, she nosed forward. One item caught her eye. Albert Wilson Harringshaw. Eve clicked on the link and waited until it opened. She scanned the page.

Albert Wilson Harringshaw was the son of John Allister Harringshaw I, and older brother of John Allister Harringshaw II.

Eve sat up, her eyes widening, her pulse high. The author of the letter was the younger brother of a more famous—or was it infamous—person? She read on.

Albert Wilson Harringshaw (October 12, 1860–May 7, 1915) was an extremely wealthy American businessman and sportsman, and a member of the famous Harringshaw family. He was known as a Gilded Age playboy, who was often seen with Helen Baxter Price, a well-known actress and reputed prostitute, even though he was engaged to Anne Fulton Hopkins, a prominent socialite, whose family had lost much of their money in land speculations and in the stock market panic of May 1884.

Albert Harringshaw purchased a brownstone for Miss Price in the fashionable Madison Square neighborhood and he seems to have continued the relationship in secret, even after his marriage to Anne Hopkins. There were many rumors and secrets as to the ultimate fate of Miss Price, many accounts having her meeting a younger man and moving to France with him. From there she seems to have quietly fallen into obscurity.

Albert Wilson Harringshaw died on the RMS Lusitania in 1915.

Eve studied the photo of him, caricatured by *Spy* for *Vanity Fair*, 1885. He was dressed dapperly in a white shirt, white bow tie, dark tail coat and trousers, dark waistcoat vest, and top hat. He had been quite handsome, with tawny red-gold hair, a waxed mustache and a devil-may-care look in his shining eyes.

Eve scrolled down and read the biography of the Harringshaw family.

The Harringshaw family is an American family of British origin that was prominent during the Gilded Age. Their success began with the shipping, steel and railroad empires of John Allister Harringshaw I. The family extended their vast fortune into various other areas of industry and philanthropy. John Allister Harringshaw I built a grand mansion on Fifth Avenue in New York City, and luxurious "summer cottages" in Newport, Rhode Island.

Eve searched the link for John Allister Harringshaw II and found it at the bottom of the page. She took a sharp intake of breath and clicked on the link. The page refreshed and a black-and-white photograph of John Allister Harringshaw II looked back at her.

Eve made a little sound of surprise. He looked so alive—so real, staring back at her. The room suddenly fell into a deepening silence, and the quality of light changed as the candles flickered. Eve raised her eyes from the screen and glanced about, as if feeling the presence of someone else in the room. A cool draft made her shiver and she wished the radiator heat would come rattling on. It was cold outside and going down to 42 degrees, or so the weather people had said.

She returned her attention to the laptop and the photograph of John Allister Harringshaw II, enlarging the photo, narrowing her eyes on it, and becoming completely absorbed by it. John Allister Harringshaw II looked back at her with piercing dark eyes and the clean chiseled features and fine sharp nose of an aristocrat. He wore a top hat and tails and appeared to be about thirty years old, maybe older. He was tall, straight and handsome, remarkably handsome, with a natural authority and a stern dignity.

Eve could not picture this man writing the letter that lay on the side table next to her. This man seemed cool, aloof and worldly, perhaps fiercely practical and well-schooled in the art of wealth and privilege. As handsome as John was, Eve was not overly impressed by him. The more she stared into those eyes, the more she felt he was a dark, cold and brooding man. He probably frightened his servants, his clients and any subordinates who worked for him.

Then it struck her. Was this photograph taken after John had written the letter to Evelyn or before? Eve examined the photo caption more closely to see when the photo had been taken. The date was written in small type. December 1885.

Eve swallowed and read his brief biography.

John Allister Harringshaw II was born in New York City in 1854, the second son of John Allister Harringshaw I and Alice Mayfair Gibson. He attended the St. Paul's School in Concord, New Hampshire and Harvard University. For a time, he managed the family estate and became active in real estate development, building several notable New York City hotels, including The Continental Hotel and The Hotel Dickenson.

He was engaged to socialite Elizabeth Ashley Loring, but they never married, and it was speculated that some scandal or the potential for such was the reason, although it never appeared in the press of the day. It has, however, surfaced in two of eight biographies written about the Harringshaw family.

John vanished from business and society for a time (most biographers claim he moved to southern France) while his brother, Albert Wilson Harringshaw, assumed the responsibilities of managing the estate.

John reappeared after his brother's death in 1915 and once again took over managing his family's estate, but he seldom appeared in society and he never married. When he died in 1921 at age 67, his net worth was US $95 million (equivalent to over US $2 billion by today's standards).

The Harringshaw family's prominence lasted until the mid-20th century, when the family's great Fifth Avenue mansion was sold and turned into The Collermore Art Museum.

Eve studied a photo of the Harringshaw mansion and she tried to recall if she'd ever been to The Collermore Art Museum. No, now that she thought about it, she never had. Eve looked up, her face bright with a new idea. She would visit the museum and walk the house where John Harringshaw II and his family had lived. Now that would be an electrifying and novel adventure.

Eve found The Collermore Art Museum website and read about it. It housed exhibitions of European painting and decorative art, as well as some Hudson River Art, American lithographs and watercolors from the New England Watercolor Society, including Winslow Homer and John Singer Sargent.

The museum was open six days a week, closed on Monday.

As Eve sat contemplating her visit to the museum, two thoughts entered her mind. First, she'd promised to call Granny Gilbert and convey the contents of the letter. Second, she wondered if she should contact the Harringshaw estate and let them know she had a letter they might want. Eve was sure she'd get a good price for it.

She closed the lid of the laptop, shut her eyes and heard the radiators pop and hiss. Heat at last.

At ten minutes after 9 o'clock, Eve dialed Granny Gilbert's number and waited as it rang. Five rings later a woman's small, friendly voice answered. It wasn't Granny's.

"Hello, may I speak to Granny Gilbert, please?" Eve asked.

There was a pause. "Who's calling?"

"My name is Eve. I was in the antiques shop yesterday. I have some information I promised to share with her."

Another pause. "I'm Granny's daughter, April. Granny had a stroke last night. She's in the hospital."

Eve straightened. "I'm so sorry. Is it serious?"

"Yes, I'm afraid it is. She's had at least two others this year, but none as serious as this one."

Eve switched the phone to her other ear. "She was so kind to me yesterday. I hope she recovers quickly."

"Thank you. Is there something you want me to tell her?"

"No… no, it's not important. But can I call again in a few days to check up on her? Would that be all right?"

"Yes, of course. That's very nice of you. You said your name is Eve?"

"Yes, Eve Sharland."

"Okay, Eve. Call anytime you wish."

EVE SLEPT RESTLESSLY THAT NIGHT, and when her alarm buzzed at 6 a.m., her quilt was wrapped tightly around her. Georgy Boy came in, tail swinging, and leaped up on the bed, licking her ear and nuzzling her cheek until she unwound herself.

"Okay, Georgy Boy," she said, walking stiff-legged into the kitchen.

Later, as she ate breakfast and sipped her second cup of coffee, Eve wondered again if she should contact the Harringshaw family about the letter. Once again, she decided she wasn't ready to share it with anyone else just yet. The letter seemed sweetly private somehow, and she suspected that John Allister wouldn't want historians nor his descendants to see a letter that was obviously intended for one person only, a person he loved deeply and had probably regretted losing for the rest of his life.

As odd as it seemed, Eve felt like a kind of caretaker, a confidant and, dare she think it? A secret friend. She still felt goosebumps on her neck and arms whenever she realized that only she and John Allister knew the highly emotional contents of his letter.

No, Eve would not contact the Harringshaw family. Not just yet.

EVE HAD THE MORNING OFF from the doctor's office that day, but spent a busy afternoon at the Women's Free Clinic in lower Manhattan. There she worked with two doctors giving routine GYN exams, Pap smears, and HPV testing, as well as counseling women on such issues as family health, emergency contraception and STD testing and treatment. She also spent a half hour with a woman she'd seen before, who'd been beaten by her husband. She was struggling to get herself and her son out of a homeless shelter and into permanent housing. Eve promised to call her social worker to offer any help she could.

At 5:10, Eve piled into a cab and instructed the driver to take her to The Collermore Art Museum at 650 Fifth Avenue. As they pressed through traffic, a ripple of excitement made her restless and she willed the driver to move faster through the clotted rush hour traffic.

When the landmarked building came into view, Eve craned her neck and took in the mansion, with all its Victorian and Gilded-Age splendor. It was a massive structure, built of marble and pink brownstone, with turrets shooting into the sky, mansard roofs, dormer windows, elaborate balconies and rich stained glass. It was difficult to believe that this mansion had ever been anyone's private residence.

Eve paid the cab driver and sprang out, anxious to get inside. She hurried across the walkway, passed through the double glass doors and entered a wide and spacious white marble lobby. She turned in a circle, gazing in awe at the jewel-like stained glass windows, the oak and cherry woodwork, and the ornate decorative stenciling. It was beyond anything she could have ever imagined owning.

She paid the entrance fee and browsed the quiet rooms, stepping lightly across parquet floors, scarcely giving the artwork hanging on the walls a glance, as her imagination expanded, creating scenes of extravagant parties and spectacular dinners, with stylish women dressed in lavish, colorful gowns and men in fashionable tuxedos. She wondered if John Allister had ever brought Evelyn here, but then she dismissed it. Whoever Evelyn was, she obviously did not move in the same circles John Allister did. So what was it about her that had attracted John? He could have had any wealthy and socially connected woman he wanted and, according to the biography, he was, in fact, engaged to someone else. Eve recalled her name: Elizabeth Ashley Loring.

After she'd strolled through most of the rooms, Eve asked a pleasant, gray-haired security guard if there were any paintings of the Harringshaw family. He wasn't aware of any, and a search of her museum brochure confirmed he was right. It was soon closing time and she had to leave.

Outside, under a stormy sky, Eve hailed another cab and started for home, traveling through Central Park. She gazed out at the trees, many of which were already bare. As the sharp wind rattled them, more leaves fell and sailed and scattered like fleeing birds. Again, Eve's thoughts turned to Evelyn. In a strange sort of way, Eve felt a kinship with her. She felt an ineffable longing and sadness for Evelyn, a poor young woman who had fallen in love with a fabulously handsome and wealthy man. How in the world had it happened? How could a poor girl meet such a rich guy back in those days? It was an old story, probably as old as the human race itself: poor girl meets rich boy.

Eve would call her father later to see if he had located the family tree and perhaps then Eve would find out who Evelyn really was. Maybe they *were* related. Wouldn't that be the craziest coincidence?

CHAPTER 5

"IT'S ME, DAD. Did you find the family tree?"

"Yeah, I've got it here. Your mother and I were looking at it during dinner. I'd forgotten a lot of it already."

Eve relaxed in her chair, staring at the letter that lay beside her. The lantern was still on the hearth, candlelight illuminating it. Georgy Boy was lying in his bed near the hearth, the candlelight gleaming in his warm eyes.

"Did you find any information about Evelyn Sharland?" Eve asked, anxiously.

Her father cleared his throat. "Why are you suddenly interested in her? You didn't care at all when I was doing all the research."

"I don't know, Dad. My marriage was in the toilet then and I was working mega hours. I don't know. What did you find out about her?"

Her father cleared his throat again. "Okay, whatever. So Evelyn Sharland was born in 1860 in Concord,

New Hampshire into a Quaker family. They were pacifists and antislavery, among other things. There's not that much here about her except that she seems to have moved to Manhattan in about 1883."

"Why?"

"Don't know why."

"Does it say what she was doing? What kind of work?"

"I'm not sure, but one census in 1884 listed an Evelyn Sharland working for the Western Union Telegraph Company, which was located at 195 Broadway."

"What did it say her occupation was?"

"Telegraph operator."

"Really? I didn't know women could work those jobs," Eve said. "Is there a home address for her?"

"232 East 9th Street."

The same address as the one on the envelope, Eve thought, springing off the couch with rubbery agility, so excited she could barely contain herself. Georgy Boy lifted his head, looking at her with a strange curiosity.

"Did she marry?" Eve asked.

"I don't know. I don't think so. There's not much information on her after 1884."

"Is there any information about her death?"

"There was a letter from a cousin that says Evelyn died from typhoid in 1885 or 1886."

Eve lowered her head. "Typhoid?"

"Yes. She was twenty-five or twenty-six years old. That's about all I have. So when are you coming for a visit? You haven't been home in six months."

Eve sat back down, distracted.

"Eve? Did you hear me?"

"Yes, Dad. I'll be home for Thanksgiving."

Her father's voice dropped into concern. "Have you heard anything from Blake?"

"Blake? Oh, God no, and I hope I never will. That's over, Dad. We're divorced. Why do you keep bringing him up?"

"Well, he calls here sometimes, asking about you."

"Tell him to stop calling. He should have called when we were together instead of running around with that married woman, who, by the way, won't get a divorce now that he's available. Look, I'm sick of thinking about him and I don't want to hear about him anymore. Okay, Dad? We're divorced." She softened her voice. "It's over, Dad."

"Okay, okay… It's just that… Are you seeing anybody?"

"You and Mom must have had one of your long dinner conversations about the kids and the grandkids."

"We just worry about you, Evie, that's all. Why don't you think about moving back down here? Ohio's a good state. You could find a good job here."

"Maybe I will someday. Not now. I like New York and I like where I work. I've made friends here, and now that Blake is out of my life, I feel much better. Stop worrying. I'm fine. I've got to go now, okay? Give my love to Mom. Bye."

Eve made a cup of Earl Grey tea and returned to stare into the candles. She slumped deep into the chair, sure now that she and Evelyn Sharland *were* related. Evelyn was her great grandfather's sister, Eve's distant aunt. With that realization came a thin edge of anxiety, as if the coincidence was just a little too bizarre and way too poignant. The dates of Evelyn's birth and death almost certainly confirmed that she had been John

Allister's true love. When Eve turned to view the letter once again, as it lay on the side table, she felt it was more alive than ever.

Poor Evelyn had died from typhoid fever, probably as a result of drinking contaminated water. Eve had never actually seen a patient with typhoid fever, and she didn't recall the symptoms, so she *Googled* it. As she read, she frowned. Evelyn had not had an easy death. She probably had a persistent fever, as high as 104°F. She would have experienced headaches, loss of appetite, stomach pains, weakness and probably a rash. Diarrhea most likely occurred in the second or third week, in combination with a declining fever. Finally, assuming she had a severe case, she had ulceration and perforation of the intestinal wall which led to death.

Eve closed her laptop and shut her eyes. Could John Allister's doctor have saved Evelyn's life? Probably not. There were no antibiotics in 1885.

What would have happened if Evelyn had never contracted the disease or if she had survived? Would John Allister have risked losing everything and married Evelyn?

According to the letter, he would have.

Eve reached for the letter and read it again, for at least the fifteenth time. What affected her most were two particular paragraphs. Eve read them again, slowly, completely absorbed, her bright eyes taking in each word, as if she were hearing them from John Allister's own trembling lips.

You told me in your last letter that you still have the lantern. How that touched me, Evelyn. How that moved me to tears. If health permits, please light the lantern once more, the lantern that first brought us to-

gether on that snowy night, and then read this letter again, and think of me kindly. Remember the good and pleasant times we had together; recall the sequestered timeless minutes when I held you in my arms and recollect the tender kisses. Evelyn, pray to God that he will allow us to be together again, either in this world or the next, and that our good and true love will then be blessed and come to full flower.

The light from the lantern will forever symbolize our eternal and unceasing love. Please, dear Evelyn, please light the lantern and remember me with forgiveness, and with compassion and love in your heart.

Eve folded the letter, holding the pages loosely in her hand, its words once again having a surprising and powerful emotional effect on her. She thought about the regrets and old actions of her own life, wishing she'd made different choices—at least better choices— one of which was marrying Blake. She regretted that and, oddly enough, she also regretted their divorce, for it signified failure, and Eve did not like to fail. But Blake had been cheating on her. The divorce had been a no-brainer.

Blake had often implied that the failure of their marriage was her fault.

"You're too much scientist and not enough romantic," he'd said to her more than once.

Had that been true? Perhaps she'd never really been in love with Blake. But then why had she married him? She *thought* she was in love with him. Her friends were all getting married and it seemed like it was time for her to, as well. He was a lawyer and she was a nurse practitioner, both professionals. It seemed like a good match. But emotional things had always confused her, and muddled her usually clear, precise thinking. Emotions were unseen things, hard to catalogue things, mixed up and nebulous things. That's why Eve liked science, with its rules, procedures and documentation. Of course there were things science couldn't explain, but, even then, one could analyze, extrapolate or speculate.

Love and emotion seemed to have no rules or practical procedures. During her marriage, Eve had felt like a little sailboat lost in a tossing sea, without help or direction. There were too many feelings she couldn't understand, taking her into uncharted seas.

A few months after she and Blake were married, she began to feel lonely and empty, even when they were together. It was true Eve had been working mega hours, including some weekends and holidays. That certainly hadn't helped the relationship, and it had made her mother question Eve's commitment to the marriage.

"Maybe you just don't want to be with Blake," her mother had said. "Maybe you're working to stay away from him and your marriage. Have you ever thought about that?"

As the weeks and months passed, Eve would look at her husband from across the bed or the kitchen table, or from across a room, and she'd feel an aching in her soul. She felt a cool distance between them that grew wider every week, until they'd become strangers, living together as if programmed in some sterile computer simulation. Their love-making became perfunctory and almost tense. Blake surely wanted more, and that was no doubt the reason he started an affair with another woman. But why a married woman?

"Because she's there for me," was Blake's angry and accusing answer. "Married or not, whenever I need her, she's there for me."

Of course Eve had to accept some blame for the divorce, and after Blake had moved out, she'd stared at herself in the mirror, struggling to understand what made her tick. She'd even tried therapy for a few months.

At one point, her therapist asked her, "Eve, have you ever been in a loving relationship with a man?"

Eve winced at the thought. She didn't like the question. She recalled her sharp answer. "Of course I have," she'd said, no doubt sounding extravagantly defensive.

And of course it was a lie. While she'd had a few relationships in college and one nine-month relationship before she met Blake, none had touched her or moved her, at least not in the way Evelyn Sharland and John Allister Harringshaw had apparently been moved. Eve had never felt that depth of feeling those two must have felt, and this fact made her sad and confused.

Eve blew a sigh from her pursed lips. She wished she could read the letter Evelyn had written to her lover, John Allister. It had moved him to tears, and he didn't look like a man who was emotional or prone to easy tears.

Eve closed her eyes and recalled John Allister's photograph. He had been so very handsome and so very aloof. Eve had often been attracted to aloof men. What did that say about her?

She smiled a little. She wished she could have met John Allister Harringshaw II. If he was anything like the letter he wrote, he was a true romantic, perhaps of the old school. Cool and distant in public but warm and spicy in private. Eve chuckled to herself at the thought. How many men today could write such a tender, romantic and heartfelt letter as John had written to Evelyn?

The tragedy was that Evelyn had never received the letter. She'd never lighted the lantern. She'd never granted the forgiveness John Allister had prayed for, longed for, and asked her for. Consequently, in a very real sense, their relationship had remained incomplete and their love for each other unrequited.

How sad. What a waste of love, in a world where love is so hard to find.

Eve absently fingered the heart-shaped pendant that hung around her throat. She'd forgotten to take it off after she'd arrived home. For some reason, she'd felt compelled to wear it every day since she had bought it. It comforted her somehow.

It made her think of Granny Gilbert. She reached for her phone, touched the number, and waited until she heard her daughter's quiet voice.

"It's Eve Sharland, April. How is your mother?"

"She's a little better. She can't talk easily, but she seems to understand what I say to her."

"I'm so glad she's better," Eve said. She paused for a moment. "April, is your mother well enough for me to read her something?"

"Yes, I think so."

"When I was there the other day, I promised to let her know what was in an old envelope I found at the shop. It was a letter."

"Oh, she'd love that. My mother always loved history and old things. It might cheer her up. Hang on a minute. I'll take the phone to her."

A few minutes later, April was back. "Eve, I told her what you said. She's very excited. I'm going to put the phone to her ear."

Eve spoke slowly. "Granny, it's Eve Sharland. I hope you're feeling better and that you have a speedy recovery."

Eve pressed the phone more tightly into her ear. She heard Granny's small, brittle voice, straining to get the words out. "Thank... you. The letter... read. The letter."

"Yes, Granny. I think you'll find it fascinating."

Granny coughed into the phone and then struggled to speak. "The letter... the same name. You have the same name... Evelyn."

Eve waited, surprised. "Yes, Granny. Yes. We have the same name."

"Read it..." Granny said in a hoarse whisper.

Eve started reading, slowly and carefully pronouncing each word. At this reading, Eve felt the power of the letter even more keenly, felt the sentiment and emotion more intensely. When she was finished, she was quiet for a moment.

"What do you think, Granny?"

Eve waited. "Are you there?"

April came back on the line. "Yes, she's here, Eve. She had tears in her eyes. Hang on a minute, she's trying to tell me something."

Eve adjusted her position in the chair and switched the phone to her other ear.

"Eve... my mother just said, thank you. She said she wished they had had their chance. She said they deserved their chance at love."

"Yes," Eve said. "Tell her I feel the same way. And tell her how much I loved her shop and how much I love the heart pendant watch."

April said, "Granny wants you to find a good man and get married."

Eve laughed a little. "Okay. Tell her I'll work on it."

After Eve hung up, she took in a deep breath, closed her eyes and whispered a little prayer that Granny Gilbert would be returned to health.

Later, after a glass of white wine, Eve sat in her chair, glancing about the living room, smiling with satisfaction. Everything was neat and clean, the bookshelves perfectly arranged, the floors glossy, and the sense of order and tidiness giving her a sense of well-being. Georgy Boy lay sound asleep, his nose twitching. He was probably having a dream, chasing a squirrel or a rabbit. She had a good home, a pleasant and comfortable home. There was only one problem: she was alone. For a while, after the divorce, she'd been content to be alone. Now, it was getting old. Now, the nights seemed longer and emptier. Now, she seemed too secluded and tucked away in some back closet, away from the close touch and intimate whisper of a friend and lover.

Eve finished her wine and drifted into a sinking melancholy, feeling a familiar tug of isolation. The radiators hissed, her mantel clock ticked, Georgy slept and the apartment seemed an island surrounded by a vast dark sea. She looked down at the letter that lay in her lap and gave it a sweet, dejected smile. Granny was right. It was too bad that Evelyn and John Allister never had their chance at love.

She nodded off to sleep. Minutes later she was jolted awake by an idea. It was one of those dreamy ideas, vague and shadowy.

Why didn't Eve do what Evelyn had not done? Why couldn't Eve light the lantern? Why couldn't she open the letter and remember John Allister with kindness and forgiveness? Why couldn't Eve wish the doomed lovers the happiness and reunion they'd so longed for but were denied in life? After all, weren't Eve and Evelyn related? Yes, of course. It was a splendid idea!

That morning, Eve had been excited by the prospect of lighting the lantern, and so she'd taken it to a local hardware store to buy oil and new wicks. She knew the owner and he was happy to replace the wick for her, showing her how to make sure the wick fit snuggly in the burner sleeve. Then he trimmed it with scissors. Finally, he showed her how to load the oil, which was easy enough, but something she'd never done before. She'd never been on a camping trip in her life and, besides, this was an antique lamp.

On hands and knees at the hearth, Eve carefully filled the oil lamp font to seven-eighths capacity, as instructed. Georgy stirred, watching her sleepily as she put the burner with the wick in the lamp and allowed the wick to soak for ten minutes, while she read the letter again. Then she placed the lantern back on the hearth and opened one of the four, now cleaned, panes of glass. She reached for a box of kitchen matches and, just before she struck it, she paused, feeling a fluttering in her stomach and a dry throat. She sat back on her knees, amazed at herself, because she was not the new-age type, or a believer-in-the-occult type. But some-how, it seemed like the right thing to do, to perform a kind of personal ceremony honoring two lovers who'd been denied the chance to come together and express their love.

She, Eve Sharland, had found the lantern and the let-ter and this one simple act of lighting the lantern might finally put to rest Evelyn Sharland's and John Allister's longing and unrequited love.

Eve lifted forward, struck the match and watched it blaze. With perfect concentration, she reverently lit the wick. To her surprise and delight, the wick took the flame and flared. Eve closed the open glass window-pane and stared, entranced, as the lantern glowed, its light illuminating the room. Her eyes opened in wonder and satisfaction, her sharpening eyes lowering onto the open letter that lay next to her.

"Okay, Evelyn and John. This light is for you. And John Allister Harringshaw the Second, I am remember-ing you with kindness and with forgiveness. Rest for-ever in peace."

Suddenly, Eve felt a cold draft of air blow in. It star-tled the candle flames. They flickered and danced. Eve wrapped her arms around her chest for warmth, glanc-ing about, trying to locate the source of the draft. The windows were shut tight and the front door was closed and locked.

She felt light-headed—her vision began to blur. She blinked and wiped her eyes and, when the room seemed to tilt and sway, she placed her hands on the floor to anchor herself.

Another draft of wind swept in. She shivered. It was a cold wind, nothing like anything she'd ever experienced before in this room. Maybe she had left a window open somewhere. She tried to push to her feet, but the room shifted and swayed. Eve dropped hard to the floor. An earthquake!?

The room stilled. Silence. Dead Silence. A loud quiet that hurt her ears. She thought, *I must be coming down with some virus.*

When the fireplace began to melt from view, when the walls shimmered with a kind of bluish sparkling light, Eve stared in dazed astonishment. She looked down and the floor seemed to be dissolving beneath her, swallowing her up. What was she sitting on? Another puff of frigid wind tossed her hair.

Eve was terrified now. Her body tensed. She glanced about, watching the room glitter with bluish light, feeling dizzy and disoriented—she didn't feel properly anchored in her body. Then she threw a darting glance toward Georgy Boy. He had vanished! She frantically tried to reach for him, but she couldn't move. She was a block of stone.

She snapped a look at the lantern, and her eyes were drawn into its bright, buttery flame. Yes, the flame. It had all started when she'd lit the lantern. It must be that. The flame. The light. Had to be. She had to put out the light. Now!

With great, struggling effort, she got to her hands and knees and reached for the lantern. It took all her straining effort to lift the pane. She clumsily reached for the candle snuffer near the candelabra. In slow motion she struggled and wheezed and finally capped the flame.

The lantern went dark, gray stringy smoke rising toward the ceiling in twisting curls.

Eve flopped backwards, bracing herself with her hands, her breath coming fast.

The shimmering lights vanished, the floor felt solid under her, and the room became warm and comfortable. Georgy Boy was there, gently sleeping, as if nothing had happened. Eve shifted her gaze to the candles. The flames were steady and calm.

Eve swallowed away anxiety. She stared soberly, not blinking. What had just happened? It took all her courage and strength to look at the lantern. It sat inert and still, an old relic from another time and place. But was it just an old relic? What the hell had just happened?

Trembling, her eyes lowered on the opened letter. For a long time, she listened to the ringing silence, her breathing shallow and staggered. And then her gaze slid away into the shadows of the room.

CHAPTER 6

Eve made her way to bed, feeling feverish and mildly disoriented. Whenever she closed her eyes, she saw images of dissolving walls; felt as if she were falling through the bed. At midnight, she took her temperature. 98.4 degrees. Normal. Still, she could have a virus. Her nurse's brain mentally scanned the list of probable causes. A reaction to the lamp oil? A migraine? She'd never had migraine headaches, but the visual distortions pointed to that.

She found a bottle and shook out a sleeping pill, hoping that after six hours' sleep, she'd feel better.

When her eyes popped open at 5:34 a.m., she still felt shaky. Her restless dreams had been filled with images of John Allister in his top hat, and of that damned lantern expanding out and up until it was the size of a skyscraper, throwing its bright yellow light out across the entire city, and beyond.

She threw on some jeans and a coat and took Georgy Boy out to the sidewalk, hoping the morning air would clear her head. It worked. Back inside, she leaned over the bathroom counter and stared at herself in the mirror. Her eyes were clear. She took her pulse and her temperature. Both were good. She declared herself fine. She was feeling fine.

But as she walked into the kitchen, she realized there was something—some emotional residue from last night's incident—that still made her uneasy. She was afraid to look in the living room, afraid to look at the lantern.

I have to get rid of that thing, she thought, adding milk to a bowl of oatmeal. *I'll mail it back to Granny Gilbert.* She stirred the oatmeal vigorously. *The letter needs to go too.* She'd find someone in the Harringshaw family and either deliver it in person or mail it to them.

She didn't want to think about the lantern, or the letter, or Evelyn, or John Allister Harringshaw anymore. And she wasn't going to speculate as to what had happened the night before. It had all been too disconcerting and frightening.

Eve considered herself to be a rational and courageous person, who didn't scare easily. She didn't believe in ghosts, in the paranormal or in UFOs. Whatever had happened probably had more to do with a small virus or a migraine or something she'd eaten. Maybe it was stress. She'd been seeing a lot of new patients, requiring a lot of time on the computer. And she never got enough sleep.

On her way out of the apartment, Eve kissed Georgy Boy goodbye, avoiding even a passing glance at the lantern and letter. Once outside, Eve gazed up at her bay windows, as if she half-expected to see something or someone looking back at her. She continued on with reluctant strides, finally hailing a cab. She wasn't in the mood for a bus today.

The office was boiling with activity at 8:15 and Eve was seeing patients by 8:30. She tried not to allow last night's events to distract her in any way, but suddenly the words "Central Park" kept playing in her head, like the lyrics of a song you can't shake. Without realizing it, she started humming an old Frank Sinatra song her parents had liked, about autumn in New York. How had it gone?

Lovers that bless the dark
On benches in Central Park
Autumn in New York...

Eve tried to be focused, pleasant and methodical, falling into the hectic rhythm of the work, but the song and the physical sensations of the night before would suddenly rush through her body again and she'd have to stop and take a deep breath. She took medical histories and examined ears and throats and abdomens, and even removed stitches from the foot of a 12-year-old girl who bantered on about some reality TV show Eve had never heard of, but she couldn't shake the odd feelings of the night before.

Just before noon, she had a consult with the M.D. on staff, Richard Mandel, a thin, high-strung man in his early 40s with wild, gray hair and steady eyes. They were in his office, discussing a new patient, when Eve paused.

"Do I look okay to you?" she asked.

Eve was standing near his small, narrow desk. He glanced up from a stack of papers he'd been sorting through and squinted at her. Eve and Richard had gone out to dinner a couple times when she was going through her divorce, but they remained just colleagues and causal friends.

"Now that you mention it, you do look a little pale. Are you feeling okay?"

Eve chose her words carefully. "I feel a little odd. Sometimes when I look around, things look a little fuzzy... a little out of focus. This morning, when I was taking a history, the man's voice seemed to echo—no, that's not it—it seemed to sound hollow and far away."

Richard sniffed. "Could it be a migraine? Or an ear infection? Any dizziness?"

Eve shook her head. "No..." She hesitated. How could she ever explain what had happened without sounding crazy? "It's probably just... well, I took a sleeping pill last night. That's probably it."

Richard nodded. "I can't take those things. They make me paranoid. After I wake up, I feel like I'm being followed, and that every kid I pass is actually a big person hiding in a little body. And they all want to mug me." He chuckled. "Crazy, huh?"

Eve nodded, gently lifting her eyebrows and giving him an uncertain smile. "Yeah... a little."

She started for the door.

"Get some rest," Richard said, more soberly. "And let me know if you need anything."

Eve turned back. "Thanks, Richard, I will. I'm heading off to the clinic now. See you Monday."

LATE THAT AFTERNOON, Eve canceled dinner reservations with Joni and her boyfriend. She still felt too shaky, and she had a strong compulsion to get rid of the lantern. Once it was out of her life, maybe the words "Central Park" would stop playing in her mind like some incessant refrain. And that song! It had become a real distraction by the end of the day.

Before she left the Clinic, she called April to check on Granny Gilbert's medical condition and to ask her if she could return the lantern to her.

When April said hello, Eve knew from the sound of her voice that something had happened. "Granny passed away early this morning," she said softly. "She died peacefully, with her family by her side."

It was almost dark when Eve arrived home, feeling downcast and worried. She collapsed her umbrella and brushed the beads of rain from her brown raincoat. The weather people had said the temperature would probably drop, turning the rain into snow flurries.

She didn't remove her coat or boots. Instead, she took Georgy Boy out for a quick walk before feeding him. He was happily gobbling his food when she wandered into the living room and lingered by the leather couch, deep in thought, her arms folded across her chest. She stared into the dark fireplace—focusing on the lantern. What should she do with it? If Granny hadn't died, she could have mailed it back to her. She didn't have the heart to just throw it out. Maybe she should sell it to an antiques dealer or put it up for sale on eBay. But Granny wouldn't want that; she'd been fascinated by the lantern and the letter, and probably would have kept them both if Eve hadn't been so persistent and aggressive. And how Granny had loved hearing John Allister's loving words! Now that Granny was gone, only Eve knew the letter's contents and, for some strange reason, she felt a responsibility to honor John's privacy.

In the silence of the living room, the lyrics to the song played louder and louder in her head, circling around in her brain like a mantra that wouldn't let go.

Lovers that bless the dark
On benches in Central Park
Autumn in New York...

Suddenly it hit her. That's where she should take the lantern! She should take it to Central Park and leave it on a bench, and then whoever was meant to have it would find it. Let fate decide.

Eve grabbed John Allister's letter, her eyes falling on one particular sentence.

If health permits, please light the lantern once more, the lantern that first brought us together on that snowy night in Central Park, and then read this letter, and think of me kindly.

Eve stepped toward the hearth. That's exactly what she would do. She put the letter and some matches in her coat pocket, pulled a deep breath and reached for the lantern, picking it up by the loop handle. She stood rigid, holding it away from her, like it was some dangerous animal that might bite. She waited to see if anything happened. Nothing did.

In the kitchen, while Georgy Boy swarmed her ankles for attention, she found a plastic bag with handles and carefully lowered the lantern inside. At the front door, she sat on her haunches and stroked Georgy's head. "I'll be back in a little while, Georgy Boy," she whispered. "I won't be gone long."

On her way down the stairs, she reached for her phone and saw a text from Joni.

Hope you're feeling better.

Eve texted back. *Still not feeling great.* She paused, her heart suddenly racing. Should she tell someone what she was doing? No. It was too weird. Still...

Her fingers seemed to move of their own volition. *If you don't hear from me by morning, please come over and check on Georgy.*

She touched SEND and then continued on her strange mission.

Outside, the rain was replaced by drizzle, which shimmered in the streetlights, making the world appear like an impressionistic painting. Eve had forgotten her umbrella, so she pulled her hood up, ran to Broadway and hailed a cab. She slid in, closed the door and sat still and silent.

The driver, dressed in a white turban, with a gray beard, waited patiently for her to tell him the destination. Finally, he turned slightly, his face in profile.

"Where to, Miss?"

What was she doing? How could she ever explain her actions to anyone? Even now, she was conflicted and puzzled, her back straight, her eyes fixed ahead, her plan of action suddenly seeming ridiculous. She was going out in the rain to light a lantern, read a letter and then leave the lantern on the bench? What if someone saw her? What would they think? Nuts!

"Central Park. East 66th Street," she said, in a small, tentative voice.

The cab jumped away from the curb and pulled into light traffic. Eve shook her head at the absurdity of what she was doing, but felt certain that this was the right course of action. She was grateful to see the rain turning to snow as the taxi crossed the park at West 96th Street and turned right on Fifth Avenue.

At East 66th Street, Eve paid the driver and stepped outside, taking the lantern with her. She entered Central Park and walked briskly west across the damp walkway, under the soft glow of the amber park lights. The wind had shifted and there was a chill in the air, the kind of chill that signaled the cold breath of winter was finally moving in. It was October 24th. Eve buttoned the top button of her raincoat, wishing now she'd worn a heavy sweater underneath it, and trudged on.

Despite the hour and the weather, lovers strolled hand in hand, and tourists with maps and cell phones sought direction and landmarks. She took the walkway leading to the lovely Bethesda Terrace and the Central Park Mall that runs through the middle of the Park from 66th to 72nd Streets.

It was an area once referred to as an "open air hall of reception" by its creators, as the Mall was designed so that a carriage could dislodge its passengers at the south end, drive around and then collect them at Bethesda Terrace, where the view of the Lake and Ramble was a popular point of interest.

There was a soft moan of wind as Eve strolled along the broad path under a canopy of American elm trees, many of them having already shed their leaves. The path was framed on either side by a wrought-iron fence. It was the only straight line in Central Park, nicknamed the "Promenade." Minutes later, Eve arrived at her destination, The Poet's Walk, also known as The Literary Walk, at the southern end of The Mall. Here were four statues of renowned writers, Fitz-Greene Halleck, Robert Burns, Sir Walter Scott and William Shakespeare.

Shaking off her nerves, Eve found an empty park bench near the comfortable, buttery glow of a park light. She removed two tissues from her purse and wiped beads of water from the bench. She sat, instantly feeling the chill on her buttocks and legs.

She watched a parade of people stroll by, some students with backpacks, their faces lit up by cell phones as they read or texted. An elderly man with a cane stuttered along, his old dog on a slack leash, walking stiffly on his arthritic legs, his ears and head down, his tail inert.

Sweethearts drifted by, bodies close, chatting and laughing, their hands stuffed into their pockets as the snow flurries fell lazily across the park lights. And there were tourists, pausing to study the statues. When they noticed the snow flurries, their faces brightened and their hands jutted out to catch some fat flakes.

Eve let out a long breath. What was she doing here? Okay, she knew why she said she was here. To leave the lantern. But a part of her knew it was also to see if the strange events of last night would happen again, even though what she was about to do was so foreign and so blatantly uncharacteristic of her that she shook her head again in utter disbelief.

She had once thought about becoming a doctor. Becoming a nurse practitioner had been easier and less expensive. She liked medicine, and she prided herself on her rational, calm and reasoned thinking. She made decisions quickly, and she was logical. All well and good.

So what she was about to do was not rational nor did it make any logical sense whatsoever. Carrying an old lantern to Central Park in a snowfall made no sense at all. But here she was. She could rationalize it by saying she was a scientist and scientists conduct experiments, don't they? Scientists must be open-minded skeptics who are not afraid to try things—even outlandish things—if the result can help illuminate and educate. Right?

Was that truly why she was here? Maybe, or maybe it was because of her fear: her fear of that damned lantern and the experience she'd had the night before. If so, she had to overcome it. She was stubborn enough not to be bullied or frightened by some over-imagined event or by some ridiculous occult incident, whatever it was. No way. She'd face it and walk through it. That was her nature, or so she believed. It was what her parents had always said about her.

Okay, fine then. It was time to repeat the events of last night—again, a simple scientific experiment. Eve was going to light the lantern just as she'd done when she'd been alone in her apartment. But this time, she wouldn't be alone. She'd be around people in Central Park. If something weird happened, people would notice. They would corroborate the event. They would help document the experiment, and these would be people she didn't know and had never met. All the better.

When Eve reached for the lantern, she felt her heart pulsing in her throat. She lifted it from the plastic bag, anchored the bag with her cell phone and purse to keep the bag from sailing away on the wind, and then she set the lantern down to her left, beside her. A handsome man in a blue parka glanced her way, intrigued by the lantern, but he kept walking and, once he'd passed, he didn't look back.

Eve reached into her pocket for the book of matches and took in another sharp breath, suddenly feeling her body temperature rise. Really? Was she really *that* nervous?

She opened the glass pane and struck a match, cupping the trembling match flame in her hand to protect it from the breeze. She hesitated, swallowed away a half lump in her throat and lit the wick. The lantern filled with warm, golden light.

Eve lowered the glass pane and stared into the soft, scintillating light. It comforted her, soothed her, and drew her deeply into the blue-fringed, rich, quivering flame. A man on roller skates bobbed and danced and then whisked by, waving at her as he meandered away. But Eve didn't notice him. She was mesmerized by the light, bewitched by the light, immersed in the light. She put her hand in her pocket to pull out the letter, but she was too entranced by the light, and when nothing happened, she began to relax. She grew lethargic and sleepy. Her eyes fluttered, opened wide, fluttered again and closed.

It seemed minutes passed before she opened them. When she blinked, her eyes were stuck closed, as if glued. With an effort, she forced them open. To her astonishment, she saw strange multicolored lights dappling her vision, like carnival lights or whirling Christmas lights. A puff of wind blew the hood from her head and, on impulse, she reached for it, but her arms felt heavy and slow and the hood seemed miles away.

She saw her hands moving in a blur, in confused motion.

Someone was standing over her. It was a man, an out-of-focus man, staring at her with concern. He spoke. His words came out slow and garbled. Eve couldn't understand a word. His voice was a grumble that reminded Eve of a bowling ball thundering down the alley toward the pins. And then he just melted away and disappeared.

Eve felt the bench move and jump. It began a slow, wobbling motion—up left, down right—bang. Hard. Eve grabbed hold, her knuckles white, eyes round with fear. The bench vibrated and shook, then began to spin violently. Eve was pitched about, as if she were on a thrill ride at an amusement park. She held on to the bench tightly with both her hands, trying to anchor herself, her eyes shifting, searching for help, her heart thumping wildly. She tried to cry out for help but she couldn't find her voice.

When a yellow smoky fog blew in and enveloped her, Eve was completely disoriented and dizzy. She shook her head, blinked her eyes and glanced about in desperation.

She didn't know if she was upright, sideways or on her back, but she released her hands and reached up, feeling like some helpless turtle. She felt that pit-of-the-stomach sensation of plunging down and rising up, drifting, drowning in a misty fog. She must be dying. Leaving her body. Again she tried to force out a scream, but it was only the hollow wheeze of a frightened child.

She heard distant voices, but she didn't see anything except boiling fog whipping around her, scattering leaves, snow and loose pages of a newspaper. The sharp wind tossed her about like a rag doll. She threw up her hands to protect her face, as the wind swept in harshly, making rattling sounds, moaning sounds. All she could do was surrender, let herself go, a quivering twig being hurtled down a raging stream into the freezing darkness, being tossed into a spiraling abyss.

CHAPTER 7

He looked long and steadily at her. Eve stared back, dazed, frightened, struggling to focus on the blurred face that loomed out of a smoky fog. He had tawny red-gold hair, and a waxed mustache that gleamed in the glow of the park light. He wore an ankle length overcoat with a brown fur collar, a golden silk scarf and a large diamond ring on his pinky finger. He had a good, lean jaw, a handsome face and rich, sharp eyes that were studying her peculiarly.

"Madam, are you in need of assistance? Are you in distress?"

Eve blinked around, trying to orient herself, struggling to catch a breath. She saw a halo around the park lights; saw people strolling past; noticed a light snow was falling. She felt drugged and disoriented, as if she'd taken a sleeping pill and was trying to wake up.

Something wasn't right or something was different or something had changed; the sounds, the air, the light.

Everything was different somehow, but Eve was too blunted and dazed to understand exactly what.

She was still sitting on the park bench and it was snowing, but there was a deeper quality to the silence; the park lights were a rich amber, and the people who passed wore clothes that were heavy-looking, long and dark. She watched men amble by, men with beards and mustaches and top hats and tuffs of hair growing on their heavy jowls.

"Madam?" the man, repeated. "Can I be of any help to you?"

Eve struggled to come out of her dozing dream, at least that's what it felt like. She swallowed and tried to speak. Nothing came. She tried again. "I'm... I'm... Okay. I'm..." her voice faded into a cold wind.

"Are you quite sure?" he said, his voice low and formal. Eve speculated that he was over thirty. She couldn't place his accent. New England? British?

Her blue eyes were startled and uncertain. She became aware of many curious stares as people strolled past. Some paused mid-stride and stared at her, while others hurried away as she stared back at them, their eyes enlarging on her and then dropping away.

Eve tried for dignity, straightening, raking a strand of hair from her forehead. She ventured another look at the man. He, too, was staring at her in a strange way.

She slowly found her voice. "Yes, I'm sure. I just... Well, I just don't feel so good."

And then she heard it. The rhythmic trot of a horse's hooves. She saw a dark carriage loom out of the snowfall from her left. It glided by and moved off right into the hazy depth of the park.

Eve had never seen a carriage like that in the park. At least not in this section of the park. She'd seen carriages in the park and she had even ridden in one, but this particular carriage seemed different. It was larger, and it was being drawn by two raven-black horses, lit by side lanterns.

"Can I drop you somewhere?" the man said. "My carriage isn't far."

Eve's head lifted. "Your carriage?"

And then she saw the high crowned derby he held in his hand. He'd taken it off when he'd approached her, a real gentleman. He placed it on his head. "Yes. I have a carriage close by." He indicated to his left. "I will be happy to drop you wherever you wish."

Eve took in his face, appraising it. She had the odd feeling she'd seen it before. There was something familiar about it. It was an attractive face, with full sensual lips, high cheekbones and lively, interesting eyes.

"I... don't know. I mean..." Eve struggled to put two words together. She was still confused, her thoughts tangled. "I can get a cab."

A sharp thought struck, and she whipped her head right. She felt for her purse. It wasn't there! She jerked about looking for it, feeling for it. It was gone! The lantern was gone too, and her cell phone and the plastic bag she'd placed it on. All were gone!

"Is something wrong?" the man asked.

"My purse!" Eve said, with panic rising in her voice. "My purse is gone. My cell phone is gone."

The man lifted an eyebrow. "Your cell... phone?"

Eve shot up, turning her back to him as she frantically searched underneath the bench, behind the bench and around the bench.

"Yes, my cell phone. My purse and my cell phone are both gone! Dammit!"

She turned to face him, her eyes moving. Her mind reeled, and she fought to orient herself. She touched her head to steady it and shut her eyes, struggling to think one clear thought, but everything was spinning and she couldn't grab one coherent thought. She stood on the edge of raw panic.

After another thorough search of the area, Eve stood before the bench in defeat and confusion. The man was staring at her, blinking. Resigned, her shoulders slumped. Someone must have taken them when that storm struck—when that fog moved in. When whatever had happened, happened.

Fighting alarm, she wrapped herself with her arms, searching the night for help. For answers. Everyone who passed turned to stare at her. What was the matter with these people? Why were they looking at her? They were all dressed so somberly, in black, men wearing black hats, women in long dresses, brushing the ground. Eve struggled to think, to construct a sentence to explain how she felt. Her brain was a mass of jumbled wires. She shut her eyes again, as if to shut out the world. She inhaled two deep breaths. When she opened her eyes, the man was still there, trying to smile, but it was more of a twitch.

Another carriage came into view, and then another, snow now falling more heavily, swirling, glazing the trees and the benches, sparkling under the park lights. She felt weak and unsteady. What the hell had happened? What was going on? She turned her eyes on the man, suddenly feeling cold, hungry and completely lost.

"I want to go home," she said, feeling desperate now. "Can you take me home?"

"Yes, of course. Very well, then. I will ensure you arrive safely."

He indicated again toward a walkway. "Shall we?"

He started, and when she didn't move, he turned, waiting for her. Eve took a few hesitant steps, walking slightly behind him, down a winding dirt and gravel path she'd never taken and didn't know existed. She remained watchful and cautious, passing the man sideways glances. He was too well dressed to be a mugger or a thief. His coat was luxurious cashmere, his boots a rich, glossy leather, his demeanor, one of class and comfortable wealth. Old school wealth.

The temperature must have dropped ten degrees and Eve's teeth began to chatter. Her feet felt like icicles. Her raincoat was no match for this cold. She pushed her hands deep into her coat pockets and continued on until they came to a carriage path, again, one she didn't recall ever seeing.

As Eve listened to their footsteps scratch across the path, she became aware of the eerie silence. It was unnerving. And there were distant sounds that were unfamiliar to her in a city she'd lived in for eight years. This whole experience was giving her the creeps.

"We are almost there," the man said.

Eve just wanted to go home, take a hot shower, eat something and go straight to bed.

She watched the man puff on a cigar as he moved in an easy, stately manner, as if he were some lord of the manor, some costumed actor right out of one of those 19th century Masterpiece Theatre episodes.

When Eve saw the man's carriage, she stopped short. Under the park lights, it looked sleek and stylish, like something from another century. It was an enclosed carriage, with a black enameled sheen, hard top roof, glowing side lamps and glass windows. Two sleek horses, one chestnut and one midnight black, stood waiting, white vapor puffing from their nostrils. One horse pawed at the ground, as if restless. An elegant coachman sat perched and waiting, wearing a top hat, dark uniform and royal blue cape, reins and whip in his gloved hands.

The man stopped and turned to her. "Is anything the matter?"

Eve didn't know where to begin. What wasn't the matter? Everything was the matter. Why would they take a carriage through the park? Why not just hail a cab?

Eve drew herself up. "Why don't we just grab a cab?"

He lowered his eyes on her. "I think you will find my carriage is much more comfortable, madam."

Madam? Eve didn't know what to say. Her mind was still filled with cotton. She felt shaky and fragile, as if she could easily fall and break into a thousand pieces. She just wanted to get home as fast as possible.

"Okay, fine," she said, turning from him. "Fine. Let's take your carriage."

The coachman stepped down and was waiting with an open door when Eve approached. She glanced at the stoic coachman, and he gave her a little bow. He took her hand and helped her inside. She sat on a soft leather seat and slid over when the man entered and sat beside her.

The carriage door closed and Eve tensed up, feeling scared and nauseous. She saw a hand warmer muff beside her. She reached for it and inserted her hands inside. It was all fur, soft and warm.

When the carriage lurched forward and gained some speed, she flinched. She heard the faint jingle of harness and the clop of horses' hooves. She smelled the man's sandalwood cologne and noticed the soft cushiony leather as she settled in the seat. Eve felt the man's eyes on her and she stole a quick glance at him.

"Where to?" he asked.

"Oh… yes. I live on West 107th Street between Broadway and Riverside."

The man looked her over and for a long moment they stared at each other. "Are you sure?"

Eve tried not to sound irritable. "Yes, of course, I'm sure. I've lived there for over a year now."

The man turned and looked out the window, folding his hands in his lap. The coach moved on. Eve watched snowflakes dancing across the windows.

When the man spoke, it was in a deep, even voice. He did not look at her.

"Young woman, have you fallen down? Have you hurt yourself in some way? Do you know where you are and where you came from?"

His words struck like a blow to the stomach and she made a little sound of anguish. Yes. Something was very wrong. She glanced about, feeling as if she were in a waking dream that made no sense. In a whirlwind of emotion and memory, her mind began to compute, think and reason. She licked her dry lips as an image of the lantern flame flooded her eyes. The lantern! Evelyn's lantern. John Allister's lantern. The lantern that had so frightened her!

The man turned, meeting her gaze. She had a feverish, wild look, as if she'd just seen a disaster. He tried to give her a reassuring smile, but it failed. Then he looked genuinely worried.

At first, Eve refused to acknowledge it. She was a smart, educated and reasonable woman. She did not believe in the occult—in fantasies.

"Madam, are you quite yourself?" the man repeated.

"No... No, I'm not all right. I'm... Just lost or something. I'm... definitely not myself."

He continued to stare at her. She grew snappish and disoriented. "I don't know what's going on, okay?"

"Shall I take you to a doctor?"

Eve looked at him again. She focused. She froze. "A doctor? No, no, I don't need a doctor. I need..." Her voice trailed away.

At that moment, Eve knew the unthinkable had happened. The impossible had occurred. The unimaginable had materialized. The mind-blowing, Earth swinging-off-its-orbit had happened—or she had completely lost her mind.

But no! She wasn't dreaming. Her pulse was strong. The sights and smells were real. The man seated next to her, retro dressed and looking like an actor from a costumed drama, was also real. The smell of the leather was real. The people back on the promenade dressed in those period clothes were real. The carriages were real. It was all real!

Her neck stiffened as one frantic thought chased another. How could it have happened? How did it happen?

Eve took in a quick breath to try to calm her galloping emotions. She had come to full wakefulness now, and it was a nightmare. An awful, dizzying nightmare!

"You look quite pale," the man said, with some unease, seeing her swallow hard and squirm.

Eve's heart pounded and she was sure her blood pressure was off the charts. Her face flushed hot. Suddenly she felt like a trapped animal in a burning barn. All she wanted to do was burst through that carriage door and tear off into the night and run and run until she collapsed or escaped or found herself home with Georgy Boy.

"My dear woman, have you left the Bloomingdale Asylum? Shall I take you up there?"

Eve looked at him, trying to process and understand. Of course, he thought she was crazy. Out of her mind. Of course he did. Wouldn't she, if the roles were reversed?

"No. No. No Asylum. I'm fine. Fine," but she heard her own frazzled voice. She didn't sound fine. She sounded like she was insane.

"Do you work for the Towers Nursing Home? It is up in that area."

Eve tried to relax, tried to let the reality of what had happened sink in, but she couldn't stamp down the rising panic. She began to tremble.

"No... No. Never mind. Forget about 107th Street." Eve instinctively felt her forehead with the back of her hand. She was burning up with fear.

"I'm just a little confused. I just need to sleep or something. I need food or something. I just need to rest. I'll be fine in the morning."

"May I ask you for your name, madam?"

Blinking rapidly, Eve shot him a look. "My name?" She felt as if she couldn't breathe.

"Yes. If you would be so kind. What is your name? Perhaps I can help you find your family or some friends. They can help you."

Eve looked at him again, carefully, certain she'd seen him some place. She was convinced of it. She couldn't speak. She just stared.

He lifted his regal chin, now trying to summon patience. "Young woman, I cannot help you if you will not let me. You are obviously in some sort of distress. I just want to help you."

Eve continued staring at him, straining to remember. She finally found her voice. "What is... What is your name?"

"My name? Forgive me. I would have introduced myself earlier, as any gentleman would, but you seemed in such anguish." He gave a little lift of his head, as if he were a king.

"I am Albert Wilson Harringshaw."

Eve's mind locked up. Her poor brain couldn't take another blow. It stalled and then it shut down. She felt herself droop and weave. She was slipping away into dark shadows. She felt herself slip away, and there was nothing she could do about it. She began to fall from a great height into a dark pit.

Her eyes rolled back into her head and she wilted, falling to her right. Her head struck the glass window and she was out.

CHAPTER 8

When Eve came to, she realized she was lying on a divan, covered by a rose crochet blanket. She lifted her torso and looked around slowly. The room was a plush Victorian parlor groaning with possessions: large, gilded mirrors; hanging gas lamps; ornate framed oil paintings of white clouds, cherubs and angels; and jade, marble and porcelain figurines, displayed on claw-footed mahogany tables. The décor was mostly burgundy: burgundy love seat with matching chairs and velvet burgundy drapes. There was a gold and marble fireplace with a crackling fire, and a lush carpet with floral patterns of plum, rose, and lavender.

Eve stared in a half-dream/half-waking state, caught between two worlds, staring up at the gas lamps and the blue-edged flames caught behind the etched patterns of the glass shades. She seemed to hover for a time, like a ghost, before she became fully conscious.

Someone had removed her raincoat and her boots, leaving her dressed in a light blue sweater, a patterned button-up blouse and designer jeans, not exactly Victorian attire. On an impulse, she searched her neck for the gold pendant. It was there. The lantern, her purse and her cell phone had all disappeared, but the heart pendant had not. It gave her small but welcomed comfort.

Where was she? She lifted up on elbows and blinked around, her eyes now fully open. She heard muffled voices coming from an adjoining room, a woman's voice, and a man's deep authoritative voice. They were arguing in whispers and sighs.

And then it struck her. The nightmare of what had happened back in the park and in the carriage. Albert Wilson Harringshaw's carriage. The park bench. The lantern! Blistering fear slowly crawled up her spine, and again she felt the pulsing animal instinct to break and run. Several deep breaths helped to calm her agitated mind. She had to stop the spreading raw panic that seemed to fill every atom of her body.

She had to think and reason. Eve's father, the FBI agent, used to say, "There is nothing you can't handle in this world if you don't lose your head. You are equal to whatever comes at you." Yes, but what world? What world was she in?

Eve dropped back down on the comfortable divan, her eyes taking in the black-varnished wood with burgundy upholstery and buttons. Her chest was still heaving.

She placed her arm over her eyes, willing herself to go back to sleep. Maybe when she woke up the next time, she'd be back in her own bed and back in her own time. Georgy Boy would come bounding onto the bed and lick her face, and everything would be right with the world. She heard her own whispery voice say "Georgy Boy."

And then she heard the loud ticking of a grandfather clock and the soft hiss of the gas lights. Eve was not stupid. She couldn't deny what had happened to her—she couldn't pretend it was just a dream—because she knew it was not a dream. Either she was lost in some nightmarish hallucination, she was going insane, or—the unbelievable and unthinkable had happened—she had somehow traveled back in time.

Years ago, while she was studying for her degree, Eve had taken mental health courses at NYU. She'd seen patients who believed themselves to be famous people, and she'd worked with patients diagnosed with paranoid schizophrenia. But she didn't have any of those symptoms. She was the same rational person in the same body, but she suddenly found herself some-where in the past, or lost somewhere in the depths of her own crazy mind.

She fought to clear her mind and think. As she heard the whispery argument continue in the next room, she forced herself to review the events and face the facts as she saw them. What exactly had happened? Twice when she'd lit the lantern, strange things had happened. The melting away of floors and worlds. Colored lights and cold winds. A feeling of falling and flying. Those had all happened. She did not imagine any of them.

And all of these events had occurred after she'd lighted the lantern—after she'd stared at the flickering light. That golden light that seemed to envelop and swallow her. But the whole thing was just too incredible and ludicrous. It was just a flame.

She sought answers in the air, struggling for any rational thought. Did that light somehow open a window into the past? Did she somehow fall through it? Was that even possible?

As crazy, silly and outrageous as it sounded, once again Eve couldn't ignore the apparent fact that because of the lighted lantern, she had been changed—transported to another place and time. What other possible explanation was there? She'd seen it all with her own eyes. She had experienced it. This was a reality. It was here, now. She was lying on a divan in a Victorian parlor under gas lamps. She'd met and seen Albert Harringshaw with her own eyes. Yes, this was reality and, whatever had been the cause of the incident that had brought her here, she was stuck in this reality. At least for now, she was pinned to it, like a pin in a pin cushion.

All because of that stupid lantern. The lantern she'd been attracted to back at Granny Gilbert's little antiques shop. Why hadn't she just let Granny Gilbert keep it?

Eve's rational mind still worked to reject the idea of time travel. How could an old lantern have the power to send someone back in time? It was silly. It was the stuff of fairy tales, novels and movies. It was the stuff of stories told around campfires or in bedrooms deep into the night when you couldn't sleep. There was no scientific foundation for it. There was no plausible or reasonable explanation. And yet, here she was. She was alive, breathing, thinking, and being. She was very much HERE.

"So, what now, Eve?" she said, whispering to herself.

And what about Albert Wilson Harringshaw? Did the lantern somehow have a homing device, or a beacon, or a GPS chip that was able to beam him to her while she sat on that park bench? And why him, and not his brother, who wrote about the lantern in his letter, for whom the lantern was so important?

Eve rolled her head from side to side, her entire body a mass of anxiety and tension.

When she heard footsteps approach, she shut her eyes tightly. It was the little girl response. If you can't see the monster, maybe it's not there, so you squeeze your eyes even tighter and pray. "Go away, monster. Please just go away."

But it didn't go away.

Eve sensed someone standing close by. Reluctantly, she opened her eyes.

A gray-headed, portly man stood over her. He appeared to be in his middle fifties. He wore a black wool suit, a waistcoat and a white shirt. His small, dark, watery eyes were curious, widening on her as he fully took her in, her face, her hair and her clothes. He had florid cheeks, a bulbous nose and mutton-chop whiskers. Eve's first thought was that he looked like a big Muppet.

He cleared his throat. "I am Dr. Eckland." His voice was rich and formal.

Eve rolled her head further right to see Albert Harringshaw and a woman—a full-figured, attractive woman, with gleaming chestnut hair swept up to the top of her head, with bangs frizzled over her forehead. She wore a gorgeous, long, deep purple two-piece silk bustle dress with buttons up the front and an elaborate hem. It had a low waist and a low bust, supported by what must have been a corset. A dazzling double string of pearls adorned her neck, and she gave off scents of rose and lilac.

The doctor cleared his throat again. He indicated toward his two companions. "I believe you have met Mr. Harringshaw?"

Eve nodded, still focusing on the woman's fabulous dress.

Dr. Eckland turned to the woman. "May I introduce you to Miss Helen Baxter Price?"

Miss Price gave Eve an indulgent smile. Eve flashed back to the description of Helen Price in Albert Harringshaw's biography on Wikipedia, and the coldness grew inside her. This was *the* Helen Price she'd read about, his mistress.

Eve calculated that Helen was about her own age, and she saw an immediate distrust and hot jealousy in Helen's eyes.

Eve nodded again. She was still too overwhelmed with her new reality to speak. She felt fragile and scared, not wanting to do or say the wrong thing to push herself off balance.

The doctor reached for a chair and lowered himself onto it, keeping his gaze on Eve.

"May I ask, what is your name?"

Eve swallowed. "Eve..."

"What is your last name?"

Eve had the presence of mind to avoid using her last name. If she *had* gone back in time to 1885, and if Evelyn Sharland was alive and well, Eve did not want to raise any suspicion.

The doctor waited. All three waited. Helen gave an arrogant sniff.

For some inexplicable reason, Eve suddenly thought of Jackie Kennedy.

"Kennedy. My name is Eve Kennedy."

The doctor blinked in satisfaction. "Is it Miss Kennedy or Mrs. Kennedy?"

"Miss."

Helen lifted her chin in dissatisfaction.

"Miss Kennedy, how do you feel?"

Eve wanted to laugh out loud. She felt crazy and freaked out. "I'm tired. I'm just very tired."

"Miss Price's housemaid will be along shortly with some refreshments. They may help you regain some of your strength," Albert Harringshaw said.

"Do you recall striking your head when you fainted, Miss Kennedy?" Dr. Eckland asked.

"No, not really."

"Does your head hurt?"

"No, I don't think so. No," Eve said, looking about. "Where am I?" she asked.

Albert Harringshaw broke in. "You are on 24th Street. To be exact, you are at 16 West 24th Street in the Madison Square neighborhood. This is Miss Price's brownstone. Miss Price is a trusted friend. I did not know where else to bring you after you fainted."

Eve slowly sat up, removing the cover from her legs and swinging them to the floor. She looked down at her white socks. Everyone else did too. She tried not to wiggle her toes, but she couldn't stop an old habit.

When she passed a glance at Albert Harringshaw, she saw a twinkle of desire in his eyes. Immediate displeasure registered in Helen's eyes. Eve didn't need or want this.

"Miss Kennedy," Dr. Eckland said, "Mr. Harringshaw reports that he found you in Central Park, sitting on a park bench, obviously distressed and disoriented. He said your manner of dress, your agitation and your confused demeanor compelled him, as a gentleman, to stop and offer his assistance. Do you recall why you were in Central Park or what caused your troubled state of mind?"

Eve looked down. She certainly couldn't tell them the truth. She needed time—time to think things through. Time to gather her thoughts and come up with a fake story and a plan of action. Too much had happened too fast.

"Frankly, Dr. Eckland, I don't remember," Eve said, slowly shaking her head.

He leaned back in mild surprise. "Do you have friends or family we can contact for you?"

Eve wrinkled her brow, dramatically, as if struggling to remember. "I don't know. I just don't recall. My mind is a blank."

"But you do recall your name," Helen said, with an edge to her voice.

"Yes... thankfully, I do recall that. My name is Eve Kennedy."

Albert stepped forward, his reddish-gold hair burnished under the gas lamplight. The ends of his waxed mustache were twirled up to gleaming perfection. There was an attractive, roguish appeal about him, Eve thought. No doubt about that. He had a smooth, privileged confidence, just as she'd seen in that old black-and-white photograph on Wikipedia.

"Were you involved in an accident, Miss Kennedy?" Albert asked. "Did you suffer some trauma?"

"I just don't know," Eve said, wishing the food would arrive. She was ravenous.

"Miss Kennedy," Albert Harringshaw continued, "You fainted at the sound of my name. I have had many reactions to my name in the past, but I must confess, I have never had a lady faint from the sound of it. Do you know who I am?"

Eve gave him a vacant grin. "I have heard of you, sir."

Albert beamed with splendid pride as he squared his shoulders. "Well, I must say, I am greatly flattered that you do not know the names of your friends and family, but you do recall mine. Quite flattered, Miss Kennedy."

Eve looked at Helen, who was not happy. *I just made a big mistake*, Eve thought.

Helen moved toward the center table, to a bouquet of flowers, the color in her face rising. She leaned over and took in their scent.

"Where did you get your clothes, Miss Kennedy?" Helen asked, turning to reveal a suspicious eye. "I must admit, I have never seen anything quite like them. They are, I am forced to say, somewhat indecent. And your hair style fascinates me. But a woman in pants seems, forgive me for saying so, rather radical and immodest. Are you, by any chance, a member of some new suffrage movement?"

Eve knew enough history to know what Helen was talking about. The Women's Suffrage Movement was part of the Women's Rights Movement. They fought for women to gain the right to vote and run for office,

among other things. Eve had read that some suffra-
gettes wore a kind of modified slacks.

Albert spoke up. "Miss Kennedy says she does not
recall where she came from or what has happened to
her, Miss Price," he said, coming to Eve's defense. "I
think it is rather unfair to suggest that Miss Kennedy is
immodest and radical, under the circumstances. We
simply do not know the cause of her unfortunate situation. And we must help her find out."

Eve wished Albert hadn't come to her defense. Pink
jealousy was written all over Helen's face. Eve would
need friends in a world where she had no contacts, no
family, no money and no acquaintances. Being a woman, Helen could help in ways that Albert probably
couldn't or simply wouldn't. Albert was from a prominent and wealthy New York family. He had surely
brought Eve to Helen's, probably against her wishes,
because he could never have taken Eve to the Harringshaw mansion on Fifth Avenue.

The room went silent for chilly moments.

That's when Eve realized that her manner of speech
and the way these people spoke were entirely different.
Their speech patterns, inflections, and choice of words
were much more formal and yet filled with silent meaning. Eve did not want to add more mystery to herself
by speaking modern slang. She would have to modify
her speech.

But how? The first thing that came to mind was
Jane Austen. Eve had read all of Jane Austen's novels
and she loved them. If Eve could replicate those speech
patterns, it would help and, in time, she might be able to
pass for a Victorian woman.

Eve knew that Jane Austen was British and not American, and that Jane Austen did not live in the Victorian period. Nonetheless, Jane Austen would have to do. Think Jane Austen dialogue, she said to herself: formal, last names, no profanity, no contractions and no slang.

Eve faced Helen. "I do apologize for my clothes, Miss Price," Eve said, feigning contrition. "I was shocked and dismayed when I saw myself in them. I cannot imagine how I came to be dressed this way or what happened to me in Central Park."

Eve lowered her head and her eyes, trying for a humble expression. "I am so grateful you have taken me in like this, Miss Price. It is most generous and kind of you."

To Eve's ears, her words sounded a bit forced and awkward. Was it too much?

Helen's hard stare melted a little, but only a little.

"Never mind about the memory loss now, Miss Kennedy," Dr. Eckland said. "What you need is some nourishing food and a good night's sleep. Now, if you will permit me, I will take your temperature and your pulse and do a quick examination."

Dr. Eckland reached into his black leather Gladstone medical bag, withdrew a stethoscope and went to work.

Helen's maidservant, Millie, entered the room from a side door, just as Dr. Eckland was concluding his brief examination. Millie was in her early 20s, thin, shy and quiet. She wore a white uniform, a light blue apron, and a cap bonnet that made her seem even younger.

She placed an oval silver tray on the center table near the flowers. It held cheese, pickled fish, nuts, cider cake, ham, fruits and bread. She gave a little bob and a bow and retreated, returning minutes later with a second tray holding a silver tea set.

While she poured four cups of tea, Dr. Eckland replaced his stethoscope into his bag and pulled out a light blue bottle. He extracted the cork, poured a teaspoon of reddish-brown liquid, and offered it to Eve.

"What is that?" she asked.

"Laudanum. It will do you good."

Eve's dull mind struggled to recall what Laudanum was. But before she could, the spoon was in her mouth and she swallowed, wincing at the extremely bitter taste.

"Miss Kennedy, your pulse and coloring are both a little high. It is obvious you have been through some kind of unpleasant ordeal which your mind has chosen to forget, at least for the time being. Before bed tonight, I want you to take another spoonful of Laudanum. It will help you relax and sleep. In the morning, if you do not feel better and if your memory has not returned to full capacity, Mr. Harringshaw will contact me and I will perform a more thorough examination."

Eve spoke up quickly. "I trust I will be much better by morning, Dr. Eckland. Thank you for your advice and help."

"Surely, I deserve some recognition," Albert Harringshaw crowed, with a little twist of a flirtatious smile. "After all, I am the gentleman who came to your assistance when you were in great distress."

Eve feigned embarrassment, thinking, *He's a smooth one.*

"Forgive me, Mr. Harringshaw," Eve said. "Yes, thank you for all you have done. You have all been so kind to me."

Helen took a cup of tea from Millie. "If you are not improved by morning, Miss Kennedy, have you any plans as to what course of action you might take?"

Albert came to Eve's rescue yet again. "We shall not talk of plans just yet, Miss Price. We must allow our guest to eat, rest and recover herself first. These things cannot be rushed. They take time. Miss Kennedy has obviously had a very trying day."

Helen moved away from the table, her hot gaze lingering on Albert's face. "Whatever you say, Mr. Harringshaw," she said, with mild bitterness in her voice.

Eve stepped to the table and helped herself to cheese, ham, nuts and bread. As she ate, she wondered if she'd survive the night. Would Helen slip into her room with a knife and plunge it into her chest? Watching Helen's dark expression, she wouldn't put it past her. And what was Eve going to do with Albert? He was obviously intrigued by her. Eve had seen enough movies and read enough novels to know that in late 19th century America, men held the power in industry, politics, real estate and the home. Women had no power at all.

Just then, Eve noticed Millie coyly looking her over, wonder in her eyes. Did Millie detect something unique about her movements and overall demeanor? What was she thinking?

Eve took a sip of her tea. "This is very good," she said with a smile, looking directly at Millie. "Thank you."

Millie blushed.

"That will be all, Millie," Helen said, sharply.

Millie bobbed a bow and retreated.

After Millie's exit, Eve gathered her courage. "Forgive me for asking, but what is the date?"

Dr. Eckland looked startled, Helen suspicious, and Albert amused. It was Albert who answered.

"It is Friday, October the 24th."

Eve cleared her voice, staring down at the carpet. "And the year?" Eve asked, softly.

Dr. Eckland laid his tea cup aside, his eyebrows arching dramatically. "Surely you know what year this is, my dear. Surely."

Helen straightened her back and spoke coldly. "Perhaps she belongs in a hospital, Dr. Eckland."

Albert once again rose to Eve's defense, obviously ready to assist her in any way.

"It is 1885, Miss Kennedy. October 24, 1885."

Eve lifted her eyes to meet his warm and engaging eyes.

"I thought so," Eve lied, feeling some of the life drain from her body. "Just making sure."

And to herself, she thought, *How am I ever going to get back home?*

CHAPTER 9

E ve was awake at rosy dawn, staring out her third-floor bedroom window onto 24th Street and the thin dusting of snow that covered it. As she lifted her eyes and searched the horizon, she saw, to her astonishment, church spires instead of skyscrapers. The New York City skyline that rose up in massive towers of glass and steel—a skyline that people from all over the world loved and recognized—was simply gone, or, more accurately, it had not yet been conceived of, never mind built. Stretched out before her were low storied brownstones, chimneys belching smoke, long gray warehouses and the spires of countless churches.

Across the street was a double line of brownstone houses, all similar in style, that reminded Eve of her brownstone in the twenty-first century. She watched a Hansom cab trot across the cobblestones, while people strolled along the sidewalk, a man wearing a bowler hat, and two women in long coats and hats decorated with feathers. The hats were worn perched at the front of their heads over elaborate hairstyles; their dress hems were swaying about their ankles. A scruffily dressed newspaper boy no more than 7-years old came into view, a bundle of papers tucked under his arm. He hurried downtown against a headwind.

Eve stared transfixed as oxen pulled a huge dray loaded with lumber along the narrow street, the driver hunched over the reins, his wide-brimmed hat pulled low over his forehead and a cigar clinched between his teeth.

She sat uneasily on the broad window sill, watching this foreign world unravel past her like a movie set, like something out of a dream. She felt light-headed and a bit nauseous from the Laudanum. Thank God she'd recalled what was in the stuff before she took the prescribed spoonful before bed. She'd learned about it in nursing school. It had been widely used in the Victorian Period for everything from menstrual cramps to tuberculosis. If memory served her, it was 10% opium and 90% alcohol, flavored with cinnamon or saffron. It was awful tasting and highly addictive.

Eve felt numb and resigned as she stared out at her new world, a world so foreign and so alien that she might as well be on another planet. The white and blue cotton floral nightgown she wore was soft but large on her. Helen had sent it up with Millie, along with two day dresses that Eve had barely looked at the night before. Exhaustion and stress had taken over, and she'd fallen fast to sleep after pulling on the nightgown and flopping down onto the bed.

Eve's attention slowly shifted from the outside to the inside. She glanced about, feeling chilled, trapped, marooned and isolated. Her family didn't exist, her friends, her career, and dear sweet Georgy Boy, none of them existed now. They had not even been born. How crazy and strange was that? Would they ever be born or would she be long dead before they were born? The disorienting thought made her head spin.

In this world of 1885, she didn't know anyone, didn't know the culture, didn't know the city and had no idea how she was going to survive. As she sat there, each thought straining, each emotion aching, she felt that nauseating rise of panic again, just as she had last night when she'd realized she was not hallucinating.

Eve had fallen asleep hoping and praying that she'd wake up and the entire fantastical nightmare would be over. But it wasn't over. She'd pinched herself, touched the walls to make sure they were solid; she'd felt her skin. She was here. However it had happened, she had to face the fact that it had happened and she was now living in 1885.

At least she had slept well in the 4-poster bed, in this rose-colored room. Luckily, the sleep had revived her physically and given her some clarity of mind.

She closed the gold velvet drapes and crossed the room to the oak writing desk. She stared down at it. There was no one to write to, and that gave her a sad, empty feeling. She sat on the stylish settee, upholstered with deep diamond-tufting in white silk, and she felt like a queen on her throne. Such elegance. Even if Helen had money, Albert Harringshaw was surely footing the bill. If Eve had to guess, she'd bet it was the latter. Even in 1885, a New York brownstone had to cost a lot of money. And Eve was surprised by the room's warmth. The fireplace was now only smoldering embers, but the room was still warm because of a cast iron sectional radiator, similar to the one she had in her apartment on West 107th Street, over 130 years into the future.

Eve sat on the settee massaging her forehead, listening to the tick of the mantel clock. Her mind suddenly filled with images of her parents and friends; of her colleagues and her patients. What about Georgy Boy? Had Joni received Eve's message? Would she realize something was wrong and take care of him? Surely somebody would. But wait a minute, none of those people existed. Georgy Boy wasn't even alive! Her parents weren't alive. Eve hadn't been born yet! So who the heck was she then?

Eve put her head in her hands. But they *were* alive somewhere, in the future, wherever the heck that was. She was proof of that, wasn't she? She shook her head, fighting back tears.

Yes, her parents had to be alive somewhere. So what were they doing on this early Saturday morning so far into the future? Having brunch? Going to the movies? Was Joni having a latte at Starbucks while Georgy Boy waited anxiously on the sidewalk?

Had Eve been missed? Had the police found her cell phone and purse? Had someone filed a missing person's report? What if she never returned? Would anyone ever know what had happened to her? No, of course not. How could they? She had just disappeared—been erased from the day and the year and the roll call of the twenty-first century. Eve sighed, audibly, pushing fear and anxiety from her mind.

She lifted her head and wiped her tears. Enough of that. No more indulging in what happened, what ifs and what could be. She had to pull herself together and focus on goals and action. She had to come up with a plan. She had to find a way to survive in this time first, and then she'd set about making plans on how to return to her own time.

First things first. She needed money and a place to stay. Helen Price had already made it obvious that she wanted Eve out. Eve had seen the dark suspicion in Helen's eyes, and whenever Eve noticed Helen watching her, Eve saw jealous calculations going on behind those eyes. They were the eyes of a cold predator—an adversary, a competitor.

Albert Harringshaw had also eyed Eve with peculiar suspicion, as had Dr. Eckland. These were not stupid people. They were educated and worldly wise. They knew Eve was different from them in some profound and mysterious way, but they couldn't quite put their finger on it. How long would it be before they acted on their suspicions? Eve didn't fit into any known social or cultural slot in a time when everybody fit into a social category or slot.

It was surely Eve's aura of mystery that had captured Albert's attention right from the start. He'd been noticeably infatuated by the ambiguity of her behavior and her clothes. Dr. Eckland had tried to match Eve up with some image of reality, some familiar pattern from his vast life experience, but he couldn't, and he'd remained puzzled, curious and cautiously aloof.

He must have thought something like, "Here is a specimen I have never seen the likes of before. What exotic island has she arrived from?"

But what troubled Eve the most was Helen. Eve had met and treated many patients in her time: sane, crazy and everything in between. She was certain that Helen was a very dangerous woman. After all, her entire image and survival depended on holding on to Albert Harringshaw. And Helen surely knew how to play any game she needed to play in her world and in her time. Eve had just been born into this world and she was a baby who hadn't even learned how to crawl yet. Helen was a runner—perhaps even a sprinter.

In the short term, Eve would have to disarm Albert's attraction to her, and then get out of Helen's house as soon as possible. For that, she'd need money and a way to make a living.

Finally, the most pressing problem was: how could she ever get back to her own time? She didn't have a clue.

Eve struggled to contain a yawn, and then she stopped trying. Her attention turned back to the bed. It seemed to beckon her, entice her to bury her worries into the pillows, cover her head with the comforter and escape once more into sleep. Eve wanted to get back into that bed and sleep forever.

Minutes later, she was under the soft, warm sheets, her hair deep in the pillow, sound asleep.

A RAP ON THE DOOR awakened her. She sat up bolt erect.

She found her rusty voice. "Yes?"

"It's Millie, Miss. I have your breakfast."

"Come in."

The door opened and Millie entered, carrying a silver tray. She crossed the room and gently placed it on the side table next to the bed. It held a teapot, covered by a cozy, a white porcelain cup and saucer, a matching pitcher of milk and a silver plate cover.

"Thank you, Millie."

Millie gave a thin smile, her eyes lowered.

"What's for breakfast?" Eve asked, looking at the tray.

"An omelet, kidneys and bacon, and fresh bread, Miss Kennedy."

Eve's eyebrow lifted, and she grimaced. "Kidneys?"

"Miss Price ordered them for you. She likes kidneys."

Eve forced a smile. "How nice of her," she said, trying to hide her sarcasm.

"Will there be anything else, Miss Kennedy?"

Eve decided to seize the moment. "How long have you been working for Miss Price, Millie?"

"A little over a year."

"Do you like it here?"

Millie blinked fast, her eyes still lowered. "Yes, Miss Kennedy."

"How long has Miss Price lived here?"

"Over a year."

"So you were employed here just after Miss Price moved in?"

"Yes, Miss Kennedy."

"You can call me Eve when we're alone, Millie. It's okay."

Millie stared at her twisting hands. "Will that be all, Miss... I mean..."

Eve saw that Millie was flustered.

Eve pressed on. "Millie, has John Allister Harringshaw ever come to this house?"

Millie glanced up, her eyes moving. She opened her mouth to speak and then stopped.

"It's okay, Millie. I won't tell anybody. I promise."

Millie lowered her voice. "Mr. John Harringshaw wouldn't come here."

"Why?"

Millie shifted her weight. "I am not supposed to talk about these things, Miss Kennedy. Miss Price would be very angry with me."

Eve leaned back against the headboard. "Okay, Millie. I don't want that. I wouldn't want you to get in any trouble because of me."

Millie leaned in and whispered. "He came only once."

Eve straightened. "When?"

"Months ago. He and his brother got into an argument."

"Over what?"

Millie glanced about as if the walls had ears. "Over Miss Price."

"Why?"

Millie's voice was barely audible. "Mr. John Harringshaw wanted his brother to…" Millie searched for the right word. "… To break off the relationship because of Mr. Albert's engagement to Anne Fulton Hopkins."

"But Albert refused?" Eve asked.

Millie nodded.

"Is Mr. Albert still engaged to Miss Hopkins?"

Millie nodded.

Eve let the thought settle.

Just then, there was a hard knock on the door.

"Miss Kennedy, it's Helen Price, may I come in?"

Millie seemed to turn to stone. Her eyes registered terror.

Eve cleared her throat and nodded encouragement to Millie. "Yes, Miss Price. Please come in."

When Helen swept in, like an opera diva making an entrance, Millie curtsied, bowed and turned to leave the room. Helen's stern voice stopped her in her tracks.

"You were in Miss Kennedy's room much too long, Millie. What took you so long?"

Eve spoke up. "My apologies, Miss Price. I was asking Millie too many questions about this delicious looking breakfast."

Helen narrowed her eyes on the tray, noticing that neither the teapot cozy nor the silver plate cover had been removed. Helen smiled, but there was no mirth in it.

"I see. Leave us, Millie. You have a lot of work to do."

Millie bowed. "Yes, Miss Price."

Millie fled the room, shutting the door quietly behind her.

Helen wore a light gray day dress, with a bodice, skirt and overskirt. The corset must have been drawn tight, as her waist was quite slim compared to her shoulders and bust. Eve had to admit the woman possessed a certain sexy allure that most men would find attractive, although by twenty-first century standards, she would have been considered plump.

"I do hope you had a comfortable rest," Helen said, with the same indulgent smile she'd given Eve the night before.

"Yes. The bed is very comfortable, and the room is lovely."

Helen gave a little lift of her chin. "I have been hopeful and optimistic that with a good and restorative night's sleep, Miss Kennedy, your impaired memory would return to you, either in whole or in part."

Eve considered her words carefully. "I have recalled certain events and faces," Eve said, purposefully making her speech sound formal and vague. "I feel certain I came to New York recently, and that I am originally from some other place. But then again, there is so much more I simply cannot recall, no matter how hard I try. But I am sure I will recall everything, given a little more time."

Helen's expression darkened. "Yes, I see. More time."

"I promise not to be a burden, Miss Price. I do have plans."

There was a small silence between them.

"Plans?" Helen asked, her tone lighter. "Plans are good things to have. By the way, the dresses that Millie hung in your closet belonged to my sister. She is about your size, so I am hopeful they will fit. You will let me know if I can help you in any other way."

"Thank you, Miss Price, you have been more than helpful."

"All is well then. Please enjoy your breakfast."

Helen turned to leave, then recalled something. She faced Eve, thoughtfully.

Eve watched Helen reach into a flap pocket mounted onto a skirt panel and draw out a brown suede drawstring purse. She stood there for a time in reflective anxiety.

"Mr. Harringshaw left this for you last night. It is a sum of money. Since you lost your possessions, as well as your memory, Miss Kennedy, Mr. Harringshaw felt it was his duty, as a gentleman and as your rescuer, to offer his assistance in this way."

Helen pursed her lips as she grudgingly approached the silver tray. She lowered the purse on the tray next to the teapot, turned swiftly and withdrew to the door, waiting.

Eve stared at the purse, conflicted. If she took the purse, she'd be obligated to Albert, and run the risk of further jealousy and hatred from Helen Price. If she didn't take the money, how would she get out of that house and try to find a way to make a living?

She was trapped. She had to take it.

"Please tell Mr. Harringshaw how grateful I am for all his help. And let him know I will repay him just as soon as I can."

Helen kept her back to Eve as she opened the door. She left the room without a response.

After Helen was gone, Eve turned her head left and stared hard out the window. Her mind had completely cleared now. The shattered pieces of the events of the night before had come together; the shock and the emotions had gradually begun to dissipate, and a theory had begun to form in Eve's head. She began to take a mental inventory.

The lantern. Evelyn Sharland's lantern. John Allister Harringshaw and the letter. She'd found them in Granny Gilbert's shop. The lovers had never been able to express their love. Evelyn had died of fever. John had never recovered from her death. Was it possible that Eve could somehow find them and change the course of history? Could Eve prevent Evelyn's death? Could she somehow meet John Allister and convince him that he should marry Evelyn?

And if she managed to bring Evelyn and John together, how would she get back home to her own time?

Eve teetered over on her side, gathered herself into a fetal position, and closed her eyes.

"I've got to find that lantern," she whispered. If she had any chance at all, she would have to get that lantern.

CHAPTER 10

Eve sequestered herself in her room all day Saturday. Although Dr. Eckland and Albert Harringshaw both came by to see her, she refused to see them, claiming she was still recovering from her ordeal and didn't feel well enough to accept visitors.

Not to be put off, Dr. Eckland huffed about in Helen's parlor, finally insisting that he would come by Monday evening to conduct a thorough examination, whether Eve consented or not.

"I am afraid this Miss Kennedy is a typical, overwrought female who can only be rightly healed by a strong and practical physician such as myself," he'd blustered to Helen and Albert. "And only by the stern application of my medicine," he'd added, as he fumed out of the house.

Albert Harringshaw had listened to the doctor with mild amusement. He was well aware that the doctor's dramatic and outraged performance was given solely for him, so that Albert, his benefactor, would witness the doctor's steely dedication and conscientiousness. Thus being satisfied and impressed, Albert would keep paying the doctor's invoices.

Eve knew that Helen would prefer that she stay tucked away in her room, away from any possible contact with Albert. Eve was certain that Helen was concocting some plan to get Eve out of that house and forever out of Helen's and Albert's lives.

On Sunday, when Millie told Albert that Eve still wasn't seeing visitors, he composed a note to Eve and instructed Millie to deliver it immediately. When Eve read it, she sighed and shook her head.

Dear Miss Kennedy:

I cannot hide my disappointment at not being able to visit with you either Saturday or Sunday. I am hopeful that my communication finds you in improved spirits, with your health virtually restored. I look forward to our next meeting with pleasure and anticipation. Meanwhile, if you have need of, or wish for, anything whatsoever, please contact me, as I am your most dedicated and humble servant.

—Albert Harringshaw

Eve folded the page and tossed it into the fire. She watched it curl, crinkle and burst into flame. She could only hope that Helen had not seen Albert's note. His brazen flirtation with Eve added yet another layer of anxiety that she didn't need or want.

On Sunday evening, Millie reported that Albert and Helen had gone to dinner at Delmonico's and then they were off to the theater.

Eve did not understand how Albert could be engaged to one woman, probably a wealthy woman of his own class, and be out running around with another. Weren't there social conventions in 1885?

When Millie arrived with Eve's dinner that night, Eve took the opportunity to ask her about it. Eve was sitting at the oak desk, documenting her thoughts and feelings, and bullet-pointing possible action plans. Millie delivered the dinner tray on the side table and started for the door.

"Millie, I am slowly recalling facts about my life, and I am certain now that I have only recently arrived in New York. I suspect I am a small-town girl who doesn't know much about this city. I was wondering if I could ask you some questions."

Millie paused at the door, about to reach for the doorknob. "I suppose so, Miss Kennedy."

"Millie, how can Albert Harringshaw be seen in public with Miss Price when he's engaged to a woman of his own class?"

Millie turned to face Eve. She shrugged. "He's very rich, Miss Kennedy. Rich men can do what they like. Most of the papers don't report it. I guess Mr. Harringshaw pays them off. At least that's what I hear."

"I wonder how Miss Price and Mr. Harringshaw met," Eve said.

Millie lowered her voice to a conspiratorial whisper. "The cook, Mrs. O'Brien, said Mr. Harringshaw met Miss Price when she was performing at the Fifth Avenue Theatre. She was very popular. A lot of rich men used to wait for her at the stage door."

"Miss Price is an actress?"

"She was. Mr. Harringshaw demanded she leave the theater after he bought her this house. Mrs. O'Brien said that Miss Price insisted he purchase it for her or she wouldn't leave the theater. So she picked out this house, and he bought it for her. He pays for everything."

"And do you know anything about Albert's brother, John?"

Millie shook her head. "Just what I told you. He's engaged to Elizabeth Ashley Loring. Her family is very rich too. Their engagement was in all the papers."

"When did they announce their engagement?"

"The first of February, just before the great blizzard."

"Blizzard?"

"Yes," Millie said, nodding. "You must remember the February blizzard. Unless you weren't in the city then. If you were, you'd never forget it. The telephone lines all came down, and the wind was so frigid that horses froze to death, and children, too. Many children who lived on the streets died from the cold."

Eve sat still, her eyes probing Millie's animated face. "Yes... I think I remember." She paused. "You said John Allister Harringshaw came here once. Did you actually see him?"

She nodded. "Yes. John Allister and Albert were in the parlor arguing. I was just inside the door to the service entrance. I was going to bring them tea and sandwiches, but when I heard them arguing, I waited. The door was open just enough for me to see them standing near the fireplace."

"What does John Allister look like?" Eve asked, eagerly.

Millie's eyes filled with a dreamy haze. "He's tall and very handsome, much more handsome in person than the sketches of him in the newspapers. But he's quite different from Mr. Albert. He's quite severe and restrained in his manner. He refused to meet or talk to Miss Price. I heard him tell Mr. Albert that he was a philanderer and should break off his relationship with Miss Price immediately and marry Miss Anne Hopkins. He said that Mr. Albert was scandalizing society and soiling the reputation of the Harringshaw family."

"What did Albert say?" Eve asked.

"Mr. Albert laughed and told his brother he was a hypocrite. He said he knew about the poor girl John Allister was secretly seeing. He told his brother not to try to push into his personal affairs, when his own were soiled and tarnished and disrespectful to society and to the Harringshaw family. Albert said that if John Allister ever approached him again on the subject of Miss Price, he'd live to regret it. Albert said he'd expose John's poor little wench to the entire world."

Eve straightened, her eyes round with interest. "Did Albert say who the poor girl was, Millie? Did he say her name?"

"No, Miss Kennedy."

"What did John Allister say?"

"He did not say anything. I could see he was quite enraged, but he did not speak. He got very quiet. Then he left the house abruptly, without another word, and he has not been back, as far as I know."

"How long ago was this, Millie?"

"About two months ago."

Eve went into thought. "August?"

"Yes. Around the middle of August. It was a very hot night."

Eve looked down at the floor, her mind racing. On the desk was the suede purse filled with cash that Helen had given her.

"Millie… is sixty dollars a lot of money in the city?"

Millie pressed her lips tightly together, her eyes falling on the purse. "Oh, yes, Miss."

"How much is that? I mean, can I buy a lot with sixty dollars?"

Millie looked at Eve, struggling to understand.

"I know it's a strange question, but it's very important."

"You can buy a lot of things with sixty dollars, Miss Kennedy."

Eve went for another approach. "How much do most working people in the city earn in a week?"

Millie shoved her hands into her blue apron pocket. "Well, my brother's a carpenter. He makes sixteen dollars."

"For forty hours a week?"

"Oh, no, Miss. He works at least sixty hours a week."

Eve ran a hand through her hair. "Wow. We *have* come a long way," she said, forgetting herself for a moment.

Millie squinted a perplexed look.

"That's a lot of hours, Millie. How many hours do you work a day?"

"At least twelve, six days a week. Sometimes more."

"That's more than seventy hours a week."

"Yes, Miss."

Eve shut her eyes and massaged her forehead.

"Will that be all, Miss Kennedy?"

Eve opened her eyes, an idea forming. "When is your day off, Millie?"

"Monday."

"Millie... I was wondering. Could you show me around? I mean, show me around the city? I do not feel confident going out by myself, and I have some errands to run. I could use a companion and a tour guide—someone who knows the city. I'll pay you, of course... say five dollars."

Millie's face lit up. "Five dollars! That is a lot of money, Miss."

"Will you be my tour guide on Monday, Millie?"

Millie beamed. "Yes, Miss Kennedy. Yes."

Eve looked toward the closet where the two dresses hung. Eve had examined them earlier, and she didn't have a clue how to wear the things or what exactly she'd wear under them, or how she was supposed to look in them.

"Millie, can you show me how to dress like a real city lady?"

Millie stared at her with curious fascination, and then she lowered her gaze. "Miss Kennedy, I do not wish to be impertinent, but where did you get those clothes you were wearing the night you first arrived?"

Eve scratched the end of her nose. "From a place that's far away from here. Very far away."

"But how did you get here?"

"I don't know."

Millie suppressed a giggle. "I've never seen shoes like the ones you had on."

Eve deflected the conversation. "Will you show me how to dress, Millie?"

Millie twisted her hands, her eyes twinkling with enthusiasm.

Millie threw herself into it, presenting Eve with all the garments she'd need. First there were the drawers and the chemise and the corset, then the petticoat, the corset cover, the bustle, the underskirt, the skirt, the bodice and the beaded capelet.

Millie took the dress from the closet and held it up. It was an elegant brown wool bustle dress, with a velvet trim that came with matching round-toed boots. With great pride, Millie presented each garment and then meticulously assisted Eve as she put them on, including the dreaded corset.

Surprisingly, the boots and the dress were a satisfactory fit, except that the corset restricted Eve's breathing. With all the undergarments and the pleats, the hem and the length of the thing, she felt like a dressed up turkey.

Next came the makeup.

"Just lightly powder your face," Millie said, applying the powder. "Miss Price likes rosy cheeks, lipstick and eye shadow in moderation. She used to apply a lot more makeup, but Mr. Harringshaw asked her to use less after she left the stage."

Then Millie worked with Eve's hair. Since Eve's hair was shoulder length, Millie pulled it back and then parted it in the center, creating two long, curly fringes that hung on either side of her face.

When she'd finished, Eve stood up and stepped hesitantly before the full-length mirror, looking at herself critically, and then standing back two steps. Little by little she adjusted the dress to her hips, wriggling a bit to fit the corset and adjust the shoulders. Eve turned first left, and then right, feeling the gravity of the bulky dress, like it was an anchor. She swung it about, listening to it rustle, first ambiguous, then self-conscious and finally, pleased. The transformation was remarkable, and she turned to view a stranger: a smartly dressed woman from another time and place, staring back at her with the hint of a proud grin.

"You look so beautiful," Millie said, taking her in. "The dress fits you perfectly."

Eve shook her head. "I look like a big chicken."

Millie laughed. "I've never heard such a thing, Miss. Please do not think me disrespectful, Miss Kennedy, but you look much improved in these clothes. The clothes you wore when you arrived were plain, and somewhat immodest."

Eve turned toward her. "Thank you for all your help, Millie. What would I have done without you?"

Millie blushed and averted her eyes.

"Where shall we meet tomorrow?" Eve asked.

"At the Washington Monument at Union Square? Do you know where that is?"

Eve smiled, warmly. "Yes, Millie. I do. I'll see you there at 9 a.m."

After Millie left, Eve strode to her desk and managed to ease down, feeling the fight of the bustle and corset. She definitely felt different in Victorian dress, more formal and certainly more constrained.

Eve plotted her next move. From her telephone conversation with her father—that now seemed a lifetime ago—she'd learned that, in 1884, Evelyn Sharland had been employed as a telegraph operator at the Western Union Telegraph Company, at 195 Broadway. One year later, she might still be working there.

It was time to meet Evelyn. Eve hadn't yet figured out what she'd say to her when they were face to face, but she'd think of something before tomorrow.

CHAPTER 11

At 8:20 on Monday morning, October 27th, Eve left her room and descended the stairs, fully dressed in the bustle dress, an ankle length navy coat with a cape attached, gloves, a bonnet with straw and feathers, and a parasol. Seeing her from the partially opened parlor doors, Helen slipped out and met Eve at the bottom of the stairs.

Helen looked her over coolly, with unintentional admiration for Eve's style and poise.

"Well, Miss Kennedy. You are on your way out, I presume?"

"Yes, Miss Price. I am."

"Have you completely recovered your memory and your health?"

Again, Eve chose her words carefully. "I am better, thank you. I thought a walk would improve my overall constitution, especially since the day is so bright."

"Yes, it most certainly is a bright day, with plenty of sunshine. Will you meet someone, Miss Kennedy?"

Helen was a nosey one, Eve thought. "Perhaps I will be fortunate in that regard, Miss Price."

The vagueness of her answer stirred Helen's annoyance and suspicion. "Indeed. I wonder who the fortunate person might be."

Eve smiled, warmly. "One never knows, Miss Price. In my case, I am simply wishing for a peaceful walk and some restorative fresh air."

"Ah, yes. I think fresh air will do you a world of good, Miss Kennedy."

Out of the corner of Eve's eye, through the partially opened parlor door, she saw the back of a man. He was well built, with good shoulders, wearing a dark woolen suit. His hair was black and curly, but she couldn't see his face.

Silence hung in the room, while Eve speculated and Helen calculated.

"I should be going," Eve finally said.

Helen stepped back and Eve started for the front door, its ornately cut glass window covered by a fine French lace, tinted now by glowing morning sunlight.

"Enjoy your day, Miss Kennedy. I look forward to hearing all about it."

Eve did not turn as she opened the door. "Thank you, Miss Price, and a good day to you."

Outside, in the unusually chilly autumn day, Eve took in her new world with the brand new eyes of a child. The sky appeared bluer, the air an odd mix of smells: horse manure, burned leaves and coal dust. She noticed the heavy, wrought-iron lamp posts and the streetcar tracks threading along the cobble streets. The trees were ablaze in autumn golds and reds, leaves sailing and drifting, carpeting the sidewalks.

She spotted a two-wheeled Hansom cab, pulled by a single horse, and she waved it down. It trotted over to the curb and stopped. The driver sat in the rear on a high seat from which he could look over the top. Eve opened the cab door and pulled herself and the bulky dress inside. She sat back, feeling like a trussed up goose. The corset was tight and binding, the dress a mass of heavy silk and velvet. Eve wiggled and shimmied, trying to loosen the thing. A panel slid back, revealing a small open square in the roof. Framed in it, she saw an eye and part of a gray, bushy mustached face waiting for her to state her destination.

"Union Square," Eve said.

The panel slid closed.

The cab driver clucked at the horse, jiggled the reins, and the cab jolted forward and gathered speed, heading downtown. It swung onto Broadway, fighting its way through wandering pedestrians, the loud tangle of fine carriages, clanging trolleys and horse droppings.

Rested and more acclimated to her surroundings, Eve found her new world strangely thrilling as she watched 1885 slide by her window in full living color. She saw bearded, cane-swinging men in tall shiny silk hats, and others in high crowned derbies, most wearing ankle-length topcoats. They seemed to glide as they walked, chins up, backs erect.

Eve was fascinated by the women's fashion. On the unusually chilly day, many had donned hats, ribbon-tied under the chin. Most wore short, tight-waisted cutaway winter coats; some carried muffs and others wore gloves. On their feet were button shoes, which appeared and disappeared under the sway of long skirts that were mostly bottle-green, maroon, brown or black.

She was amazed at the crowds, the traffic and the determined energy and relentless pace that she had previously thought was particular to twenty-first century New York.

As Eve watched it all in curious wonder, she had a sudden peculiar thought. In her time—the twenty-first century—all these people were long dead, their backgrounds, childhoods, challenges, loves and hates, all gone. It was as if they'd never existed. In her time, they were forgotten ghosts, where only the famous were dimly remembered: the U.S. Presidents, the famous writers, or the super-rich with names like Astor, Vanderbilt or Carnegie.

But Eve was having a rare and unique privilege. She was seeing them alive again, moving through their lives in 1885, just as she had moved through hers in the twenty-first century, the days, weeks, months and years slipping by like a daydream. Here they were, alive again, real flesh-and-blood human beings, with careers and families, hopes and dreams.

She had somehow stumbled into their time, like a drunken woman, like an alien from some other planet. Why was she here? What strange, ineffable trick had sent her here?

As the cab approached Union Square, the great statue of George Washington loomed ahead. Eve had been to Union Square many times in the twenty-first century, but she didn't recall seeing the statue of George Washington. Here it was conspicuous and grand, standing on a granite base in a fenced enclosure in the middle of the street.

Eve spotted Millie dressed in a simple long coat and hat, standing meekly on the sidewalk, near a lamppost. Eve called up to the driver and pointed at Millie.

Millie lit up, waving. She advanced to the cab, stepped in, closed the door and sat.

She looked Eve over, proudly. "Don't you look fine, Miss Kennedy. Yes, you do look so fine in your outfit."

"Millie, we're out of the house now, call me Eve. Please."

"Okay, Miss... I mean... But you do look really fine."

"Thanks, Millie, but it wasn't easy. The maid who helped me dress this morning is a bit of a bitch."

"A bitch?" Millie asked, meekly embarrassed.

"You know what I mean. She's not so nice," Eve quickly noted.

"Yes, Miss," Millie said, averting her eyes. "You mean Mrs. Barker."

"You have to admit, Millie, that Mrs. Barker does have quite a bark."

Millie giggled in her hand at Eve's little joke. "Yes. But she has a good and kind heart, Miss. She just doesn't like the extra work on Monday, when I am off."

"Well, I can't blame her for that," Eve said.

Millie looked outside. "Where would you like to go?"

Eve looked pointedly at Millie. "I need to go to a pawnshop."

Millie was startled. "A... pawn... shop?" she repeated, haltingly.

"Yes. Do you know where I can find one?"

The driver called down. "Where to, ladies?"

Millie was a little flustered. "Well, I know there are some pawnshops in the Bowery."

Eve called up. "The Bowery, driver."

"Any place specific in the Bowery, Miss?"

"I'll let you know," Eve said. "Can you please just drive along?"

"Whatever you say, Miss," the driver said, curtly.

The cab lurched ahead.

"I never thought you to be the kind who would ever go to a pawnshop, Miss," Millie said.

Eve felt into her dress pocket for the heart pendant watch. She didn't want to part with it, but she needed money. She needed freedom from both Helen Price and Albert Harringshaw. She had to get out of that house.

"It's an emergency, Millie."

Millie sat back, studying Eve with new eyes. From the first, she'd known there was something different about Eve, but it was an elusive thing, not easily grasped—it was out of her reach and understanding. And that first night, Millie had seen the impact Eve had made on Miss Price, Albert Harringshaw and the doctor. They had studied and observed Eve with wary, curious eyes, as if she had come from some far-off primitive island or, even more shocking, as if she were an incarnate ghost from a séance. And Miss Price loved to go to séances.

There was an edge of easy confidence about Eve that Millie had seldom witnessed among women, and it made Eve attractive and exotic. Millie was delighted to be with Eve on this adventure, because she knew, instinctively, that Eve would inevitably lead her to exceptional experiences and untraveled highways. Millie's life was anything but an adventure. Her days were filled with long, arduous hours of hard work and end-less weeks with nothing but more work to look forward to. Being with Eve was like sailing away on a clipper ship to the far corner of the world.

The cab circled around Union Square and steered onto the Bowery.

Eve turned to Millie. "How old are you, Millie?"

"I am twenty-two."

"Were you born in New York?"

"Yes. But my parents came from Ireland in 1854. My mother was a domestic and my father was a carpenter, but he couldn't always find work. And then after I was born in 1863, he was killed in the war."

"Which war?" Eve asked.

Millie eyed her strangely. "The Civil War. My father was killed at Gettysburg."

"Oh, of course. I'm so sorry," Eve said, quickly. "Is your mother still alive?"

"No, she died of consumption."

"Tuberculosis?"

"Yes. Yes, they call it that now."

"It must have been hard for you to lose her. I'm sorry again."

The finer shops soon fell away and Eve took in cobbler shops, hardware merchants, barber shops, four-story flop houses, beer gardens, banks, theaters and saloons—and there were many saloons. Men stood slumped in their doorways, smoking cigars, their hats roguishly askew on their heads. Some blank and suspicious eyes looked back at her.

"Do you live with your brother now?" Eve asked.

"Yes, and my older sister, Kathleen. My younger brother was killed two years ago."

"How tragic. How?"

"He got in a knife fight down at Bandit Roost."

"Bandit Roost. What is that?"

Millie gave a little shake of her head. "You don't know the city at all, do you, Miss?"

"No, Millie, not *this* city."

"Bandit Roost is down on Mulberry Street. A lot of gangs are down there. My brother was a wild boy. My older brother, Michael, tried to keep him in line, but he couldn't watch him constantly, could he?"

"Of course not. I am sorry for your losses, Millie."

"He was a good lad," Millie said, staring ahead, as if she could see him.

They moved on, soon surrounded by beer hall dives, music halls and the obvious bordellos. There was a seediness about this part of town, a stink of stale beer and sweat. Eve saw people with the tired, worn faces slouching along the streets, carrying bundles or babies. Their eyes were watchful, guarded and sullen. Men wore heavy beards or mustaches; many had rounded shoulders in their old, heavy coats.

Eve spotted a faded green shop sign that read PAWNSHOP. She called to the driver to stop.

Millie glanced about, suddenly nervous. "Here, Miss Kennedy?"

"Why not, Millie? There's a pawnshop."

Eve handed the cabby the fare and pushed the door open. She stepped out, with a tense and alert Millie on her heels. Eve adjusted her dress and hat, gave a nod of her determined head, and pressed forward, across the crowded sidewalk, past street vendors and their carts. Eyes watched her, guarded, watchful and sullen.

Just then four boys went tearing across the sidewalk. They were no more than seven or eight years old and shabbily dressed. They charged through the crowds, their eyes wide with hope, their faces pale with fright. They turned sharply on their heels, darting out of sight into a narrow alley. A middle-aged, well-dressed man came into view, darting glances about, his face pinched in anger.

"Those street urchins stole my wallet! Where did the rascals go?"

Two men pointed at the alley. A stout policeman with a bushy mustache appeared, and the victim drew up to him, jabbing a pointed, lighted cigar at the alley. Both men hurried off in pursuit.

"Watch your purse down here, Miss Kennedy. There are pickpockets everywhere," Millie said.

"I take it ladies don't come down here very often?"

"Often, Miss Kennedy? Never."

"Whatever," Eve mumbled with a flick of her hand. "You gotta do what ya gotta do."

As they approached the shop, Eve noticed an over-printed ad on a brick building. It read *Charles Fletcher's Castoria.* "Must be a laxative," Eve said, at a whisper. She glanced about at the food carts, the push carts, and the hanging linked sausages. "God help me," she said, as she turned to look at the three-story pawn-shop. The broad sign above the door read,

PAWNBROKER'S SALE STORE

Eve stood back, looking into the plate-glass win-dows framed by round columns. She saw a hanging trumpet and trombone, racks of jewelry, a tea set, ornate vases, a dusty typewriter, cutlery and gold watches.

Eve sucked in a breath, opened the heavy glass front door and entered, hearing the bell jounce on its coiled spring. She glanced up at it, startled, then gathered her courage and advanced.

Outside, Millie's forehead wrinkled up as she approached the pawnshop. She heaved out a sigh, looked both ways, and followed Eve inside.

The long room was lit well by overhead gas lamps. A wooden floor creaked under Eve's boots. She passed between two long, wooden display cases covered in glass, holding jewelry, gold watches and jade figurines. On the wall, she noticed a glossy leather handgun holster, just like the kind they wore in the Wild West.

Eve walked to the front counter where a man in a gray, bushy mustache stared at her doubtfully. A younger, thinner man on the other side of the room leaned casually against a display case, puffing on a cigar. He seemed mildly amused. His dark hair was lacquered back off his forehead and his small wary eyes and dark beard made him look a bit evil.

Millie took in the scene and chose to stand close to the door, in case she'd have to make a run for it.

Eve walked boldly up to the older man. He watched her with bland curiosity as she withdrew the gold pendant watch from her dress and laid it on the glass counter.

"How much will you give me for this?" she asked.

The man's eyes slowly moved down Eve's neck and chest and then rested on the pendant.

"Where did you acquire this?" he asked, gazing at Eve in dark flirtation, his eyes roaming her pretty face and lively, unflinching blue eyes.

"What does it matter where I acquired it? I acquired it. It's here. How much?"

He didn't move. He stared.

"You don't want it?" Eve asked. "I'm sure there's somebody in this town who will."

He snorted a laugh and reached for it.

Eve put on a brave, calm act, but her heart was thumping in her chest, and she was sweating under the big heaping bundle of a dress.

Mr. Bushy Mustache held the pendant in his hand. He popped the catch and lifted a dark eyebrow. It was ticking. He closed it and examined the filigree on the back. He made a little grunting sound. He reached for a loupe and tucked it into his right eye. He squinted a careful look at the pendant. He popped the catch again, zeroing in on one particular detail. He grunted again, smiling with an expression of shady discovery.

Eve blinked rapidly. Millie kept throwing startled glances out the window.

The man removed the loupe, placing it, and the pendant, down on the counter.

He squared his beefy shoulders. "Is this some kind of joke?" he asked, pursing his lips, his jaw out in a kind of challenge.

"What do you mean?" Eve asked. "It's a pendant. I just want to sell it."

"There's a date etched into the base at the inside. It says 1890."

Eve felt heat shoot up her spine and flush her cheeks. "1890?" She began to stutter. "Well... obviously there's some kind of... mistake. I mean, it couldn't be 1890, could it? This is 1885. How could the etching say 1890? You're seeing it wrong."

"Not unless I drank too much Irish at Grand's Saloon on Saturday night and lost my mind and five years. Miss, where did you get this?"

Eve's mind was racing. Why hadn't she noticed the date on it? How could she have missed that? Okay, she hadn't looked very carefully. She thought fast.

"It was a gift. A gift from a good friend."

She reached for it, but the pawnbroker was faster. He snatched it away and held it tightly in his palm. He grinned, darkly. "Somebody is playing a joke on you, Miss, or maybe you're trying to play a joke on me."

"Give it back!" Eve demanded.

He threw a glance at his partner. "Imagine. 1890."

The partner laughed, blowing a plume of cigar smoke toward the ceiling. "Maybe the engraver can't see so good there, Colin. Maybe his old woman hit him on the head with a pan and he don't know where he is anymore."

Both men laughed, while Eve licked her dry lips.

Mr. Bushy Mustache held the pendant up, twirling the chain, watching the pendant spin and catch the light. "I'll tell you what. I'll give you three dollars for it. Now, that's a good price."

Right on cue, the other said, "That's a damn good price. Don't let that one get by you, madam."

Bushy Mustache said, "I like a good joke as much as the next sucker. 1890. Imagine that. I'll keep it as a good luck charm and give it to my first born."

Both men laughed again.

Eve considered. She didn't know if that was a good price or not, but she needed money and she needed to get out of there. "Okay, fine. I'll take it."

ON THE WAY OUT OF THE SHOP, Eve heard the men laughing rowdily. She didn't turn around as she left, with Millie swift on her heels.

Eve stood on the street, trembling.

"Are you all right, Miss Kennedy?"

"Yeah. Yeah, I'm fine. Those guys gave me the creeps."

Millie gave Eve an inquisitive squint. "Did the engraving really say 1890?"

"Of course not, Millie. They were just being the irritating assholes that they are."

Millie flinched at the curse word, looking down and away.

Eve shut her eyes, realizing her mistake. "Sorry, Millie. It's been a stressful few days. Forget I said that."

Millie eyed her, searchingly. "Where to now, Miss?"

Eve opened her eyes. "The Western Union building on 195 Broadway. There's a woman there I want to meet. She may be my ticket back home."

"And where is your home?" Millie asked.

"Never mind, Millie. I'll tell you some day. Let's go."

Just as Eve was about to swing up into the carriage, she caught a glimpse of a man turning away.

He wore a long greatcoat and derby hat, but it was his build that caught her eye. He was a tall, well-built man, just like the man she'd seen in Helen Price's parlor. Was Helen having Eve followed?

CHAPTER 12

The Broadway commercial district was overrun with telegraph and electrical lines strung across streets and the tops of buildings. To Eve it looked like a chaotic mess, designed by a madman. The cab moved through the snarling, tangled traffic and Eve wondered why there were no signal lights—or at least some policemen directing traffic. They arrived at Broadway and Dey Street, and Eve looked out to see a massive turreted building topped by a clock tower.

"Impressive," Eve said, nodding her head. "It has ten floors."

"A girlfriend of mine applied to work here, but she didn't get the job," Millie said. "She said they don't hire many women. It has a passenger elevator and a hundred operators that work in shifts twenty-four hours a day."

"Look how it dwarfs the Goodyear Rubber Goods building," Eve said. "Wish I could take a picture of this thing. Wouldn't that be something, Millie? You and me in a Selfie in front of this building. Now that would be something to post on *Facebook*."

Once again, Millie looked confused.

"Oh, never mind, Millie," Eve said, lightly. "I'm just blabbing on about nothing."

They left the cab and ascended wide cement steps, passing between monumental columns as they approached the heavy glass doors. Millie paused.

"Miss Kennedy?"

Eve stopped and turned. "Yes?"

"Maybe I should stay out here," Millie said, her eyes lowered.

"Why?"

"I am not as bold as you are, Miss Kennedy. I feel uneasy."

"But why?"

"Who is it you are looking for?" Millie asked. "May I be so bold as to ask?"

Eve stepped over to her. "Yes, Millie. Of course. The woman who works here is a sort of acquaintance. She might even be a distant cousin."

Millie didn't lift her eyes. "Miss Kennedy, has your memory returned? Do you recall now where you came from and how you chanced to be on that park bench in Central Park?"

A gust of wind nearly blew Eve's hat from her head. She grabbed it and held it down firmly with a heavy hand. Eve narrowed her eyes, assessing the words, the problems, and the issues. "Millie, do you trust me?"

Millie raised her eyes. "Yes, Miss Kennedy. I do trust you."

"Okay then. I am not going to tell you where I came from or how I got here. At least not now. Maybe I will, some day. We'll just have to see. You'll just have to trust me. Can you do that?"

Millie considered Eve's words. She nodded.

"Good. All right. You can stay out here if you like. This shouldn't take more than a half hour. If you get cold, just come inside. Okay?"

Millie nodded again.

Just as Eve turned toward the entrance, she spotted the man again, standing down on the sidewalk about forty feet away, leaning back against the base of a streetlight, a newspaper covering his face. His build was the same. Hair the same. Hat the same. Clothes the same. Eve frowned and sighed. So Helen *was* having Eve followed. Had it been Helen's idea or Albert's? Did it matter? Should Eve confront him? Maybe in time. Not now.

Eve pivoted and entered the building through the heavy wood and glass doors. The Western Union Lobby had an impressive domed ceiling, with large display windows and hanging bronze gas lamp chandeliers. Eve walked briskly across the shiny black and white stone tiles to the polished oak lobby desk. Standing behind the desk, elevated above her like a judge, was a man in his late 40s, dressed in a black suit, a tie and a very stiff, high collar white shirt. His frame was narrow; his face angular and somber. He reminded Eve of an undertaker in some old movie. He leaned, looked her over and sniffed, pompously.

"Yes, madam?"

"I believe you have an employee by the name of Evelyn Sharland working here. If possible, I would like to speak with her."

"Employees receive a half hour lunch break between the hours of 12 p.m. and 1 p.m., depending on the work flow and that, of course, is also at the discretion of the manager on the floor. Employees may or may not receive a lunch break."

Eve glanced at the wall clock. It was 10:35. "I see. Is there any way you can tell me if Evelyn Sharland is actually employed here?"

"You just told me she is employed here," he said, coolly.

"No, I said I believe you have an employee by that name."

He sniffed again, looking away from her. "That information would be ascertained through the Personnel Department, but they do not give out that information to the general public."

"Okay, can I wait for her?"

"If in fact she does work here, she will not come this way or leave the building until her shift is over. Employees have lunch on the premises."

"What time does she get off work?"

"I wouldn't know. Some work later than their required shifts."

Eve summoned patience. This guy was being purposely difficult. "Okay, if she were to work a normal shift, what time would she get off?"

He shuffled through some papers. "This building runs twenty-four hours, madam. I do not know if the woman works the day or the night shift."

Eve stood up a little straighter, ready for a fight. "What time did you begin work today, sir?

The question startled him. He glanced up and kinked his neck. "I begin at 8 a.m."

"And what time do you finish?"

He sniffed again. "At 8 p.m."

"And your replacement will begin his shift at 8 p.m.?"

Now he was annoyed. "Yesss," he said, clipping the word off sharply.

"So if Evelyn Sharland began her shift at 8 a.m., she'd most likely leave at 8 p.m.? Is that correct?"

His gaze was cold and direct. "I would presume so, madam. Now, if you will excuse me, I have work to attend to."

Eve felt heat rush to her face. "Well, haven't you been gracious and helpful, sir? Where I come from, we would call you a royal pain in the ass. Good day, sir."

His lips tightened, and he scowled at her. Eve whirled and walked away.

Outside, Eve breathed out her irritation and saw Millie coming toward her.

"Did you speak with her, Miss Kennedy?"

"No. I don't even know if she works here. You know what, let's grab a cab and go to..." Eve shut her eyes, allowing her annoyed brain to clear so she could recall the address. "Let's go to 232 East 9th Street. Do you know where that is?"

"Yes," Millie said. "It's not too far away."

Eve stole a glance toward the street. She didn't see the man. He wasn't at the lamppost, and he wasn't hanging around on the sidewalk, but Eve had the feeling he was around, and he was watching her.

IN THE CAB, EVE LAID her head back on the hard, tufted leather upholstery and shut her eyes for a while. They rode in silence, while Eve listened to the trot of the horse. When she opened her eyes, she stared out the window, deep in thought. She watched a gray-bearded man dodging through the traffic; she saw two women in long dresses and big hats walking so grace-fully and elegantly, as if they were in a dance. How did they move so easily in those dresses? Eve watched car-riage wheels revolving, the spokes catching the sun-light; she saw horses trotting by, heads held high, their coats burnished brown and golden in the light.

Eve sat preoccupied with her own survival; with finding Evelyn and the lantern so she could return to her own time. She felt clumsy, startled and out of sync in this time and place. Her body was still trying to ad-just to the pace and rhythm, to the language and mode of speech, to the sharp earthy smells and the strange clothes, and to a thousand other things that seemed to assault her and throw her off-balance.

Her brain was not wired to this time. She had not been born for this time, and she felt a big empty hole in her heart. She missed her family and friends. She missed Georgy Boy and her work. She missed her life in the twenty-first century. It had been a good life—except for her marriage and divorce—but that was all over, and she had been looking forward to a new and richer life. She'd hoped to meet a guy and fall in love again, get married and begin a family.

That was all gone now, the possibility of it seeming more remote every hour. Her life—the trajectory of her life—was over, at least in that time. She had to face the fact that she might never be able to return home, and that singular thought both depressed her and terrified her.

"Are you okay, Miss Kennedy?" Millie asked, seeing the anxiety in Eve's face.

Eve lifted her chin a little, hoping to show courage. "Yes, Millie, I'm fine. Just fine. I'm hoping Evelyn works the night shift. She might be home now."

"What happens if she is not home?" Millie asked.

Eve sighed. "Then you can take me on a tour of the city."

Millie brightened. "Oh, I would like that. There are so many things to see."

The cab drew up to the curb, Eve paid the driver, and the two ladies climbed out, lifting their hems to avoid trash, litter and manure. Eve's heart sank as she looked around at the shady, unfortunate neighborhood. She saw block after block of desolate, five-story row houses, neglected and shabby. Dirty children in tattered clothes sat on steps, or hid in the shadows of doorways, staring with the distant, emotionless eyes of the old and forgotten. Boys were playing ball in the street, their voices sharp, their fists ready. They looked rough and threatening.

Eve looked at Millie's downcast face.

"I don't like the looks of this, Millie."

"These are five story walkups, with four apartments on each floor," Millie said. "I have been in buildings like them. There is not much sunlight, and the air doesn't circulate very well."

Millie folded her hands, staring down at the craggy pavement. "My brother and I used to live just down the block. When he began making more money, and I got my job with Miss Price, we moved to a nicer place uptown."

Eve tried to project an impression of strength, but she looked about bleakly, flattened by the heavy, depressing mood of the place.

Eve lifted her shoulders and then dropped them. "Well, okay, Millie, let's see if Evelyn is home."

At the broken, leaning wooden stairs, a little girl of about ten-years old sat staring warily, with a proud, defiant expression.

"Hi there. My name is Eve."

The little girl didn't respond.

"Do you know if Evelyn Sharland lives here?"

The little girl searched Eve's eyes, and then she looked at Millie.

"Gone," the girl said.

Eve swallowed away disappointment. "You mean she doesn't live here anymore?"

"Gone. Moved," the girl repeated.

"How long ago?"

She shook her head.

"Do you know where she moved to?"

The girl shook her head again.

"Did someone help her move? I mean, did she leave with somebody?"

"She's gone."

Eve wilted. No Evelyn. No lantern. No chance to get back home.

Eve stood staring at the little girl, hoping for some different answer that she knew would never come.

"Thank you," Eve said, softly.

Eve stared up into the sky, watching a stringy white cloud drift over. Pigeons wheeled and darted over chimneys and sloped rooftops. She was about to walk away when it suddenly struck her. This was the address

John Allister Harringshaw had written on the envelope in December—addressed to Evelyn Sharland.

Eve looked at the little girl again, lowered her voice and smiled. "Does Evelyn's mother live here?"

The little girl nodded. "Yes, on the fourth floor."

Eve passed Millie a look of relief.

"Do you know the apartment?"

"Three."

"Thank you so much," Eve said, giving the girl a warm smile.

Eve reached into her pocket for some money, but Millie laid a hand on her wrist to stop her. She shook her head.

"I wouldn't, Miss. Not here. There are many eyes watching, if you know what I mean."

Eve reluctantly obeyed.

Eve led the way into the apartment building that was cold and foreboding. It was a place of shadows, trapped earthy smells, human sweat and dim lighting. They mounted the squeaking wooden stairs, using the rickety banister sparingly, afraid the thing would come apart.

On the fourth floor, they strolled along a dusty, thread-bare carpet until they came to a door that had a tarnished tin number 3 nailed to it.

Eve felt a hitch in her throat and she gulped it away. She could be close to finding her way back home, if the lantern was inside.

She knocked lightly. There was no sound. She knocked again, more forcefully.

The door swung open so swiftly that it startled both girls. Standing before them was a thin, pale woman, with crinkled gray hair and dull gray eyes. Her hair was tied up in the middle and secured in back with a bun. Her shoulders were wrapped in a blanket, and Eve thought the woman looked so sad and forlorn that she probably hadn't smiled in years.

"Yes, who is it?" she said, in a low, scratchy voice.

Eve stepped back, instinctively. "My name is Eve… Eve Kennedy. I am looking for Evelyn."

The woman's frosty eyes didn't blink. "She's not here," she said, curtly.

"Do you know where I can find her?"

"No, I don't. She moved out. I don't know where."

"Do you know anyone who might know?" Eve asked softly, wishing she could enter the place and look around for the lantern.

The woman's eyes flamed. "If I knew that I would have told you, wouldn't I?"

Eve lowered her voice. "Are you Evelyn's mother?"

The woman waited, looking over Eve's shoulder into the dim light, staring at nothing. "Yes, I am."

"Is Evelyn still working for Western Union?"

Mrs. Sharland's lips trembled. She looked away. "Did you work there with her?"

"No. I am just a friend."

Mrs. Sharland's eyes cleared. The anger melted away, and the woman began to soften. In that instant, Eve saw that this woman and Eve's father had similar noses and chins. It was startling. Eve could actually see some of her father in this woman. This was, after all, a relative—a very distant relative.

"My daughter is sick…" Mrs. Sharland said, sorrowfully. "She moved out to protect me. I told her not to. I told her I didn't care. I told her I'd take care of her, but she didn't listen. She left and she wouldn't tell me because... Well, as I said, she didn't want me to catch it."

Millie stared down at her shoes. Eve suddenly felt great compassion for this woman, living alone in a broken down tenement in a cold, gray room.

"If I may ask," Eve said, "Do you know what illness your daughter has?"

"Tuberculosis."

Millie gasped, a hand covering her face. She turned and moved down the hallway as if she'd seen a ghost.

Eve stared at the woman, seeing her quiver in the cold, numb with distress. Her heart opened in sympathy.

"I have to go," Mrs. Sharland said. "I have a lot of work to do. I'm a seamstress and I'm behind."

Eve wouldn't be able to enter and look around. The lantern probably wasn't there, anyway. Evelyn had probably taken it when she moved, or maybe it was never there.

Eve took a five-dollar coin from her purse and offered it to Mrs. Sharland.

The woman looked down at it, strangely, as if she didn't understand.

"Please take it, Mrs. Sharland. Please. Evelyn would want you to."

Mrs. Sharland's trembling hand lifted to take it, then she stopped. "Who are you?"

"Just a friend. I will try to find Evelyn and help her if I can."

Eve pressed the 1885 five-dollar Liberty Head Half Eagle gold coin into Mrs. Sharland's hand. Mrs. Sharland's eyes misted up as she stared down at it. She tried to speak, but she faltered.

"If I find Evelyn, Mrs. Sharland, I will let you know."

Eve gave her a reassuring smile, then turned and walked toward the stairs.

OUTSIDE, EVE AND MILLIE WALKED for a time in silence. They walked past sagging houses and gray dilapidated neighborhoods and they saw men sleeping on fire escapes and in doorways and hiding out in alleys, looking back at them with gaunt, hollow eyes.

They soon arrived in a cleaner, safer-looking neighborhood, and Eve relaxed her shoulders.

"What kind of work do these people do?" Eve asked.

"Store clerks, wagon drivers and factory workers. A little of whatever they can find. Some are employed by the Manhattan Gas Works and the Turpentine distilleries. Some work in the saloons."

The air smelled of coal oil, resin and pine sap.

"This is not the city I thought it would be," Eve said. "Not that I thought about it all that much."

Millie looked long and steady at her. "So you planned to come here, Miss?"

Eve chided herself for confusing Millie once again. "Don't listen to me, Millie. My head is still messed up. Sometimes I don't know where I am. Sometimes I don't even know who I am."

A dark cloud covered the sun, and the wind swept in sharply, rustling the leaves. One crimson maple leaf sailed down and stuck to Eve's coat. She grabbed it and held it up to the sky, studying its intricate vein work to see if it was real, as if she were still trying to prove to herself that she was living and breathing in 1885.

"I am sorry for what I did back there," Millie said. "It's just that the word 'tuberculosis' brought back such terrible memories about my mother."

"I understand. It was a shock. It wasn't what I'd expected either. I thought she had typhoid fever. I've got to try to find Evelyn, and fast."

Millie turned. "Why did you think she had typhoid fever, Miss Kennedy?"

"I don't know. I just didn't think she had tuberculosis."

"She won't survive, Miss," Millie said, softly. "I am sorry to say that, but no one seems to survive that awful illness. The coughing is terrible."

Eve lowered her head, lost in stern concentration. These were the days before penicillin. It wouldn't be widely used for infections until the early 1940s. So there were no antibiotics and no sulfa drugs. Nothing. How did physicians treat tuberculosis in 1885? By doping people up on Laudanum? Eve recalled seeing only one case of tuberculosis when she was in school, during her clinical hours. The doctors had prescribed Isoniazid and Rifampin, and the patient had been taking antibiotics for six months. So was Millie right? Was Evelyn doomed to die?

During their walk, Eve occasionally stole glances over her shoulder. Once she was sure she saw the man following them. But he was skilled, like a flickering shadow. There one minute, gone the next. He was starting to irritate her. What did he want? What was he looking for?

They hailed an Omnibus pulled by four horses and climbed aboard. Eve deposited two nickels in the fare tin box, and the two women sat down on a wooden bench as they started their journey uptown.

Millie became the tour guide, pointing out places of interest, but Eve was too engrossed with her thoughts to pay much attention. At 42nd and Park Avenue, Millie pointed to the Grand Central Depot. Eve nodded, seeing the three story red brick and white stone structure, but it meant nothing to her. At West 39th Street, Millie indicated toward the Metropolitan Opera House. Eve nodded distractedly, hearing the endless clatter of wheels on cobble, and the neighing and whinnying of horses prancing for the right of way.

Eve was surprised to see that up here, in a nicer neighborhood, a stout policeman dressed in a tall helmet and white gloves was directing the flow of traffic with a thin baton, as if he were an orchestral conductor.

At the Croton Reservoir at 42nd Street and Fifth Avenue, they exited the Omnibus and approached the massive, fifty-foot granite walls that surrounded the above-ground reservoir. Eve was amazed by the edifice.

"This supplies the city's drinking water?" Eve asked.

Millie nodded. "Yes. You haven't seen it before?"

"No." Eve kept glancing back over her shoulder, looking for their shadow. She didn't see him.

"It's a man-made lake," Millie said, looking up. "Along the tops of the walls are public promenades that offer pleasant panoramic views. I've walked them several times. Shall we walk, Miss Kennedy?" Millie asked, seeing Eve was lost in thought.

On the way uptown, it had occurred to Eve—for the first time—that she could have already altered the natural course of history, albeit in some small way. Her presence in this time could have some impact that could dramatically, or not so dramatically, change the future. Wasn't this the problem all science fiction and time travel stories dealt with? She recalled watching the movie *Back to the Future* with her ex-husband, Blake, as well as his favorite episode from the original *Star Trek* series, *The City on the Edge of Forever*.

If you change the past, do you change the future?

Millie repeated her question. "Miss Kennedy... would you like to take a promenade along the reservoir?"

Eve snapped alert. "Yes, yes, of course, Millie. Let's go."

They climbed the great flight of stone steps to the top, where they had an unobstructed view of the river, the city, and the New Jersey Palisades. Eve looked down a Fifth Avenue that was completely altered from the one she knew. This was a narrow, quiet street, with magnificent palatial residences. She stopped walking, shading her eyes from the sun, hoping to recognize the Harringshaw mansion. Then the thought came to her. Did John Allister know that Evelyn had moved and where she had moved to?

If she could find Evelyn and if, by some chance, she could save her life, would that change the course of history? Would it change her own life?

"Miss Kennedy, are you all right? You look pale again."

Eve stood there gazing out at the brownstone mansions, transfixed. She thought she saw Saint Patrick's Cathedral, but it looked all wrong.

"Is that Saint Patrick's Cathedral?" she asked Millie.

"Yes."

"There are no spires."

"No, Miss Kennedy," Millie said. "The cathedral is not finished yet."

Eve looked away. There was no Rockefeller Center or Saks Fifth Avenue, and there was no 42nd Street Library or Bryant Park, because she was standing on the spot where they would appear many years later.

Eve stared, disconsolate. Suddenly, she had vertigo. Everything seemed to be spinning around her. All that she had seen and experienced—all the conversations, the images, the possibilities and the confusion—was too overwhelming. Her brain simply could not absorb it all. She felt exhausted and unstable.

Millie watched in concern. Eve was standing absolutely frozen, hardly breathing.

"Miss Kennedy, are you ill?" She looked at Eve with the eyes of a frightened child.

Eve struggled to find her voice. "I need to go home, Millie. I just need to get out of here. Please, I need some water. I need some sleep. Just get me out of here."

CHAPTER 13

Late that evening, Eve lay quietly in bed, staring at nothing, merely resting in the soft yellow glow of the gas lamps. She listened to the burning logs in the fireplace as they snapped and hissed, and was comforted by the sound of a horse's hooves clopping across the cobbles. She had finally come up with a plan.

When she had arrived back at Helen Price's house that afternoon, Helen had met her in the foyer. Eve told her she wasn't feeling well, and that she was going straight to her room. From Helen's forced, empathetic tone, Eve knew she wasn't pleased that Eve wouldn't be moving out anytime soon.

Eve immediately plunged into a deep sleep and awoke at 6:30, just as the cook placed a dinner tray at her door and knocked softly. Helen was housing and feeding her, despite her own jealousy, strictly following Albert's orders. But it was he who was pulling the strings.

After eating, Eve paced the room for several hours, struggling to fight back mounting fears and quivering irrational impulses to check herself into a hospital and feign illness for a while, just to escape from everything. But of course that was no solution, because she might be committed to an insane asylum. She felt lonelier and more homesick than any little girl ever felt at summer camp.

Sometime after 9 p.m., she slowly pulled herself together and came up with a plan that might allow her to escape Helen Price's house and establish roots of her own, at least until she could find Evelyn Sharland and retrieve the lantern which might allow her to return home. She crawled back in bed, hoping to rest quietly until sleep would once again provide a welcomed escape.

She was startled when she heard a soft knock on the door. She lifted up on her elbows.

"Yes?"

"Miss Kennedy, it is Dr. Eckland here. May I enter?"

Eve had assumed she'd see him soon and had incorporated him into her plan. "Yes, Dr. Eckland. Come in."

Dr. Eckland entered quietly, standing erect in the glow of the fire, dressed in a black cutaway coat with silk lapels and a winged collar, black-and-white striped pants, and a black ascot tie. His black leather medical bag was in his hand.

"How are you feeling this evening, Miss Kennedy?"

"Much better. Thank you."

"Really? Miss Price told me you looked quite pale this afternoon. I expected to hear that your condition had worsened."

"Not at all, Dr. Eckland. I just needed to sleep. I am much better. The outing today did me a world of good, even if it tired me out."

"I am glad to hear it! Very glad to hear it. Please excuse the late hour and my dress. I just came from the theater."

He unbuttoned his coat. Across his vest hung a heavy gold chain with a watch on the end tucked into his vest pocket. He clicked the watch open and checked the time.

"It is even later than I thought. Nonetheless, if you would permit it, I would like to examine you."

Eve sat up and braced her back against two pillows. Dr. Eckland found an upholstered chair and drew it up next to her. After he took her wrist to check her pulse, she casually asked her first question.

"Are you married, Dr. Eckland?"

"I was. My wife is deceased. Five years now."

"I am sorry to hear it," Eve said. "Do you have any children?"

"I have a daughter and a son. My daughter is about your age. She is married, living in Chicago. My son is an adventurer, I guess you might say. He moved to San Francisco two years ago. I have not seen him since, although he does write now and then."

"What type of work does he do?"

"He builds marbleized mantels and sells stoves and ranges. He says business is booming out there. I guess he's amassing a small fortune. He says San Francisco will be larger than New York someday."

Dr. Eckland released her wrist. "Your pulse is strong and normal, Miss Kennedy. How is your diet? Have you been eating?"

"Yes, although I am not so fond of mutton."

"Mutton is good for you. Eat it. It will give you strength."

Eve tried to think of a smooth transition into the next subject. "Dr. Eckland, in my travels today, I heard someone speak about tuberculosis. The woman said her sister had it."

His voice deepened. "Tuberculosis? Well, of course I have seen my share of it as a doctor, as well as scarlet fever and smallpox."

"Where would a woman in New York go for treatment, if she had tuberculosis?"

Dr. Eckland took this in with a little nod. "If the woman is from a good family, they would see to her care, of course. Perhaps they would employ a private nurse or she would be sent to Davos, Switzerland or Saranac Lake, New York. Rest in the open air is of paramount importance. There are special houses and cabins built to allow easy access to the outdoors. Of course, going away causes a long separation from home and family so it can be a hardship. And the financial cost is a consideration."

"What if the woman doesn't have much money?" Eve asked. "What if she cannot afford to go away?"

"Well then, that is a different matter. She might be admitted to the Knickerbocker Hospital here in Manhattan. It is a fully equipped hospital."

"Where is that?"

"It is located on Convent Avenue and 131st Street in Harlem. It serves primarily poor and immigrant patients and it is the only general hospital north of Ninety-Ninth Street. During the war, it served as a temporary Civil War tent facility for returning Union Army invalids. I offered my services to some of those poor fellows in those dreadful days."

Dr. Eckland took a handkerchief from his rear pocket and dabbed at his forehead. "Those are not good memories for me, Miss Kennedy. I saw many a brave man die there. Many a good and brave man."

"I am sure they benefited from your skill and kindness, Dr. Eckland."

He replaced the handkerchief, shaking his head. "My skills were often not good enough, I am afraid, but I did my best. I rest at night confident that I did my best."

Eve saw him grow sullen as he reflected.

"Dr. Eckland, are there any hospitals close by that treat patients with tuberculosis?"

"Let me think. There is Gouverneur Hospital in the Financial District. It serves the European immigrants on the Lower East Side. It opened just this year. Its original purpose was to treat accident cases; however, I learned recently that it is the first public hospital in the country to create a tuberculosis clinic."

He pulled out his stethoscope. "It also has a female ambulance surgeon in its employ, something I find personally questionable, but I suppose that is the way of the world these days. But as I said, I have heard from colleagues that there are a number of female tuberculosis patients at the clinic."

Eve let that settle for a moment, while Dr. Eckland checked her heart and lungs.

"Dr. Eckland, how do you treat a patient with tuberculosis?"

He cleared his throat. "Why this sudden interest in tuberculosis, Miss Kennedy? Surely you do not think you are suffering from that dreaded disease?"

"No. No. Just curiosity, I guess."

"Well, this certainly is not the usual topic of conversation for most young women."

He examined her throat, ears and eyes, and then his eyes quizzed her face. "Of course, Miss Kennedy, I realize you are not like most young women I have met."

Eve shifted nervously under his gaze. "No? Surely I am not so different," she said, with a forced smile.

Dr. Eckland breathed in. "There is something, how do I say, uncommon about you, Miss Kennedy. I am a lover of the theater, and I sometimes have the keen impression that you are playing a part, and that the authentic you lay somewhere hidden behind a veil or a mask."

Eve struggled for calm. Was it that obvious? Was he on to her? "Well, I do have a curious nature, Dr. Eckland. I admit that. Perhaps that is what you are detecting."

And then, before Dr. Eckland could answer, she asked again. "So, how do you treat tuberculosis?"

Dr. Eckland sat up a little taller, inflated by his knowledge and his desire to expound upon it.

He lowered his voice. "It is a terrible disease. Highly contagious. Transmission occurs when the patient exhales, coughs, or sneezes. Preventing its spread has become one of the most pressing problems we face, and the primary motivation for most public health campaigns these days. Of course we are more modern now than in the past, and we have learned many things not previously known. For example, we now require all treating nurses and doctors to wear masks, as must all friends and relatives who come to visit. Sanitary conditions are of vital importance."

"Have you found any effective medications for it?"

"Medications?" Dr. Eckland repeated. He shrugged. "Isolation, good clean air and prevention are what is called for, Miss Kennedy."

Eve's head tipped to one side as she thought. "I suppose it is always fatal?"

Dr. Eckland stared into the fire, soberly. "Are you familiar with the writer George Sand, whose given name was Amantine-Lucile-Aurore Dupin?" the doctor asked, speaking the French name perfectly.

"No, I'm afraid not."

"But you are familiar with Frédéric Chopin, the great composer, are you not? Surely you have heard his *Nocturnes*?"

Eve had heard of them, maybe in her high school music appreciation class. "Yes... I know of him."

"Chopin died of tuberculosis in 1849. Mademoiselle Dauroe Dupin, his, shall we say, mistress, wrote to a friend that 'Chopin coughs with infinite grace.' It was a sad end to a great and young composer, and it has been a sad and tragic end to many persons, Miss Kennedy, including a nephew of mine. He died tragically from the disease at 12 years old. It was a ghastly end, poor boy."

"When was that?" Eve asked gently.

"In 1883. I remember it well because the very next week I had to attend the Harringshaw costume ball. I did not wish to, of course, but, well, the Harringshaws have been good patients of mine. I felt it was my duty."

Dr. Eckland shifted his eyes back to Eve. They were sad, and Eve was touched by this. She could see that Dr. Eckland was a sensitive man and probably as good a doctor as he could be. This emboldened her to trust him, at least a little.

He tapped his knee, suddenly remembering something. "Oh my, the Harringshaws are having another one of those balls on December 4th. I suppose I will have to go. Well, yes, of course I must go. Unfortunately, my daughter will not be in town to accompany me. I shall have to find someone else. Well, no matter. Anyway, Miss Kennedy, tuberculosis is almost always a fatal disease."

Eve lowered her eyes. "I am sorry to hear that."

After a brief silence, Eve turned to the doctor. Dr. Eckland sat back, and in the gaslight, his bushy muttonchops and earnest expression gave him a professorial countenance.

He folded his hands, his expression earnest. "Now, how is your memory, Miss Kennedy? Do you have any recollection as to who you are and where you came from?"

Eve smiled, nodding her head, ready with the answer. "As a matter of fact, Dr. Eckland, I do recall something of my past."

He leaned forward, twisting his hands, his interest sharpening. "Please tell me, Miss Kennedy."

"I am a nurse, Dr. Eckland. Today, I remembered that I am a nurse."

His voice was hesitant, low, his expression doubtful. "A nurse? Are you quite sure?"

"Yes, Dr. Eckland."

"So that explains your interest in tuberculosis. What else? What else do you recall?"

"I am from Ohio."

"Where in Ohio?"

"I am not exactly sure, but I know it's Ohio."

"Do you recall family and friends? Perhaps you have a husband? Surely a young woman as attractive as you, if you will permit me to say so, is married."

Eve hesitated for a moment. "Since I am not wearing a ring, I am sure I do not have a husband. I feel positive about that. As for my family, well, I can see faces, but I am not sure if they're *my* family. It's still a little blurry."

Dr. Eckland sighed. "Miss Kennedy, this is promising. Yes, this is very promising indeed."

Her voice took on urgency. "Dr. Eckland, can you help me get employment as a nurse?"

The question seemed to startle him. "Employment?" He glanced about the room, as if seeking the answer. "Well, I don't know."

Eve inclined forward. "I know I'm a good nurse, Dr. Eckland. I am a very good nurse. I know that for sure."

"That all may be well and good, young woman, but do you have a diploma from a reputable nursing school, such as Broad Street Hospital, where I see patients?"

Eve was ready for this. "Obviously, I don't remember where I received my training, Dr. Eckland, but I would be happy to work for low wages until I could prove myself."

"That is quite impossible, Miss Kennedy." He shook his head. "And even if I could arrange it, how could we trust that your memory for nursing practices is intact?"

She leveled her determined eyes on him. "Dr. Eckland, can I work with you until I prove myself? You can watch me, study me. You will see I am a good nurse. I must work to earn money. I do not want to be a burden on Miss Price or take advantage of Mr. Harringshaw's generosity."

"My dear Miss Kennedy, whether you are a good nurse or not is beside the point. You need a diploma. Surely, you must know that. These are modern times. We simply cannot let you practice the profession of nursing based on your word, with no credentials from a reputable institution. I am sorry, but it is quite impossible."

He softened his tone, offering her a reassuring smile. "Miss Kennedy, do not worry about being a burden to Mr. Harringshaw. He is a kind and generous man who is only too happy to support you in your time of need."

Eve knew that was coming and she was ready for him. She folded her arms, turning deadly serious.

"Dr. Eckland, would you want your own daughter to accept Mr. Harringshaw's many overtures and generosities?"

Dr. Eckland stood abruptly, stammering to get a word out. "Miss Kennedy, that is not seemly. It is not a fair or an appropriate question. It just isn't seemly."

"It may not be seemly, Dr. Eckland, but you know what I mean. I want to work and find my own place. Isn't that what you would want for your daughter, if she were in my place?"

His mouth twitched, and he blinked rapidly as he struggled for words. "Miss Kennedy, I am heartened that you are feeling better. Yes, very pleased and heartened."

He turned for his medical bag and started for the door. He reached for the doorknob, but Eve's voice stopped him from opening it.

"Won't you please help me, Dr. Eckland?"

He paused, only for a few moments, keeping his back to her.

"Miss Kennedy, I cannot say I am not... impressed by you."

He turned to look at her. "You have a good mind and a worthy ambition, for a woman, and I sense that you are in need of help. Yes, I see all this."

He stood there in the soft aura of firelight, avoiding her eyes. "I will see what I can do for you, Miss Kennedy. I cannot promise anything, but I will see what I can do. Good evening."

He turned and left the room.

Eve's shoulders slumped. What did 'I will see what I can do' mean? Dr. Eckland was a kind man, she could see that, but could she wait for his help or should she seek help elsewhere?

"Just keep pushing," her father used to say, "And the door will eventually open. It never fails."

EVE SLEPT SURPRISINGLY WELL that night. She arose early and was dressed by the time Millie knocked and entered, carrying Eve's breakfast. Millie looked downcast, avoiding Eve's eyes as she set the tray down on the nearby side table, bobbed and turned to leave.

"Millie? What's wrong? Are you mad at me for something?"

Millie waited obediently by the door.

"No, Miss Kennedy. I have a lot of work to do is all."

"Millie, did Miss Price say something to you about me?"

"I have to go, Miss Kennedy."

"She did, didn't she? How did she know we were out together? You left the carriage a good two blocks away from the house."

"Please, Miss Kennedy. I don't want to lose my job."

"All right, Millie. Can you do me a favor? Can you bring me the morning paper, please?"

Millie bowed. "Yes, Miss." She bowed and left.

While Eve chewed the fresh bread—which tasted better than any she'd ever eaten in the twenty-first century—she figured out how Helen knew she and Millie had been together the day before. It was the shadow. The jerk who had been following them.

Eve flushed with anger. She was tired of being trapped, followed and patronized. She was tired of being a woman in 1885, powerless and subjugated. She knew Albert Harringshaw would be calling soon, maybe even that night, and he would expect something in return for his favors. Who knows what he would say or do? He would want to make a move sooner or later, and Eve didn't want to be around when he did. She had to take some action and get away from this place as soon as possible.

Millie returned with the folded morning paper and did not make eye contact when Eve thanked her. She promptly left with another bob of a bow.

Eve snapped open *The New York Sun* for Tuesday, October 27, 1885. She skimmed the front page: A policeman had hired a convict to kill his wife, but the attempt had failed. There was yet another banking scandal. A bald and bearded politician assured the readers that he was going to clean up the crime and graft in the city.

Nothing new under the sun, Eve thought, glancing at the paper's name and then chuckling at her own pun.

Shifting through the paper, she finally located the real estate section. She perused it until she saw what she was looking for. She jotted down the address and gulped down her last bit of tea, calculating her next move. It was risky and it might backfire, but she was desperate.

She reached into the folds of her ankle-length skirt and took out the draw string suede purse, the same purse Albert Harringshaw had placed the sixty dollars in. She counted the contents. Forty-two dollars. Based on the ad she'd seen in the paper, that would be enough to hold her for a month.

Eve glanced outside the window. It was another clear blue day, with cool temperatures. She slipped into her button up boots, put on a pill box hat and her long coat, picked up her gloves and left the room.

She glided down the stairs rapidly and moved to the front door, before Helen, wherever she might be, could see her.

Outside, Eve walked briskly in the bright morning sun until she spotted a Hansom cab. She hailed it and climbed inside.

"Gramercy Park."

CHAPTER 14

Eve's cab bumped and bounced along Fifth Avenue through heavy traffic, cracking whips, aggressive carriages and clanging street cars. Her lips were pressed tightly together, her face determined, her body tense. She thought she was being followed—in fact, she *hoped* she was being followed. She was ready to confront the guy, even though she was not especially looking forward to it.

When the carriage arrived at Gramercy Park, Eve tapped the roof and the cab edged to the curb. She paid the driver and climbed out with one foot onto a concrete carriage step designed to help passengers down to the sidewalk. How civilized, she thought.

She paused to look around, feeling a snap in the air. Strangely enough, the Gramercy Park area was similar to the one in the twenty-first century, except it was more picturesque. There was a quiet park with benches and trees, shimmering with autumn colors. Four gas lamps still glowed around a curving walkway that led into a peaceful, circular area. Surrounding the park were stylish brownstones; cast iron, horse-topped hitching posts; and cobbled streets.

Eve watched as a chic, deep olive-green, enclosed carriage drifted by, pulled by two magnificent, prancing white horses. There was a woman passenger inside, sitting very erect, wearing a midnight purple coat and a flamboyant feathered hat. The liveried driver wore a top hat and deep olive uniform, with a woolen blanket draped across his lap.

Eve turned to orient herself and locate her destination. A second carriage passed, canary yellow with shiny black fenders, its black horses proud and fine, their harnesses shining. Behind the glittering glass window, a man in a silk top hat looked her way, a cigar protruding from his white mustached mouth.

Eve became aware of her surroundings, certain that she was being followed, even though she couldn't yet spot the familiar shoulders of the man.

In front of the four-story brownstone at 4 Gramercy Park West, Eve saw a sign in the window:

ROOM AND BOARD 1 VACANCY

After climbing the six steps, Eve lifted the gold knocker and let it fall. She waited. The door opened gently and a young girl stood looking back at her. She wore a pale cotton dress and a long blue apron. A white dust cloth, folded into a turban, covered her upswept, ash blonde hair.

"Hello," Eve said, cordially. "I'm here to look at the room."

The young woman's voice was feathery soft. "We only have the one on the second floor back."

"That's fine. May I see it?" Eve asked.

The girl stepped back and allowed Eve to enter the foyer, with emerald green and white tiles, polished cherry wood walls and a small gas chandelier.

The girl closed the door, turning to Eve. "My name's Marie Putney."

"I'm Eve. Eve Kennedy."

Eve followed Marie up the carpeted stairs. At the second floor landing, Marie turned right, gesturing, and Eve followed. Marie opened the door to a room that was larger and cleaner than Eve had expected. It had two large windows, covered by lacy, starched curtains that looked out on a courtyard. Under one window was a window seat, cushioned in maroon velvet. There was a double bed, a rocking chair and a dark wood dresser with a white marble top that held a pitcher and a bowl.

The blue and tan carpet wasn't new, but it was by no means thread-bare. The wallpaper was light green with a pattern of exotic parrots and rosy floral bouquets, and on the wall hung an oil painting in a gilded frame depicting young maidens in bonnets picking flowers in a lush, sun-drenched meadow.

"It's nice," Eve said.

"You'll share a bathroom with the other boarders. It's just down the hall."

"How much?" Eve asked.

"It's eight dollars a week. That includes breakfast and supper. Breakfast is from seven to eight and supper is at six."

It felt right. Eve could already feel herself beginning to relax. "I'll take it," she said, passing one last glance around the room. "I like it. It seems quiet."

"It *is* quiet here and we keep it clean. We do require references," the young woman said. "At least two."

Eve stiffened, forcing a reassuring smile. "Yes, of course... I've just arrived from out of town, here on family business, and I'm afraid my original accommodations didn't work out. I am, as they say, at my wit's end. Would it be possible for me to move in now and then provide you with the references in, say, a week or so... maybe sooner?"

Eve thought about Dr. Eckland. Surely, he would help.

Marie folded her hands, her expression conflicted.

"I can pay for two weeks right now," Eve said, quickly. "I assure you I am quiet, respectable and dependable. I would be grateful to you, Miss Putney."

"Well, it is highly unusual, Miss Kennedy. The house belongs to my grandfather, and he is quite resolute about such matters."

"I could speak with him, if you think it would help," Eve said, swallowing away a dry throat.

"Grandfather suffers from occasional bouts of indigestion, gout and rheumatism, so he's not around much, and he doesn't like to be disturbed."

The silence stretched out as Eve stared down at the floor and Marie pondered her decision.

"All right, Miss Kennedy. I won't say anything to grandfather, but please provide the references as soon as you can."

Eve took a little breath. "Thank you, Miss Putney. Yes, I will."

"Grandfather often has supper downstairs if he feels up to it and, if you meet him, please, let's keep this little secret between the two of us. Will you have many bags, Miss Kennedy?"

"No, not many. I traveled lightly."

"Will you be staying long?"

"I'm not sure. It depends... well, it depends on my family. As I said, I can pay for two weeks in advance."

"That won't be necessary, Miss Kennedy. One week will suffice."

Outside, Eve strolled easily along the sidewalk, feeling she'd taken a giant step toward achieving independence. Still, there were many obstacles. The key was to conserve the money she had left and get a job as fast as possible so she could sustain herself and look for Evelyn Sharland.

She walked purposely slow to see if her shadow was around, but there was still no sign of him. As she strolled, her mind worked with eager restlessness. If she did find Evelyn, could she help her survive, or at least help prolong her life? And if she prolonged her life, would that change history? Was it even possible to change history? Did it matter?

Had Eve somehow, in some small way, already changed history? She was, after all, a wildcard—an extraterrestrial in this time and place who was not born here and was never meant to be here. She was not originally a piece of this 1885 puzzle. She was a separate piece from another puzzle in the twenty-first century.

So why was she here? Why had the lantern—its mesmerizing light—brought her here? Was there a reason? Was it by chance? By accident? Did it happen because of some kind of quantum anomaly, not that she had a clue as to what that really was. Was there any logical explanation for it?

Perhaps the lantern had somehow absorbed and held the lovers' tragic feelings of love, loss and frustrated psychic energy. Is it true that even inanimate objects have some form of existence on the energetic level and in their own energy body?

Eve recalled a course she'd taken in college—an elective—about energy and objects. The idea was that material objects have energy dimensions that can be changed by accident or on purpose. Her professor, a psychologist with eccentric ideas and wardrobe, had said that objects carry energy—and they can have a spiritual interaction with the person who owns them, especially if they are particularly treasured objects. She used the example of a guitar. If a person plays a certain guitar all his life, when he dies, that guitar could have some sort of link to the owner. In another instance, she used the example of a lover imbuing a dried rose bud with spiritual significance, or magicians and witches making charms and amulets.

Eve never gave the idea much weight at the time. She thought it was rather silly. Now she wasn't so sure.

Maybe Evelyn's and John's tragic love energy had somehow become trapped in the lantern and the letter, and somehow, Eve was the instrument by which that energy was released, allowing the lovers a second chance.

Right now, all she could do was keep moving forward, try to find the lantern, and hope that when she found it, it would take her back home.

At 20th Street, Eve glanced over her shoulder and she saw him! Yes, there he was. He swiftly ducked away toward a parked carriage, where a horse was drinking from a quaint-looking water trough near the curb. Her follower snapped out a newspaper and began to read, or at least he pretended to read.

Eve looked about at the trees and the lovely brownstones. Nearby was the open campus of the Theological Seminary and a home for retired nuns. In this neighborhood, she felt safe enough to approach him. She lowered her chin, fortified herself with breath, pivoted and started toward the man in the dark suit, black overcoat and bowler hat.

When she was ten feet away, he lifted the newspaper higher to cover his face and shoulders. Eve advanced, nerves beating away at her.

"Excuse me, sir."

He didn't stir.

"Sir, excuse me."

The paper slid down slowly, and he straightened to his full height. Eve was startled by him. He was taller than she'd expected, clearly five inches taller than she. He had vivid, intelligent blue eyes, a fine handsome face with a heavy shadow of a beard, a prominent nose, a solid, determined jaw and full lips—fantastic lips— that she had difficulty pulling her eyes away from. He had a broad chest, a muscular neck and good athletic shoulders.

He stared at her as though he were about to smile, and that made him appear affable, cocky and sexy.

"Are you addressing me, madam?" he asked.

Eve detected an accent. Irish? He did look Irish, with his dark, curly hair sticking out from beneath his hat.

Eve swallowed, stepping back a little. "Yes, I am addressing you."

He shrugged and looked resigned. "Okay, then, what can I do for you? Are you lost? Looking for a place of business or a shop?"

She liked his voice. It had a sing-song baritone quality to it. It was a confident voice, a resonant, masculine voice.

Eve stood there, confused now. Was this the same guy she'd seen from the back in Helen Price's parlor?

She stammered. "Well, I… Well, I just thought that maybe you…" She stopped, hearing her shaky voice and suddenly feeling foolish.

"Yes, madam? You thought?"

Eve lifted her chin and decided to go for it. "Have you been following me?"

The left corner of his mouth lifted. Was that a grin or a sneer? Eve couldn't tell.

"You are a bold woman," he said.

"Bold or not, that doesn't answer my question."

"And a direct one. My grandfather used to say, 'It is better to be a coward for a minute than dead the rest of your life.'"

"And what does that mean?"

"It means you're not a coward, but maybe you should be sometimes. Walking up to a stranger on a public street to ask him whether he's following you may not be the best course of action."

Eve looked deeply into his eyes. She didn't see a threat. She saw playfulness, and she saw attraction.

"Is that a threat?" she asked.

He met her eyes and held them. When Eve felt the power of his gaze, she was seized by a sudden and remarkable attraction. It flamed in her like a lit torch. She blinked and looked away across the street at a Coffee House with the name **Zarcone's Tea & Coffee House** printed in gilded letters on the plate-glass window. Beneath that was written **Dealer in Coffee, Teas and Spices**.

"My grandmother used to say, 'What fills the eye fills the heart,'" he said lightly.

Eve put on a hard face, her eyes avoiding his. "Well, it sounds like your grandparents spent a lot of time sitting in the parlor working hard at being clever."

He laughed out loud, and it surprised her. He was amused by her. Was he mocking her?

"So are you following me?" she repeated, with force.

His laughter faded, and he folded his newspaper, leveling his eyes on her. "I should have been following you a long time ago, I think."

Eve felt the rise of heat again. It was unnerving how her impulsive attraction to this guy threw her off-balance. "Well okay, then, whoever you are," Eve said, hearing her voice tremble, "I just want to tell you that…"

He cut her off in mid-sentence. "My name is Detective Sergeant Patrick Gantly and you have friends in high places. Aren't you the fortunate one, madam?"

Eve didn't speak. She wasn't sure what he meant.

"You're a policeman?"

"I'm a Detective Sergeant, but you don't have to call me that. But then, why not call me that since that is what I am?"

He stood watching her, completely at ease. His face was half in shadow and half in sun.

"Then you *are* following me?"

He offered a little bow and tipped his hat. "Observing, madam. Merely observing and making sure you do not get into any harm."

"Who?" was all she could force out. Then she consciously closed her mouth.

"Who what, madam?"

"Hired you? Who hired you?"

Patrick tucked the newspaper under his arm and regarded her with a lifted eyebrow.

"Well, as my old Da used to say, 'Be kind to your enemies and lie to your friends, and pray that the one never meets the other in the local pub.'"

Eve considered it. "I'm sorry. I have no idea what that means."

He grinned that sexy grin again. "I never did either, but he said it frequently, especially after a long night at Clancy's Pub. I suspect he had some personal experience that doesn't quite translate. You probably had to be there."

Detective Gantly glanced toward the coffee house. "It's a bit cold out today. Would you care to have a coffee with me then? Am I being too bold? After all, here we are on a public street and we weren't properly introduced. But although we've just met, we are not strangers, are we, Miss Kennedy?"

So he knew her name. Did she like that? Eve was confused and aroused, and she didn't know what to say.

"Too bold?" he asked, crossing his arms.

She heard herself say, "No... not too bold. Not where I come from."

Detective Gantly looked her over, suddenly serious. "And where is that, Miss Kennedy? Where do you come from?"

Eve drew in a breath to calm her nerves. "As a girl-friend of mine used to say, 'A woman is not what she says she is, she is what she hides.'"

Gantly grinned, broadly. "You, Miss Kennedy, are quite the unwrapped secret. That is for sure."

He gestured toward the street. "Shall we, then?"

There was a break in the carriage traffic and they hurried through, heading toward the Coffee House.

CHAPTER 15

Zarcone's Tea & Coffee House was a narrow, cheerful room. On the back wall sat shelves of small, square wooden boxes containing a variety of loose, exotic teas. The proprietor, standing behind the long gray marbled countertop, was a busy, fussy man with a drooping mustache, a proud Roman nose and beady eyes always in motion. Eve saw enamelware & pewter gooseneck coffee pots and teapots with decorative Italian castle scenes. There were China mugs and porcelain cups, hand painted with roses and gold trim. There was a variety of round, heavy glass jars that contained spices, some of which Eve had never heard of. The shop itself smelled predominantly of rose, clove and cinnamon.

They sat near the front window across from each other at a white marble tabletop, on chairs with brown padded cushions. Natural light came through the plate-glass window, though gaslight chandeliers hung from the ceiling. Two lavishly dressed women sat in the back of the room, sipping tea and speaking in breathy whispers, their feathery hats nodding as their conversation grew animated.

Eve glanced about the shop, avoiding Gantly's eyes. But she felt it—a strange fascination, a feeling of rising emotion moving past the static of her thoughts. Meeting Detective Sergeant Gantly had been a surprising encounter, its outcome completely unexpected. He had removed his hat and was fingering his long, thick hair back off his broad forehead.

Eve's attraction to him had been immediate. Her first impression was of a firm-jawed man of action: forceful, resolute and decisive, with a wry sense of humor. He was unabashedly masculine, tantalizingly mysterious and certainly clever, or at least he seemed to be so. He was entirely different from modern day men, but she had yet to put her finger on why.

She stirred real cream into her coffee and watched it turn light brown. She tasted it: strong and bold, warming her chest. Her mouth twisted up in surprise.

"Wow, this is good," she said, forgetting herself. "Wow."

"Wow?" Gantly asked, amused. "What a word. It sounds a bit like the Bow Wow verse I heard as a boy."

"And how does it go?" Eve asked.

Gantly looked toward the ceiling to recall the words. "Well, let me see now… 'Bow Wow, he barked to his lady love. Bow Wow said she to her turtle dove. He bowed and wowed her with his wail, and…" he stopped, suddenly recalling the final, sexually suggestive line.

Eve looked at him. "Well, go on, finish."

He hesitated a moment. "Miss Kennedy, it is not meant to be recited in mixed company."

Eve looked at him, directly. "I'm sure I can take it. Go ahead. Finish it. I assure you I am a very modern woman."

Gantly exhaled. "Okay, but remember, you asked." He licked his lips. "He bowed and wowed her with his wail and she, impressed, did wag her tail."

Eve laughed a little. "And how old were you when you first learned that little poem?"

"Oh, ten or eleven, I suppose. My older sister taught it to me."

Patrick scratched his ear, a bit embarrassed. "I do apologize, Miss Kennedy. Wow," he repeated with a little shake of his head. "Where did you hear such a word?"

Eve thought fast. "It's something I heard in the Bowery."

"Oh, yes, that's right, you were in the Bowery. Yes, well, people hear all sorts of things in the Bowery, don't they?"

She glanced up. "So you were following me?"

"Not following. Observing. If I'd been following you, you would have never seen me."

Eve turned toward the window. "Snow," she said excitedly. "Snow in late October."

Patrick turned and, sure enough, a few flakes were sprinkled in with a light rain, melting instantly against the window as they struck and slid down.

"Ah yes, the weather in New York. One minute there's sun and the next snow, and it's not even November yet. As changeable as a weathercock."

Eve's eyes drifted back to Patrick's face, and she felt a sudden impulse.

"Sergeant Detective Gantly, are you a good policeman or a bad one?"

He shrugged a shoulder. "Depends on the day. I shot a couple of burglars over on 11th and Broadway last week. I helped capture and convict Mrs. James a while back."

"Mrs. James?" Eve asked.

"Mrs. James used to induce young girls to immigrate, and when they landed at Castle Garden, she took possession of them, body and soul. Well, I'm sure you get the picture."

"So you were a kind of hero," Eve said.

"No, Miss Kennedy, not a hero. But I do rescue damsels in distress from time to time. It is my specialty. Are you in any distress, Miss Kennedy?"

She grinned, thinly, at his flirtation. "How is it that you can just follow me around all day? Don't you have other more important duties to attend to?"

He shook his head. "No. You see, Miss Kennedy, I was handpicked for this job by Albert Harringshaw himself, and he knows people in high places and he knows how to get what he wants from those people in high places, if you get my meaning."

"No, I am not sure I *do* get your meaning."

"Shall I be direct, Miss Kennedy?"

Eve looked at him, dubiously. "Yes, be direct."

Gantly leaned forward in a conspiratorial manner and whispered. "Money helps to grease wagon wheels, frying pans and greasy hands, Miss Kennedy," he said, rubbing two fingers together. "Mr. Harringshaw has a lot of money and power in this city. I dare say he also offers some very good stock tips to those who, shall I say, have an interest in such things."

Eve understood and nodded. "So why were you handpicked?"

Patrick sat back in his chair, sighing, showing some frustration. "The Harringshaw family is famous for its costume balls, Miss Kennedy. Perhaps you have heard of them? In 1883, their fancy dress ball was the talk of the town. The invitations were hand delivered by servants in livery. The young socialites practiced quadrilles day and…"

"Quadrilles?" Eve asked. After she interrupted, she realized she'd just reverted to a twenty-first century New York conversation style, with its impatient demand for information.

"You surprise me, Miss Kennedy," Gantly said. "It is quite popular among the elite society."

Eve looked at him coolly. "Not the elite society I'm familiar with, Detective Sergeant."

He grinned. "At any rate, a quadrille is a dance performed with four couples in a rectangular formation. Not a good old Irish jig, mind you, but a spectacle to behold, nonetheless."

"And you beheld?" Eve asked.

"I did. I was part of the plain-clothes detectives assigned to keep out the curious, the pickpockets, the polished thieves and the party crashers, all who might want to spoil what turned out to be a two-hundred-and-fifty-thousand-dollar affair."

Eve did some quick calculating. In twenty-first century currency, she guessed that would be in the millions.

"And that's when you met Mr. Harringshaw?" Eve asked.

"In a manner of speaking. I stopped a jealous man from shooting him. It was over a woman, of course."

Eve sat up. "You stopped the man from shooting Albert Harringshaw?"

Patrick eyed her with pleasure, admiring the flutter of her very long lashes. She had shiny, lush blonde hair under that pill box hat, and a tender, generous mouth.

"It didn't appear in the papers. No one knew about the incident except Mr. Harringshaw, his brother John Allister, who was standing by, the jealous man, and two ladies, one who fainted dead away."

"How did you stop him from shooting Mr. Harringshaw?"

"As soon as the jealous man raised the gun to fire at Mr. Harringshaw's chest, I dove for the jealous lover's legs. We hit the floor hard. The gun went off, and the bullet shattered a piece of the glittering electric chandelier. Electric you will note, because only the Harringshaws, the Astors and the Vanderbilts have electric lights in their mansions. I assure you, Miss Kennedy, it was the stuff of melodrama."

Eve lifted her cup and drank the remaining coffee while imagining the scene. "So Mr. Harringshaw owes you his life?"

"We have never discussed it. I doubt we ever shall. But I felt it quite fitting that Mr. Harringshaw was dressed as the Count of Monte Cristo that evening." He took a sip of coffee. "Perhaps you have heard that the Harringshaws are hosting another costumed ball on December 4th? All of society will be there... and I, of course, will also be there. Working."

Eve looked at Patrick with speculation. "Will you continue to follow... to observe me, Detective Sergeant Gantly?"

He gave her a shrewd, measured look. "You are my assignment, Miss Kennedy. As long as I am assigned, I will do my duty."

"And if you are reassigned?" Eve asked, staring into her empty cup. She was gently flirting, and enjoying herself, and she knew Detective Gantly knew.

The Detective's voice dropped to a serious tone. "Miss Kennedy, I have not been able to learn anything about you—where you came from, who your family is, nothing."

She glanced away.

"I am very good at what I do, Miss Kennedy. I have located some Kennedys here in the City and they have never heard of you. I have checked past directories and government documents, including marriage licenses, and I have found nothing. Absolutely nothing. It is as if you don't really exist and yet, here you are, sitting there across from me. By the way, Miss Kennedy, are you married?"

She slanted a coy look at him. "No, I am not."

Eve was sure she saw his shoulders settle a bit. He blinked twice and almost—that is almost— imperceptibly, smiled.

Patrick gave a quick, firm nod and continued. "I have made inquiries about you within various layers of society, both high and low, and no one—not one— knows of you or has had the whiff of a scent about you. Now that, Miss Kennedy, is highly unusual and patently suspect."

"Suspect?" Eve said, finally looking at him. "I think I like the sound of that. Why suspect?"

"Who are you, Miss Kennedy?" he said, directly. "There is something about you that I cannot quite understand—no, that is not the word. Not understand, apprehend. Your walk is unusual, your language and patterns of speech are unique, and your overall manner is one I have never observed and, I can assure you, Miss Kennedy, I have observed many and various types of people from many walks of life and various lands. You puzzle me, Miss Kennedy. You intrigue me. I may be bolder than I should be by saying this, but you fascinate me, and I am not easily fascinated."

Detective Sergeant Gantly folded his hands on the table top and bored into her with his eyes. "So who are you, Miss Eve Kennedy, if that is even your real name?"

Eve was rattled and astounded by his shrewd and swift observations. Was she that transparent? Was she still that different, despite her attempts to fit in?

She shot up, hoping to throw him off with an expression of offense. "Who I am is nobody's business, Mr. Gantly or Detective Gantly or whatever name you're supposed to be called."

Detective Gantly waved her back down to her chair. "Please, Miss Kennedy, sit down."

"You make me sound like some kind of laboratory specimen, some bizarre creature to be analyzed and catalogued. Who I am is none of your business."

They locked gazes, hers firm, his searching. "Please, Miss Kennedy," he said, softening his voice. "Please do not take offense where none was intended. Please sit down."

Eve should have left, but she didn't want to. She slowly lowered herself down.

Gantly scooted his chair back, ran a hand along his jaw and crossed one knee over the other. "Miss Kennedy, I am telling you in confidence that I have been charged with following you to learn who you are, where you came from and what you are out to accomplish. I did not want this assignment, Miss Kennedy. In truth, I asked to be removed from it. I did not want to be a puppet, with my strings jerked and pulled by Mr. Albert Harringshaw, who is forcing me to follow some lost female around the city."

Eve felt the insult like a slap on the cheek. She shifted in her seat, ready to blast him back. "Then why, pray tell, did you take the assignment, Detective Sergeant?"

"I had no choice in the matter, Miss Kennedy. Inspector Byrnes himself so ordered it. I am sure you have heard of Inspector Byrnes, the head of the New York City Police Detective Department?"

Eve had never heard of him, but she thought it best to lie. "Of course I've heard of Inspector Byrnes."

"So you see, I have grown very fond of eating and staying warm in winter. So here I am."

Eve put on her best smirk. "Well, I'm sorry I'm such an inconvenience," she said. She shot up again and whirled toward the entrance.

Gantly sighed and got up. "Please, Miss Kennedy, wait…"

But she had marched to the door, yanked it open and exited.

Gantly dropped some coins on the table and hurried out after her.

Eve walked briskly in a light rain, irritated at herself for over-reacting to Patrick's insult, if that's what it was. It wasn't like her to be so dramatic and emotional. But then she was in a very vulnerable position, in a strange world, with no friends or family to turn to and no one she could trust. She didn't want this Detective sniffing around and following her every step. She already felt as though she was in everyone's crosshairs.

And yet, she felt deflated by his declaration that he was forced to follow her. For a few moments, she had felt playful and free. She had felt as if he might be someone she could trust. And he was oh, so attractive.

She heard Patrick call her from behind. A blast of cold wind slung little flecks of snow and rain into Eve's face. Seeing a tailor shop, she ducked into the protection of its doorway. Patrick came fast, a firm hand pressed down on the crown of his hat. He slipped in beside her and jammed his hands into his coat pockets, seeking words.

Eve's eyes were locked ahead, refusing to look at him.

"Miss Kennedy, you did not let me finish."

Eve watched carriages pass. She saw two sturdy horses pulling a delivery wagon with the name PYLES MOVING AND STORAGE written on it in bold black letters. She saw jets of white vapor puffing from the horses' nostrils. She saw women hurrying along the streets, some ducking into doorways like she'd done. A lumbering dray rattled along the street with rows of tied-down beer barrels.

"Miss Kennedy, as a policeman, I get certain feelings about things. I have learned to trust those feelings. It helps to keep me alive."

"Good for you," Eve said.

"I get the feeling you are in some kind of trouble, Miss Kennedy. I get the feeling you are quite alone in this very big city and you might need some help. Frankly, Mr. Albert Harringshaw will not be your helper. You are living in a house of vipers. Miss Price is a shrewd and spiteful woman, who would do anything to hold on to Mr. Harringshaw and his generous allowance to her. I will not comment on Mr. Harringshaw, other than to say I don't believe he can be trusted when it comes to a woman's honor. Now, I have already said too much."

"And *you* can be trusted?" Eve asked, still staring ahead, watching the frenetic snowflakes swirl, land and melt on the cobblestone street.

"I can be of help, and you *can* trust me, if you are honest with me."

She turned to him with a frosty stare, but the sharp blue of his eyes and the strong handsome face, with those partially opened lips, simply enchanted her. His was a face she'd never seen before, holding a contradiction of expressions: hard and tender, challenging and playful, mysterious and revealing—revealing what was surely an attraction to her. She must have revealed the same to him because she was in fact "wowed" and "bow wowed" by him, but also caught between fear and desire. Eve cleared her throat before speaking.

"And if you help me, Detective Sergeant Gantly, what do you want in return?"

He stared back at her, his eyes narrowing.

"Mr. Harringshaw also thought you might be in some kind of trouble. He asked me not only to follow and observe you, but also to protect you from any harm. So I will protect you, Miss Kennedy, from any harm."

Eve pushed down a rising, sexy thrill. "You didn't answer my question, sir."

"If you ask me what I want in return, then I would ask you to trust me. I would ask you to tell me the truth about yourself. That is what I want in return."

Eve turned away, feeling the air grow colder. And now there was only snow, dusting the tops of men's silk hats and shoulders, and the tops of enclosed carriages. She could never tell him the truth. It was impossible. She quickly changed the conversation, turning to him.

"Detective Sergeant Gantly, will you help me? Do you mean it?"

"I will, Miss Kennedy, if I can. Just tell me how I can be of service."

She decided to blurt it out. "I need a diploma from a nursing school. Any nursing school, as long as it is accredited."

He looked at her uncertainly, his mind working to understand.

She held his stare. "Surely, you know I am a nurse."

He watched her, carefully. "I have heard the rumor, yes."

"I have lost my diploma and it will take too long to request another copy. I can't get work without one. If I am to get out of that house of vipers, as you call it, then I need a job. Can you help me get a diploma? You seem to be a man who gets around, who knows the right people, and who knows how to get things done."

He pushed the bill of his hat back on his head and let out a long, audible sigh.

"Miss Kennedy, is it possible that I may have under-estimated you?"

Eve lifted her chin, imperiously, the way she'd seen Albert Harringshaw do. "I hope you have, sir. And, if I may say it, I am, in a manner of speaking, a damsel in distress who very much needs your help."

He smiled as he considered her face, her eyes and her glistening mouth.

Eve felt his eyes on her and, when she spoke, she saw her own misty white breath, and for a wonderful moment, they hovered there in a budding intimacy.

"Will you help me, Detective Sergeant Gantly?"

He looked at her with solemn purpose and, with some difficulty, he pulled his eyes from hers. He shoved his hands into his pockets again and looked skyward.

"Shall I find you a cab, Miss Kennedy?"

"Does that mean you won't help me?" Eve asked, searching his face.

He gave her a look, and she didn't know what that look meant. He left her and went to the curb. He waved down a Hansom and opened the door for her as she approached. He took her hand and helped her in-side. His hand was big and broad, but gentle. He leaned in, taking her in, and Eve thought she saw a de-licious desire in his eyes. She was sure he saw desire in hers, because she was feeling it.

"I would prefer you don't tell anyone about our meeting, Miss Kennedy, especially Mr. Harringshaw. He will want to court you, you know. That is his inten-tion. He would not take kindly to our little rendez-vous."

"Will you help me?" Eve asked, with some urgency in her voice. "Will you find me a diploma so I won't be indebted to Mr. Harringshaw and have to be courted by Mr. Harringshaw?"

Patrick gave her an inscrutable look, took her hand and pressed a folded piece of paper into her right gloved hand. He closed the door and touched his bowler. He knocked on the side of the cab and it lurched ahead. Eve twisted around, watching Patrick until the cab turned the corner and started uptown.

Detective Sergeant Gantly watched the carriage retreat, merging into traffic and disappearing into blurring snow. He stood there feeling a clash of emotion: confusion, desire, and a stirring sexual excitement he hadn't felt in a very long time. Who was this Eve Kennedy that aroused him and made him edgy? He would have to find out. He wouldn't rest until he did indeed find out who she was and where she came from.

He hailed a cab and started off after her.

CHAPTER 16

Eve instructed the driver to take her to the "La-dies' Mile," a shopping area on Fifth Avenue between 15th and 24th Streets. According to ads in the newspaper, it boasted some of the best ladies' shops in Manhattan, as well as the finest jewelers, furriers, florists and haberdashers. She had to buy her own clothes and return the ones she'd borrowed from Helen Price. This might help anchor her in this time and place, or at least help her establish her own identity.

As the cab trotted through Madison Square, through a now gentle snowfall, Eve saw a mixture of stately homes, grand theaters and luxurious hotels. The entire area reminded her of the Paris she'd seen on her honeymoon with Blake.

Eve had purposely not opened her gloved hand until she was well away from Detective Sergeant Gantly, wanting to savor the delicious moment of attraction and desire, and the warm feeling of trust. Was it a personal note? Eve smiled at the thought. For the first time since she'd landed in 1885, she felt that maybe she'd finally found a friend, someone she could trust and rely on.

She slowly unclasped her hand. It was not a personal note, but a folded bill. She smoothed it. It was a ten-dollar bill issued by the Seaboard National Bank of the City of New York.

Eve gazed rapt and moved. This was a lot of money, maybe an entire week's salary, for the detective sergeant.

Easing back into the seat as the cab was jostled through heavy traffic, she felt her longing and admiration for him swell. She couldn't accept the money, of course, but it was a kind, generous and supportive act. She would return it to him as soon as they met again.

Her heart fluttered. Would she see him again? What if he began following her and not observing? What if Albert Harringshaw found out about their meeting and decided to fire the detective? He was a jealous and possessive man, after all, who wanted total control over his lovers.

Detective Sergeant Gantly knew what was going on in that house. Were Dr. Eckland and the Detective on speaking terms? Eve sat up. She could only pray that Gantly would somehow obtain a diploma for her, after which she'd present it to Dr. Eckland and ask for his help in finding a job. Then she could continue her search for Evelyn Sharland.

It had stopped snowing by the time the cab turned onto Fifth Avenue and the Ladies' Mile. Eve was entranced by block after block of gleaming ladies' stores, the sidewalks crowded with lavishly dressed women, their grand carriages waiting for them at the curb.

Women hovered around the big display windows, pointing, gesturing and speculating, their servants waiting, attending. Eve tapped the roof, and the driver edged the cab to the curb. She paid and stepped out onto the sidewalk, quickly merging with other women as they strolled the sidewalks, pausing to gaze into the windows.

Then the sun broke through fast-moving clouds and glittered the windows, and Eve wondered if this was the first mass of department stores in the United States. Again she thought about how she'd love to take a Selfie here. That one would go viral.

She entered Lord and Taylor, hoping to buy two dresses, some underwear, gloves and hats. In the crowded store, buzzing with conversation, she moved through to the dress goods and ribbon department. Eve drew up to a thin, officious salesman in his thirties who had a florid nose and a florid mustache. When she asked him where the dresses were, she was met by a stony stare.

A finely dressed, middle-aged woman, with a no-nonsense manner and gold-rimmed eyeglasses, pushed in and approached the salesman.

"Show me some elephant's breath cashmere," she said, in a very upper class accent that sounded so affected, Eve almost laughed.

When the salesman retreated to fetch the material, Eve screwed up her courage and asked the woman what she had just ordered.

"It is a shade of woolen goods, of course," the woman answered, rather curtly.

Eve stood back and watched as a nervous woman inquired about where she could find an imported jersey.

Another woman asked for a Moliere waistcoat, an ostrich feather fan and ten yards of plum-colored velveteen. Still another fashionable young woman asked for some crinolettes.

Feeling dizzy and out of her element, Eve wandered over to the glass display cases, where she tried on some bonnets and hats. She didn't know what looked fashionable or even if any looked right for her.

Back outside in the heavy stream of sidewalk traffic, Eve decided she'd have to solicit Millie's or some other woman's help on how to shop. It was an intense, creative and baffling world she obviously knew nothing about.

EVE DECIDED TO SPEND the rest of her day looking for Evelyn Sharland, and that meant visiting Gouverneur Hospital in the Financial District. Dr. Eckland had said they treated tubercular patients there and maybe Eve would get lucky and find Evelyn. Eve sought directions to the hospital from a kindly older man, who looked like Uncle Sam in a high silk hat.

Ten minutes later, she stepped onto the crowded, elevated EL Train, which was pulled by a steam locomotive. Eve held on to a thin pole as the train rattled, puffed and smoked its way downtown like some antiquated thrill ride.

She left the train completely disoriented and wound up on Wall Street, a Wall Street that didn't look even remotely like the Wall Street of her time, except that Trinity Church was the tallest building around. There were no glass or steel towers, just brownstones on either side of the street. Vendors and delivery men driving wagons contested each other for the right of way,

189

and men in tall silk hats walked aggressively along the sidewalks, puffing on cigars, the smoke trailing behind them.

Eve drew up to a freckle-faced shoe-shine boy of about ten years old and asked him for further directions to the Gouverneur Hospital.

His weary expression and old eyes took her in with both calculation and suspicion.

"Shoe shine five cents," he said with a challenge.

Eve took twenty-five cents from her purse and handed it to him. He took it swiftly, looked down at it, and then lifted his eyes to her face. He didn't smile. He glanced about as if afraid someone was hovering in shadow, waiting to pounce on him. When he spoke, his voice was low and hoarse.

"Gouverneur Slip and Water Street at the East River. It's a bit of a walk."

Eve thanked him and started off. The sun was out now and the snow had quickly vanished, as if some artist had changed her mind and blotted it out, adding yellow beams of sunlight instead.

Twenty-five minutes later, she saw the hospital, a new three-story, red-brick building. Three young boys were playing stick ball in the street, and the hospital was surrounded by market wagons that blocked the ambulance access. That wasn't a good sign, Eve thought. She spotted a one-legged man on crutches, wearing a tattered Union Army uniform, moving toward the entrance. She followed.

Inside, Eve strolled along the highly polished floor, past an elderly couple who sat hunched on wooden chairs, staring into the void with wrinkled faces and a dull acceptance. Eve had seen faces like that when she'd worked for a time in the ER. Grief and loss are timeless, she thought, only the clothes are different.

Eve stepped over to a long oak lobby desk. A thin woman, wearing a white smock and spectacles, was shifting through some papers. Her gray hair was pulled back tightly into a bun, and when she lifted her head from a stack of papers, Eve noticed her placid, handsome face was pock marked. From her medical training, Eve recalled that smallpox had been prevalent in the 1800s, although she couldn't recall what years.

The woman's gray/blue eyes were kind. She greeted Eve with a soft, friendly smile. To Eve, who had been in this time of 1885 only four days—although it seemed like weeks—this woman's smile was the most open and welcoming smile she'd received from anyone thus far. There was no suspicion or confusion in this smile.

"Good afternoon," Eve said, softly, "I am looking for someone who may be in the women's tubercular ward. Her name is Evelyn Sharland."

The woman held her smile. "Are you a relative?"

Eve hesitated. She was a relative, but if Evelyn was here, Eve didn't want her to know it, at least not yet. "No, I'm a friend."

"I see," the woman said, reaching to her left for a folder. She opened it and flipped through some papers until she found what she was looking for. She used her index finger to slide down the page.

While she waited in happy impatience, Eve considered a range of possible introductory phrases she could use on Evelyn when they finally met. Eve grew excited at the possibility that not only was she close to seeing her distant relative, but she was also about to see the recipient of John Allister Harringshaw's Christmas Eve letter. A very touching letter. A heartfelt and heart-breaking letter. A tragic letter that Evelyn had never seen. The letter that John Allister had not yet written.

Eve felt some of the tension leave her body as she stood there, feeling strangely at ease in the place, as she often did working in hospitals and clinics in her own time. This hospital had a good atmosphere about it, maybe because it actually employed a woman surgeon or maybe because of the people who worked there. Dedicated doctors and nurses, who had a true calling to heal, made all the difference in a place. Eve had witnessed miracles of healing by nurses who cared and by doctors who listened.

Oddly enough, this hospital seemed like a little oasis in the midst of so much ignorance and suffering. It was as though Eve was finally wakening up to the reality of the world in 1885—this bare-knuckle world before child labor laws, or women's right to vote, or antibiotics; this world where men held absolute power; where children lived in the streets and slept in hay barges on the East River; where there were no social safety nets.

Eve also awakened to the grim reality of what Evelyn was facing: she was facing an almost certain death, alone. A very awful and terrible death.

Eve felt a pang of guilt and she looked down, disappointed in herself. Standing here in this welcoming hospital, she suddenly realized that her priorities had been all wrong. Instead of searching for Evelyn so she could locate the lantern and return to her own time, even if that were possible, Eve should be focusing solely on finding Evelyn to try to save her life. After all, wasn't Eve a nurse, a healer? Hadn't she felt called to that work ever since she was in high school?

The woman behind the desk raised her eyes. "I'm sorry, Evelyn Sharland has not been admitted here."

Eve sighed, feeling hope drain from her.

The woman stared with compassion. "Have you tried some of the Catholic Institutions?"

"I'm from out of town. I don't know about them."

The woman took a piece of paper and a pencil and began to write them down.

"There's the House of the Good Shepherd and the House of the Holy Family. Even if your friend is not there, perhaps she has been there or has had friends who might know where she went. I know it is an off-chance, but it might be worthwhile investigating."

She finished writing and handed the paper to Eve.

Eve took it, smiling warmly. "You have been very kind. Thank you."

"I hope you find her. I'm sure your friendship means a lot to her."

Eve was so grateful for this woman's genuine concern. On an impulse, she asked a question.

"Are you from here?"

"No, I am from Newburgh, New York."

"Are you a nurse?"

The woman's eyes were serene and intelligent. "No. I'm a doctor. I'm filling in for the receptionist, who is on a 20-minute break."

Eve stared, dumbly. "Oh, I didn't know."

"You weren't aware that there are female doctors?"

"Yes, I have heard about you. You're the surgeon?"

"Yes."

"I'm sorry," Eve said.

"No need to be." The doctor extended her hand. "I'm Dr. Long. Ann Long. And I am, as they say in the newspapers, the first female ambulance surgeon. When we first opened this hospital, it was solely for the purpose of treating accident cases. We have since expanded to include a ward for patients with tuberculosis, and unfortunately, we are overwhelmed and low on good staff."

Eve shook Dr. Long's hand, and she was struck by an exciting thought. If Detective Sergeant Gantly did manage to get her a diploma, she would return and ask Dr. Long for a job. This is where she wanted to work.

"Thank you, Dr. Long, for everything."

"May I ask your name?" Dr. Long asked.

"Eve Kennedy."

They briefly shook hands.

Outside the hospital, Eve searched for the EL train. It was time to return to Helen Price's home, and Eve dreaded it. Helen would certainly be glad to see her go, but what would Albert Harringshaw say? As Eve started for the train, she hoped and prayed he would not be at the house when she returned.

CHAPTER 17

At 5:30, Eve and Helen Price were in the parlor, Eve seated on an upholstered chair and Helen opposite her on a red velvet settee. The fire crackled, the grandfather clock ticked loudly, and both women were sipping tea that Millie had carried in. Helen was fidgety and edgy. Eve had forced a calm demeanor.

"It would simply be rude for you to leave before Mr. Harringshaw arrives at six," Helen said, in a troubled voice, avoiding Eve's face. "He will blame me for being selfish and inhospitable, and I do not wish to incur his displeasure in that regard. You must admit that he has been sufficiently kind and generous to you, Miss Kennedy. I would think that you owe him the benefit of conveying to him, in person, what your future plans are and where your living quarters are situated. Surely, you see that that is the correct and polite thing to do."

Eve breathed in nerves, resigned. "If you think it is best, Miss Price, then I will wait, although I am sure

Mr. Harringshaw is not that interested in my plans. He was just being a gentleman to a down-and-out woman."

Eve was purposely playing down Albert's attraction, for Helen's sake. But Helen's face twisted up in displeasure and her jaw stiffened.

They sat in an awkward silence, as their teacups rattled on their saucers and the fire hissed.

"As I mentioned earlier," Eve said, "I'll return the dresses just as soon as I can have new ones made."

Helen flicked at the air with her free hand. "There is no need to return them, Miss Kennedy. I have no need of them. Mr. Harringshaw had them made for my sister, and I'd prefer we not even mention the subject to Mr. Harringshaw."

Eve saw the anger flare up in Helen's face, and then she knew. Albert Harringshaw must have flirted with Helen's sister as well, and maybe he'd accomplished more than just a flirtation. Eve wasn't interested in that story, surely a painful one for Helen and, from Helen's snarly glance, she didn't want to know. Since Helen's sister no longer lived in the house, something "uncomfortable" must have happened.

Once again, Eve felt compassion for Helen. She was a woman trapped, in a sense. Her life was at the mercy and whim of Albert Harringshaw. He was in total control of the relationship. He could come and go as he pleased, and he could see and make love to any woman he chose, and there was nothing Helen could do about it, at least she didn't think so. After all, she lived in a grand house with servants, wore fine clothes, ate the best food, spent nights at the theater and dined at the finest restaurants.

Obviously, she had put up with a lot to keep her lavish lifestyle, and she was choosing to continue. But what would happen when she lost her sexy, hour-glass figure and pretty face? Surely, Albert Harringshaw would drop her like yesterday's fashion.

And so they sat in an extended, awkward silence.

Millie returned once to see if Miss Price needed anything, but Helen waved her away without a glance. Just before Millie exited through the side door, she turned to Eve, flashed a quick, covert smile and disappeared.

When the front door bell rang, both women flinched. Eve saw Helen draw an uneasy breath. Eve laid her teacup aside and stood, waiting for Albert Harringshaw to make his appearance.

Millie was at the front door in a minute and opened it. Albert Harringshaw entered. He greeted Millie and handed her his silk hat, fur-collared coat, gloves and cane. He stroked either side of his mustache with a finger, squared his shoulders and entered the parlor.

Both women were standing, Helen's face set in hope of affectionate attention and Eve's forcing a tight little smile. She was fighting a mounting hostility toward the man.

"Well, well, isn't this a pleasant sight? Two lovely ladies waiting for me in this attractive and cozy parlor at the end of a long and devilishly busy day."

Albert gave a gentlemanly bow to both ladies, but his eyes went to Eve. They were alive with secret interest.

Helen's face fell as she followed his gaze.

"Miss Kennedy, you look very well. The good Dr. Eckland tells me you are much improved."

"Yes, Mr. Harringshaw, I am feeling so much better, thank you."

"I am glad to hear it."

He turned to Helen. "And you, Miss Price, are you well?"

Helen brightened a little. "Yes, Mr. Harringshaw, I am very well."

He stood erect, posing. "I am wearing a new suit. The tailor is quite in demand these days. How do you like it?"

Eve quickly studied Albert's suit. It fit him to handsome perfection. There was an extremely narrow lapel on the rich woolen jacket, with a high button front, and a ruby stud in his stiff white shirt. His trousers were tailored to a slimmer style, and there was no crease. Eve supposed that was by design. His jacket was buttoned only at the top, allowing him to display proudly his purple silk vest and glistening watch chain.

Helen spoke up first. "It fits you to perfection, Mr. Harringshaw."

He looked toward Eve, who wanted to tell him that his ego was as big as the Empire State Building, but of course the great building hadn't been built yet, so she nodded a smile instead.

"It is a fine-looking suit, Mr. Harringshaw."

He waited for more, but Eve didn't offer more.

In melting disappointment, he turned from her and clasped his hands together, undaunted. "I was on Broadway today and it was clogged with the usual carriages, the victorias, landaus, broughams, and coupes, and all along its sidewalks, promenading in endless procession, were elegantly attired women. In that attractive throng, whom do you think I saw?"

He swung his attention back to Eve. "I saw you, Miss Kennedy."

Eve was immediately suspicious. She wondered if Detective Sergeant Gantly had followed her and then told Albert Harringshaw. It was his job, after all, but it still disappointed her.

"Oh, yes," Eve said, forcing a cheerful tone. "I did go shopping."

"And were you successful?" Mr. Harringshaw asked.

"I am afraid not. I will have to return."

Albert's eyes widened in delight. "And return you shall, Miss Kennedy. The three of us shall sally forth together, say, tomorrow, and this time you will be successful. I will insist on it and I guarantee it. We will find the finest silks and velvets for you; the most fashionable bonnets."

Helen looked down and away.

Eve spoke up quickly. "Thank you, Mr. Harringshaw, for all your many generosities, but I am afraid I must decline. You see, I am moving out of the house. Miss Price has been so kind and generous, but I think it is time I leave and make my own way. I have found a clean boarding house in Gramercy Park. From there, I will spend the next few days getting settled and looking for work."

Albert stared at her, incredulous. "A boarding house? Looking for work? What does this mean?"

"Yes, sir," Eve said, meeting his astonished eyes.

He faced Helen for answers, and when she didn't lift her eyes from the carpet, he returned his attention to Eve.

"I simply don't understand. Have we insulted you in any way, Miss Kennedy? Have we been inhospitable or unkind?" And then he glared at Helen, who refused to look at him.

"Oh, no, Mr. Harringshaw. Miss Price has been…" and now Eve gulped a little, "… like a sister to me. I am greatly indebted to her and to you, Mr. Harringshaw. But it is natural, and it is for the best that I move on with my life now."

"Have you sufficiently recovered your health, Miss Kennedy?"

"Oh, yes, completely."

Albert narrowed his eyes on her. "So your memory has returned in its entirety?"

For a moment, Eve felt cornered, but she quickly found a way out. "I have recalled enough of my memory to be able to function sufficiently in day-to-day matters, Mr. Harringshaw."

Eve saw he was displeased. "So then you are quite resolute in this course of action, Miss Kennedy?"

Eve licked her lips. "Sir, I have been a burden long enough."

Albert wrinkled his brow. "I must admit, Miss Kennedy, I do not think it is for the best."

And then—right out of the blue—Eve recalled a Jane Austen quote from *Mansfield Park.* "'We have all a better guide in ourselves, if we would attend to it, than any other person can be.' Don't you think so, Mr. Harringshaw?"

Eve watched Mr. Harringshaw consider her words. Surely, he had never read Jane Austen. His right eyebrow lifted, almost imperceptivity.

Helen Price's eyes lifted, carefully scrutinizing Eve's face, as if suspecting something. But she couldn't quite grasp it.

Eve stood ruler straight.

Albert pursed up his lips and lifted his chin, like a king about to make a proclamation. "Well, Miss Kennedy, your independent nature may be seen as admirable by some, but I deem it potentially dangerous in a woman. Although there are women who pretend courage and independence, I have found, through experience, that most need and indeed want the emotional and physical strength and protection of a man. Nonetheless, as I see that you have made up your mind in this matter, there is little else to be done."

Eve let out a little trapped air through her nose.

He clasped his hands together. "Now, I think a celebration is in order. Ladies, powder your noses and wear your finest. Tonight we dine at Delmonico's."

Eve opened her mouth to protest, but then quickly shut it. She would not win this battle, and she knew it. She would have to move first thing in the morning.

ALBERT HARRINGSHAW'S GRACEFUL, black carriage drew up to the Fifth Avenue and 26th Street Delmonico's Restaurant at eight o'clock The liveryman dropped down to open the carriage door, and Eve and Helen emerged, followed by the proud and kingly Albert Harringshaw.

They entered the first-floor public dining room with its glittery chandeliers, hearing the lilting music of a string quartet and seeing the white tablecloths and large gilded mirrors. Mr. Harringshaw was greeted by the effusive maître d', a thin man in white tie and tails, who swiftly tucked three menus under his arm and led the way to a table in the most fashionable part of the room. Eve smelled the perfumed air and tried not to gawk at the bejeweled women and their full, opulent gowns of buttery yellows, burgundy and deep pleated purples. They sat with their cigar-smoking tuxedoed men, all dining in supreme elegance.

As Albert passed several tables, men acknowledged him with a little head bow, while nearly all the women ignored him, their expressions icy, eyes averted, whispering. Albert seemed to enjoy the attention, as he enjoyed the covert, envious glances of men who watched Helen and Eve drift by, both captivating beauties.

They sat at a round table, with Albert facing out, flanked by his two lovely ladies. As they were presented with menus, Albert waved them away, ordering Delmonico steaks for everyone.

Helen sat in a pride of silence, boldly glancing about the restaurant, recognizing the Astors, Miss Edith Fish and Mrs. Daniel E. Fearing, all the cream of society.

Eve took it all in, mesmerized by the magnificent spectacle and the extravagant designs and theatrical performances of these society-conscious people.

Albert was bantering on about the latest theater, and about all the items on the menu he had tried, while Eve was preoccupied, unable to pull her eyes from the waiters dressed in black suits, white ties and long white aprons, gliding across the floor; the graceful turn of a lady's hand as she talked; the shimmering jewels around necks, on fingers, and in hair; the beards on nearly every man in the room, and the sheer opulence and regal bearing of these fabulously wealthy people.

When the steaks came, Eve ate voraciously. It was a scrumptious piece of meat, one of the best, if not *the* best, she'd ever tasted.

For dessert, Albert ordered Baked Alaska for all.

"The Baked Alaska is a wonder," Albert said, with proud enthusiasm. "Please tell the ladies, Andre, how the Baked Alaska is prepared."

The waiter, Andre, wore a thin black mustache, and he reminded Eve of Agatha Christie's Detective Hercule Poirot. His hands became animated as he spoke with a fluid French accent. "The nucleus is an ice cream. So *tahstee!* That is surrounded by an envelope of *zee* fluffy meringue. Just before they serve it, it is placed under *zee* influence of a red hot salamander."

"And what is a salamander?" Eve asked.

"That, madam, is a kitchen tool used to warm and brown the tops of food dishes. There is a round disk in the wire that the chef holds over your dish to brown *zee* tops of your Baked Alaska. Trust Mr. Harringshaw, madams, it is an exquisite dessert."

Just as Andre retreated, Eve saw a dark shadow pass across Albert's face. She followed his gaze. When she saw whom Albert saw, she froze. She recognized him immediately. It was John Allister Harringshaw! He was with a woman, and they were being escorted to their table by the maître d'. She was a tall, willowy brunette, wearing a gold satin gown with lace trim. Eve's first impression was that she was not a beauty. She had a long face, an aggressive jaw, and dull, evasive eyes.

John Allister Harringshaw, on the other hand, was strikingly good looking. Just before he sat, he caught a glimpse of his brother. He stiffened, and each held the other's uncomfortable gaze.

Eve's pulse surged. She sat bolt erect, feeling hypnotized by the impossibility of the moment. There he was, in the flesh. The man who had written the Christmas Eve letter. Eve had dreamed of this moment and now that it was here, it seemed strangely chilling.

She studied him—every inch of him. He was indeed tall, taller than most men of his time, and he was handsome, remarkably handsome, with piercing dark eyes, clean chiseled features and the fine sharp nose of an aristocrat, just as she'd seen in his sepia photograph on *Wikipedia*. His dark suit had four buttons and high lapels, and he wore a stand-up wing collar and a black tie with a glossy gold stick pin. His shoes were high, black and buttoned. There was a natural authority and a stern dignity about him that was both attractive and disconcerting, as if he were not completely comfortable in his own skin.

His eyes left his brother's and traveled first to Helen, where Eve saw disapproval, and then they settled on Eve. Eve's heart pounded in her ears. She sat rigid, her eyes meeting his. Somehow, she thought he might recognize *her*. It was irrational, of course, but Eve stared back in anticipation. In his eyes, Eve saw first surprise, then questions, and then indifference.

John Allister gave his brother a polite bow, and then he turned and sat down with his back facing them. Albert reached for his coffee cup and laughed mirthlessly. "My boring brother," he said to Eve. "His fiancée is a silly, unattractive, superficial sparkle. I am sure they will be very happy together."

Eve took in a quick breath. She knew her cheeks were flushed, and she saw Helen looking at her, questioningly.

"Do you find Albert's brother attractive, Miss Kennedy?" she said, with a little sneer.

Albert threw Eve a hard glance.

Eve straightened her shoulders. "I find that both the Harringshaw brothers are attractive, Miss Price. Both are truly fortunate men in that regard."

Albert considered Eve's statement. He liked it, and he smiled his satisfaction. "But of course, Miss Kennedy, I contest that I am more attractive than my brother. Do you not agree?"

Eve recalled a phrase her mother used to quote, again by Jane Austen. *Vanity working on a weak head produces every sort of mischief.* But once again, Eve held her tongue.

"You do have fortunate qualities, Mr. Harringshaw, manliness and generosity being chief among them."

That pleased him immensely, and then, thankfully, the Baked Alaska arrived.

While she ate, Eve couldn't help stealing glances at John Allister. She was so close to him and yet so far away. If she could just get him alone, she'd ask him if he knew where Evelyn was. Perhaps there was still time to help save her life or, at the very least, Eve could make her more comfortable with care and treatment. And then there was the issue of the lantern. When Eve found it, would it perform as it had before, and send her back to her own time?

CHAPTER 18

E ve spent the next few days settling in at the boarding house and looking for Evelyn, venturing out on day trips to visit the various infirmaries and charitable hospitals Dr. Long had written down for her. She took the Second Avenue El north to the Knickerbocker Hospital in Harlem, but Evelyn Sharland was not a patient there, nor had she ever been a patient there, nor at any other hospital, clinic or infirmary Eve searched. The task made Eve especially grateful for twenty-first century technology like the telephone.

During her travels, Eve often glanced back over her shoulder to see if Detective Sergeant Gantly was in sight, but he wasn't. She paused in doorways and searched for him. She sat on benches and looked for him. Riding on the El train, she stole furtive glances, but he wasn't there. Had he abandoned her? Was he "following" her and not observing? Had he been fired and put on another case? She simply didn't know. But she was disappointed. Greatly disappointed.

Detective Sergeant Gantly had agitated her emotional landscape, leaving her with a swelling discomfort, a tickle of desire, and an unwanted attraction. He'd given her a pure emotional high that had surprised and unnerved her, and she couldn't shake it loose. In that first meeting, the man had moved her like no man had ever moved her before, and she began to wonder if it was simply the weird circumstance of her being in another time... and so lonely.

The night they met, she had a sexy dream about him. He'd come up from behind, seized her hand and yanked her into a darkened alleyway. He'd pressed her against a wall and kissed her, long, wet and warm. When Eve had awakened, she was perspiring and wanting—wanting more. Much more. She'd shut her eyes, longing to return to the dream—to him, to his strong hands, to his wall of a chest, to his firm, commanding kiss.

After that dream, Eve considered searching the local precincts to try to find him, with the pretense of returning the ten-dollar bill, but she didn't know if that was something a woman would do in 1885. She suspected it wasn't. Would his fellow detectives get the wrong impression if she showed up, with a ten-dollar bill in hand? Yeah, of course they would, because even in the twenty-first century they'd probably get the wrong impression. And even if they didn't, Detective Sergeant Gantly would suffer many unpleasant jokes and end up despising her for it.

The other reason she didn't search for him was simple: she needed the money. She was running low, and she'd need money to survive until she could find some sort of job.

Albert had offered her more money, and to put her up in a fine apartment near Madison Square, but Eve had refused, politely but firmly. Albert didn't like being rebuffed, but he'd accepted it with reservation, probably feeling certain Eve would soon run out of money and become desperate. He was waiting, patiently.

Eve had hoped that Detective Sergeant Gantly would have appeared by now, and her instincts had told her that he'd procure her a diploma if he possibly could. Apparently, she'd been wrong. The ten-dollar gift was most likely a polite send-off: "Goodbye and good luck, strange lady from another planet."

Millie had come for a visit over the weekend and they had gone shopping, with Millie escorting Eve to a few less expensive shops. Millie also knew a good, inexpensive seamstress, and Eve was finally about to have one dress of her very own.

At the fitting, the seamstress had argued for a narrow look for Eve. From neck to knee, the dress would be straight. Below the knees, the skirt would flare out and form a shallow train. The dress still required a bustle, but it would be moved to a lower position. The narrow dress would also demand a correspondingly small hat that the seamstress had in stock, for a much cheaper price than they charged at the stores on the "Ladies' Mile."

On Monday afternoon, November 2nd, under a cold, gray metallic sky, Eve was returning home from the seamstress. As she approached Gramercy Park, she saw him. Detective Sergeant Gantly was sitting on a park bench, long legs crossed, reading a newspaper. He was dressed as before, with a heavy overcoat and bowler hat. He glanced up over the paper and acknowledged her with a touch of a hand to the brim of his hat.

Eve stopped, staring, breathing, her pulse escalating. She stood proudly erect, determined not to fall into sensual dreaminess over this man, because it was simply not in her nature. So she stood there, waiting, and then their eyes met and there it was, an unmistakable spark. Despite herself, a new and insistent burn flared through her body, and there was a tender sweetness about it that melted her.

Then all at once, she was angry at him, irrational as that seemed. After all, hadn't he flirted with her the last time? Wasn't he supposed to be following her and watching out for her?

The detective neatly folded his paper and stood up. He started toward her and, as Eve examined his face, she thought she saw a stormy mood. This confused and worried her. Had he somehow found out about her—learned the truth about where she'd come from? Did he think something romantic had happened between her and Albert Harringshaw? One thought chased another as she noticed white clouds of vapor leaving his partially open mouth.

When he was within fifteen feet of her, a little smile formed on his lips. She relaxed her tight shoulders and, as he drew up to her, he rested his eyes on her face.

"Good afternoon, Miss Kennedy."

"Good afternoon, Detective Sergeant Gantly. I suppose since you were waiting for me, you weren't following me?"

He knew what she was really saying, and so did Eve.

"I have been on other assignments, but..." He paused and looked up into the gray rolling clouds. "I have also been around."

Eve wondered if he was telling her the truth, but then decided he was. That pleased her.

"Shall we take a walk, Miss Kennedy?"

Eve nodded, and they started off along East 20th Street, neither speaking for minutes. A delivery wagon rattled by, led by a sturdy horse which advanced in an easy rhythm, an unlighted kerosene lantern swaying under the rear axle. Eve paused when she saw the lantern, her mind flashing back to her own time and the lighted lantern that had brought her here.

"Anything wrong?" he asked.

"No... Nothing."

A policeman with a walrus mustache, dressed in a knee-length blue coat with brass buttons and tall felt helmet, was walking his beat. Detective Sergeant Gantly acknowledged him with a nod, and the policeman tapped his cap with his baton. They walked on, hearing the vendors hawking their wares, and the newsboys shouting out the latest editions.

A woman in a feathered black hat and a cape over her shoulders walked by and around the corner, holding her long skirt an inch above her ankle as she climbed into a carriage.

"Where do you work?" Eve asked.

"I work out of the fifteenth precinct station house on Mercer Street."

"And what were some of your other assignments?"

"You would probably find it boring."

"Try me," Eve challenged.

"All right. I've been looking at mug shots."

"Hmm… I didn't know there were mug shots in…" She caught herself. "So you've been looking at photos of criminals?"

He gave her a sidelong glance. "Yes, Miss Kennedy, and some of us have been assigned to explore the relationship between appearance and criminal behavior. We have compiled a record of, let's say forgers, to see if all forgers look alike, or if all murderers look alike, or if all burglars have the same facial features."

"And what have you found?"

He smiled. "I find it particularly fascinating, Miss Kennedy, that you find this conversation both proper and interesting."

"I do," Eve said. "I find it very proper and very interesting."

"Frankly, I am skeptical about the whole thing, but some of my superiors are excited by the research, as are members of the press and many Americans. You have probably read about it in the newspapers."

"No, I haven't, but I would think that criminals are much too clever to get themselves categorized by appearance or by face and head type."

"And you would be right, Miss Kennedy, at least according to my experience."

Snow flurries suddenly appeared and Eve held her hand out to catch some.

"How do you like your new accommodations?" Detective Gantly asked.

"The boarding house is very comfortable and pleasant."

"I am glad to hear it."

"Detective Sergeant, are you married?"

Eve looked at him. The skin tightened around his eyes, and his mouth firmed up. "You can be direct, Miss Kennedy."

Eve hadn't planned to ask. The question had just jumped out of her mouth. Now that it was out, she waited for his answer.

"I was married. She and my little girl passed away a little over a year ago, during child birth."

Eve lowered her eyes. "I am sorry. Truly sorry."

"Thank you, Miss Kennedy. It is kind of you to say so."

They continued on and, even though there was a small breeze and a gentle snowfall, Eve was comfortable in her flower pot-shaped hat tied under her chin, her woolen coat and her hands tucked into a muff, a gift from sweet Millie.

"Why do you want to locate Evelyn Sharland?" Detective Gantly asked, mildly.

Eve's neck tightened. Okay, so he *had* been following her, and he knew what she was up to.

"Personal reasons."

"Would those personal reasons have anything to do with the Harringshaw family?"

"She's a friend."

"You didn't answer my question, Miss Kennedy."

"I don't have to answer your question, Detective," Eve said, more sharply than she'd wanted. She softened her voice. "She's sick. I just want to help her."

"Is that why you came to New York?"

Eve thought about that. "I suppose so. Yes, you could say that."

It occurred to her again, although more deeply each time she considered it, that this must be precisely why she was propelled to this time: to find a way to help Evelyn, or help change the outcome of Evelyn's and John Allister's relationship. What other reason could there be? But how could she change the outcome when she couldn't even find the woman and, if she did, this world of 1885 had no effective medical way to save her from her disease?

"Are you related to Miss Sharland?" Patrick asked.

Eve started to speak and then stopped. "Why are you asking me these questions? Because you work for Mr. Harringshaw?"

"Because, Miss Kennedy, I do not know who you are, where you came from or what you want. If your intention is to embarrass the Harringshaw family because of Evelyn Sharland's relationship with John Allister, or to seek money from them, I will have to prevent you from doing that."

Eve stopped short, turning sharply to face him. "Do you really believe I want money from them? Do you really believe that?"

He searched her eyes. "Then why this charade, Miss Kennedy? Why won't you tell me who you are—and don't tell me you're Eve Kennedy."

She shook her head. "I'm disappointed in you, Detective Sergeant Gantly."

The world became still and quiet. Snow landed on his shoulders and melted. A carriage drifted by, the horse's hooves clopping along the cobblestones.

He inventoried her face with calm eyes, expressionless. "Whether you believe me or not, I am trying to protect you, Miss Kennedy. You seem to have dropped in from some other world, and you have no idea about the power of the Harringshaws."

"I don't give a damn about the Harringshaws or their power."

He lifted an eyebrow. "Is that so?"

"Have you told Albert that I have been searching for Evelyn Sharland?"

He was quiet. When spoke, his voice was small with regret. "Albert? So you call him Albert, his Christian name?"

She waved his comment away. "It's not what you think. Where I come from, we call people by their first names."

He blinked slowly. "Where you come from?"

"So you *have* told Mr. Harringshaw then," she said, resigned.

He stared at her, his eyes growing progressively cold. "You greatly disappoint me, Miss Kennedy."

Eve felt the cut of his remark. She lifted her chin in defiance. "Well, it seems we disappoint each other, don't we?"

He gave a sharp nod. "So it would seem."

"Okay, fine then."

He sighed and reached into his inside coat pocket. He drew out a robin egg blue envelope and handed it to her.

"What's this?" Eve said, taking it, blinking fast and feeling the flush of anger.

"Until you trust me, Miss Kennedy, I have done all that I can for you." He touched the brim of his hat. "Good day."

Eve watched him walk away in the now blowing snow. He paused to buy a paper from a corner news-boy, touched the boy's cap affectionately, said a few words that made the boy grin, and then moved away with the paper tucked under his arm. Detective Gantly already had one newspaper under his arm. He probably bought a newspaper from that boy every day, and probably from many more boys.

Eve turned cold, shivering in regret and irritation. Turning her attention to the envelope, she slid open the flap, drew out the heavy bond paper and unfolded it.

It was a diploma.

City of New York

Department of Hospitals

Blessing Hospital
School of Nursing

THIS IS TO CERTIFY THAT

EVELYN KENNEDY HAS COMPLETED THE ESTABLISHED COURSE OF INSTRUCTION AND PRACTICE IN THE SCHOOL OF NURSING IN THIS HOSPITAL AND HAS SATISFACTORILY PASSED ALL THE REQUIRED CLINICS AND EXAMINATIONS.

THIS **12 day of February 1884**

SUPERINTENDENT: **J. Paxton Edwards**
SUPERINTENDENT OF NURSES: **Ellen M. McManus**

Staring dumbly, Eve saw there was also a handwritten note clipped to the diploma.

Miss Kennedy:

Do not be concerned about the Superintendent or the Superintendent of Nurses in the event a potential employer contacts them. They will corroborate any inquiries regarding your credentials. I trust this will aide you in gaining satisfactory employment.

Please destroy this note, promptly.

Best regards,
Detective Sergeant Gantly

Eve's staring eyes searched for the Detective, but he had faded away. She slowly turned and shambled back to the boarding house. Would that be the last time she saw Detective Gantly?

She would go see Dr. Ann Long at the Gouverneur Hospital the first thing in the morning and ask for a job.

CHAPTER 19

Two weeks later, on November 16th, Eve left her room at suppertime and went downstairs to the large front parlor that opened off the hall. There was a cozy fire in the fireplace and the room was furnished comfortably, with a large, brocaded settee against the wall, an upright piano, a leather rocking chair and two upholstered chairs.

Eve stepped over to the partially opened sliding wood doors, hearing the murmur of voices and the clink of dishes. She gently rolled back the doors and was greeted by Marie Putney, who stood before a partially set, heavy, oak dining table. On the windows were drawn blue velvet drapes, fringed with little gold balls. A glass-fronted cabinet, displaying blue and white china, sat in the corner of the room.

"Good evening, Eve," Marie said with a friendly smile. "Mr. Putney is so much better today and he is joining us again for supper."

Seated at the head of the table was Elijah Putney, Marie's grandfather and the owner of the brownstone boarding house. He was a thin, older gentleman who wore thick wire-rimmed spectacles, and had neatly combed silver hair, a white beard and a pale complexion. With a grimace, he worked to heave himself up as Eve stepped over to meet him.

"Please don't get up, Mr. Putney," Eve said.

"Forgive me, Miss Kennedy," he said, slowly returning to his seat, with a deep straining sigh. "Forgive these old bones, but I am an old man whom Father Time likes to keep working on in a variety of ways."

He patted the chair next to him. "Please sit down next to me, Miss Kennedy. I haven't seen you in nearly a week. Marie told me you are working as a nurse at the Gouverneur Hospital."

Eve smiled. "Yes, for almost two weeks now."

"And how are you getting along then?"

"Very well, Mr. Putney. Now, as to your gout, did you try the cold compresses? Have they helped to lessen the inflammation and ease the pain?"

Mr. Putney smiled, broadly. "Yes, Miss Kennedy, they have, as you can see by my presence here tonight. Marie has insisted I follow your advice and so we have been placing ice on my toe joint for twenty-to-thirty minutes several times a day. And I drink a lot of water."

"Good," Eve said. "The water will help your body stabilize uric acid to a normal level."

"Uric acid?" Marie asked, placing napkins at the five table settings.

"Yes. A gout attack happens when there's already higher than normal levels of uric acid in the body and it has built up around a joint."

Cornelius Adams, seated at the other end of the table, looked at Eve carefully from over the top of his *New York Express* newspaper. He wore a clean shirt with a high collar, a mother-of-pearl vest, a gold watch chain, a long black coat, black pants and wire-rimmed spectacles. At forty-two years old, he was neat, precise and measured with his words. He worked as an accountant for an insurance company.

"I would think that cold would agitate such a condition, Mr. Putney. Didn't your doctor prescribe Laudanum?"

Eve leveled her cool eyes on him. "I assure you, Mr. Adams, I have treated gout many times in the past. What I prescribed has been very effective. Laudanum will do very little good."

Mr. Adams wiggled his nose, like Samantha Stevens often did in the old TV show *Bewitched*. Eve had loved watching it on *HULU*. She nearly laughed out loud.

Mr. Adams' small eyes narrowed. "So you know better than Dr. Hamilton, Miss Kennedy? I recognize that you are a nurse, but I am dismayed that you have taken the liberty of overriding Dr. Hamilton's treatment and prescribing your own."

Mr. Putney cut in. "Well, in any case, Mr. Adams, I have tried Miss Kennedy's treatment, and it works and I am the better for it. Thank you, Miss Kennedy."

Mr. Adams went back to reading his paper with an air of indifference. On the back page of the paper, Eve saw an advertisement that caught her attention.

COCAINE
TOOTHACHE DROPS
Instantaneous Cure
Price 15 Cents

Nellie Tanner entered the dining room, a nervous diminutive woman who could have been cast as an elementary school teacher in any Hollywood movie. And, in fact, Nellie taught at an all-girls school near Madison Square, specializing in preparing her students for Vassar. She wore a black dress with a high neck and tight sleeves that covered her arms with little white ruffles at the wrists. Her mostly gray hair was pulled back into a tight bun.

She sat and acknowledged everyone, her back ruler-straight, her thin lips tightly compressed.

The last boarder to arrive for dinner was Thomas Finch, a clerk at the courthouse. He was short and broad, perhaps thirty-five, with reddish blond hair, chipped green eyes and a large mustache growing from both the upper lip and cheeks. The whiskers from the cheeks were styled, pointing upward. Although he was not unattractive, he exposed crooked teeth when he smiled, so between the teeth and the odd mustache, he looked a little sinister. His eyes shined noticeably brighter whenever they took in Marie, as they did now while she was systematically carving the turkey and presenting each boarder with a plateful of food.

The conversation centered around the weather, which was cold for November; President Grover Cleveland's rejection of several veterans' pension bills because he believed them fraudulent; and the President's support of the gold standard.

Eve was impressed with her fellow boarders' knowledge of current events, noting that they all read more than one newspaper per day.

Nellie turned to Eve. "How do you like your new job, Miss Kennedy? You have not spoken much about it."

Eve didn't know where to begin. Although the hospital was clean and sanitary, the level of medical knowledge and procedures seemed shockingly primitive. And while Dr. Long was a gifted doctor and surgeon, she struggled against a male-dominated profession that considered her a second-class doctor, barely worth acknowledging.

"What kinds of patients have you been seeing?" Mr. Putney asked, delicately chewing a piece of turkey.

The boarders all lifted their eyes to Eve, waiting.

"Yesterday I saw a man who had been kicked in the head by a horse. He survived but has lost much of his memory and some of his speech."

"Isn't that too bad," Nellie Tanner said, her face set in concern.

"Just this week, Dr. Long and I have treated patients with overdoses of morphine, cirrhosis of the liver and gunshot wounds."

"Oh my," Marie said. "Those poor souls."

All eyes had widened on Eve. They stared with keen interest, and she wondered if she was a kind of TV reality show for them. She continued. "Young mothers have brought their children in with scarlet fever, measles and smallpox. Most of the children who come to us are under-fed. They have deep coughs, ear aches, belly aches, head lice and rashes. Two women have died in childbirth."

"It's a sad business," Mr. Putney said, shaking his head. "A very sad business indeed. We must remember all of them in our prayers, Marie. Yes, we must."

Marie spoke up. "Yes, grandfather, we shall remember them. What about the tuberculosis patients you spoke about last week, Miss Kennedy? Are they improving?"

Cornelius Adams' voice was sharp. "More importantly, are you staying clear of them? They are highly contagious, you know. We certainly don't need to be worrying about that awful disease entering this house."

Eve looked at him pointedly. "Dr. Long has not allowed me to see them, for that very reason. Everyone wears a mask when they enter their room, but so far there are only two nurses caring for the five patients. I have not seen any of them."

"Well, I am glad to hear it," Mr. Adams said, heaving out a sigh. "I am very glad to hear it."

Just then the doorbell rang. Marie pushed back her chair and left the dining room to answer it. Minutes later, she entered the dining room, carrying an envelope. She handed it to Eve.

"A messenger boy delivered it. He's waiting for your reply. He's so dirty. I'm going to give him a turkey sandwich."

Eve thanked Marie and opened it. Meanwhile, Marie placed some turkey on some white bread and packed the sandwich down.

Eve read the message.

Miss Kennedy:

I have located Miss Evelyn Sharland. Please keep information to yourself. Meet me tomorrow evening at 7 p.m. at Dorlan's, an oyster restaurant in Fulton Market.

If you can't meet, let the messenger know. If you can, simply destroy this communication.

Sincerely,
Detective Sergeant Gantly

Eve stared at the message, utterly transfixed. Marie waited for Eve to answer, but Eve didn't stir.

"Is everything all right, Miss Kennedy?" Marie asked.

Eve was caught between excitement and dread. Everyone at the table had stopped eating, watchful and curious, waiting for her reply. Eve felt the heavy weight of the moment. A hundred thoughts and emotions leaped up, nearly engulfing her. To finally meet Evelyn was so fantastic that Eve couldn't quite take it in. Why hadn't Detective Gantly told her how she was? Was she dying? Was she okay?

And then there was the possibility of seeing Detective Gantly again. In the last two weeks, she'd mostly managed to push him out of her mind, knowing that her attraction to him was an unwanted complication and she shouldn't indulge in it. And yet, her subconscious mind wasn't buying it. She'd had two more dreams about him and, in the quiet moments after waking, she'd fantasized about kissing him and feeling his hands on her body.

"Miss Kennedy," Marie said, waiting. "Will there be a reply?"

Eve shook awake. She folded the message and returned it to the envelope. She cleared her throat.

"No, Miss Putney, there will be no reply. Thank you."

The dining room was quiet. Eve could feel everyone's eyes on her. She must have looked strange, and she felt strange. After all these weeks, she still did not feel a part of this time, nor did she feel sure about what she would do once she met Evelyn Sharland.

"You're sure that everything is quite all right, Miss Kennedy?" Mr. Putney asked.

Eve forced a smile. "Yes, Mr. Putney."

"I hope it wasn't bad news," Nellie Tanner said, obviously wanting to know what was in the message. "I so dislike bad news. It's so hostile to the blood and digestion."

"No, it's not bad exactly. Just... a work thing. No worries."

"A work thing? No worries?" Mr. Adams said. "You have the most interesting way of expressing yourself, Miss Kennedy. Quite entertaining."

"Where did you say you were from?" Thomas Finch asked.

"Ohio."

"What city?"

"You've probably never heard of it," Eve said, preoccupied with thoughts of Evelyn Sharland and Detective Gantly.

"*I'm* from Ohio," Mr. Finch said. "A town just north of Cincinnati. I'm sure I'll have heard of it."

Eve barely heard him. "Really? How nice," she answered as she prepared to leave the room.

"Please excuse me," she said in a louder voice. "It's been a long day and I have a long day tomorrow. Good night."

Their eyes held questions, and when they went back to eating, each seemed lost in his or her own thoughts.

CHAPTER 20

Eve rushed by the coffee shops and oyster saloons of Fulton's Market, an area crowded with well-dressed men and ladies. She found Dorlan's in the heart of the city's thriving publishing industry. It was the haunt of cub reporters, newsboys, press tycoons and famous writers. Everyone went to Dorlan's.

Detective Sergeant Gantly was standing by the entrance, dressed as always in his black greatcoat and bowler hat. When he saw her, he put his hand to his hat in acknowledgement.

The gas lamps threw a cone of light on the walkways, and it made the night seem a bit eerie and out of focus. She strolled up to Detective Gantly and smiled at him, trying to suppress a blush from a mounting sexual attraction.

"Hello, Mr. Detective," she said, playfully.

He lifted an eyebrow. "Mr. Detective?"

She shrugged. "Why not? It takes a lot of energy to call you Detective Sergeant Patrick Gantly," she said, batting her eyelids ever so slightly.

He watched her for a moment, showing no expression. Then he grinned. "Shall we go inside?"

Dorlan's was loud and crowded and swirling with cigar smoke, but Patrick Gantly led the way, pressing through the mass until he found an empty two-top wooden table in the back corner of the room. He held a chair for Eve and she slid onto it, removing her gloves and hat. He sat opposite, removing his hat. He folded his hands on the tabletop, noticing that her blonde hair seemed to give off light and her eyes sparkled in the lamplight.

"I guess we're eating oysters?" Eve asked.

"You can also get a slice of beef or ham and a side order of beans. That's what most people order."

Eve looked about at the yellow gaslights, and then out the windows as shadows of people moved across them.

Not being used to smoke—especially cigar smoke— Eve coughed. "I'll have whatever you're going to have," she said.

When the fat, heavy-mustached waiter came over, his white apron spotted with grease, Patrick ordered beef, ham, two side orders of beans, 12 oysters, pickles, raw onion and olives. He ordered a beer for himself.

"I would love a beer as well," Eve said softly. "Possible?"

The waiter looked at Gantly with a raised, bushy, black eyebrow. Patrick nodded. "Why shouldn't you, Miss Kennedy? In this den, no one will even notice."

The waiter shrugged a right shoulder and retreated into the boisterous crowd.

"You have a strange appetite," Eve said, with a hint of a grin.

He stared at her. "How is the new job?" he finally asked.

She held his eyes. "Thank you for that. You ran off before I could tell you how grateful I was. How did you manage to get the diploma?"

"Some people owed me a favor. I collected. That's the way the city works, Miss Kennedy."

Eve propped her head up with the palm of her hand, looking at Patrick boldly. He didn't disengage from her stare and so they sat there, gazing into each other's eyes. Eve felt a strange magic envelope her, felt herself opening, as if a door had swung open and she was hovering somewhere between reality and fantasy. Here she was in this strange world with a man that disturbed and thrilled her like no other man ever had, in any time or place. She felt giddy and a little drunk on this guy, whose piercing eyes seemed to see into the veiled secrets of her heart. Could he see what she was feeling? Did he feel it?

Eve felt a surge of intrepid feelings. She wanted to be next to him, feel the heat of him, the man of him. It was as if she was losing a part of her mind—the mind she had always known and had been comfortable with.

"Why are you staring at me, Miss Kennedy?"

"I could ask you the same thing."

"I stare because I can't make you out. You're a puzzle and I can't find all the pieces."

"Am I a woman of mystery then, Mr. Detective?" she said, playfully.

"You are that. But I will find you out, Miss Kennedy. Given a little more time."

"Where is Evelyn Sharland?" Eve asked, directly.

Detective Gantly sat back in his chair, folding his arms across his chest. "She was living in Hoboken, New Jersey with her brother, but is now in the temporary care of a physician."

Her eyes slid away from his steady gaze. His words hung in the smoky air, even as she tried to take them in. Finding Evelyn was a game changer. It presented Eve with a new set of problems and possibilities.

Eve raised her eyes. "The last time we met, you said you'd done all you could for me. Thank you for this."

"I found her because Albert Harringshaw requested it."

Eve shot him a look of surprise and disappointment. "I see. So that's the way it is."

"No, Miss Kennedy, you don't see and that is not the way it is. The Harringshaw brothers are not getting along, and I am finding myself caught in the middle of something I'd rather not be a part of. If John Allister finds out I am, for all practical purposes, working for his brother... well, let me put it this way, he has connections too. I could easily take the fall when things get particularly dirty. And they will get dirty, Miss Kennedy. They always get dirty, because money is constantly changing hands in this city. I have seen this happen to others within the department. One detective, who got tangled up with the Astors over a certain daughter he had nothing to do with, shot himself in the mouth. I hope I'm not being too grossly inappropriate, Miss Kennedy."

He waited for her to respond. She didn't. She was still listening intently.

"Miss Kennedy, the rich don't give a damn one way or the other about the people who work for them. We're just convenient pawns to be pushed and shoved about on their broad and opulent chess board."

Eve nibbled on her lower lip, taking it all in. "Detective Sergeant Gantly, you do not seem like the kind of man anyone could push or shove around."

Their mugs of beer arrived, cold with foamy heads. He sipped his.

"I would fight, of course, but I would be defeated."

"Why are you telling me this?" Eve asked.

He leaned forward, sliding his mug of beer aside and glaring at her. "Because I want to know how you, certainly not a woman of his class, arranged to meet Albert Harringshaw, one of the richest and most powerful men in the country. Why are you looking for Evelyn Sharland and what is it that you want? I don't believe in coincidence, Miss Kennedy. You are plotting something and I do not want to be caught in either your trap or the Harringshaw trap. I have repeatedly requested to be relieved of this assignment, but all my requests have been emphatically denied. I am assuming you and Albert Harringshaw are plotting something, or maybe you're plotting something with someone else, although I have not been able to find out who that someone else is. Perhaps Mr. Albert Harringshaw wants to get rid of me because he does not want to owe me for his life. I do not know the reason yet, but I warn you, if the day comes when I am disgraced and fired from my position, I will have my revenge."

He snatched his beer and drank it half empty, his eyes burning.

Eve let it all settle for a time. It was not what she'd expected. Nothing was working out as she'd thought it would. Now, she felt as though *she* was in a trap and she had no idea how to get out of it.

When their food came, they merely picked at it, their eyes wandering the room. Eve watched men in silk bowler hats jabbing fingers into chests, laughing and shouting opinions, their cigars curling blue-gray smoke. The packed bar held mugs of beer, jars of pretzels and shot glasses. Eve saw only two women, who were richly and stylishly dressed, standing with a distinguished man, who had the sheen of wealth all about him.

What an odd place, she thought, her mind a tangled mess. What was she going to tell Detective Gantly? She couldn't tell him the truth; if she did, he'd think she was out of her mind. More minutes passed as she watched him eat the ham, bread and pickles. Still, she had to say something.

"I am related to Evelyn Sharland," Eve blurted out.

Gantly stopped chewing and lifted his head, waiting for more, his eyes hard and focused.

"My meeting with Albert Harringshaw was entirely accidental, and that is the truth. He found me sitting on a park bench in Central Park when I was in great distress. I had had some kind of breakdown and, even now, I am not sure what caused it—although I am sure some of it had to do with hearing that Evelyn was not only involved with John Allister Harringshaw, but that she was sick with tuberculosis. I am a nurse, Detective Gantly. I am a very good nurse and I came here to find her and help her. I still have some memory lapses, but I know for certain that I must go to Evelyn and see if I can help her in some way."

Detective Sergeant Gantly studied her closely, alert to her every gesture and tone of voice. He was trained to know if people were telling the truth. He drained his beer mug, watching her. He ate beef and onions and he watched her.

Eve ate a little and turned from his harsh gaze.

"How did you hear that she was sick? Did she or someone else in the family write to you? Why haven't I been able to find even one person who knows who you are?"

Eve couldn't compete with his practiced, experienced, skillful and suspicious mind.

"Take my word for it, Detective Gantly. I heard about Evelyn and I came. That is the honest truth."

He ate, pensively. "Miss Kennedy, what perplexes me the most is why you insist on being vague and evasive. How can I take your word for anything when you will not reveal the factual truth about yourself?"

Eve leaned forward. "If you tell me where Evelyn Sharland is and if I can somehow help her, perhaps then I can tell you the whole truth."

He sighed and then shook his head. "No... Not this time, Miss Kennedy. It is your turn now. It is your turn to give something back. I have gone the extra mile for you every time, and every time you keep putting me off."

She sat stiff-shouldered. "Please... I may be able to save her life. Every day that passes, she gets worse. Please tell me where she is, for her sake, not for mine. Please."

"And what can you possibly do for her?" he asked.

"I don't know unless I see her. Please tell me."

They sat in silence, loud conversation all around them.

OUTSIDE, THEY WALKED AIMLESSLY for a time, neither talking. Finally, Detective Gantly hailed a Hansom. Eve looked at him inquiringly, but he ignored her. He said something to the driver, helped Eve in and then slid in next to her.

They still didn't speak as the cab trotted uptown. They came to the theatrical section of Broadway. The area was packed with shiny carriages, the sidewalks alive with theater-goers in evening dress, excitement all about them.

As the cab moved on to 4th Avenue and 24th Street, Eve saw a theater sign under glowing yellow globes. It was the Lyceum, a three-story building. She saw easel posters near the entrance. **Annie Russell!** was printed in large block letters.

Eve stole a glance at Patrick, but he refused to look at her.

Detective Gantly had wanted to separate from Eve back at Fulton's Market. In fact, he'd been wanting to separate from her ever since he'd met her. He knew she was lying to him, and he despised lies and liars. He dealt with them every day of his life. And yet, he couldn't stay away from her. There was a sexy allure and mystery about the woman that absolutely enthralled him, almost as if he had drunk some magic love potion. He thought about her during the day and had dreams about her at night. He could not drive her out of his thoughts, and that disturbed and irritated him.

As he sat there so close to her, his hands formed into fists so they wouldn't reach for her and kiss her. He was simply perplexed and bewitched by her.

He stared out the carriage window as they came to the city's nightclub district. He'd told the driver just to drive, it didn't matter where, so he could think and spend time just sitting with her, inhaling her scent, inhaling her essence. So here they were near Fifth Avenue and 32nd Street, in the area known as *The Tenderloin*. The name referred to the extortion payments the police extracted from both legitimate and illegitimate businesses in the area. Every cop knew this area, and many made a good living off it. Reformers called it Satan's Circus.

They passed saloons, brothels, gambling parlors, dance halls, and clip joints. The whole area was buzzing with life, "a carnival of the damned" the Detective often called it. He'd seen too many drunks, thieves and whores to last a lifetime and yet, at 35 years old, he knew he would see a lot more before his career was over, if he lived long enough.

He finally ventured a glance at Eve, but she didn't seem fully present. She was lost in her own thoughts, and he would have given a month's salary to know what she was thinking. So they moved on in silence.

"What was your wife like?" Eve finally said.

Her question threw him off guard. He turned from her. "She was a good, practical woman; a religious woman who prayed for my black heart every day and night. Heaven is a better place for her being there. I am the worse for it."

Eve turned to him. "That's a kind and good thing to say."

He looked at her earnestly, his eyes settling on her lips. "It's the truth."

"Did you always want to be a policeman?"

"It's what was presented to me. My father was a policeman."

"Is he still alive?"

"No. He passed five years ago."

"Do you have any family living in New York?"

"No, my sister died of the fever a few months before my father. She was a gentle soul, and I believe that is what finally did him in. The pain of her loss cut him deeply."

Detective Gantly tapped the ceiling and told the driver to take them to Gramercy Park. They returned to silence.

When the cab drew up to the curb on 4 Gramercy Park, Detective Gantly faced Eve. She waited for him to speak, but he seemed to struggle.

Eve felt a new rush of desire for him. She wanted him to kiss her, to hold her. As trite as it sounded, Detective Sergeant Gantly was the man she'd always fantasized about, even if unconsciously. It was as if he'd been standing in the distant shadow of her mind, waiting for her, waiting for the right moment, beckoning to her, whispering for her to come in for a long, warm kiss.

"All right, Miss Kennedy. I will take you to see Evelyn Sharland."

Eve smiled, relieved. "Okay," she said, not knowing whether these people ever said "Okay" or not. "Okay, you'll come with me. I'd like that. I'm very grateful."

Her answer melted some of his suspicion.

"All right, then. How about Sunday? I will come for you at 10 a.m., and the carriage will be parked at the end of the block, out of sight from the boarding house. Will that be convenient?"

She nodded, and they hovered next to each other, Eve willing him to kiss her. He didn't. He left the cab, circled it and opened the door, offering her his hand. After he helped her down from the cab, their hands stayed joined for a second longer than necessary, but neither dared look at the other.

She walked to the porch, turned and waved. He tipped his hat, turned and re-entered the cab.

Eve watched the cab move away, drifting in and out of the yellow cones of lamp light. She released a long, restless, disappointed sigh.

His hand had been so strong, yet so gentle.

CHAPTER 21

Sunday morning was bright and cold, with a thin sugary glaze of snow in the crooks of trees, on park benches and on the roofs of parked carriages. Detective Sergeant Gantly was right on time, waiting by the Hansom, watching Eve as she approached.

She was wearing a plum-colored bustle dress, a fitted wool coat, a hat and gloves. She'd swept her hair up into a new style, with bangs frizzled over her forehead, in a style similar to the one Helen Price wore.

As he watched the sunlight catch her, Detective Gantly felt a little catch of longing, but he hid it, as he always did when he was with her.

"Good morning," Eve said, brightly.

He tipped his hat and opened the cab door.

Inside the cab, they sat opposite each other and talked politely about the snowy weather, the chill in the air, and President Grover Cleveland's recent Proclamation 273, which declared Thursday, November 26, 1885 to be a national holiday set aside for prayer and thanksgiving.

"And will *you* celebrate Thanksgiving Day this coming Thursday?" Eve asked, hoping to lighten the mood.

"Unfortunately, I must work that day, Miss Kennedy, so that others may celebrate." He spoke matter-of-factly, without resentment.

Eve nodded, accepting his formality, wondering when he would allow her to see his playfulness and humor again. She remained quiet as they made their way to the Christopher Street landing. A great crowd had already gathered around the pier, as the ferry to Hoboken was almost ready to board.

Eve and Detective Gantly left the cab silently and walked down the cobblestones toward the throng: farm women holding baskets, their children clinging to their coats; workmen and draymen in floppy, wide-brimmed hats, huddled in groups, some smoking pipes; a priest staring out at the wide gray Hudson River; and Catholic nuns, heads down, speaking in whispers, as if in prayer.

There was a loud, shrill blast from the ferry whistle, and the children held their ears and made ugly faces as the crowd prepared to board.

Soon they were strolling up the steep ramp, stepping onto the wide open deck. Gantly steered Eve away from the cabin, knowing that the body odors, the cigar and pipe smoke, and the loud, vulgar conversations would not be appropriate for her.

Soon the ferry sputtered away from the dock, its deep-throated engines churning up the water, vibrating the floor beneath the passengers' feet. Eve and Gantly stood at the railing on the open deck, upwind of the wind and coal smoke, and stared out at the glittering Hudson River.

Gantly looked at Eve. Her eyes were a vivid light blue, her complexion white and smooth, her lush hair glowing in the sunlight. She smiled at him and said, "Hello," although over the din of the engines and loud talk, he only saw her mouth form the word.

He nodded and managed a small, tight smile. What else could he do? He couldn't relax his controlled face and expression, for if he did, his desire for her would be obvious. She'd know that as cold and direct as he could be, and as wounded as he'd been since his wife's and baby's deaths, he wanted to hold Eve, protect her, love her and cherish her. The larger part of him held back, of course, because he still didn't trust her.

Eve too projected a calm exterior to Patrick Gantly, though inside, Fourth of July fireworks were going off. It was exhilarating. Even standing among this mixed crowd, Eve felt a warm intimacy just being next to Patrick, as if they were already lovers, enjoying the new pleasure and the eager thrill of being in each other's company.

As the ferry churned ever closer to Hoboken, Eve now believed, without any doubt, that she was fulfilling her destiny in some inexplicable way. Whatever crazy magic had brought her to this time, surely it must have had a purpose—to help Evelyn with her illness, as well as to bring her and John Allister Harringshaw together. What else could it be?

But Detective Sergeant Gantly was an entirely different matter. Though she was still conflicted about him—confused, delighted, and scared—she was falling for him in a big way. Maybe she already had. And what in the world was she going to do about it?

When the ferry rode a wave, Eve instinctively moved a little closer to Patrick. She noticed he didn't move away. There was a quiet dignity about Patrick—in the line of his back and in the tilt of his head—and Eve wished she could tell him the truth about where she had come from. Maybe he could help her make sense of it all! But she didn't have the courage, at least not yet. Maybe someday soon.

Patrick drew closer to her and, even though there was a cold wind racing across the river, Eve felt warm.

They were only inches apart as Hoboken came into view. When a bell rang, everyone around them began to gather their belongings and move toward the exit. They were among the last to leave the ferry.

At the dock, Patrick found a cab, and they started off, passing warehouses, lumber mills, factories and saloons. Soon they were traveling along a tree-lined street away from the city, turning left away from the river, navigating a dirt road through open land and rickety-looking houses.

"This is not what I expected," Eve said.

"What did you expect?"

Eve had never been to Hoboken in her own time, even though she knew it had had a renaissance of sorts, with renovated brownstones, condominiums and a thriving bar and restaurant scene. She also knew that Frank Sinatra had been born there.

"I don't know. Not this. How did you find Evelyn?"

He folded his arms, staring ahead, his head lifted in mock arrogance. "You have your secrets, Miss Kennedy, and I have mine. Let's just say I have a network of paperboys, street urchins, and a few friends you probably wouldn't care to meet."

Eve playfully punched him in the arm. He turned, feigning shock. "Brutality will not help you, Miss Kennedy."

And then they locked gazes, hers open and warm, his filled with want and longing. He lifted a gentle hand and touched her cool cheek.

When he spoke, his tone was reflective, his voice feathery soft, filled with his lilting, Irish accent. "If each could learn as well as I, to profit by my pain, there's ne'er a man beneath the sky, would ever love again."

Eve looked at him gently.

He lowered his hand to his lap and looked out the window. "Where did that come from?" he muttered to himself.

Eve kept her eyes on him, hearing the steady trot of the horse. "Yes, where did it come from?"

He refused to look at her. "Something my grandfather used to say after his dear wife passed. He was never quite the same. He died only a few months after she."

"Do you often think of your wife?"

"I do. We were married less than two years. She was English, if you can believe it, from Manchester. Came over with her mother."

Patrick turned to Eve, his eyes narrowed. He had the drawn face of a mourner. "And what of your parents, Miss Kennedy? Where are they from? Is Kennedy your actual name, and please do not lie to me, because I know it is not."

Eve began twisting her hands. "How much further?"

"Tell me?" Patrick said, his voice strong, almost demanding.

Eve swallowed. "Sharland. My real name is Eve Sharland."

Neither moved for a time, as the cab pitched and ramped over the old ruddy road. Patrick slowly eased back into the seat.

"Evelyn Sharland?" he repeated, working to process the new knowledge.

"Yes."

"So you really *are* related to... to the Evelyn Sharland we're about to see?"

"Yes. I am a distant relation."

The cab turned right and started down a narrow street lined with new brownstones on either side.

"Why did you change your name? Are you running from something—from a husband? Maybe an abusive one. I see a lot of that."

Eve blurted out a laugh. "Oh, God, no. I divorced him."

Patrick looked at her in a strange way. "Divorced your husband?"

Eve nodded firmly. "Yes. I didn't love him. He was, to put it bluntly, unfaithful. So I divorced him."

Patrick scratched the side of his neck, processing this.

"Does that shock you?" Eve asked.

"I must admit, Miss Kennedy or Sharland or whoever you are, I am constantly surprised by you."

"It is the truth, and you wanted the truth."

"Are you running from the police back in Ohio then?"

The cab drew up to the curb and stopped.

Her eyes were cool and direct. "I am not running away from anyone, Detective Gantly. Stop being a cop for a minute and really look at me. Do I seem the type who is plotting a crime? Do I look devious and calculating, or do I look like a woman who is in a very difficult situation who finds herself very attracted to a certain detective?"

Before Gantly could speak—or even try to, since he didn't know what to say—Eve turned her gaze out the window. "Is this where she is?"

He only nodded.

She turned back to him. "Please trust me. I will tell you everything when I can, when it is right to tell you. I'll tell you everything and you still won't believe me. For now, please continue to call me Eve Kennedy. Please."

He ran a hand over the shadow of his beard and looked at her with a disappointing shake of his head.

"It is unfortunate, Miss Kennedy. Unfortunate that you won't trust me. I had believed that we could be... friends."

"Friends?" Eve asked, probing his face. "Only friends?"

"Friends are honest with each other, Miss Kennedy. Lovers trust and share all secrets. I fear we cannot be either."

Eve's shoulders sagged as she sighed audibly.

He pushed the door open and stepped down, offering her a helping hand. After asking the driver to wait, they stood looking at the handsome, three-story brownstone that was surrounded by a heavily spiked wrought-iron gate.

"Did you contact her?" Eve asked.

He shook his head.

He swung the gate open for her.

"It's a nice enough neighborhood," Eve said, feeling hopeful as they mounted the stairs.

Eve lifted the gold knocker and let it strike the heavy door. They waited.

When it opened, a young, white-aproned, white-capped maid stood alert, looking back at them.

"Yes?"

"I am told that there is an Evelyn Sharland living here," Eve said.

The maid's eyes darted about in sudden alarm. "Well... I."

Eve heard a deep, stern voice coming from inside the house.

"Well, who is it? Who is it?"

The maid bobbed a bow and turned. "It's a woman and a man looking for Miss Sharland, sir."

A man suddenly appeared from nowhere, an imperious scowl on his face. He was short and thin, wore a dark suit with a dark blue ascot, and his clean black beard was trimmed to a point.

"Who are you and why are you here?" he demanded.

"I am a relative of Miss Sharland's and I would like to see her."

"That is quite impossible."

Patrick stepped forward. "And why is it impossible, sir?"

"She is not well and cannot, under any circumstances, receive visitors."

"Miss Kennedy is a nurse and a relative, sir," Patrick said, with authority. "You may be assured that Miss Kennedy only has Miss Sharland's welfare in mind."

The man lifted a proud chin, puffing out his chest. "I am Dr. Horace A. Begley, and whether this woman is a nurse and has my patient's welfare in mind or not, it is of no concern to me. This is my house and I cannot and will not allow it."

Dr. Begley backed away and was about to close the door when Patrick wedged a big foot inside to prevent it from closing.

The doctor stared with shock and anger. "Sir, release your foot this instant or I will have to summon the police."

"I *am* the police, sir. Now we are here to see Miss Sharland, and you can either cooperate with us or you can find yourself down in the local precinct under the questioning gaze of detectives."

"This is outrageous!" Dr. Begley thundered. "On what charge would you have me down for then, sir?"

Patrick grinned sardonically, presenting a threatening expression Eve had never seen before. Patrick drew out his badge, presenting it for the doctor to see.

"On any charge I may wish to provide, doctor. The New York Police Department works very closely with The New Jersey Police Department. I happen to have a cousin who is a detective here. I have not seen him in two months. Shall I see him today and catch up on old times?"

Dr. Begley swallowed back rage and humiliation, and Eve saw his Adam's apple move. His eyes twitched and his mouth twitched. He lowered his eyes and stepped aside to let them enter.

It was warm inside the elegant foyer. Off the hall-way was the living room, which was expensively deco-rated in burgundy and gold. A fire gleamed in the hearth.

Dr. Begley pointed to the staircase that led to the up-per rooms. "Miss Sharland is in the first room on the right," he offered, face tightly closed, not moving.

Patrick removed his hat and indicated toward the staircase. "Please escort us, Doctor. If you would be so kind."

The doctor smoothed out his suit jacket and snorted. He marched up the stairs like a soldier going boldly into battle.

Upstairs, he opened the door to Evelyn's room and backed away, refusing to look inside.

"I want it known that I will contact Miss Sharland's brother. He has put Evelyn in my exclusive and profes-sional care, and he has been responsible for the pay-ment of my fees."

Eve looked at him carefully before entering the room. "What is his name, Dr. Begley?"

The doctor feigned surprise, his eyes widening. "You are a relative and you do not know his name?" he asked.

"Just answer the lady, doctor," Patrick snapped.

"Clayton Sharland."

"Thank you, Dr. Begley," Eve said, mildly.

Eve hesitated before entering the dark room. She had come a very long way to see this woman, the love object of the Christmas Eve letter; to see the distant rel-ative who, in Eve's time, had been dead for many years.

Eve entered. She smelled lye, soap and vinegar, a good sign, she thought. At least Evelyn was in a clean place. All Eve could see was the shadow of a four-poster bed, a chest of drawers and a chair. She went to the window and gently parted the heavy blue velvet drapes until a slice of light entered the room, illuminating the gray bundle that lay on the bed.

Dr. Begley and Patrick remained standing, framed in the light of the doorway. Eve stepped over to the bed and looked down at Evelyn, who was sleeping. Eve drew in a quick, startled breath, astounded to see that she and Evelyn had very similar features. Except for the long red hair that lay scattered on the pillow around her face, they could have passed as sisters. Evelyn looked so vulnerable and thin under the quilt. She had a scattering of freckles but was as pale as the snow, her chest rising and falling erratically. Eve touched Evelyn's forehead. It was hot and damp.

Eve turned to Dr. Begley, who was staring down at his shoes. "What is your diagnosis, Dr. Begley?"

He cleared his throat. "When I asked this patient what her symptoms were, she said that, a month or so ago, she thought she had a cold, but then it got much worse. After my examination, I concluded she has bilious fever."

Eve had no idea what that was. "Bilious fever, you say?"

"Yes! It's a common ailment," Dr. Begley said, defensively. "You purport to be a nurse, and yet you don't know what bilious fever is?"

Eve ignored his question. "Not consumption? Not tuberculosis?"

"Consumption? No. When Mr. Clayton Sharland first brought her to me, he thought so. Evelyn herself had been told she had tuberculosis by an unscrupulous and incompetent physician in Manhattan. Upon examination, I found no blood in her sputum and no other symptoms consistent with tuberculosis. Her symptoms were fever and intestinal distress, all consistent with bilious fever. Unfortunately, since then, she has developed what I believe to be pneumonia."

Eve worked to process this, her mind spinning with ideas and possible solutions.

"What medications have you administered, doctor?"

He placed his hands behind his back and locked them. He remained silent for a time.

"Medications, Dr. Begley?" Patrick said, with a small dark grin.

"The medications are mine and mine alone. They are proprietary."

"Please, Dr. Begley. It would be helpful," Eve said, softly. "Please."

"I assure you, Miss Sharland is under the best of care," Dr. Begley said, largely. "I am widely known and respected, and my patients come from the highest social classes. I only agreed to accept Miss Sharland as a patient out of professional conscience, because Mr. Sharland seemed so desperate."

"And where does Clayton Sharland live?" Eve asked.

"On 12th Street and Addison. About three miles from here."

"The medications, Dr. Begley," Patrick repeated. "What medications?"

Dr. Begley exhaled audibly. "I have administered laudanum and morphine. Being a chemist as well as a physician, I have also created a personal prescription for Miss Sharland, which includes mercury, silver and arsenic compounds. They are already having an efficacious effect."

Eve shut her eyes in utter disbelief. The good Dr. Begley was killing Evelyn with his ludicrous cure. Eve's eyes opened, and she swung her attention to Patrick. "We have to get her out of here."

Patrick stiffened in surprise. Dr. Begley looked as though he'd been stricken with a heart attack.

"What!? You'll do no such thing!" Dr. Begley shouted.

"We must get her out of here," Eve said, firmly.

"Why, this is a complete and utter outrage!" Dr. Begley bellowed.

"You are killing her," Eve said. "She needs proper care and supervision. She's doped up on laudanum and morphine and God only knows what else. Arsenic alone will kill her, Dr. Begley. It is a poison. Mercury will kill her. You are further weakening her already weakened system, Dr. Begley."

"How dare you impugn my professional integrity, you... you, you nurse!" Dr. Begley roared.

Eve went to Patrick. "We have to get Evelyn back to New York to Gouverneur Hospital, where Dr. Long and I can treat her."

Patrick was bewildered and then conflicted. He looked first at Eve, then to the doctor, and then to the bed where Evelyn lay, already looking close to death.

"I tell you I won't have it," Dr. Begley yelled, bursting further into the room. "You will kill her if you move her, and I will not be responsible. Do you hear me?" he said, punching a fist into his chest. "I will not be responsible for her death! I will take this to the highest authority! I will contact my lawyer! This will not stand; do you hear me? It will not stand!"

Patrick stared hard at Eve.

And then it struck her—a hammering, throbbing thought. This moment was possibly *the* seminal moment—the very reason Eve had come to 1885! She was very likely about to alter a future event and with that, perhaps change the future of the entire world. By moving Evelyn Sharland, Eve was changing the trajectory of Evelyn's life, as well as changing the future course of others' lives: John Allister Harringshaw for one, and possibly the entire Harringshaw family; Evelyn's mother and her brother and Dr. Long, not to mention Detective Sergeant Gantly. Eve was about to rewrite history, and no matter how small or seemingly unimportant the act of change might be, who knew where it would lead? Insignificant or not, who could predict the consequences or what the final results would be?

If Evelyn survived her illness, what if she bore a child who became a U.S. President, or a spiritual leader, or some crazy dictator who started an entirely different kind of World War, or a war that destroyed the world? There were so many "what if's" swimming around in Eve's mind that she couldn't catch them all.

Eve felt a tightening in her chest. She was rigid with doubt, suddenly terrified about making a decision. She glanced down at Evelyn once more, seeing the still, gray, thin body hardly breathing, and the damp, pallid face. And then she knew what she had to do. She could not leave Evelyn to this so called "doctor" who was slowly poisoning her to death with nineteenth century medications, no matter what the outcome. To move Evelyn in her present condition was a big risk. To leave her would mean her certain death.

She turned to Patrick, her jaw set. "Please, Patrick. Please help me save Evelyn's life."

CHAPTER 22

The following Tuesday morning, Eve was on duty at the Gouverneur Hospital, dressed in her nursing uniform: an ankle-length, light gray dress with puffy sleeves, a long white apron and a heavily starched nursing cap. She was working in a large rectangular room that was clean and surprisingly well lit by tall windows. There were four occupied beds near the wall, and one isolated bed on the far side of the room surrounded by a privacy curtain. Evelyn Sharland occupied that bed.

One wall held supply cabinets, a table to prepare medicines, and a glass-fronted cabinet filled with instruments. There was also a deep sink for washing hands and instruments. An upper shelf held sterilization equipment.

In the middle of the room were two examination tables, each surrounded by a privacy curtain. Eve was standing near them, studying Evelyn's chart, waiting for Dr. Long to appear so they could give Evelyn her daily examination.

On Sunday night when Eve and Patrick arrived at the ER with the semiconscious Evelyn, Dr. Long had thoroughly examined Evelyn and diagnosed her as having typhoid fever, or bacillus eberthella typhi, with acute onset of pneumonia.

Dr. Long had not minced words. "Frankly, Eve, any number of factors can be contributing to Evelyn's already serious condition: exhaustion, internal hemorrhaging, and ulceration of the intestines."

Eve felt helpless. If only this so-called Gilded Age had antibiotics at their disposal.

Not only was Dr. Long pessimistic about Evelyn's chance of survival, but she had also chastised Eve for bundling her up and transporting her back to Manhattan, when Eve could have found a charitable hospital, infirmary or clinic in Hoboken. The trip across the Hudson in the dead of winter did not show good judgment, Dr. Long had said.

Eve did not defend herself, but she still felt she'd done the right thing, the only thing she could think to do at the time. Eve didn't know anything about hospitals in Hoboken, but she did know Dr. Long and the nurses at Gouverneur Hospital. If anyone could help save Evelyn's life, it would be Dr. Long and her dedicated staff of nurses and assistants.

Detective Gantly hadn't opposed Eve's decision. He had lifted Evelyn from her bed, and then carried Evelyn downstairs into the cab, and then onto the ferry. He did not challenge Eve or complain. He had simply been supportive and magnificent.

On the ferry traveling back to Manhattan, he sat with his arm around Evelyn's thin body, holding her close to him for warmth as she shivered. Eve had bundled her up in two woolen gowns, with heavy socks, boots and a woolen hat, and Patrick had wrapped her in his great-coat.

She and Patrick hadn't spoken much during the trip back across the river to the hospital, but Eve stole glances at him. When their eyes met, she smiled warmly and gratefully at him. He smiled back and nodded, as if to say, "Don't worry. Everything's going to be all right."

Back at the hospital, when Eve told Dr. Long about Dr. Horace Begley, Dr. Long frowned and shook her head.

"Yes, I know about Dr. Begley," she'd said, sourly. "He was once the director of the Moore Charitable Hospital in Brooklyn until many of his patients had great difficulty surviving what he called his *progressive* treatments and medications. He did have an Astor as one of his patients a year or two ago who, surprisingly, survived an illness despite the good doctor's bumbling treatment, and that helped establish Dr. Begley's dubious reputation. You did the right thing in getting Miss Sharland out of his care, Eve."

Dr. Long looked troubled as she entered the room, accompanied by another nurse. Eve looked up from the chart.

"Miss Kennedy, Evelyn Sharland's brother, Mr. Clayton Sharland, is at the admitting desk. He's demanding to see you."

Eve inhaled through her nose. "Yes, well, I expected this. I thought he'd come yesterday."

"Shall I go with you?" Dr. Long asked. "He's very upset. I've asked two orderlies to stand by close, just in case."

"No… I'll be fine."

"How is Miss Sharland this morning?" Dr. Long asked.

Eve looked nervously toward Evelyn's bed, feeling helpless without antibiotics. All she could do was feed her and try to make her warm and comfortable. "The fever hasn't broken. She's very weak. I don't know if she's strong enough to fight it."

Dr. Long took the chart from Eve. When she smiled, it changed the shape of her face. Dr. Long looked surprisingly pretty when she smiled, even with the old, pocked scars from smallpox.

"Don't worry so much, Eve. If she wants to live, she'll live. Do you know her? Does she have something to live for?"

Eve considered the question. She thought of John Allister Harringshaw. What would he do if he knew Evelyn was here? Would he come? Would seeing him again give Evelyn something to live for? How could Eve get in touch with John Allister?

"There might be something," Eve said, lost in thought.

Dr. Long gestured with her chin toward the door. "You'd better go talk to Mr. Sharland before he comes bursting in here. I told him his sister was much too ill to have any visitors, and that she was still contagious."

Eve walked toward the admission desk with her shoulders back and her head up, hoping it would give her the appearance of confidence, and not arrogance.

Clayton Sharland stood near the admission desk in a dark suit and coat, twirling his bowler hat, looking grave and irritable. Behind the desk, Maggie, the admitting nurse, had her head so far down near the desk that she almost looked like she was dozing. She was obviously frightened by Clayton Sharland, who was a big man, though not as big or as broad as Detective Sergeant Gantly. He had craggy features, a full, black beard, and steady, angry eyes. Those eyes were burning as Eve drew up to him, her hands locked behind her back.

"Good morning, Mr. Sharland, I was hoping to…"

He cut her off. "You silly, stupid woman! What have you done with my sister?"

Eve took a calming breath, smelling alcohol on his breath. His eyes were clear and directed at her like the muzzles of a gun.

"If my sister dies, I will personally break your neck, and it will be a great pleasure."

The violence of his words and expression shocked and terrified her. She stepped back as if stricken. She wished Patrick Gantly were nearby.

She swallowed and struggled for composure. "Mr. Sharland, I just wanted…"

He cut her off again, taking a step forward, jabbing a finger at her face. "And what is this business about you telling Dr. Begley that you are related to us? What foul lies you have told! What black and terrible lies! Why have you lied and snatched my dying sister from the only man who could have possibly saved her dear, sweet life, and brought her here to be treated by a female doctor? A woman doctor!? Why have you done this, Miss Kennedy, or whoever you are? Why have you done this to my poor sister, Evelyn? Why?!" he shouted, showing his crooked teeth. "Tell me or so help me God I'll strike you and not feel the worse for it! I'll break your neck and I promise you I will never feel one day of remorse while I rot in jail."

Eve took another step back, her entire body trembling. And then, from some small place in her soul, she felt a flicker of courage, a small twinge of conviction. When she heard the words escape her lips, she was stunned.

"Because I am going to save Evelyn's life, Mr. Sharland. And if I don't save her life and she dies, I will gladly offer you my neck, Mr. Sharland, and you can break it in as many pieces as you like."

Eve watched his shoulders relax and his expression change from rage, to confusion, to suspicion. His eyes became misty with pain as he struggled to comprehend.

They lapsed into silence. Somewhere, they heard a ringing bell. Was someone ringing for a nurse? It finally faded.

Eve released her locked hands from behind her back and relaxed them at her side.

"Mr. Sharland, if I could have consulted you on Sunday, I would have. But time was of the essence. I had to make a difficult decision. I ask you now for your forgiveness for acting so rashly, but I truly believed that the medications Dr. Begley was administering to Evelyn would have killed her faster than the typhoid fever would have. Dr. Long is a female physician, yes, but she is a good and dedicated doctor who works tirelessly for all her patients. She trained at the finest hospitals. She studied in Vienna and Switzerland. She is doing everything possible to help Evelyn.

I brought Evelyn here, Mr. Sharland, because I want her to live, and I believe she *will* live."

He fixed his hard eyes on her. "Who are you? Why did you tell Dr. Begley that you are a relation?"

Eve had an answer ready and, in this day and time, how would anyone ever know if she was lying or not? "We *are* distant cousins, Mr. Sharland. I am from Ohio. I have a grandfather there, Amos Sharland, who told me that since I was moving to New York, I should look Evelyn up. When I learned of her illness, well, of course, as a nurse, I wanted to find her and help make her well again."

That was it. Eve didn't want to say more. Simple was good. She waited while Clayton considered her words.

"I've never heard of Amos Sharland."

"He did not mention you either," Eve said, quickly. "He only mentioned Evelyn."

Clayton ran the flat of his hand across his thick heavy beard, his eyes looking at the floor and the walls, as if he was realizing for the first time where he was. He'd been lost in a kind of wild, angry fever.

"So we are related then?" he said, gently.

Eve nodded. "Yes, Mr. Sharland, we are related, and I am going to do all I possibly can to bring Evelyn back to health."

His face softened and Eve was surprised to see that the man she'd thought was forty-years old was actually much younger, probably no more than thirty-two.

"She is the dearest of women, Miss Kennedy. Evelyn is the dearest and kindest person I have ever known. Can you save her precious life?"

Eve honestly didn't know, but she had to show confidence. "I promise you, Mr. Sharland, I am going to do all I can to bring her fully back to us."

That obviously touched him, because Eve saw his eyes well up. He didn't wipe them, and so a tear broke away and rolled down his cheek.

"Have you told your mother about Evelyn, where she is and that she does not have tuberculosis?" Eve asked.

His face hardened again. "She has banished the both of us, Evelyn for her relationship with a certain gentleman, and me for supporting her. Our mother is quite religious, Miss Kennedy, but in all her religious fervor, she seems to have forgotten charity and forgiveness. Can I see Evelyn?"

"Not now, Mr. Sharland. She is either unconscious or delirious. She has had brief moments of lucidity and she has tried to speak but then she lapses back into unconsciousness."

He stared, sadly, with a bowed head. "I understand." They stood silently for a few moments, and then he took out his pocket watch. "I have to get back to work, Miss Kennedy, or I will lose my job. It has taken nearly all I have in savings to pay Dr. Begley for his services. How much will you charge me?"

Eve smiled. "Nothing, Mr. Sharland. We are related. There will be no charge."

His lips trembled, and he looked away from her, fighting tears and emotion. He nodded, not meeting her eyes.

"When do you think I will be able to see her?"

"It is not easy to predict. You can try again in a few days, Mr. Sharland."

Eve turned to the admitting desk and took a piece of paper and a pencil. She wrote down her address and handed it to him.

"This is where I live. You are always welcome to visit me."

She handed him a blank piece of paper. "Please write down your address and, when Evelyn improves, I'll send a messenger with the news."

He took her address and then wrote down his own and handed it to her. He started to speak, but then decided against it. He gave a quick nod, turned and walked away.

Eve leaned back against the desk and sighed out tension. She shut her eyes and, in a moment of blackness, Dr. Eckland's face suddenly appeared. Her eyes popped open.

"Yes!" she said aloud. "Yes. Of course."

CHAPTER 23

After work on Wednesday evening, the day before Thanksgiving, Eve took a cab to Dr. Eckland's home, composing what she was going to say to
him on the way. Dr. Eckland's brownstone was just off
Fifth Avenue, on a quiet, tree-lined street, north of the
Albemarle Hotel, where Lily Langtry lived. Eve had
never heard of Miss Langtry, the famous actress, but
everyone at the boarding house certainly had, and they
were greatly impressed that Eve was going to visit the
eminent doctor who had treated Albert Harringshaw.

Eve paid the driver and started toward the front
stairs, hoping Dr. Eckland wasn't entertaining and that
he wouldn't think her too bold. She knew of no other
way to contact John Allister. She couldn't just send
him a note or a letter. He didn't know her or trust her.
No doubt her note would be ignored, if it ever even
reached him. Eve would have asked Dr. Eckland to
contact John Allister, but since Albert and John were
feuding, it was unlikely Dr. Eckland would risk cross-

ing Albert in order to contact John Allister for her. And if he did, John Allister would surely dismiss her as another one of Albert's mistresses, or worse.

But Eve had to get in touch with John Allister. She had to tell him where Evelyn was and that she did not have tuberculosis. She was sure he'd want to know, and Eve wanted Evelyn to see John. It might help her fight off the illness and survive.

Eve had recalled a conversation she and Dr. Eckland had had while she was still living in Helen Price's brownstone, while he was examining her. He'd mentioned the Harringshaws' costume ball. *"The Harringshaws are having another one of those costume balls on December 4th,"* he'd said. *"I suppose I will have to go… Unfortunately, my daughter will not be in town to accompany me. I shall have to find someone else."*

Eve also recalled something else he'd said to her, *"I will see what I can do for you, Miss Kennedy. I can't promise anything, but I will see what I can do."* She hadn't called upon him to help her find a job, but he had willingly written her a reference for the boarding house.

Eve used the heavy knocker to knock on Dr. Eckland's front door. The door was opened by a frosty-haired man, complete with a frosty mustache. He was in his sixties, dressed classily in white tie and tails, and he stood looking back at her blankly, as if he were a living, breathing manikin staring out blankly from a department store display window.

Eve cleared her throat. "Is Dr. Eckland available?" she asked meekly.

His eyes didn't move. Was he breathing? "Who may I ask is calling, please?"

His voice was deep and greatly affected, like a butler in an old 1930s movie.

"Eve Kennedy. I am a former patient of his."

His right, white eyebrow lifted, like Spock's in *Star Trek*. "Former, did you say?"

"Yes, sir."

"Is he expecting you, madam?"

"No."

"If you are not expected, Dr. Eckland will not be available. You are welcome to make an appointment."

"If you announce me, sir, I believe he will see me." Then Eve decided to drop *the* name that she was sure would get her in. "Tell him it's about Mr. Harringshaw."

The butler blinked twice and finally focused on her. She saw that he really was alive and not frozen. He stepped aside.

"Please come in, madam."

Eve stepped into the white marble foyer, framed in cherry wood. The butler took her coat, hat and gloves and then led the way to a parlor off to the left. He opened the heavy oak door and indicated into the room.

"Please be seated, Miss Kennedy, and I will see if Dr. Eckland is available."

"Thank you, sir," Eve said, as formally as he had addressed her.

He closed the door and left Eve alone in a glorious room decorated in gold, with gothic furniture. It had heavy proportions, dark finishes, elaborate carvings and ornamentation. A fire was crackling in the fireplace.

She sat in an upholstered chair near the fireplace and waited, smelling wood smoke, leather and furniture polish. Her thoughts drifted, as they often did, to Patrick Gantly. She had not seen him since Sunday and she missed him. Before he left her in the hospital corridor, he had looked at her oddly when she handed him a ten-dollar bill and thanked him for the loan.

"You are an independent woman, Miss Kennedy."

Eve gave a little nod, waiting for more. He didn't offer more, and he didn't take the money.

"Please take it and thank you," Eve had said. "It was a very thoughtful and generous thing to do."

"It was a gift, Miss Kennedy. I will not take it back, and it is in bad taste to ask me to take it back."

Eve shrugged and stuffed it into her apron. "Okay. Fine. Thank you."

"Yes, quite independent, Miss Kennedy, and you will always be thus, I think."

"Thus?" Eve said. "Always be thus?"

"I will be clearer then. You will always be occupied with your work, won't you, Miss Kennedy?"

Now Eve understood. She had an independent spirit at a time when most women could never be independent. They couldn't own property; they couldn't vote; they couldn't go to saloons and drink alone without being thought a prostitute. If a woman lived alone, she was called a spinster, a derogatory name. A woman couldn't work on Wall Street or run a corporation or certainly never, ever even think about running for political office.

"Do you have a problem with that, Detective Sergeant Gantly?"

"A problem?" he asked, a bit taken back by her slang.

"Yes, do you have a problem with the fact that I'll always be occupied with my work? Recently, I have even thought about becoming a doctor. Would that be a problem, Mr. Detective?"

"You have a defensive tone, Miss Kennedy."

"Yes, I guess I do because I am feeling defensive."

"And you are flushed. We have both had a long, challenging day, Miss Kennedy. I should go."

"You haven't answered my question," she pressed.

The overcoat Patrick had used to wrap Evelyn in was hanging across his arm. He shouldered into it.

"The problem is, Miss Kennedy, I happen to very much admire your conviction and your spirit. It is rare to witness such strength and dedication, even in a man." He held up a hand to stop her before she could speak. "And I mean no disrespect, Miss Kennedy."

He turned and started for the exit door. Eve called after him and he turned. She closed the distance between them.

Her eyes traveled over his face, his wonderful, handsome, masculine face, and his full waiting lips. "I'm sorry, Patrick. I guess I'm tired, stressed and edgy."

He was dead still. "Patrick?"

"Do we have to be so formal? Can't we just call each other Patrick and Eve? I mean, is it so awful? Would anybody fall over dead?"

"You are constantly surprising me, Miss Kennedy." He took in a little breath. "You do surprise me and I find that I am always delighted by the surprise."

He moved closer to her, and she felt that wonderful rush of excitement. If this were the twenty-first century, she'd stand up on tip toes and kiss him. She would ask him out for a drink. She might even ask him back to her place. But this was the Gilded Age and there were conventions and strict morals, at least in public, and women could not be so bold without being thought a hussy.

"Patrick, thank you for what you did today. Thank you for saving Evelyn. It was a very kind and generous thing to do."

"Is that what I did? Did I save Evelyn or did I want to spend my entire day with you because I wanted to be with you? I wonder."

They stood, their eyes exploring, wanting.

"Good evening, Miss Kennedy."

He turned, started walking away, and then he stopped and looked back over his shoulder. "I will drop by in the next few days to see how Miss Sharland is doing. Will that be all right, Miss Kennedy?"

Eve smiled. "Still so formal, Patrick? Do we always have to be so formal?"

"You have not told me the truth about yourself, Miss Kennedy. You are still holding a large part of yourself in shadow. Perhaps someday, when you trust me completely, we can be less formal."

He smiled, tipped his hat and left.

THE DOOR OPENED and Dr. Eckland appeared, dressed in a blue velvet smoking jacket, looking surprised and worried. As Eve stood, he came over to her.

"Miss Kennedy. What brings you here? Haynes, my butler, said you mentioned the Harringshaws. Are you in any distress?"

She waited until the gilded mantel clock dinged seven times, and even then she wasn't sure how direct or indirect she should be. She spoke in a low tone.

"Dr. Eckland, please forgive me if I am too direct. Are you still planning to attend the Harringshaw costume ball Friday next, on December 4th?"

He looked at her with interest, his lips pursed slightly. "Why yes, of course."

"Are you escorting anyone, I mean a lady?"

He unbuttoned the top button of his jacket and then buttoned it again. "I was, Miss Kennedy. I was to escort Miss Emmaline Fish, but I received a note from her only yesterday stating that her brother had passed away from complications of a gunshot wound. It seems the poor man shot himself. Bad business, Miss Kennedy. Unfortunately, he was a troubled young man who often took to drink and immoral living. As a friend to Miss Fish, I tried to counsel the poor man about such things, but I fear he was not inclined to take anyone's advice."

"I am sorry to hear of his death, Dr. Eckland."

"I treated the young man for fevers when he was a boy. It is a sad thing, really. Terribly sad."

Eve took a breath and gathered all her courage. "Dr. Eckland, would you consider letting me accompany you to the ball?"

He was gently surprised. He tilted his head in analysis.

"Have you been invited?"

"No, Doctor, I have not."

"Ah, so you want me to invite you to the Harringshaw costume ball, Miss Kennedy?"

"Yes. I would so love to attend, if you would consider it appropriate for me to accompany you."

Dr. Eckland unbuttoned and buttoned his jacket again as he glanced over at the shining fireplace.

"Would you like a glass of port wine, Miss Kennedy?"

This was the first time since she'd arrived that anyone had offered her an alcoholic beverage. She'd had to ask for the beer at Dorlan's restaurant.

"Yes, Dr. Eckland, I would love a glass of port."

He walked over to a tall, gargoyled cabinet with a glass front, opened it and took out a decorative canister and two crystal port glasses. He poured the 20-year tawny port, turned and handed a glass to Eve. They touched glasses, which tinged like a little bell.

"To Thanksgiving," he said.

"Happy Thanksgiving," Eve said.

He smiled, warmly. "Yes, a happy Thanksgiving, and why not?"

Eve felt the sweet, velvety port slide down her throat and soothe her chest. It was by far the best port she had ever tasted, not that she was any authority, but her ex, Blake, had known about wine and port. She'd tasted a few.

"This is very good," Eve said.

"I am glad you like it, my dear. Now, Miss Kennedy, I want to explain something to you about this Harringshaw costume ball. It will be a grand social affair. All of New York society will be attending."

Eve suspected where he was going with this. "I understand, Dr. Eckland. I know I'm just a nurse with no name or title."

He made a sweeping gesture with his hand. "No, it is not that, Miss Kennedy. My grandfather was Theodore Eckland, who came to the New World to fight with George Washington at Brandywine, Pennsylvania, and then again at Yorktown. He was an officer and a gentleman, Miss Kennedy, who held high office during the time that George Washington lived in New York, and afterwards. Although the Eckland name is not as well-known as Astor or Vanderbilt, I am proud to say that it is a revered and respected name. Whom I choose to accompany me to any social occasion is of my own choosing, Miss Kennedy. No, I am speaking about an entirely different matter."

He leaned toward her, suddenly flush with excitement. "We have to come up with a costume for you."

Eve's eyes flashed with new life. "Then you will allow me to accompany you, Dr. Eckland?"

He gave a little courtly bow. "It will be my honor, Miss Kennedy. I shall be the envy of every man, and most especially, if I may add in all candor and with all due respect, of Albert Harringshaw."

Eve feigned calm, but her pulse sped up. She couldn't care less about Albert Harringshaw. It was John Allister she needed for a few private moments.

Dr. Eckland drained his port glass and set it aside. "But there is still the matter of your costume. We have precious little time, my dear. Have you given it any thought?"

"What will you be wearing?" Eve asked.

Dr. Eckland puffed his chest out proudly. "I will be costumed as Don Pedro, Prince of Aragon, from Shakespeare's, *Much Ado About Nothing*. In my view, he is one of the most thought-provoking characters in the play. I shall wear a large feathered hat, a blue velvet jacket with golden buttons, tights, and the most pointed shoes you can imagine. My costume will be the stuff of great and glorious gossip, Miss Kennedy. In short, I am going to enjoy myself immensely."

His attention sharpened on her, his enthusiasm growing. Eve had never seen him so animated. He appeared 10 years younger. "But enough of that. What costume shall we create for you, my dear? I know the best seamstress in New York and I will see that she works on it night and day."

"What will it cost, Dr. Eckland?"

"The cost!?" he snorted. He waved the question away. "Damn the cost! Excuse my language, Miss Kennedy, but the cost is irrelevant. Completely irrelevant."

"But I must pay for it," Eve said.

"Don't be ridiculous, my dear Miss Kennedy. It will be in the hundreds of dollars. Perhaps a good one thousand or more."

Eve's eyes widened. "What? No, Dr. Eckland. That's too much."

He ignored her words as he circled her, hands locked behind his back, speculating and calculating. "We'll hear no more of it, Miss Kennedy. Now we must concentrate. We must think. We must plan."

He brought a finger to his lips, narrowing his eyes on her. An idea struck, and he jolted awake with excitement.

"I have it, Miss Kennedy! Yes, of course. You will be Rosalind!"

Eve's eyes shifted. She was embarrassed to tell Dr. Eckland that she didn't know who Rosalind was. He noticed her lack of response.

"You don't like Rosalind, Miss Kennedy? Rosalind from *As You Like It*?"

Eve knew *As You Like It* was a Shakespeare play. She'd seen a production some years ago at Shakespeare in the Park in New York.

She blurted out, "Yes. Yes, of course I know Rosalind."

Dr. Eckland clasped his hands together. "Yes, it will be fine. You are a bit like Rosalind, Miss Kennedy. She is one of Shakespeare's women with a very strong character and a profound message. Being of a high class, she fights and overcomes the limitations placed on women in the society of the time. She is strong, charming, and knowledgeable. Yes, Miss Kennedy, you will be Rosalind. Now let's see, as to the dress. First of all, you will not be corseted. Not in Rosalind's time. The dress will be a cream, satin and beaded gown, with a velvet over-gown. Yes, I can see that quite clearly. Okay, well, maybe we don't have to be so decisive just yet. But, at any rate, we will lower the neckline so that we can capture the lurid eyes of the men and the jealous stares of the women. Yes?"

Eve stared at him, incredulous. "Dr. Eckland, I suspect you have a little of the rebel in you."

He grinned broadly and gave her a little wink. "Oh yes, my dear, and all of it can be expressed in Shakespeare. Shakespeare makes all respectable vice, moral—and all respectable morals, vice."

They fell into easy laughter, and then Dr. Eckland poured them both another generous glass of port. They toasted.

"It will be a glorious night, Miss Kennedy. A glorious night indeed!"

In the cab on the way home, Eve smiled to herself, allowing herself to forget, for a few precious moments, both Evelyn Sharland and all the heightened emotions she'd been carrying around for days. She needed to smile, to laugh a little. She had become as tense as a guitar string, and Dr. Eckland had provided her some much-needed relief by being so comical and entertaining in his excitement about dressing Eve in a lavish gown and walking arm in arm with her down some grand staircase at the Harringshaw mansion. Eve felt a little like Cinderella, and she was actually looking forward to the occasion.

As the cab drew up to the curb outside her building, Eve noticed a lavish carriage was parked nearby, its side lamps glowing. Eve paid the driver and stepped out at the same time she saw Albert Harringshaw emerge from his carriage. Her heart sank. What did he want and why was he here? Whatever it was, it was not good.

CHAPTER 24

The moon was nearly full, sailing out from behind purple clouds, washing the world in a silvery light. Albert Harringshaw approached her, a lighted cigar between the fingers of his right hand, his face set in a fixed smile, a practiced smile that held little warmth. He wore a long coat with a fur collar, leather boots and a tall, silk hat.

He exuded class, wealth and, to Eve, suspicious behavior. She managed a weak smile as he drew up to her.

"Good evening, Miss Kennedy. It is an enchanting evening, is it not?" he said, touching the brim of his hat. "The moon is most beguiling."

"Yes, it is quite lovely. I see you have been waiting for me."

"Yes."

"Not too long, I hope."

"Not at all. When a lovely lady is involved, it is never too long a wait, only too long between visits." He grinned, assured that his line was a clever one.

Eve thought, *Well, aren't you the practiced bullshitter of all time, Mr. Full-of-Himself-Harringshaw?*

"You are very kind," Eve said, still forcing her smile.

"I wonder, Miss Kennedy, if you would accompany me to supper?"

Eve glanced toward the house. "I was just going in to supper. They're keeping a plate for me, since I am late."

"You would do me a great service, Miss Kennedy, and there are some items I would like to discuss with you."

Eve thought, *Oh God, items. What does that mean?*

"Items, Mr. Harringshaw?" she said aloud. "What items would those be?"

He looked back at his stately carriage. His livery man was waiting patiently by the opened door.

"It would be so much more pleasant to discuss them over supper at, say, The Hotel Brunswick. They have eleven French chefs in their kitchens and the Burgundy wine selection is without equal."

Eve didn't like the sound of the word "hotel." She didn't know if there was some connotation attached to it, some suggestion of impropriety, or some social expectation that she knew nothing about.

"I am a simple girl," Eve said modestly, looking down and away.

Albert was perplexed. "I don't understand, Miss Kennedy. A simple girl? Please enlighten me as to your meaning."

"Mr. Harringshaw, perhaps we could discuss the issues at a less lavish dining establishment. As you can see, I am not really dressed for such extravagant dining."

He looked her over anew. "You surprise me, Miss Kennedy."

Again, she didn't know if that was a bad thing or a good thing, and his expression did little to enlighten her. He was a blank page.

"Nevertheless, I am your servant, Miss Kennedy, and we shall dine at a humbler establishment."

He smiled broadly, exposing all his white teeth, and then offered his arm. Reluctantly, she took it, imagining what Gantly would think if he were watching from a dark corner shadow.

Inside the carriage, Eve sat in comfortable luxury as they traveled uptown toward Broadway.

"How is Miss Price?" Eve asked.

"She is quite well, and she told me to send you her kind regards."

Oh, I'm sure, Eve thought, sarcastically. The woman has no idea where her rich benefactor is, unless, of course, Helen hired a private detective to follow Albert around. But why would she? She had no power. All she could do is accuse him of infidelity, which he would either refute or not refute. It didn't matter to him either way. He had nothing to lose. Helen had everything to lose.

The restaurant was a glitzy, mirrored, pseudo-posh Broadway restaurant with white tablecloths, plenty of brass railings, and gilded framed paintings of what Eve supposed were popular actresses of the day.

Once again, the maître d' made a sputtering fuss over having Albert Harringshaw as his guest, and the couple drew the adoring eyes of female patrons as they were shown to their private table. A drawn burgundy drape, tied back by a creamy sash, could easily be released to enclose them in even more privacy, and Eve quickly assumed that Mr. Harringshaw had closed it when he brought other women to this restaurant.

Eve hoped Albert wouldn't release the sash. What would she say if he did? She didn't want to hurt his pride, incite his anger or make an enemy. She also didn't want him coming on to her because it would be difficult for her to hide the fact that she despised him.

"I hope this is to your liking, Miss Kennedy."

"It is, Mr. Harringshaw."

Once again, he ordered without consulting her; first, a bottle of Champagne, and then the dinner:

Soup: Chicken, a' la Reine
Relishes: Olives, Mango Pickles,
Celery and Assorted Sauces
Meat: Roast Turkey stuffed, cranberry sauce and Giblet Gravy
Vegetables: Peas and Baked Potato
Dessert: Mince Pie, Jellies, Cheese and Candies.

After the Champagne had been poured, Albert ran a finger across his waxed mustache. He raised his glass and Eve raised hers.

"Let us drink to being thankful for our new and budding relationship, shall we?"

Eve didn't like the sound of that either. She offered a stingy smile as they toasted and drank.

After he'd replaced his glass on the table, Albert took her fully into his gaze. "Miss Kennedy, I wonder if you appreciate the excellent situation you are in."

Eve had no idea what excellent situation he was talking about. "Well, I am grateful for all the help I have received, Mr. Harringshaw. Without your generosity when I first arrived, I do not know what I would have done."

He waved his hand as if to bat the comment away. "But beside all that, it is time we looked to the present… and also to your future."

"My future?" Eve asked.

"Yes, an attractive young woman like yourself surely has more plans than just being a nurse in some lower East Side hospital."

His comment surprised her. Most women didn't have careers in the Gilded Age, so what was he thinking? That she should go to medical school? Probably not.

"Well, as a matter of fact, I do have plans, Mr. Harringshaw."

"You do?" he asked, surprised.

Of course, she couldn't tell him about her plan to save Evelyn's life and contact John Allister so that he could visit Evelyn and offer marriage. She certainly couldn't tell him that she had to find Evelyn's lantern and return to the twenty-first century.

"Yes, I am thinking of going to school to become a doctor."

His face fell a little. "A doctor?! Why, whatever do you mean?"

"Yes, there are women doctors, Mr. Harringshaw. Surely you are aware of Dr. Ann Long at the Gouverneur Hospital? And there are others."

"I am aware, but I do not approve, Miss Kennedy."

Eve leaned a little forward. "You don't approve of what, sir?"

"Women make good nurses and midwives, but doctors? As I see it, being a physician should be a purely male occupation. Men are less prone to emotional reactions, and they don't possess the... natural frailties that all women possess by their very nature. The male physician understands, by his experience of having a mother, how the weaker sex simply does not have the strength and fortitude for such a profession. And frankly, Miss Kennedy, what sane and reasonable man would allow himself to be treated by a woman? It is utterly preposterous. Surely you grasp the truth of my various arguments, Miss Kennedy, and understand their sound and rational particulars?"

Smugly, certain that his opinions offered irrefutable proof that he was right beyond any doubt, he reached into his coat, drew out a glossy gold cigar case, snapped it open and reached for a cigar.

"Do you mind if I smoke a cigar?" he asked.

Eve shook her head and then watched him light it and blow a plume of blue-gray smoke toward the ceiling.

It took all her twenty-first century strength not to blast him with expletives that would make a sailor blush. Instead, she reached down deep into her patient soul and managed a very tight, meager smile.

"That is very interesting," she hissed through clenched teeth, maintaining her straining smile.

"I knew you would see my point, Miss Kennedy. But in any event, I was speaking about an entirely different matter. I want to suggest to you that I could be, let us say, even more generous—even more helpful—than I have been in the past."

Eve knew what was coming, and she wasn't surprised. She had long prepared her statement for when he made the romantic pass she knew was inevitable. She was about to say, *"You are so kind and generous, sir, but I will be returning home to Ohio to take care of my dear sweet father and I don't know when I'll be able to return. I just received the letter yesterday. I'll be leaving any day now."*

But Albert didn't say what Eve thought he was going to say. What he said totally paralyzed her.

He puffed on his cigar, thoughtfully. "Miss Kennedy, I know you are in the process of plotting to blackmail my brother, John Allister. You see, I know all about Evelyn Sharland, where she is and what her current condition is."

Eve stared, stunned. "What?!"

Albert waved a cloud of smoke away and lowered his voice. "Don't get me wrong about my brother, Miss Kennedy. He has it coming. Frankly, I wish I had thought of the blackmail business. But never mind about that. I know you need money and I know you are probably working with some silent partner to achieve your ends. I regret that I have not yet been able to locate your silent business partner."

Eve's face fell apart. "Silent partner?"

And then the waiter arrived and deposited the two bowls of soup. Albert picked up his spoon and began to eat. Eve remained still and stunned.

"Please eat, Miss Kennedy. You have absolutely nothing to worry about. That is, if you listen to me carefully. I have worked it all out for you and I believe you will be exceedingly delighted by the outcome."

Eve was all ears, feeling her body fill up with a cold, liquid fear.

"Miss Kennedy, your little scheme will not work. My brother, for all of his masked morality and romantic stupidity, is a highly intelligent man. If he hasn't yet found out about your little plot, he soon will. You will be caught, Miss Kennedy, promptly prosecuted, and then imprisoned in the Tombs. Do you know about the Tombs, Miss Kennedy?"

Eve shook her head.

"Ah, yes, you are new to our city. The Tombs is the informal title of The New York Halls of Justice and House of Detention. The women's prison, which occupies the Leonard Street side of the Tombs, contains some 50 cells under the supervision of a chief matron who, I am told, is not known for her kindness or genteel manner. Frankly, Miss Kennedy, she can be downright unpleasant to the extreme."

Albert paused, staring up at the ceiling, as if trying to recall something. "Now let me see, what did the great author Charles Dickens say about The Tombs when he visited New York? Something like '*What is this dismal fronted pile of bastard Egyptian, like an enchanter's palace in a melodrama*?'"

The Christmas Eve Letter

Albert went back to eating. Eve had not touched a bite. She was waiting for the next shoe to drop. She knew Albert had more to say—much more to say.

"What do you want, Mr. Harringshaw?" she asked, struggling to get the words out, because her throat was constricted with fear.

He slid his soup aside. He smiled coolly, and there was calculation and lusty intention in his eyes.

"I find you a madly attractive woman, Miss Kennedy. You are a bit thin, yes, but you have a bold charm and a vast mystery which I have never before encountered. I find I cannot keep my mind on business matters for thinking about your many, special qualities. My imagination spins out fantasies about you, Miss Kennedy, and that keeps me awake at night. Do I sound like a foolish Romeo, Miss Kennedy? Yes, I dare say I do."

Eve felt sick. She knew what was coming.

"I suggest, Miss Kennedy, that whoever your partner is, you have already compromised his trust, unless, of course, you had planned all along to, shall I say, use your particular feminine gifts to capture the attention, and I dare say, the affection of Detective Sergeant Gantly."

Eve stared at him with vacant appraisal. She breathed in, absorbing another shock wave.

Albert indicated toward her champagne. "Please, Miss Kennedy, have another taste of the Champagne. It is of the finest vintage—at least as fine as this establishment can provide."

Eve kept her round, startled eyes on him as she finished half of her Champagne, and then drained the glass.

"Yes, well now, that is better, is it not? Miss Kennedy, let me conclude our business so we can enjoy our little pre-Thanksgiving Day dinner and get better acquainted."

Albert crushed out his cigar in the ashtray. The waiter drifted by and promptly refilled Eve's Champagne glass and cleaned the ashtray.

Albert presented her with the easy, confident smile of the triumphant. "Miss Kennedy, you have won. Yes, you have achieved your goal and then some. Oh, perhaps it will not turn out as you had planned, but I propose that it will be much improved and more to your liking. You will achieve money, position and much more."

Eve took another long drink of the Champagne.

Albert continued. "I am about to secure for you a very elegant brownstone not far from Madison Square. It is flesh colored, with a handsome sweep of brownstone stairs, stout stone balusters leading to the front door, and plush curtains behind lace sheers in the windows. I am certain you will find it both comfortable and luxurious. You will find me a generous man, Miss Kennedy," he said, and then lowered his voice to an intimate whisper. "I am generous in all matters, Miss Kennedy, and I am sure you take my delicate meaning. I am confident that you will find our relationship to be both a satisfying and profitable one."

When their main course arrived, Eve nibbled at her food, mostly pushing it around on her plate. Albert, on the other hand, ate voraciously.

After dessert, Albert sipped his coffee, his eyes lingering on Eve.

"I am aware that you will have to contact your partner and let him know of your sudden change of plans. If he gives you any trouble at all, just let me know. I will see to it."

Eve was still struggling to think. She was so flabbergasted that she couldn't latch on to a single thought long enough to put together a coherent sentence. Finally, she composed one.

"What makes you think I have a partner, Mr. Harringshaw?"

"Miss Kennedy, I have dealt with many types of villains over the years who were after the Harringshaw money. They have all been handily defeated with great dispatch. Now, it is obvious to me that you needed a man for this particular crime, Miss Kennedy. Men are always the brains behind such things."

Eve felt suppressed rage arise. She worked to keep her voice even. She worked at keeping her emotions in check. She worked at not throwing her glass of Champagne into his face and walking out.

"There is no man, Mr. Harringshaw. I have no partner. I can assure you that."

He smiled, patronizingly. "All right, Miss Kennedy. As you say. It is admirable that you want to protect him. I understand that you assume I will have him caught and put in The Tombs. I understand you, and I salute you. It is an admirable quality. This further adds to your allure and mystery, Miss Kennedy."

Eve's thoughts were whirling with panic. She needed time. Time to think. Time to come up with options. Time to think about how to get back to her own time, and as fast as possible. There was no way she was going to let this son of a bitch get his hands on her.

She smiled, but her eyes were cold. "I will need some time, Mr. Harringshaw."

"Time for what, my dear? Trust me. You have no other options. I will have your new home ready for you in three weeks, a week or so before Christmas. On second thought, I have an even better idea. I will be away in Chicago on business, so things might be held up. So let us say that you will move in on Christmas Eve. That will be a marvelous Christmas present for the both of us."

He narrowed his dark, serious eyes on her. "Miss Kennedy, I firmly request that you move in at that time, on Christmas Eve day. I will of course arrange all furnishings and servants, and I will have a seamstress at your call whenever you wish, for day-dresses, gowns, coats and hats—for anything you want. Your wish will be my command."

"And what of Miss Price, Mr. Harringshaw?"

"Miss Price. Oh, well, Miss Price has so many suitors. Alas, she is in the process of casting me by the wayside, even as we speak. Do not worry your pretty head about that, my dear."

Eve knew he was lying. He would either continue to see Helen Price at his convenience, or he had already given her the boot.

Eve swallowed away nausea. "I have no choice in this matter, do I, Mr. Harringshaw?"

"Oh yes, my dear, of course you do. I can have Detective Sergeant Gantly arrest you tomorrow morning for the crime of blackmail. There will be plenty of evidence. You can rest assured that Inspector Thomas Byrnes will have all the evidence he needs to make the arrest and secure the conviction. But I know you are much too wise to take that course, Miss Kennedy. And, besides, we will have sterling times together. I am even considering a cruise to Europe. You would enjoy that, would you not?"

Eve recalled the research she had done on the Harringshaw family before she'd been propelled back into 1885. The Wikipedia entry had stated that Albert Harringshaw had been killed on a ship called the Lusitania in May 1915. Thirty years in the future.

Eve nodded. "I see. Christmas Eve," she said, feeling urgency building in her chest. And then she had a thought: Had Detective Sergeant Gantly been working with Albert to close the trap on her from the very beginning?

CHAPTER 25

On the Sunday evening after Thanksgiving, Eve sat beside Evelyn's bed at Gouverneur Hospital. The typhoid fever symptoms had abated, but Evelyn was still not out of danger. Her body was desperately fighting pneumonia, which Eve was fighting with the only available remedies at her disposal: clean, boiled water and a broth made with garlic cloves, lemon juice and honey. She had once taken a course on Naturopathic Medicine and she crossed her fingers now, hoping these ingredients would build up Evelyn's immune system and help her fight off the infection. Dr. Long had given her approval to try it, and so Eve spooned some into Evelyn's mouth whenever she was semiconscious.

Eve also found tea tree oil in Chinatown and diluted it with olive oil. After stirring the mixture, she and the other nurses applied it to Evelyn's neck and chest, rubbing gently so that the oil was completely absorbed. They had done this several times each day.

Eve had just finished such a chest rub. She sat quietly now, staring at Evelyn's emaciated face. Although Evelyn was sleeping more peacefully than when she'd first arrived, Eve had still not been able to speak to Evelyn, other than to say, "Good morning" or "How are you feeling?" Evelyn stared back at her with the foggy, distant eyes of a person who was mostly in another world.

Ever since her dinner with Albert Harringshaw, Eve had been on an emotional roller coaster ride. She'd slept restlessly, eating little and fighting a mounting anxiety. She had not seen Detective Sergeant Gantly, and she didn't know whether that was good or bad. Her mind kept flip-flopping, one minute hating the man and the next minute unable to believe that he would set her up in Albert Harringshaw's elaborate lusty trap. But then surely Detective Gantly had seen Albert in action in the past. She wondered if Helen Price had been similarly caught in his web or if she had willingly agreed to be a *kept* woman.

Eve had to face it. In this Gilded Age, when women were subjugated and marginalized, many women would have jumped at the opportunity to be the mistress of one of the wealthiest and most handsome men in New York City, if not the world. They would be flattered and overjoyed, just as Albert was sure she would be. Even with her hesitation, his belief and, unfortunately, his ardor, had not been diminished in the least.

But what of Patrick Gantly? She had thought—no, believed—that he was a good man. Eve knew he'd been attracted to her. The evidence was apparent and obvious. After all, he had helped her get her nursing diploma; and he had warned her about Albert, saying,

"I don't believe he can be trusted when it comes to a woman's honor."

Eve shut her eyes, recalling another conversation she'd had with Detective Gantly.

"I am assuming you and Albert Harringshaw are plotting something. Perhaps he wants to get rid of me because he does not want to owe me for his life. I don't know the reason yet, but, I warn you, if the day comes when I am disgraced and fired from my position, I will have my revenge."

Eve slumped down in her chair. Despite it all, whenever she thought of Patrick Gantly, her heart warmed, she grew aroused and she could not believe he had plotted against her with Albert Harringshaw. She knew, intuitively, and from his warm and tender glances, that he cared about her. Okay then, why hadn't he come to help her? Surely he knew about Albert Harringshaw's vulgar proposal—no, not proposal—his royal decree.

Eve dozed off. When her eyes opened, Evelyn was looking at her with soft, clear eyes. Eve sat up, alert, noting that Evelyn's entire face seemed lit up from within. It was a pretty face, kind and welcoming.

"Evelyn?"

Evelyn smiled. "I've seen you." Her voice was rusty and low.

"Yes. I'm your nurse."

"I saw you in dreams."

"You've been very sick."

"Yes, with tuberculosis," she said, her smile vanishing. "I'm going to die."

"No, you're not going to die. You don't have tuberculosis. You've had typhoid fever and pneumonia, but you're improving. Every day you're getting better and stronger."

Evelyn worked to comprehend. "No, the doctor said tuberculosis. He told me."

"He was wrong, Evelyn. The doctor misdiagnosed you. You don't have tuberculosis. You never had tuberculosis."

Eve saw tears form in the corners of Evelyn's now glistening eyes. There were no tissues in 1885, so Eve took a clean handkerchief from her pocket and dabbed at Evelyn's eyes.

"It's okay, Evelyn. You're improving. You're going to be healthy again. You are not going to die."

Evelyn couldn't stop the tears. "I apologize..." she said, and then she began to sob and cough. Eve stood and handed her the handkerchief, placing a gentle hand on her back, whispering words of comfort until the coughing ceased and Evelyn lay back into an exhausted peace. After she'd wiped her eyes clean, she focused on Eve standing above her.

"I prayed for help," Evelyn said. "I prayed so hard for someone to help me."

"We're going to get you well, Evelyn."

"And you're here..." Evelyn said in a whispered reverence. "There you are. I saw you in my dreams. You were so far away, across a bridge, and I waved to you. It seemed that you were in another time and place where there were things flying in the air, and there were vehicles that moved without horses and they were moving about so fast, and with such ease. I waved to you and you waved back to me. They were such strange dreams."

Eve's gaze never wavered as she listened. She felt the hair on the back of her hair stand up as Evelyn continued.

"I saw you running in a lovely green park under golden sunlight, and a dog was beside you, barking and leaping," Evelyn continued. "You were playing and laughing and you looked so happy. I kept calling for you."

Eve eased back down into the chair, unsteadily. "Those were interesting dreams," was all she could answer. What else could she say?

"Evelyn, your brother, Clayton, knows you're here. He's been by several times to sit with you and talk to you when you were asleep."

Evelyn stirred, trying to sit up. "Clayton...?"

"Don't get up, Evelyn. Please, just lie back and rest. You need lots more rest."

"But Clayton took me to that doctor. I don't remember where. He said he was a good doctor, and he'd help me, but I didn't want to go. I didn't like it there. I thought I was going to die. I felt so ill, so dreadful there. It was so dark and gloomy. I was so alone. I don't want to go back there. Ever."

"It's okay. You will never go back there. Never. I promise you. Clayton is happy you're here."

Evelyn nodded, her memory sharpening. "My mother? How is she? Does she know where I am? Has anyone told her?"

"Clayton said he would stop by and see her this morning, Sunday. This is Sunday, November 29th. He said he wasn't sure she'd let him in, but I encouraged him to go and tell her where you are, and that you did not have tuberculosis."

Evelyn shut her eyes for a moment. "November the 29th? Oh my. Oh my, my, so much time has passed. I have been ill for so long. For so very long."

Her voice grew soft and distant. "I wonder where he is... I wonder where... I told him to go away. I told him..."

She stopped, her eyes suddenly opening wide. "Where?"

"Where is he?" Eve asked. "Is that what you want to know?"

Evelyn met her gaze. "No... I mean to say... Well, it doesn't matter. It doesn't matter now. Not now. Oh, my dear mother. I wonder how she is. She wouldn't take any money from me after I met..." and then she stopped again. "Oh, I am so wretched. I am such a wretched woman. I deserved this terrible illness."

Eve pushed to her feet. "Evelyn, don't say that. Please relax now and don't upset yourself. Let's not talk anymore. The important thing is you're getting better and better. I'm going to leave now so you can rest."

"Don't go yet," Evelyn said, reaching weakly for Eve's hand. "I don't even know your name. What is your name?"

Eve let the silence draw out. Once again, she felt the impacting collision of past, present and future. She was staring into the face of Evelyn Sharland, the woman who had never received John Allister's letter declaring his devastating remorse and his undying love. If he could do it all over again, would he risk all and marry her?

Eve had changed the future—Evelyn was alive. All Eve had to do now was to keep Evelyn alive and get

John Allister Harringshaw to the hospital to see her. Eve was positive once the two lovers were reunited, the natural course of events would take care of the rest. Surely, Evelyn and John Allister would risk everything for their true and enduring love.

"Won't you tell me your name?" Evelyn asked.

"It's Eve. Eve Sharland."

Evelyn looked at her, thoughtful and confused. "Sharland? Eve Sharland? Evelyn Sharland, the same name as mine?"

"Yes. We are related, distantly related."

Evelyn's eyes slid away and slowly closed, fluttering. "I am so tired. So very tired. I must sleep now."

"Yes, Evelyn," Eve said. "Sleep for as long as you like."

Eve reached for the case-notes clipped to the wall above Evelyn's bed and logged in all the pertinent information before she left the room.

Walking toward the nurses' desk, Eve saw him: Detective Sergeant Gantly walking heavily toward her, his face set in stern concentration. She paused near a gurney, waiting for him, her arms folded. Two nurses passed her, glancing back over their shoulders, one with a girlish grin on her face. They'd seen the two of them together before.

He closed the distance between them and stopped about three feet away. They both remained silent, each sizing up the other.

"We have to leave," he said.

"Leave?"

"Yes. We have to leave the city."

"What are you talking about?"

Detective Gantly took her by the arm and conducted her to an open door that led into an empty office. They stepped inside and he left the door ajar so that only a sliver of light entered the room, falling on the floor like a narrow yellow plank.

"Miss Kennedy, you must know what I'm talking about."

And she did, although she had no idea where he was going with the conversation.

"Why we?" she asked, with a raised eyebrow. "*We* have to leave the city? Why?"

"I told you about them. I told you the Harringshaw family was powerful and dangerous."

"And where have you been for the last three days?" Eve said forcefully, trying not to assume the tone of an angry, ignored lover.

He lowered his voice. "I have a friend in San Francisco. We can go there."

"You keep saying we," Eve said. "Why would *we* go anywhere?"

He sighed a jet of air through his mouth. "Because you cannot stay here, and neither can I."

"Why? What is Albert doing to you?"

"Albert Harringshaw will probably have my hide sometime after the costume ball. He will be in Chicago for most of December and when he comes back, he will want you in his doll house and he will want me out of the way, permanently. He knows about us."

Eve dropped her arms to her side. "Permanently? That sounds very bad. Are you just being melodramatic?"

"No, Miss Kennedy, I am not. Even detectives can find themselves unwittingly caught between the wealthy and powerful, and the officials who want some of their wealth and power. If someone gets in their way, they simply remove them. So you see, Miss Kennedy, whether that sounds melodramatic or not, that is just the way it is."

In the dark, cool room, Eve shivered. "I see. And you want me to go with you to San Francisco?"

He stared intently, a beam of light illuminating his face. "We could get to know each other, Miss Kennedy. We could become properly acquainted."

Eve shook her head again. "Properly acquainted? What does that mean, Mr. Detective?"

He didn't blink. He didn't move. "Miss Kennedy, it means that I am very attracted to you, as you are to me. Don't try to deny it. And don't play the silly female role. It doesn't suit you. You're much too smart for those games."

Eve was silent. He waited.

"I can't leave New York yet," Eve whispered. "I haven't finished what I came to do."

Gantly's voice took on an edge. "And, pray tell, Miss Kennedy, where did you come from and what did you come here to do?"

"I can't tell you yet."

He turned in impatient frustration and rising anger. He scratched his hard jaw and faced her. "Why am I not surprised? So you plan to move into Mr. Albert Harringshaw's pleasure palace then?"

"No! Of course not."

"Then tell me now! Who are you?"

"I can't. But I will tell you soon. I promise."

They stood, shifting their weight, searching for words.

Eve stepped close to him, only a foot away. She reached out to touch his hand and then stopped. He inched closer to her. Their eyes met, shiny in the door light, desire building. Eve felt a sudden fever for him, an animal want and need so strong that she pulsed with it.

Patrick was alive with longing and fighting hard not to show it. It was the first real intimate moment they'd had, and they held it, silent, breathing, throbbing.

"I don't know how to say what you want to hear," Gantly said.

"Just say what you feel, Patrick."

A nurse passed outside, her head down, reading a chart. They ducked away from the light.

He stood over Eve, looking down. She felt the heat of him. She dared to look up at him. They stood in silhouette, waiting, calculating.

"I want to touch you, Miss Kennedy. I want very much to kiss you. I want us to be together, as close as two people can be."

And then he grabbed her shoulders and kissed her, the tip of his tongue plunging, tracing and exploring her lips and mouth, pulling her into his hard, wide chest. Eve arched back, stunned by crazy pleasure. She kissed him, long and warm, her body awakening from a long sleep. They remained locked in a kiss for timeless minutes, and Gantly felt her lips sweeten and flower.

When they finally disengaged, he moved his hand to her cheek. His touch was lightly sensual, and it made her a little drunk with pleasure.

"A lovely woman you are, Eve. Lovely indeed. I spend hours thinking about your loveliness and your stubbornness."

Eve smiled at him, an intimate smile. "I've missed you, Patrick. I thought you'd forgotten me."

"Never. I've been busy working for us."

She took in a breath as his tongue traveled down to lick her neck. They moved back to the light that was leaking in from the hallway, and they turned slowly, as if dancing. Eve closed her eyes and made a little sound of pleasure as a new sensation engulfed her. And then she gently broke from him, looking up.

She whispered. "Where can we meet, away from everything? You must know a place where we can be alone together for a while."

He stared at her in serious delight. "I have old ways, Eve."

She waited for more while her pulse raced. "Okay... What does that mean?"

"I want our love to be right. To be true. I want it to last and to have the right kind of beginning."

Eve stared, first in puzzlement and frustration, and then in admiration. She leaned her forehead against his chest. "Okay, Mr. Detective. Okay."

"I want us to marry, Eve."

Eve didn't move, but her entire body was on fire for him. "Marry?"

"You flame my thoughts—every thought, Miss Kennedy. You ask me where I have been for the last three days. I have spent them plotting our escape to San Francisco. That is all I have thought about. Perhaps I would not have asked you to marry me so suddenly, if things were not so dire and urgent. But now, I must ask you. It will be much easier for us to travel if we are husband and wife. Will you come with me, Eve?"

Eve lifted her head, staring into his eyes. "We've just touched, Patrick. We've just kissed. We don't really know each other."

Her lips were gently parted and moist, her left eyebrow slightly arched. Patrick was struck by a spasm of sexual energy.

Eve saw a sudden surprise in his eyes, then pleasure and finally an invitation.

"We know all we need to know, Eve Kennedy. We will touch, Eve, and I promise you we will certainly kiss… and we will love. I will never stop loving you, whether you agree to marry me or not."

CHAPTER 26

On the evening of December 4th, Eve and Dr. Eckland arrived at The Harringshaw mansion for the much celebrated and publicized costume ball. The mansion stood on the north side of Fifth Avenue, ornate and imposing, surrounded by wrought-iron gates and fences.

When Eve stared out the carriage window to take it in, her mouth opened in surprise. This was not the museum she'd seen and visited in the twenty-first century. This was something out of another world.

The mansion was made of pale yellow brick, handsomely trimmed in chocolate-colored stone, with turrets, gables, pyramids, peaks and towers that reached into the sky. There were fireplace chimneys, wrought-iron balconies, and acres of slanted surfaces, shingled in slate, trimmed in aged green copper, with countless windows, both dormer and flush, round, square or rectangular. It was a magnificent sight, and being one of the first personal residences to be completely lit with electricity—at a cost that was unimaginable to those who read about it in the newspapers—it seemed from another world.

Eve gazed upon the mansion, overwhelmed by its opulent glory, its soft glow and its massive structure. There was nothing to match it, even in the twenty-first century. This was wealth only dreamed of in fairy tales or created by special effects in a Hollywood movie.

Eve glanced at the red and brown brick houses down the street and wondered what those people thought of this mansion, living in its vast and magnificent shadow.

Fifth Avenue was congested with well-dressed curiosity-seekers, who were being held back by the police. Eve darted glances up and down the street to see if she could see Patrick, but he was nowhere in sight.

A canopy had been constructed over the Fifth Avenue entrance to help shelter and protect guests from both the curious and the light snowy weather. Dr. Eckland's carriage joined a line of carriages that pulled up and dropped guests under the canopy, to be greeted by footmen in burgundy livery and powdered wigs.

Eve and Dr. Eckland were helped from their carriage and Eve, dressed in her petticoat, gown, and long tailored winter coat, was assisted down a thick, red carpet. She and Dr. Eckland were then escorted past the potted trees and statues, to the front entrance, and then into the grand, glittering and endless rooms of the mansion.

Eve entered the Harringshaw's gleaming spacious lobby, her body a knot of nerves, her awed eyes searching the space. She took in the scent of roses, vanilla, cigar smoke and oak, the latter coming from the grand fireplace in the far right of the great hall where a giant spruce Christmas tree stood towering and gleaming.

Eve saw sprigs of holly and shiny red berries wedged behind picture frames and clocks, twisted around the chains of chandeliers, arranged in vases, fastened to the tops of draperies and pinned into women's hair.

They joined the receiving line and Eve linked her arm into Dr. Eckland's. He patted her hand reassuringly and smiled as they waited to be announced.

"You are the prettiest woman at the ball," Dr. Eckland said, proudly. "I have already received countless covetous glances. You don't know what that does to an old man. Well, it makes him feel like a young buck again."

"Thank you for bringing me, Dr. Eckland," Eve said. "And thank you again for the lovely dress. It's much more than I could have ever imagined."

"Not at all, my dear. It is not the dress we'd first conceived of, but a beauty, nonetheless. It has been a great pleasure, I assure you."

Eve's low-cut, sleeveless dress was made of orange brocade, shading from the deepest orange near her feet to lighter shades in the bodice. The figures of flowers and leaves were outlined in gold and white, with iridescent beads. Her underskirt, visible only on the sides, was light yellow, as was the satin train, which was richly embroidered in gold, and lined with a deep green. To top it off, Eve's powdered white wig was dressed high, with a wide orange ribbon on the side.

Eve was well aware of the men's wandering, wide eyes and the women's curious and jealous stares as she stood there, aloof and proud, like a princess. In any other circumstance, it would have been delightful fun.

Dr. Eckland wore a broad-rimmed feathered hat, a blue velvet jacket with golden buttons, a long, golden sash across his chest, black tights and blue velvet shoes, with curved-up toes.

Eve took the opportunity to glance about at the astounding array of costumes, jewels and flowers. She saw princes, monks, cavaliers, highlanders, queens, kings, dairy-maids, bull-fighters, knights and nobles. And there were men dressed in red hunting-coats, with white satin vests, yellow satin knee-breeches and white satin stockings. Their ladies wore red hunting-coats and white satin skirts, elegantly embroidered.

"Did you know, Miss Kennedy," Dr. Eckland said, "that the owners of all the greenhouses and hothouses for fifty miles have been working overtime for weeks to supply flowers for this occasion?"

Great vases of flowers exploded out and tumbled over each other: peonies, tulips, gladiolas, African daisies, hydrangeas, white lilies, yellow lilies, and tiger lilies, and most of all, roses, thousands of roses of every shade of white, pink, yellow, orange and red.

Eve thought it looked like a costume drama from a Hollywood movie, except that it was real.

And then they were announced. "Dr. Morris Waldo Eckland and Miss Evelyn Kennedy," the broad chested man with a basso voice bellowed out.

Dr. Eckland led Eve down a grand marble staircase into a white marble reception hall. They strolled under a vaulted ceiling and glistening chandeliers illuminated by electric lights. Eve saw lavish jewelry on throats, around necks, in hair-combs, in ears, and sewn onto capes and bodices and buttons. Pearls, diamonds, emeralds and rubies were reflected by the light, adding a sheen and luster Eve had only ever imagined.

They approached another wide, grand, marble staircase that led to upper rooms. It was wide enough for eight people to stand shoulder-to-shoulder. Ladies in silks and velvet glided up and down, past paintings by European and American masters, and sculptures from Greece, Italy and China.

They entered a luxurious music room, filled with a golden harpsichord, two glossy grand pianos, a harp and twenty-to thirty pink silk upholstered chairs. Two large cabinets, carved from the finest wood and ivory that the world could offer, held violins and lutes.

In one lavish salon were silver platters filled with caviar, crudité, fruit and nuts and tarts topped with strawberries. On another table were crystal wine glasses, champagne flutes and heavy golden goblets. Livery dressed in blue velvet coats, silk pants, white gloves and powdered wigs poured champagne and the finest red wine, as guests drifted by.

What was this world? Eve thought. *How could these people be so rich amidst so much poverty, with so many children living on the streets*? But of course this kind of thing was still happening in the twenty-first century. It was mind numbing.

At exactly 11:30, the ball began with a hobby-horse quadrille, the first of five quadrilles where the young people of society danced down the grand staircase in lavish costumes. Eve watched, astounded, as Caesar danced with Bo Peep and Marie Antoinette danced with a cowboy. She turned to see a woman wearing the most striking and odd dress Eve had ever seen: an emerald satin dress with an embroidered black velvet demon on the front, trimmed with the heads and horns of little demons. The woman was dancing with a man dressed as a priest.

Eve stared, entranced. She saw a Joan of Arc dancing with a pirate, and various men dressed like French noblemen dancing with young women dressed as nymphs and gypsies.

She tried to make sense of this world that was completely outside anything or anyplace she'd ever experienced. She was on another planet, and she truly did feel like an alien, watching these wealthy, dream-like figures adorned in splendor, posing, flirting and dancing.

And then Eve saw Albert Harringshaw, dressed in a full-skirted purple velvet coat, with knee-breeches of fawn-colored brocade trimmed with silver point, and a waistcoat trimmed with real silver lace. He wore white stockings, buckle shoes and a powered wig. He stood next to a plump, fidgety woman who looked like Queen Victoria. Dr. Eckland whispered that the woman was Albert's fiancée, Miss Anne Fulton Hopkins.

Eve watched Albert smile and pose and present a refined, even suave portrait of a gentleman. Eve knew he was a selfish, pompous, womanizing, entrapping, male chauvinist jerk, and she pitied any woman who would have to marry him.

Just as Dr. Eckland left her side for a few moments, Albert suddenly turned and noticed Eve. He stiffened in surprise, his eyes wide with amazement. For a second he was angry, but then he quickly recovered, smiling faintly and turning away. A moment later, he glanced back over his shoulder, and his warm, lusty eyes widened with new pleasure. He obviously liked her costume.

Eve ignored him. She was glancing about, looking for John Allister, when Dr. Eckland drew up with two crystal flutes of Champagne. They toasted and drank as Eve craned her neck, continuing her search.

And then a stiff, refined, arrogant woman drifted over and said a proper hello to Dr. Eckland. She had once been his patient. Dr. Eckland introduced Eve to the 40s something, sour-looking Duchess of Cambridge, who wore a head dress made of diamonds. Sapphires, rubies and emeralds studded the front of her blue satin dress.

"Miss Kennedy, is it?" she said, her eyes flickering across Eve's face and then quickly away with obvious disregard and disinterest. "How very nice for you," she said, frigidly.

The Duchess turned to Dr. Eckland, ignoring Eve. "Have you seen John Allister Harringshaw, Dr. Eckland? I am told he is most attractive, though sadly he is engaged to a Miss Elizabeth Ashley Loring, who, I am told, has very little money."

"How very nice for her," Eve said, imperiously. "How very, very nice for her."

"I beg your pardon?" the Duchess said, turning to face Eve again, her hard eyes focusing anew on her.

"I only meant that having no money and then marrying into a wealthy family like the Harringshaws would make that very, very nice for her, would it not?" Eve said, with a mockingly coquettish grin. "I mean, actually, that would be very, very nice for anyone, would it not, Duchess? Say, even for me."

The Duchess's face registered shock and offense. "What blatant impertinence," she exclaimed, with an affronted sniff and a lift of her chin, before passing Dr.

Eckland a hot glance of indignation, and then striding off.

Dr. Eckland flushed. "Miss Kennedy, please. That was insensitive."

Eve grinned. "Yes, Dr. Eckland. I thought it might be. I was hoping it was."

And then Eve saw John Allister standing next to a beautiful, gushing fountain in what resembled a garden, covered with plants and roses and lilies of the valley. He stood next to the same woman Eve had seen him with at Delmonico's, his fiancée. John was dressed in some sort of duke's costume, with a three quarter blue brocade coat, white silk lacey shirt, black silk knee-breeches and a powdered wig. Miss Loring was wearing an ankle-length pink dress with a white, fur-lined collar, a stunning diamond necklace and a gray cape. She appeared sullenly bored, while John Allister appeared distracted and lost in brooding emotion.

How could Eve get John Allister alone long enough to tell him about Evelyn? She turned to Dr. Eckland.

"Dr. Eckland, have you ever spoken to Miss Loring?"

"Well, yes, on one or two occasions. She is a pleasant woman, if reticent in conversation and rather short in the art of small talk."

Eve took Dr. Eckland's arm, wrapping both of hers around it and pulling him in closer to her. "Would you do something for me?"

"Of course, my dear. Of course I will."

"Will you have a little talk with Miss Loring while I have a little talk with John Allister?"

Eve saw sudden alarm on the doctor's face. "Miss Kennedy, I am not sure if…"

"Don't worry, Dr. Eckland, it won't take long. It's just that I have heard so much about him and this will probably be the only time I will be able to speak with him."

The doctor blustered. "Well, I just don't know. I mean, Mr. Albert Harringshaw wouldn't approve, would he?"

"Mr. Harringshaw won't mind, I assure you. Please, Dr. Eckland. I promise you it will only be a friendly little chat."

"Friendly? Well, I hope so, Miss Kennedy. I certainly hope it will be a friendly exchange, and not a woundingly sarcastic one as you had with the Duchess."

Dr. Eckland reluctantly strolled toward the fountain where John Allister was staring blankly into space. Miss Loring held a flute of Champagne, but it was obvious that it held no interest for her.

As Eve advanced, it was also obvious that they had no interest in each other. They had not uttered one word to each other the entire time Eve had been watching them.

John Allister did not notice as Eve approached, but Eve felt anxious and scared. She had no idea how he would react to her and to her information, and Eve knew that Albert Harringshaw would see her talking to his brother. What would he do?

Eve also knew that Detective Sergeant Gantly was around somewhere, although, mostly likely, he was hiding in the shadows, in the hidden hallways, or back staircases. Eve wished she could see him. It would help give her confidence.

So there he was: the real John Allister Harringshaw, tall, with an aristocratic bearing, long sideburns, a thin, well-trimmed mustache, looking supremely indifferent to his luxurious surroundings and to the woman next to him. This was the man who had written—or was about to write—or now perhaps would never write the Christmas Eve letter. The man Eve had traveled decades into the past to meet, at last.

CHAPTER 27

E ve raised her eyes to study John Allister's impassive face. She swallowed and cleared her throat as Dr. Eckland made his introductions.

"Good evening, Mr. Harringshaw and Miss Loring. What a great occasion, and what a spectacular assembly, all gathered within this incomparable and magnificent mansion."

Talk about bullshit, Eve thought. He was really laying it on thick. But then these people were the royalty of their day. They were adulated and followed by a hungry press and public, just as the movie stars in the twenty and twenty-first centuries would be.

Miss Loring only nodded, saying nothing.

John Allister turned first to see the doctor and then to Eve. He fixed them both with a cool, dubious stare.

"Good evening, Dr. Eckland," John said, flatly. "I trust you are well."

"Yes, Mr. Harringshaw, I am quite well, thank you. May I present Miss Eve Kennedy, a former patient of mine?" Dr. Eckland said, nervously. "She graciously agreed to accompany me this evening."

Miss Loring looked Eve over with no visible reaction. She remained in her bored, dreamlike state.

John Allister settled his eyes on Eve. He saw a pretty face, with sharp intelligent blue eyes, a small mouth with full lips, and a fine neck. He saw strength in her face and he saw something else: something familiar. Did he know this woman?

Eve noticed the recognition.

"Excuse me," John Allister said. "Would you be so kind as to repeat your name?" he asked Eve.

"Eve Kennedy."

"Evelyn Kennedy?" he said formally.

"Yes... Evelyn Kennedy."

Eve thought, *Did he see the resemblance to Evelyn Sharland? Is that the reason for his sudden interest?*

Eve and Evelyn did have the same nose and mouth; the same chin.

Dr. Eckland leaned toward Miss Loring. "Miss Loring, I saw some of your watercolors some weeks ago at an afternoon tea. Perhaps you could tell me something about them."

Miss Loring blinked, awakening from her daydream. "How kind of you to recall my little paintings, Dr. Eckland. I am not, I fear, a particularly gifted artist."

"On the contrary, Miss Loring, I rather thought your sleigh ride paintings were charming. Simply charming, and they are so appropriate now that snow is falling and we are approaching the Christmas season of peace and good will. Perhaps we could refill our glasses and you could tell me more about them."

And they moved away, with Miss Loring suddenly animated, delighted to discuss her watercolors. John Allister hardly noticed they'd left. He was still trying to place Eve.

"Have we met before, Miss Kennedy?"

"We have, Mr. Harringshaw, although I am afraid you will remember the occasion with some distaste."

"Distaste?"

"We met at Delmonico's. Last month, I was dining with your brother and Miss Helen Price and you and Miss Loring came by."

John Allister's expression turned dark with disappointment. He turned his face from her. "Yes, I recall now."

Eve glanced around and stepped a little closer to John Allister. The splashing, hissing water from the fountain was a kind of white noise that muffled their conversation to any person who might happen by.

"Mr. Harringshaw, I need to speak to you about a delicate matter."

He leaned back slightly. "A delicate matter?" His voice took on an edge. "Miss Kennedy, I can assure you I am not interested in discussing any subject that concerns my brother or his… questionable affairs or affiliations."

"It does not concern your brother, sir. It concerns you."

John Allister pursed up his lips in misgiving. "Me? What could you possibly know that would concern me? I have my doubts, Miss Kennedy, and I find this entire insinuation already quite irregular. My dear woman, this is not the forum for shadowy communication."

Was this the same man who had written that tender, pleading and loving letter? Eve thought.

Eve breathed in courage and determination. "Mr. Harringshaw, I am speaking about Evelyn Sharland."

He straightened up, his eyes round with shock. "Evelyn?" he asked, nearly breathless.

"She does not have tuberculosis. Evelyn is recovering from typhoid fever and pneumonia at the Gouverneur Hospital. I am a friend, as well as one of her nurses. I thought you would want to know."

Eve watched John Allister's face slowly fall apart, passing from pride to suspicion to recognition and finally, to a soft, aching tenderness. It was a remarkable and revealing transition. Eve saw, clearly, that this man *was* capable of immense feeling and profound love. It was written all over his handsome face and grateful expression.

"Can it be true? Can it truly? Is she saved from death?"

"Yes, Mr. Harringshaw. Evelyn is getting stronger every day."

He shut his eyes and nearly staggered. "Thank God," he whispered, and when he opened his eyes, they held tears. "Thank God. She told me of the tuberculosis, of course. I told her I would get help. I told her I would send her to Europe for treatment. I told her I would do anything to save her dear, sweet life. She did not respond. From her silence, I thought it was agreed. I made the arrangements to send her to Davos, Switzerland, but she just vanished, with only a note telling me she wanted to protect me from the dreaded disease. It said she did not want me to go through any further scandal she was sure the disease would bring. She said she loved me too much for that. I tried to find her, Miss Kennedy. Dear God, how I tried, but her mother refused to see me and her brother threatened me with going to the press, not that I minded that, but I knew it would only exacerbate the situation and bring further distress to poor Evelyn. Thank God she will survive, Miss Kennedy. Thank God dear Evelyn will survive. Thank you for telling me. You have taken a heavy burden off my shoulders, Miss Kennedy."

Eve drew closer, noticing that they were drawing curious stares.

"She is not completely out of danger yet, Mr. Harringshaw. Evelyn is still quite ill, but a visit from you would do wonders to improve her health. I am convinced of it. She has called your name many times when she was semiconscious. She called you Allister."

Eve saw he was fighting back a towering emotion. "Yes, that is what she called me. Allister, never John. She said she loved the name Allister, and that it fit me so well."

He slowly recovered from his emotion and squared his shoulders in determination. "I will see her. I will go to her right away. I must see her."

Eve hadn't counted on his sudden resolve, believing she'd have to argue and persuade him.

"Shall we go together, Miss Kennedy?" he asked, excitedly.

"Won't we draw attention to ourselves and then also to Miss Sharland, Mr. Harringshaw? Should we not wait perhaps until tomorrow? I can then prepare her for your visit. I am afraid your showing up unannounced might give her quite a shock."

He thought about her words, blinking, considering, and then he pulled on either side of his brocade coat and settled his shoulders in obvious frustration.

"You do make sense, Miss Kennedy. It is unhappy for me, but you do make sense. I want Miss Sharland to heal, not to fall back into illness because of my boyish impatience. Yes, you make all the arrangements, Miss Kennedy, and I will arrive the first thing in the morning."

And then Albert Harringshaw wandered over, and Eve tensed with revulsion. John Allister turned cold and irritable, as if his brother had just awakened him from a magnificent dream.

"What do you want, Albert?" John Allister said, sharply.

Albert looked at his brother with superb indifference. "What are you plotting, dear brother?"

"Nothing that would be of interest to you or to any of your hired ruffians."

Albert shined his crafty eyes on Eve. "Miss Kennedy, what a most pleasant surprise to find you here, and looking so very ravishing in that elegant gown and wig. I find, Miss Kennedy, that every time we meet, I am stimulated and fascinated by your craft and your ingenuity. It is really quite extraordinary. Are you and my brother conducting some kind of business?"

"It is not any of your affair, Albert," John Allister said, tartly. "I don't blunder into your business and I'd appreciate it if you stayed out of mine."

Albert chuckled. "John, oh John, how you do go on about things."

Albert looked at Eve. "Did you know, Miss Kennedy, that when we were boys we often played blind man's bluff? I easily found John because he was so transparent, boring and unimaginative. He would often hide in the same places. He presented no challenge; no challenge at all. I could read little John like a book, a very simple book."

Eve spoke to Albert on reflex, as if nudged by some unseen force. "And I bet your brother, Mr. Harringshaw, could also read you like a book, a book containing only four words: 'You first, after me.'"

John Allister laughed. "Well said, Miss Kennedy. Well said indeed."

Albert narrowed his cold, offended eyes on Eve.

"Perhaps, Miss Kennedy," Albert said, "You should learn to hold your clever tongue when you are in the company of your superiors."

Eve felt a volcanic rage she had been suppressing for weeks. She couldn't hold it back any longer. "Superiors, Mr. Harringshaw?" Eve said, her eyes burning. "You, sir, are not my superior in any way, nor are you anyone else's superior, as I see it. Just because you were born into a family that possesses more money than you need or know how to spend wisely, doesn't give you the right or privilege to think you are anyone's superior. I have met better breeding on a subway car in the middle of the night. Your supposed superiority shows, sir, that *you* are inferior because you lack sensitivity and depth of feeling, and you have no consideration for anyone else other than yourself. You, sir—in short, sir—are a bully."

The two men stood in a stunned silence. John Allister stared at Eve, first in utter shock, and then in swelling admiration. He began to laugh, his entire body shaking from it.

Albert's face was red with rage, his eyes pointed at Eve like threatening weapons.

"No one talks to me like that, you silly woman. No one. You will regret your caustic, insulting and impudent words for the rest of your life, Miss Kennedy, you can be sure of it."

He swung about and retreated, leaving Eve trembling with emotion, but not regret.

"Hurrah, Miss Kennedy!" John Allister said. "Hurrah, indeed! No one has ever had the courage to dress Brother Albert down like that. No one, not in his entire life. I, myself, never had the courage. Well done, Miss Kennedy!"

Eve turned quiet, the anger and adrenalin draining out of her, weakening her. The false strength was now being replaced by fear and dread. She'd just made a colossal mistake. A stupid mistake.

"Don't worry about him, Miss Kennedy. He's harmless."

Eve knew better. She knew that Albert Harringshaw was anything but harmless—quite the contrary. Eve knew he meant everything he'd said to her and more. If she stayed in New York, he would make her life a living nightmare. She had just sealed her own terrible fate.

And then she thought of Patrick and San Francisco. He was somewhere nearby, and he was waiting for her answer: would she marry him and move to San Francisco with him? He wanted to leave as soon as possible, the sooner the better, before something unseen happened to him and before she was trapped.

Eve's mind was whirling, one thought bouncing off another. Patrick had surprised her with his declaration of love and his wish to marry her, and at first, she had been thrilled by the news, indulging in delicious thoughts of making love to him, and of the two of them getting acquainted, as only newly married lovers do, in both simple and intimate ways. But now she wasn't sure.

Did she love Patrick? She was certainly physically attracted to him—more to him than to any other man she'd ever met. But marriage in this time and place? Move to San Francisco in 1885 and start a new life? She just wasn't sure. She was a modern woman and, even though Patrick had said he would give her all the freedom she wanted or needed, did he really understand what that meant? And even if she lived with someone who gave her her freedom, women in 1885 had little power and she was unlikely to gain much more, even if she did become a doctor.

Eve had boxed herself in. If she stayed in New York, Patrick would leave and she'd wind up as Albert's sex slave, or rotting in some women's prison.

Suddenly, in her mind's eye, she saw the lantern. Could she find it? Did Evelyn even know where it was? Did it exist? Eve had to find out, and fast.

John Allister turned to her, deep in thought. "Miss Kennedy, what is a subway car?"

At that moment, Eve caught movement out of the corner of her eye. She turned, hearing gasps, seeing faces stretched in fear, shock and fascination. The room turned to ice as people stood transfixed, all eyes focused on a woman who stood near two marble statues.

Eve stared at the woman in disbelief. She wore a bright red dress, a black cloak and a hood covering her head, obviously dressed as Little Red Riding Hood. She was only 10 feet from Albert Harringshaw. Eve watched in disbelief as the woman pulled a derringer from a black muff and pointed it directly at his chest.

Eve was close enough to see the derringer's silver blue finish and pearl grip panels. In that stunned silence, the lilting strings of a distant string quartet filled the space, its haunting music wafting down from some upper room, as if the gods were serenading these startled mortals, frozen in a tableau.

The woman spoke in a harsh, threatening contralto. "Mr. Albert Harringshaw!"

Albert stood stark still, alone, everyone near him having escaped to the periphery. Fear was slowly creeping into his eyes. His body was stiff, his eyes shifting, calculating escape. But there was no escape.

"You have ruined me, Mr. Harringshaw, a virtuous woman who has been deprived of her virtue and then tossed aside like some tarnished buckle. Well, sir, I will be the last woman you ruin. I, Mr. Harringshaw, will put you where you belong: in the lowest grave, in the lowest rung of hell!"

When the woman removed her hood, there were gasps.

Eve drew in a stunned breath. It was Helen Price!

Albert held up a pleading hand. "Miss Price, please lower that derringer. You are quite mistaken about me and my intentions. They are honorable, I assure you."

"No, sir, I am not mistaken and your honor, sir, is a sham, a twisted, selfish perversion. I have had you followed, sir. I know what devilish business you are up to. Now say a quick prayer, Mr. Harringshaw, before I send you straight to the devil where you belong."

Albert's face was white, drawn and grim. "Madam, please," he said, his voice pinched with appeal. "Please, I am not the man you think I am. Please spare me. I beg you."

Then Eve saw him: Patrick! He was too far away to reach Helen Price. Eve saw he was edging his way toward Albert Harringshaw. Did Helen see him? No, her cold, dark stare was only focused on Albert, her target.

Helen leveled the derringer just as Patrick sprang for Albert.

Eve screamed, "No!"

The derringer POPPED. Women screamed. Men ducked away and Eve watched in horror as Patrick pounced on Albert and they tumbled onto the floor.

Then there was chaos, as two men charged Helen, snatching the derringer from her trembling hand. They held her by her shoulders, and as she looked at Albert and Patrick lying on the floor, she burst into tears, screaming.

"Is he dead? Tell me he's dead! Tell me he's dead!" she wailed.

Eve broke for Patrick, falling to her knees on the marble floor before the two men, both lying dead still. Dr. Eckland was by her side in seconds, slowly lowering to one knee.

"Who took the bullet, Miss Kennedy? Can you see? Who took the bullet? We must first find it and stop the bleeding."

And then Albert's eyes opened, still filled with shock. He looked at Patrick, and in a kind of panic, he pushed back away from him on hands and feet, freeing his body and legs.

Without moving him, Eve frantically scanned Patrick's body—and then she saw it: a small red hole in the upper right of Patrick's black coat revealed that he had taken the bullet.

"It's Patrick!" she exclaimed.

John Allister quickly appeared. "Is there something I can do?"

Dr. Eckland said, "Get my carriage. We've got to get this man to a hospital."

"No, I'll get mine. We'll take him in my carriage," John Allister said.

John turned to a servant and gave his command.

The crowd moved in for a closer look. Dr. Eckland waved them back. "Stand back, for God's sake. Stand back and find me some water and clean bandages. For God's sake, stand back so we can help this man!"

Patrick was lying on his stomach, his head turned so that half of the left side of his face was visible. When he opened a milky eye, struggling to look at Eve, she leaned in close.

"Patrick, take it easy. We're going to get you to the hospital."

He managed a half grin. "Marry me?" he said, in a hoarse whisper.

CHAPTER 28

Patrick was unconscious when he arrived at Gouverneur Hospital, and was immediately operated on by Dr. Long, with Dr. Eckland and Eve assisting. The derringer Helen Price fired was a single shot .41 caliber. Dr. Eckland had seen similar wounds when he was a physician in the Civil War, and so his assistance was invaluable. With his help, Dr. Long explored the muscle near Patrick's right shoulder, found the lodged bullet, and then carefully removed it.

Eve's job was to ensure the wound was cleaned and bandaged. Patrick was then wheeled to one of the hospital's two private rooms and covered with warm blankets. Eve wished she had an IV drip, monitors and, most especially, antibiotics. What worried her was the possibility not only of infection but also of blood poisoning. Either could kill him. Without antibiotics, Eve could only hope and pray. She pulled a chair up next to his bed and sat there, monitoring him, tucking in the blankets, spooning water between his lips and wiping the beaded perspiration from his forehead.

Hours later, both Dr. Long and Dr. Eckland came by and ordered Eve to bed, but she refused. Dr. Eckland finally laid a gentle hand on her shoulder, sighing heavily.

"My dear Miss Kennedy, we have done all we can for him. Dr. Long performed a difficult and delicate operation with great skill. I was quite impressed, and I told her so. She is a talented surgeon, as I saw with my own eyes, so let us be grateful for her good hands. Mr. Gantly is young and strong, and it is not a mortal wound. Now we must leave it to Almighty God."

It was after 4 a.m. when Dr. Eckland left. Eve sat by Patrick's bedside, watching him breathe erratically and talk incoherently. She fought back tears and anger. Why did he take the bullet intended for Albert Harringshaw? Why didn't he let Helen Price shoot the bastard? He's the one who deserved to be lying there fighting for his life, not Patrick.

Albert had been so scared after the shooting that he didn't even bother to drop by and ask about Patrick's condition. He fled the house, taking a back entrance, even leaving his fiancée to find her own way home. So much for the chivalrous, courageous gentleman, Albert Harringshaw. To Eve, he was a feckless, blowhard chicken shit.

As the first early morning light crept into the curtain-covered window, Eve's chin slowly lowered onto her chest and she fell asleep. When she awoke an hour later, she checked to see that Patrick's condition was stable, and then she reluctantly moved to a temporary cot in the nurses' quarters.

She slept just a few hours until 9 a.m. She washed, dressed, ate a small breakfast and began her rounds, starting first with Patrick. There was little or no improvement.

As Eve stepped into the hallway, she was met by Dr. Long, who promptly handed Eve the morning paper. She made a small twist of a frown.

"You won't like it."

Eve hesitated before taking it.

"Don't let yourself feel anger over this," Dr. Long said. "It's not worth it."

Eve held her eyes for a moment before she read the big, bold headlines.

ALBERT HARRINGSHAW NARROWLY ESCAPES DEATH AT THE CELEBRATED HARRINGSHAW BALL
CRAZED WOMAN FIRES SINGLE SHOT BUT MISSES
MR. HARRINGSHAW STANDS BY BRAVELY

Eve read the first two paragraphs of the story. There was no mention of Detective Sergeant Gantly taking the bullet for Albert and saving his life. It said that Albert Harringshaw was brave, and that the crazed shooter had entered the ball under false pretenses, singling him out because he was from *the famous family*.

Eve dropped the paper to her side, feeling a sudden anger that flushed her face scarlet. "Stood bravely!?" she said, shaking the paper in outrage. "Albert Harringshaw brave!? He's an egotistical coward! What kind of journalism is this? It's all a bunch of lies, and there's no mention anywhere of Detective Gantly, who saved the bastard's life!"

Dr. Long looked long and hard at Eve, readjusting her spectacles.

"Miss Kennedy, I understand how you feel, but harsh words won't help. Anger won't work. It is a poison that will only eat you up inside. It will only harm you, not those arrogant and ignorant men out there in the world who want to protect their power and authority, and who think all women belong where they want us to belong, bowing meekly to their every command and obeying their every wish. They believe we are weak and frail, and just a little bit stupid. Over the years, I have endured every insult possible, directed toward my family, my character, my abilities and my profession. I have been called an old spinster, a silly woman, a man-hater and much, much worse. I no longer get angry, Miss Kennedy, because I know in my heart of hearts that who I am and what I offer has value both to me and to my patients, who are poor and sick and the outcasts of society."

Eve saw Dr. Long was weary, but her expression was resolute; her speech strong, filled with conviction. Her graying hair was pulled back tightly into her characteristic bun and when she removed her spectacles, she looked younger than her forty-four years.

"We must, of course, fight on for our equal rights, voting being one of them. And we shall fight on, as long as we have breath in our bodies; but let us not give these misguided men the satisfaction of seeing us angry. Instead, let them see our calm resolve and our fervent passion for truth, equality and justice for all. Let us be resolved to continue our fight with dignity and patience, Miss Kennedy. Mr. Albert Harringshaw is a poor, wretched man who has the power to pay off any newspaper reporter, any politician and any policeman in this city. These are the times we live in, Miss Kennedy, and we must face it and be resolute and persistent in our attempts to change the balance of power. But in the end, Mr. Harringshaw cannot pay off his own guilty conscience. I believe that will be the final death blow to him and to all those who subjugate women and who abuse their power and authority."

Eve stared at Dr. Long in admiration. Eve knew from her history that it would be 1920 before the 19th Amendment to the U.S. Constitution granted American women the right to vote, and decades longer before they could have credit cards, or be educated at the best colleges, or receive anything like equal pay with men. Dr. Long would never live to see these advances in women's rights, and that made Eve sad—but also extremely grateful for Dr. Long and all the women who helped lay the foundation for the women's rights movement. It was only because of them that Eve was able to live as a free and independent woman in the twenty-first century.

When John Allister Harringshaw II arrived at Gouverneur Hospital at 11 a.m., his presence created a flurry of gossip and activity. No one of his class had ever visited the hospital before, causing many of the nurses to step from rooms, hoping to catch a glimpse of him at the admission desk.

Minutes later, Eve walked briskly down the hallway to meet him. He faced her with anxious eyes and a gentle sorrow, as he removed his silk hat and gloves and took Eve's hand.

"It is so pleasant to see you again, Miss Kennedy. I would have been here sooner, but the snow made traveling difficult. We have more than seven inches so far."

Eve stared at him carefully, unsure about him. Perhaps it was the lack of sleep and the emotions of the last twenty-four hours that made her suspicious and cautious.

"I'm sure you're here to see Evelyn," Eve said.

He nodded, nervously twisted the brim of his hat. Eve watched him swallow.

"Yes... And how is Detective Sergeant Gantly?"

"He's resting. Only time will tell. The operation was successful. We can only hope infection doesn't set in."

"He was terribly brave, Miss Kennedy. Only one newspaper mentioned his gallantry, I am afraid. The family lawyers saw to that, hoping to avoid a scandal."

Eve stayed mute.

"Miss Kennedy, will you please take me to see Evelyn?"

As they walked past two tall windows, Eve saw big flakes of snow striking the glass and heard the moan of the wind as it circled the building.

Eve stopped outside the hospital room and turned to John Allister. "Where is your brother?"

"He's on a train to Chicago."

"Did he say when he'd be back?"

"I do not know. We did not converse, Miss Kennedy. May I see Evelyn now?"

Eve pushed the door open and stepped aside to let John Allister enter. He did so meekly, his mouth twitching nervously. He saw seven hospital beds on the far left, and then he followed Eve's gaze to the far right of the room, where a curtain surrounded a single bed.

"How is she, Miss Kennedy?"

"Her fever has broken, but she's still very weak. She's not completely out of danger."

"May I speak to her?"

"She may be asleep."

"I won't wake her. If I may just sit for a time?"

Eve led him across the room, past the examination tables, to Evelyn's bed. Eve gently drew back the privacy curtain and watched as John Allister crept forward, apprehensive and eager.

When he saw Evelyn lying still, her red hair pooled about her head, the freckles on her cheeks and nose, and her small, puckered mouth, tears glistened in his eyes. He turned his head aside so Eve wouldn't see him cry.

Eve left him to retrieve an old wooden schoolhouse chair. She carried it over, placing it beside the bed.

"Please sit down, Mr. Harringshaw."

He removed his overcoat and Eve took it, as well as his gloves and hat. As he slowly lowered himself into the chair, Eve placed them in a nearby closet. By the time she returned, John Allister had regained his stately composure. He sat staring down at Evelyn with such loving tenderness that Eve was moved. It was abundantly clear now that John did love Evelyn. Watching his worshipful gaze, Eve could believe at last that this truly was the man who had composed that beautifully written Christmas Eve letter.

They remained in silence, each watching Evelyn sleep.

"It was in a snow storm just like the one we're having now that Evelyn and I met, Miss Kennedy. It was

last February, in the evening, as darkness had just settled in. I was in my carriage moving up Broadway,
watching the gusting snow cover the sidewalks and the
streets. It was already hanging heavily in the trees. I
saw men and women bent against the blowing snow,
men touching the rims of their derbies, women's hands
snug in their muffs. Horse hooves were sliding, stag-
gering for a footing. I was not in a particularly happy
state, and I was lost in my own thoughts."

John Allister leaned back and closed his eyes, as if
watching an inner movie.

"We were suddenly struck violently by an omnibus,
and I was smashed hard into the left side of the carriage
as it tipped and slammed hard into the Earth, nearly
knocking me unconscious. I heard screams, the cry and
neighing of horses, and frantic footfalls on the cobblestones. I was so stunned that I was paralyzed, unable to
think or act. And then suddenly, I saw a light, a soft
light, and I heard a gentle voice—the voice of a woman
that I thought was the voice of an angel. I struggled to
find the voice and the face of the creature who was calling to me."

John Allister's eyes opened on Evelyn and he smiled
warmly. "It was Evelyn. She had managed to open the
carriage door from the other side and light up the carriage with a lantern. 'Sir,' she said, in the most sooth-
ing and gentle voice; 'Sir, are you all right? Can I be of
help?'"

John nodded. "It truly was the face of an angel. I
hope you will not think me a romantic fool, Miss Kennedy, but it was a face I'd seen in my dreams. It was a
face I knew so well. It was the face of a girl I knew I'd
fall in love with. And then there was all that lovely red

hair and the burning, chipped green eyes; the laughing freckles, the soft and pure white skin."

John Allister leaned forward, reached out his hand and nearly touched Evelyn. He stopped, his hand trembling.

"Yes, Miss Kennedy, and now you know that I am a romantic fool and that I thought I had lost my dear girl, my dear love, my dearest Evelyn, forever."

John Allister shifted his eyes to Eve, who was standing to his left. "I am so grateful to you, Miss Kennedy, for bringing her back to me and for saving her life."

Eve had never witnessed such a moving declaration of love—such an outpouring of honest feeling. In her time, the twenty-first century, John Allister's declaration would be considered gushing, cheesy and corny, but Eve felt the tender, passionate authenticity of his feeling, and she was touched by it.

"What will you do, Mr. Harringshaw?"

He knew what she meant.

He looked down at the floor. "I did not sleep last night, Miss Kennedy, for thinking about our particular situation. All I know for certain is that I will not let Evelyn get away from me again. I love her too much. If we stay in New York, the scandal will be a devastating one for my family. Evelyn is poor, with no money and no social connections. I have come to the conclusion that Miss Sharland and I will marry and move to London or Italy. It doesn't really matter as long as we are together. We will discuss it together and come to a decision."

"Have you thought about Evelyn's mother?" Eve asked. "She is so alone in that broken-down tenement."

"Yes, I have thought about her, Miss Kennedy. I will set up a trust so that Mrs. Sharland will have no financial worries for the rest of her life. Evelyn would want that, and I want only for Evelyn to be happy."

"And what will happen to Helen Price, Mr. Harringshaw?"

John Allister stood up and locked his hands behind his back. "I do not know. She is in police custody and will, no doubt, be tried for attempted murder."

"Is there anything you can do to help her?"

"Not at this time, Miss Kennedy. Perhaps later."

Eve wondered how two brothers could be so entirely different in feeling and character.

And then Evelyn stirred, and John Allister shot her a hopeful glance. He leaned over.

"Evelyn... Evelyn... It's Allister, darling. Allister."

Evelyn's eyes fluttered open and then squinted as she worked to focus. She blinked several times and when she fully concentrated on John Allister's smiling face, they opened wide with a startled confusion.

"Allister..." she said, in a breathy whisper. "Is that you?"

John reached for her hand. "Yes, Evelyn, it is. It is your Allister."

Evelyn made a sound of disbelief as she held his stare. "But... how?"

Eve pulled open the curtains to let the morning light pour in. Behind the windows was a mass of falling snow, circling and spinning patterns.

"You are my Christmas present, my darling girl," Allister said, his voice filled with emotion.

Evelyn looked at him, her eyes brimming. "Allister... my dear Allister. I thought you'd never find me."

Eve left them alone. At the nurses' desk, she was startled to see a telegram addressed to her. When she tore it open, she nearly gasped. It was from Albert Harringshaw.

Miss Kennedy:

Nothing has changed.
I will expect you to be moved into the house by Christmas Eve.

—A. Harringshaw

CHAPTER 29

Over the next week, Patrick's condition continued to deteriorate. He lay in his hospital bed, either unconscious or delirious, with no signs of improvement. There were brief moments of lucidity when he was aware of Eve talking to him, encouraging him to heal; he saw, through sticky, blurry eyes, Dr. Long and Dr. Eckland conversing, their faces heavy with concern, but when he tried to speak, he couldn't find his tongue.

"Blood poisoning," he heard Dr. Eckland say sorrowfully. "Poor fellow. Poor good fellow."

Then Patrick would slip away again into delirious nightmares, where he was being chased by sharp-toothed green savages on massive black horses, sabers drawn, guns blazing. They were coming toward him, and he couldn't run away fast enough.

Ahead, he saw his dear mother standing in a dark, foggy alley, under sickly yellow lamplight, calling his name, beckoning him with her hand.

"Come home to me, Patrick. I've been waiting for you. Come back to me. Hurry… Come back to me."

In fevered dreams he was on a Clipper ship in a dark, angry storm, staring up at the three masts and the square rig. The ship was being tossed about as towering, curling waves rolled toward them in great billows, crashing against the ship, breaking over the bow, drenching him. He glanced toward the wheelhouse and was astonished to see Eve at the helm, fighting to keep the ship from spinning out of control and crashing into tall, jagged cliffs just off to the right.

"We're almost there, Patrick," Eve yelled over the thrashing tempest. "San Francisco is just ahead. Hang on just a little longer, my love. Hang on. Don't give up!"

Eve had hardly slept or eaten that week. She was losing weight. She knew Patrick would die if he didn't receive antibiotics to kill the infection. His body simply couldn't fight off blood poisoning.

On Sunday evening of December 13th, Eve left Patrick's room and climbed the stairs to the second floor, to the private room John Allister had arranged for Evelyn. Evelyn's warm pink color had returned, she had regained much of her strength, and she was scheduled to leave the hospital in a few days.

Over the past week, Eve's and Evelyn's relationship had developed into a sisterly one. Although Eve had said little of her past, Evelyn had shared most of hers. Inevitably, the conversation always veered from the present to the future, and Evelyn's marriage to John Allister and where they would end up: London, Paris or Italy. Evelyn didn't care, as long as she and Allister were together.

On that Sunday, Eve paused as she approached Evelyn's bed, seeing she was propped up reading a book. To Eve's surprise, it was *The Adventures of Huckleberry Finn* by Mark Twain.

Evelyn lowered the book when she saw Eve.

"Hello, Eve, come in."

"Am I disturbing you?"

"Of course not. How could you ever? It is always so pleasant to see you." Evelyn patted a space next to her. "Come and sit with me."

After Eve sat down, Evelyn reached for her hand. "How lovely it is to have you as my sister, Eve. I so wanted a sister when I was a little girl. I scolded Mommy for not giving me one. But then Clayton is the best brother any girl could ask for, isn't he?"

Eve smiled. "Yes, he is. I like him very much."

"And he thinks the world of you."

Evelyn noticed Eve's eyes looked dull and tired.

"Are you feeling well, Eve?" Evelyn asked.

"Yes, I am well," Eve said, not looking directly at her. "I'm just a little tired."

"Is Detective Sergeant Gantly improving?" Evelyn asked.

Eve shook her head. "No, I'm afraid not."

"What a pity," Evelyn said. "From all accounts I heard he was very brave."

Eve wanted to change the subject, so she pointed to Evelyn's book. "How do you like the book?"

"Allister bought it for me. It's Mark Twain's latest. It's very amusing, but then Mr. Twain is always amusing, is he not? I like it that Huckleberry is a bit of a rascal."

Evelyn noticed Eve's serious expression. "Eve, what is it? You look so dispirited."

Eve's forehead knotted into a frown. "Evelyn, two days ago I started to ask you something, but then Allister came in and I didn't finish."

"Yes, I remember. You said it had something to do with a lantern."

"Not a lantern, Evelyn, *the* lantern you used the night you and Allister met. The lantern you used the night of Allister's carriage accident during that snowstorm back in February."

Evelyn's head tilted to one side as she thought. "Oh, yes. I had grabbed the lantern from the rear axle of a delivery wagon that had stopped nearby."

Eve stared at her, her pulse rising. "Do you know where that lantern is?"

Evelyn was puzzled. "Why, Eve? It was just a lantern."

"It's very important, Evelyn."

"I am sure Allister could find you another one, Eve."

"No, not another. It has to be that one."

"I do not understand, Eve. What is the matter? You look so very serious. Are you sure you feel well?"

Eve sighed and tried again. "Yes, yes, I'm fine. Did you keep the lantern, Evelyn?"

Eve held her breath as she waited for Evelyn's answer.

"I think I did. I had it with me when I was helping Allister into a cab." Evelyn played with the ends of her hair as she thought. She lit up, pleased. "I did not give the lantern back because I was so concerned about Allister. I simply forgot. Yes! I remember now that in the cab, Allister pointed at it and said when he saw the lantern's light, and my face bathed in its light, he thought I was an angel. Later, of course, he admitted that he fell in love with me right there and then. He told me he would always be in love with me, and nothing could ever separate us."

"Where is the lantern, Evelyn?" Eve said, directly. "I've got to find it."

Evelyn sat back into the pillows, studying Eve. "Eve... tell me. What is this all about?"

Eve dropped her eyes for a moment and then raised them again. "Evelyn, what I'm going to tell you, you must never tell anyone. Promise me."

Evelyn smiled, nervously. "I do promise, Eve. Of course you know I will never tell a soul."

Eve looked away. "Not that anyone would believe you, anyway. Evelyn, what I'm going to tell you will sound crazy, but please, don't say anything until I have finished the entire story."

Evelyn stared, uneasily. "All right, Eve. I'll just sit here and listen. Please continue."

Eve stood up and inhaled a deep breath. She paced to the window, turned and walked back to the end of the bed.

Eve told the story, beginning from when she first entered *The Time Past Antique Shop* in the twenty-first century. She told it carefully and concisely, though highly sensitive to the startled reactions on Evelyn's face, as it moved from polite serenity to surprise and, finally, to worry and anxiety.

After Eve had finished, Evelyn sat rigid in a bewildered silence, staring into the middle distance, not blinking and hardly breathing.

Eve faced her, her arms wrapped tightly about her chest. She was shivering, and the echo of her own fantastic and impossible words still hung in the air about them.

"So you see, Evelyn, I am hopeful that the lantern's light that brought me here will also send me and Patrick forward. Back to my home in the twenty-first century. If Patrick doesn't receive twenty-first century medicine, he will die. And besides that, I want to go home. It is where I belong and where I want to be."

Evelyn lowered her eyes, staring at the white quilt pattern. Neither spoke for long, awkward minutes. Eve couldn't read Evelyn's face to see what she was thinking, so she waited, anxiously.

"Evelyn?" Eve finally asked, softly.

When Evelyn looked at Eve, she seemed to be watching her from a great distance, as if she were staring into a dark cave or at a distant, foggy mountain.

"I don't know what to say, Eve," Evelyn said, her voice low, almost a whisper. "I just don't have any words. I'm so sorry."

"But the lantern, Evelyn? Do you have any idea where it might be?"

"The lantern must be in my mother's house. Yes, I'm sure it must be there."

Eve took a hopeful step forward.

Evelyn spoke again, her voice flat and emotionless. "I wonder how Allister's letter..." She stopped, leaving the question hanging.

Eve stared into the depth of Evelyn's eyes and she saw disquiet. "You believe me, don't you, Evelyn? I mean, I know it's a crazy, awesome story, but it's true. It's all true. Do you believe me?"

Evelyn avoided Eve's eyes, looking toward the gas lamp that sat on a nearby table. She watched shadows flickering on the walls.

"Do you go to séances, Eve?"

"What? Séances? No, of course not."

"I went to one after my father died. I wanted to speak to him, but he didn't come through. He would not or could not speak, or so the medium said. I never did get to talk to him."

Eve slowly lowered her arms, searching for words. "Evelyn, I don't know how it happened, but it did happen. Everything I told you is the truth."

Evelyn smiled, weakly. "I know you would not lie to me, Eve. I know you believe something happened, a dream or something. Perhaps you have just been working so hard, or maybe you are ill. Yes, maybe you have picked up a sickness here. There are so many ill people who come through, or so Allister told me. I myself saw many fantastical things when I was sick, as I told you. Big birds that flew through the sky, and fairies and castles and awful, two-headed monsters. And I have read stories about strange things that may happen in the future, like flying machines and projectiles that shoot out into vast space."

Eve shrank into herself, slowly realizing that Evelyn didn't believe her. She either didn't have the imagination, or she just didn't have the capacity to grasp the truth. Eve struggled for any sort of words that would help convince Evelyn, but she came up empty. She'd already said everything she could think of to say.

Evelyn went on. "Once at the theater, I saw a magician who did all kinds of marvelous things, making things appear and disappear. He used lanterns to make dancing shadows where a woman would appear and then disappear in a puff of smoke. It was so entertaining, Eve. I wish you could have seen it."

Eve lowered her head in defeat. "Yes, Evelyn... I wish I could have seen it too."

The silence lengthened and Eve knew it was hopeless. She went to Plan B. She straightened up and grinned, spreading her hands wide. "How was I!? Did you believe me?"

Evelyn's bright eyes came to Eve's. "You mean?"

"Of course! It was all a great big story. A fantasy! You thought it was all real, didn't you, Evelyn? I had you believing it was real, didn't I? Admit it."

Evelyn laughed. "Well, yes, some of it, anyway. It was so wonderfully romantic, Eve. So filled with wondrous detail about where you lived in the future and about how I was dying. Oh, and I loved that sweet and loving letter that Allister wrote to me on Christmas Eve. What a great imagination you have, Eve. You should write stories. It was so entertaining. Brava!" Evelyn said, clapping. "Brava! I was so entertained and I feel so much better because of it."

After they finished their laugh, Eve pointed at Evelyn, dead serious, and winked with a little, wicked grin.

"But the lantern is at your mother's house, right?"

Evelyn laughed, shaking her head. "Yes, dear, Eve. It must be. I am sure it is there unless my mother has thrown it out. Yes, it must be there."

Evelyn sat up with a clap of her hands, suddenly alive with a new idea. "Oh, Eve, why don't you get the lantern and bring it here! Allister will be so delighted to see it again. It will bring back so many good and loving memories."

Eve flashed a broad, satisfied grin. "And so I shall get it, Evelyn. And so I shall."

CHAPTER 30

Eve descended the stairs to the first floor and wearily strolled down the hospital corridor, past the Tubercular Ward. The lights were out, and all was quiet. It was too late to visit Evelyn's mother. That would have to wait until morning. But the very thought of it—the idea—the exciting possibility that by tomorrow morning Eve would have that lantern in her hands gave her a sudden twist of emotion that both thrilled and frightened her.

What if the lantern didn't work this time? Had it only been a onetime thing? What if the lantern was the wrong one? What if this entire experience was some kind of hallucination after all? In the nearly seven weeks that Eve had been in 1885, she'd gradually grown accustomed to its sights, smells and customs. She had adjusted to the dress, to the speech and to her work, which she enjoyed and felt had great value. She had also grown fond both of Dr. Long and Dr. Eckland, who had come by twice to visit Patrick and offer assistance. Eve and Dr. Eckland had become friends, and he had even invited her for Christmas dinner, to dine with him, his cousin and some of his close friends. Eve was very touched by his invitation and had dared to kiss him on his willing cheek. It had been a sweet and tender moment.

Millie had also stopped by to update Eve on the state of Miss Price's house. All the servants had been let go, and Millie was thankful she had found another position in a house nearby, thanks to help from the cook, Mrs. O'Brien.

If Eve left 1885, she would miss her new friends, and she would miss the simpler lifestyle, a world without the distraction of technology, without the 24-hour news cycle, without the break-neck speed of modern living, without the neon signs and the loud mass and tangle of cars, busses, trucks and car alarms.

Eve was bone tired. She hadn't slept in her own bed for three days because she couldn't leave Patrick. Not now. If anything happened to him during the night—if his conditioned worsened or if the unthinkable happened and he died—she'd never forgive herself for not being there.

She was on her way to his room when she heard children's happy cries as she passed the Children's Ward. She stopped and opened the door to peek in.

Her mood instantly lifted when she saw twelve children laughing and dancing around a tall, thin evergreen tree. Eve entered the room, where the twelve beds which occupied the back wall were now in shadow. She stood there in the cheerful scene of children preparing for Christmas, some on crutches, some with arms bandaged, some thin as twigs. They were all helping

Dr. Long and two nurses decorate the tree with apples, tangerines, walnuts dipped in egg white, and strings of popcorn and cranberries. Gold-foil had been shaped into miniature stars, steamships, elves, fish and birds, and they gleamed in the tree's candlelight.

Over the fireplace, holly was strung, its red berries glistening, and the entire room was scented with evergreen and freshly baked cookies. Eve looked up to see a sprig of mistletoe just over her head. Who was that for? she wondered.

On a wooden table, two pink-cheeked girls in red and white dresses were busy stirring a pudding, occasionally pausing to taste it.

Dr. Long waved her over. "Come join the party, Eve."

Eve smiled and pointed toward Patrick's room. Dr. Long nodded with understanding as Eve left the delightful party.

EVE SAT SLUMPED BESIDE PATRICK'S BED, nodding off to sleep and then suddenly jerking awake at the slightest sound. She often blotted his damp forehead and spoke words of comfort, even though she felt a slow, creeping dread and swelling depression, as every hour brought Patrick closer to certain death.

Fatigue and despair filled every atom of her body, and she had difficulty concentrating. Her thoughts just kept slipping away into some dark space and she sat in a stupor of discontent. She knew she should try to get some sleep, so she'd be rested in the morning for her visit to Mrs. Sharland, but sleep wouldn't come.

Eve was startled to her feet when the door to Patrick's room suddenly burst open and two men dressed in black, unbuttoned greatcoats, dark suits and thin ties entered heavily. They stood staring at her, and then their cold attention turned to Patrick.

One man was tall and authoritative, with thinning hair, a bushy walrus mustache and a face bearing the harsh and ridged lines of a competitor. There was a greedy, restless motion in his eyes, which revealed a dark passion.

When he saw Eve, his brow shot up and one eye enlarged in surprise, then curiosity, and then keen interest. Eve sensed danger. She could taste the metallic fear. She felt hunted and targeted, and she instinctively took a step back.

The other man stood in a stature of command. He was a black-bearded, round bellied, florid-faced man. He wore a stubby, flat-topped plug hat low over his brow. His unbuttoned greatcoat was swept back, exposing the curve of his threatening big belly.

"Are you Miss Kennedy?" the taller man said in an accent Eve couldn't place. It was part Irish, and part something else. To her ear, it sounded similar to a modern day Long Island accent, mixed with a heavy Irish brogue.

"Yes, I'm Nurse Kennedy."

"I'm Inspector Byrnes. Thomas Byrnes." He gestured toward the other man. "That's Detective Sergeant Doyle."

Eve's fingers formed fists—an animal instinct—not that fighting the man made any sense. She'd heard about Inspector Byrnes from Albert Harringshaw and Patrick, as well as from others at the boarding house. Inspector Byrnes' brutal questioning of suspected criminals popularized the term "the third degree," which was apparently coined by Byrnes. It was widely known that Byrnes used a combination of physical and psychological torture on his suspects. Eve also knew from Patrick that Albert Harringshaw donated generous amounts of money to certain of Byrnes' personal causes in exchange for favors.

Inspector Byrnes glanced over at Patrick, who was twisting and mumbling in a semiconscious state.

"We've come to see Detective Sergeant Gantly. How is he, Nurse?"

Eve swallowed back nerves. "He's... well, he's not improving."

The men exchanged knowing glances and jerked nods.

The fat one spoke in a pure Irish accent. "It's too bad. Patrick's a good man. A fine man. We were partners for a time, you know. A good policeman, he is."

Inspector Byrnes walked to Patrick's bed and looked down at him.

"You've got to admire a man who gives up his life for another, especially when it's done in the line of duty. Greater love hath no man than this, that a man lay down his life for his friends, the good book says."

Eve thought *Albert Harringshaw was no friend of Patrick's*. Out loud, she said firmly, "He's not dead yet."

Inspector Byrnes cocked his head to one side as if to get a closer look at Patrick.

"It isn't the bullet that kills a man like Detective Sergeant Gantly, Nurse. It's the blood poison. Let's face it, Nurse, you need to call a priest. He needs to make it right with Almighty God while he still can.

From the looks of him, he's already heading down the coal shoot."

"Honestly said, Inspector Byrnes," the fat man said. "Did you know my brother was a priest? He was a good priest, he was, who worked with the poor and the needy. He died two years ago from the fever. Patrick knew him. Now God is calling the good Detective Sergeant Gantly home as well."

Eve stood resolutely, with her head up. "Patrick is very strong. He could still survive."

Inspector Byrnes' sardonic eyebrow shot up again. "Patrick, is it? You call him Patrick, Nurse Kennedy? That's not so respectful to Detective Sergeant Gantly, Nurse. You need to give a man his proper respect, woman, especially a dying man. And, Nurse Kennedy, Detective Sergeant Gantly *is* dying, make no mistake about that. Banish any fool romantic notion that he'll survive this, Nurse. I know from my vast experience that he is a dead man. Best to face it now and get him a priest. Do you hear me, Nurse?"

Eve saw the real threat in the Inspector's eyes, daring her to challenge him. She saw the brutal eyes of a predator.

The man was a nut case, Eve thought. She also sensed—no, she knew—that these two men *wanted* Patrick to die. Why? Because Albert Harringshaw wanted it?

Someone who had attended the Harringshaw ball the night of the shooting had leaked a true account of the shooting to the newspapers, and they had enthusiastically expanded on it. Detective Sergeant Gantly was being portrayed as a hero—an honest cop who had performed his duty and was dying because "*He had laid down his life for another man.*"

Dr. Long had even been interviewed by several reporters about Patrick's condition. And in the past few days, two songs had hastily been written about Detective Gantly, celebrating his selfless courage and his dedication to the poor as well as the rich. These songs were being performed in some downtown theaters "*to wild applause and to many a lady's anguished tears*" as had been reported by *The New York Herald*.

Albert Harringshaw, on the other hand, had been relegated to the back pages and, if he was mentioned at all, it was with regard to his questionable courage, considering he was supposed to be a gentleman.

So did these powerful men want Patrick dead? Probably. Once he was out of the way, his popularity would fade, he would be quickly forgotten and business would go on as usual for Albert Harringshaw and Inspector Byrnes.

Eve wished, for the hundredth time, that Patrick had let Helen Price shoot Albert Harringshaw. She wished she could go back in time once more so she could somehow personally arrange it. Yes, she would play God, judge and jury. She would stop Patrick from catching the bullet and let it strike Albert Harringshaw instead, and the world would be a better place for it.

Eve lowered her head. Now she was more determined than ever to get that lantern and get her and Patrick away from this evil.

"Have you heard me?" Inspector Byrnes said, sharply. "Get him a priest today. I know what I'm talking about."

Eve dropped her voice to a contrite whisper. "I'm sure you know best, Inspector Byrnes," she said, in a pseudo unworthy manner. "Men always know best, don't they?"

But she quickly saw that Inspector Byrnes was no fool. He wasn't taken in by her sudden, sarcastic capitulation. The inspector was enraged, feeling patronized by a silly woman.

He stepped toward her, glaring down coldly. His voice was low, filled with an acid threat.

"You have respect, woman, do you hear me? You have respect or you'll find yourself down in the Tombs where women learn respect, if they don't disappear completely from this world."

Eve felt ice thickening in her stomach.

After they left, Eve began to shiver. She turned toward Patrick and, for the first time in a very long time, she began to cry. Once she started, she couldn't stop the flow. The tears gushed out and ran down her hot cheeks. She buried her face in her hands and sobbed out the weeks of stress, the days of struggle, and the endless hours of exhaustion she had spent caring for Patrick.

Eve doubled over in pain, slowly falling to her knees, unable anymore to resist her sorrow, to think, or to reason. She wept, holding her stomach, her body a spasm of anguish. She wept until she fell exhausted into a deep sleep.

HOURS LATER SHE AWOKE, still lying on the floor, cold and stiff. She sat up, kinked her neck, and massaged her stiff, cold arms. Her eyes were swollen and sticky from crying, her face felt puffy. With an effort, she struggled to her feet, holding herself for warmth, and blundered over to the window, parting the curtains. It was still dark, but she saw a thin line of crimson on the horizon. Early morning? What time was it? Suddenly, she snapped back to reality, whirling around toward Patrick.

He was lying dead still, his breath erratic. Eve rushed to his bedside and checked his pulse. She sighed with relief. It was faint but still there, a weak little drum beat. He was still fighting. She took a fresh cloth, mopped his brow, and then washed his neck and face. She managed to get him to drink some water and then she changed his pillow case, the old one being damp with perspiration.

She had to go see Mrs. Sharland, now! Just as she was about to leave, Patrick's eyes popped open. She flinched and rushed to his bedside.

"Patrick? Patrick?"

He stared blankly, and then there was a wildness in his stare. "Remember..."

"Remember what? What, Patrick?"

His voice was low and raspy. He struggled to wheeze out a word. "Remember... me, Eve. Remember..."

"Of course I'll remember you, Patrick."

"I... love... love you."

And then he was out again.

Fresh tears sprang to her eyes, but Eve wiped them away. Her shoulders sank, and she slumped down in the chair, staring at him.

A nurse entered with some warm broth and Eve got up and took the tray, gratefully. The two nurses didn't talk. There was no need. Both knew Patrick was dying.

Eve touched his mouth and gently opened his lips to ladle in the warm liquid. She spoke to him while she worked.

"You're not going to die, Patrick. Do you hear me? You are not going to die!"

He was silent. He wouldn't take the soup. Frustrated, Eve placed the bowl on the tray and heaved out a sigh.

She stood there observing him, studying him, his every facial feature, his thick neck, his shadow of beard, his curly hair damp from fever, and then she flashed back to the day of their first meeting: his vivid, intelligent, blue eyes, his chiseled, handsome face with a heavy shadow of a beard, his prominent nose, his full lips. She'd boldly walked up to him, spoiling for a fight.

He'd lowered his newspaper and looked at her with a cocky, flirtatious grin that had completely disarmed her and made her weak in the knees. A lightning strike of sudden desire had frozen her in place.

Over the weeks and days, she'd tried to push Patrick away, but he wouldn't go. He was always nearby. He had protected her and given her money when she was desperate; he had somehow procured a nursing diploma; and he'd helped her transport Evelyn from Hoboken to the hospital. How many other ways had he watched over her when she wasn't even aware of it? And after he'd been taken off her case— reassigned shortly after a second detective reported his suspicions to Albert Harringshaw that Patrick and Eve were becoming romantically involved (Millie had heard them talking on the front stairs of Helen's brownstone)—he'd offered to take her to San Francisco as his wife, so they could both escape Albert Harringshaw's clutches.

Weak morning light began to creep into the room, but Eve stayed with her thoughts, lost in introspection and memory, recollecting the panorama of her life, both in the twenty-first century and in the nineteenth century.

Hers had not been a particularly remarkable life. In fact, it had been quite ordinary, until a few weeks ago when she'd found herself in 1885. Her childhood had been normal enough. She'd done well in school—she'd had friends and was respected by colleagues. She'd met Blake, and they'd married. They were going to start a family, but it never happened. No, there was no family and there never would be with Blake.

That was when everything had changed. Blake's lies and infidelity had affected her on every level, almost imperceptibly, like the slow freezing of a stream. Eve recognized that fact now, in a way she hadn't before.

Eve lowered herself into the chair and, as she did so, she had a kind of epiphany—a new understanding. It was as if the sun broke through dark, heavy clouds.

When she'd learned that Blake was having an affair with another woman—a married woman, with two children—Eve had felt like she'd been stabbed in the gut. It hurt so badly that she'd gone down the traditional road of suppressing, drinking, taking sleeping pills and hooking up with the occasional sex partner. She'd slowly begun to despise, blame and hate herself, and hate and despise every man she met, convinced that they were all selfish cheaters. She didn't trust them or even like them. Finally, she'd stopped dating altogether. What was the point? *Who needs them?* had been her motto.

When her divorce was final, she swore she'd focus only on her career and never—not ever—consider, not for one burning moment, marrying again. She would never be willing to step back into all that gut-wrenching emotional pain.

Now, as she sat there, remembering, feeling, trembling, she woke up, keenly aware that she had been falling in love with Patrick from the very beginning. Patrick was a man she could trust; a man she admired; a man she could open up to and share anything with, which, of course, she would have to do when he recovered. And besides all that, she was wildly attracted to him. Eve laughed a little. To think, she had to go all the way back to 1885 to find her one true love.

With her warmly affectionate eyes on him, her heart thrummed and opened, and in that inexpressible pang of love that no one fully understands, her heart blossomed. Her invisible arms reached out for him and embraced him.

And then there was a melting of anger and betrayal, and a thawing of old hurts, which ran off into splashing streams of happiness and joy. In that inexpressible and timeless moment, Eve felt truly good and soft again, and most of all, she felt an enthralling attraction and singing love for Patrick.

And at this moment, she knew, without any doubt, that Patrick's love for her was an always love; a love that would bridge any universe, any world or any time; a love that was eternal and rich and fragrant with possibilities, whether they moved to San Francisco in the

1880s or they managed to return to New York in the twenty-first century.

With moist eyes of gratitude, Eve pushed up, leaned over and kissed Patrick's moving, mumbling lips. He didn't stir.

Maybe it had all begun when Eve first read John Allister's Christmas Eve letter. She recalled again how loving it was, how it had stirred her emotions, making her sad that their love had ended so tragically. Yes, maybe it was the letter that had first begun to open her heart and launch her into a new beginning and a new possibility of falling in love.

"I'll be back in a few hours," she said to Patrick. "It's going to be okay, darling. Everything's going to be okay. Believe in love."

CHAPTER 31

Later that Monday morning, December 14th, the cab stopped at the curb of 232 East 9th Street and Eve emerged. She paid the driver and watched as the cab retreated along the cobblestones, soon lost in a foggy snowfall. The breath of the wind was like ice blowing across her determined face, and there were snow flurries falling, adding little to the four inches of snow already on the ground from a snowfall the night before.

Eve looked about vigilantly at the forlorn neighborhood, with its stacked and aging gray tenement row houses and cast-iron commercial factories, looking even more desolate and forgotten under the heavy gray metal sky.

Children hovered in doorways, their hollow-cheeked faces whipped up red by the cold, their sniffles heard five feet away. They stared back at her with a wary curiosity, their meager coats not up to the task of keeping them warm. As Eve advanced toward the front door, two dark-spirited men on the corner, wearing bowler hats and thread-bare coats, puffed cigars and measured her every step.

Inside the dingy, smoky hallway there was little warmth. A lone gas lamp hung on the wall, giving off feeble light, the flame flickering in a cold, drafty breeze. Eve heard the wind wheezing through cracks. She heard the cry of babies and smelled coal dust, which made her cough.

She lifted her skirt and started up the creaking stairs, seeing wide-eyed kids pop their heads from behind partially opened doors. She smiled at some and waved at others. None responded. On the fourth floor she turned left and walked across the ancient, worn carpet she'd recalled from her last visit, until she found the door that had a tarnished tin number 3 nailed to it. Eve recognized it.

She gathered herself, knocked lightly and waited, nerves wiggling her gloved fingers.

The door opened, squeaking on its rusty hinges. Standing before her, to her surprise, was Clayton Sharland.

"Clayton?" Eve asked.

Clayton gave her a welcoming smile. "Yes, Miss Kennedy. What a nice surprise. Please come in."

Eve did so, removing her winter bonnet and glancing about. She saw wooden crates, packed full with clothes, candles and books. She saw furniture stacked neatly near the door.

"I'm moving my mother out of here," Clayton said. "She's coming to live with me."

"I'm glad to hear it," Eve said. "Is she home?"

"She's in the back room packing up some last minute articles of clothing. I came last night and told her about Evelyn's miraculous recovery, that she was sitting up in bed, looking well and happy. I also told Mother that Evelyn had expressed an urgent desire to see her, to make amends. I urged Mother to visit Evelyn, if for no other reason than to keep the spirit of Christmas."

"That's good news, Clayton. I'm glad you're moving her out of this place."

"I should have done it long ago, but then we don't always do what we should. I am so grateful for all you have done, Miss Kennedy. Truly, I shudder to think what would have happened if you hadn't removed Evelyn from Dr. Begley's care. She surely would have died."

"Let's just hope that Evelyn is up and around for Christmas," Eve said, a little distractedly, as she scanned the room, looking for the lantern among the gathered items. She didn't see it.

Just then Mrs. Sharland emerged from the back room, still a thin woman, with her gray hair askew and her pale white dress smudged with dust and soot. When she saw Eve, she gave her a wonderful, sunshine smile that reduced her age by five years.

"Hello, Miss Kennedy," she said, stepping over to take Eve's hand.

Eve was a bit taken aback by the woman's transformation. The sullen bitterness, the low grinding speech of regret, anger and weary old age, were all replaced by kind eyes and a sweet soprano voice.

"It's so good to see you again," Eve said.

Mrs. Sharland patted her hair self-consciously. "I must look a mess. I have been packing since first dawn's light."

"You look very well," Eve said. "I'm so happy you're going to live with Clayton."

"You have been good to us, Miss Kennedy. Clayton told me what you did for Evelyn. He told me she is nearly whole again, and that is such a weight off my mind. I cannot say I understand why you have been so generous to us, Miss Kennedy, but I am thankful for your many kindnesses. If I can ever repay you in any way, please let me know."

"Well, actually, Mrs. Sharland, Evelyn wanted me to stop by to retrieve a lantern."

Mrs. Sharland paused in thought. "Lantern?"

"Yes. Evelyn said there was a lantern here. It has sentimental value to her. Have you seen it?"

"Oh, yes, of course, there was a lantern in the back closet."

Eve lifted to her full height. "Then it is here, Mrs. Sharland?" Eve said, hope rising in her chest and lifting her voice.

Mrs. Sharland turned toward the back room, a thoughtful finger to her lips. "Well, let me see now. Yes... at least it was."

She looked at Clayton. "Clayton, did you take those crates downstairs to the backyard trash?"

"Yes, Mother, an hour or so ago. I'm sure there was a lantern in the second crate. I remember seeing it."

Eve struggled for calm, turning to Mrs. Sharland. "Did you put it in one of those crates?"

Mrs. Sharland nodded. "Yes. I have not used it and I did not think Evelyn would want it."

Eve's voice took on urgency. "Then it's out back? Have they collected the garbage yet?"

"No, I do not believe so," Clayton said.

Eve swung around to the front door. "Excuse me, Mrs. Sharland. I need to get it. It's very important."

As Eve opened the door, Mrs. Sharland and Clayton exchanged puzzled glances.

"Wait, Miss Kennedy, I will go with you," Clayton called.

Eve descended the stairs and, on the first floor, she swung around the banister and down the back hallway until she came to an unlocked door. She pushed it open and stepped out into a backyard, with a leaning wooden fence and an alleyway to the right. Eve saw mounds of coal cinders, discarded brown beer bottles, and a broken carriage wheel, all partially covered by snow. She searched about, looking for the two crates, and she finally found them, pushed up against a back wall. She hurried over, just as Clayton emerged from the building and went to her.

"Do you see it?"

Eve rummaged through the crates, anxiously, searching, removing items and peering inside. But there was no lantern.

Eve shot Clayton a glance. "You do remember seeing it, don't you?" she asked.

Clayton leaned over. "Yes, it was in the second one here. On top."

Eve sighed, her breath smoking in the cold. "Damn!"

Clayton flashed her a surprised glance.

"Sorry, Clayton. Sometimes the modern woman in me comes out."

Clayton didn't know how to respond to that, so he said nothing. Eve placed her hands on her hips as she cast searching looks around the yard. She stepped over to the alleyway and peered up and down, seeing clotheslines stretched across the windows above her, and old dingy clothes blowing in the cold wind.

When she turned around to face Clayton, she saw a small, curly-blonde-haired girl emerge through the back door into the yard. She was no more than five or six years old, and she wore a thin woolen coat and a woolen cap. Eve's eyes widened. She froze on the spot, her heart in her throat. She saw the lantern! The little girl had gripped the handle and was dragging it across the ground, making a little path in the snow as she moved.

Eve hurried over, elated and fretful.

"Little girl... Little girl?"

The blonde-haired girl turned. She had a cherub-like face, with round blue eyes and a pouty mouth, as if she were irritated at being disturbed.

Eve moved closer, focusing hard on the lantern's detail. Yes, this was it. She was sure of it. It was twelve inches high, made of iron, and painted a greenish brown. There were four glass windowpanes with wire guards, and there was an anchor design on each side of the roof.

Eve smiled, entranced. How strange it was to see the lantern again back in its own time, knowing that someday, far into the future, it would wind up in *The Time Past Antique Shop*.

Emotions arose, urgency arose. She felt a wild longing to return to her own time and to escape forever from this place.

Eve sat on her haunches before the sulking little girl. Eve's eyes shifted first to the girl and then to the lantern, lying only inches away from her anxious grasp.

"Is that yours?" Eve asked.

The little girl nodded.

"Did you find it in the wooden crate over there?" Another nod.

Eve's breath sped up. "Have you lighted the lantern?" And then Eve held her breath, waiting.

The girl didn't move. Clayton had wandered over and was looking down at them both.

"Did you light it?" Eve asked, softly. Non-threateningly.

"I don't have a candle. Do you have one?"

Eve let out a breath of relief. What would have happened if the little girl *had* lighted the lantern? Would she have been transported off into another world? A better world? A world where this poor little girl would never be hungry again? Did the lantern's powers only have relevance to Evelyn Sharland and John Allister Harringshaw?

"I can get you a candle, little Miss," Clayton said, kindly.

"No!" Eve said, sharply. And then more softly. "I mean... Well, I have an idea. What is your name, Miss?"

The little girl hesitated. "Dora."

"Dora," Eve said. "Would you take a gold coin for the lantern?"

"I like the lantern. I want to light it," Dora said.

"Yes, it is a nice lantern, isn't it?"

Eve reached for her purse, took out her change purse and shook out a Liberty Head Double Eagle Head gold coin worth twenty dollars. She stretched her open hand toward Dora and smiled.

Clayton's eyes went round with astonishment. "Miss Kennedy. Forgive me, but that is a lot of money for a little girl."

Eve ignored him. "Dora, this coin can buy you many dresses and dolls and lots of goodies for Christmas. It's like a magic coin. Can I offer you this gold coin for that lantern?"

Dora stared at the coin in confused wonder. Then she looked at Eve with a puckered mouth and wiped an eye with her free hand.

Just then a tall, young, gaunt woman exited the building, throwing darting glances, obviously looking for her daughter. She spotted Dora, Eve and Clayton and she turned cautious and fretful, afraid Dora had gotten into some kind of mischief.

"Dora? I've been calling you."

Dora didn't look at her mother. She was caught between the practical item she still gripped in her left hand and the fascinating gold coin that lay on the outstretched hand before her.

The woman came over, her long, shabby, open coat flapping in the wind, snow flurries whipping across her pallid face. She grabbed and pinched her coat at the collar for warmth and stood near Clayton, calculating the situation.

Eve looked up at the woman, whose sad and suffering eyes touched Eve. She was so very thin and obviously cold, and surely hungry.

"Has Dora done anything wrong?" the mother asked.

"No," Eve said. "No, not at all. I want to purchase her lantern."

The woman's expression held questions as she stared down at Eve's open hand holding the twenty-dollar coin.

"She found it," the mother said. "She just found it in the trash."

"Yes, but *she* found it," Eve said, staring intently at Dora. "Dora found it. She is the owner now."

Eve closed her hand, reached into her change purse and took out a ten-dollar coin and added it to the twenty-dollar coin.

"It's another magic coin," Eve said, her face filled with wonder.

Eve wanted this little family to have the money. Yes, Eve wanted the lantern, but she also wanted this little girl and her mother to have a happy Christmas with plenty of food and presents.

Eve stretched out her hand again, now displaying two gold coins worth thirty dollars.

"Miss Kennedy!?" Clayton exclaimed.

"Dora... I offer you these two gold coins for the lantern. Take it or leave it."

Dora's face was filled with conflict. If Dora didn't accept her offer, Eve would have to go to Plan B, whatever that was. She hadn't come up with it yet.

Dora's mother had been guarded, but now with the real possibility of a sudden fortune, she grew suspicious and hopeful. "What are you trying to do, Miss?" she said to Eve, her voice quivering a little. "She found the lantern in the trash heap. It's not worth that kind of money. What do you want? That lantern is not worth anything."

"It's worth a lot to me," Eve said.

Eve fixed Dora with a pointed stare. "What do you say, Dora? The lantern or the magic, shiny gold coins?"

The mother was suddenly stung by a desperate need. She took a step forward. "Take the money, Dora," the woman said, in a sharp, desperate voice. "Do you hear me? Give her the lantern and take the money, girl. Take it!"

Dora was unmoving, still pondering.

The mother took two more aggressive steps forward to snatch the lantern from Dora's hand. Eve's loud voice stopped her.

"No... It's Dora's decision."

Dora's face slowly relaxed. "Are those really magic coins?" she asked.

Eve smiled. "Yes, Dora. They'll buy you many things, including a brand new lantern that you can light for Christmas."

Dora stared up into the gray, frosty morning and sighed. At last, she dragged the lantern forward, depositing it before Eve. "I'll take the magic coins," she said, her eyes now locked on them, already imagining far-off lands and sugar cookies and little pink fairies flying about her head.

"Open both hands," Eve said, with an open face, smiling brightly.

Dora did so, and Eve dropped first one, and then two coins into her pudgy hands.

Eve saw Dora's mother fight back tears and noted that the woman possessed a kind of subdued elegance that even poverty couldn't defeat.

With hopeful eagerness, Eve reached and took possession of the lantern, gripping it firmly. She climbed to her feet, feeling the weight of the lantern, feeling re-lief and optimism—and then new anxieties assaulted her. Once lighted, would it take her back to her own time? Would she be able to take Patrick with her so she could save his life?

Eve looked down at Dora, who was completely ab-sorbed in her magic coins, touching them, turning them and speaking to them in a strange language that only children know and understand.

"Merry Christmas, Dora," Eve said.

Dora looked up. "I like them. Merry Christmas."

Eve turned to Dora's mother, who straightened with dignity. Eve was impressed by her, by her fragile pride, her tears, and her obvious love for her daughter.

"Merry Christmas," Eve said, with kindness.

The woman didn't smile or speak. She just nodded.

Having what she'd come for, Eve said her goodbyes to Clayton and Mrs. Sharland and started back to the hospital.

CHAPTER 32

When Eve arrived back at the hospital, a telegram was waiting for her. To her revulsion, it was from Albert Harringshaw. She tore it open and read, feeling panicked and sick.

RETURNING EARLY. WILL ARRIVE TONIGHT, MONDAY, DECEMBER 14TH**.**
WILL PICK YOU UP FOR DINNER AT 7 P.M.
A. HARRINGSHAW

Eve angrily crushed the telegram and stuffed it into her pocket, her mind racing with ideas. Carrying the swinging lantern at her side, she marched down the corridor to Patrick's room, anxious to start the process of departure. It was time to escape from this time and place, and especially from Albert Harringshaw's grasp.

Eve was met by Dr. Long, whose face showed pinched urgency.

"Thank heaven you're back, Eve. There's been a carriage accident. Some children have been injured. Can you help us? Please come quickly."

Eve hesitated, looking first at the lantern and then toward Patrick's room.

"There is no change in Detective Gantly's condition, Miss Kennedy. Please hurry. Time is of the essence."

"Yes, of course. I'll be right there. I'll just change," Eve said, feeling the telegram like a fire burning in her pocket.

Eve slipped into Patrick's room. His face was flush with fever and he was delirious. Conflicted and agitated, she slipped the lantern under his bed and reached for a cold cloth that lay in a pan of water. She wiped his wet brow and face and spoke comforting and encouraging words. How much more of the fever and infection could he take? She couldn't wait another day to get him on antibiotics or it would be too late.

For the next six hours, until 5 p.m., Eve, Dr. Long and three other nurses helped to clean, dress and bandage various wounds, from head cuts and sprained ankles, to broken bones and lacerated tendons. They worked tirelessly, without a break, and when Eve finally glanced at the clock, her blood pressure shot up.

Albert Harringshaw would be waiting for her in two hours. Eve had to get Patrick prepared to leave the hospital. She'd been planning their escape, and it was now time to put those plans into action.

She figured she couldn't just light the lantern in his hospital room. If the lantern's light was effective, and if it did indeed return them to the twenty-first century, Eve had no way of knowing where they might land. Based on her first experience, they would be deposited in the same spot where they currently stood.

So where would that be? In someone's apartment? In a gift shop in the South Street Seaport Mall or on some street in the lower East Side? In a sewer, a subway track or an office building? She couldn't take that chance.

Her plan was to return to the same Central Park bench she'd been sitting on when she had first arrived. Eve knew for certain that the park bench existed in both times. If she and Patrick suddenly appeared on that bench, it would be dark, which would minimize the effect of their sudden appearance. So she had made the decision to bundle Patrick up, put him in an ambulance and travel to that same bench in Central Park.

Could she confide in Dr. Long? Eve came to the conclusion that she could not. Eve knew two beefy ambulance drivers, and she had solicited their help the night before. She'd told them she would have to move a patient, and that it was an emergency. Fortunately, they liked her and, because she paid them well, they didn't ask any questions.

Eve quickly changed into her street clothes, found a pencil and some paper, and scribbled down a note.

Dear Millie:

I'm going away and I'll never see you again. Enclosed is some money. Please spend it on something fun for yourself this Christmas. Thank you for all your help and for your warm friendship. I'll never forget you.

Affectionately, Eve Kennedy

Eve left the nurses' room and walked briskly down the hallway and up the stairs to Evelyn Sharland's room. Inside, she was surprised to find John Allister sitting by Evelyn's bed.

"Oh, excuse me," Eve said, peering into the room. "I didn't know you were here, Mr. Harringshaw."

He arose, smiling warmly. "Come in, Miss Kennedy. Please come in. Miss Sharland and I were just discussing you."

Reluctantly, feeling the weight of passing time, Eve stepped into the room and closed the door behind her. She leaned back against it.

"Discussing me? Oh, please, you must have more interesting subjects to talk about."

Evelyn smiled. "I was telling Allister, I mean Mr. Harringshaw, about your grand story—the one you told me about the magic lantern and the future."

Eve shifted her weight from one foot to the other. "Oh, that. Well, it was just a little something to entertain you, Miss Sharland."

"It was quite a fantastic story, Miss Kennedy. Evelyn told me some very specific things about your story that have intrigued me, one being that you said you lived in the year 2016 in an apartment uptown on West 107th Street. Of course that's all rural countryside up there, is it not?"

Eve smiled, faintly. "Yes, I suppose it is."

"Why did you specifically choose that year and use that address, Miss Kennedy?" John Allister asked, his expression deeply curious.

Eve shrugged. "Oh, who knows? I've always had too much of an imagination. It gets me into trouble sometimes."

"Did you know, Miss Kennedy, that Evelyn has a capital memory. She remembers the smallest thing, the minutest detail. That's one reason she was hired by Western Union, for her high and keen intelligence."

Eve smiled. "Yes, I can see that."

Evelyn looked at Eve carefully, with her crystal mint eyes. "Mr. Harringshaw told me, Eve, that he'd had several dreams about the night of the accident and they all included the lantern. By any chance, did you find it?"

Eve shrank a little in height, avoiding her eyes. She didn't want to lie, but she didn't have the time or the inclination to explain any further. "No... No, I didn't, unfortunately."

And then she was grateful to change the subject. "By the way, your mother is moving to Hoboken to live with Clayton."

Evelyn brightened. "Is she? Oh, how wonderful. Then you saw her and spoke to her?"

"Yes. Yes, she is much better. She'll be dropping by to see you. And I was just with Dr. Long. She said you'll be out of the hospital this week."

Evelyn sat up higher in the bed. "Yes, she stopped by earlier. I will be so happy to leave, even though you have all been so kind." She reached out her hand to Eve. "And what would have happened to me if you had not come along, Eve?"

Eve stepped over to the bed and took her hand. Evelyn squeezed Eve's hand and then peered deeply into her eyes.

"Wherever you came from, Eve, thank you for saving my life."

John Allister moved closer to Eve. "We are eternally grateful for what you have done for both of us."

Eve's voice was hesitant and low. "I will never forget you both."

"You will visit us at Christmas," Evelyn said. "You must. We will all be at Clayton's. Say you will come, Eve."

Eve looked at them both. "Of course I'll come. Thank you."

Eve left Evelyn's room and hurried down the stairs to the side entrance. Outside, she found Daniel Fallow and Jacob Jackson, the ambulance drivers, smoking cigars and leaning back against the box-like horse-drawn ambulance. Darkness had already dimmed the world, and the side lanterns on the ambulance glowed.

"Good evening, gentlemen."

They touched their bowler hats. "Miss Kennedy."

"Is it time?" Mr. Fallow, a broad stocky man, asked.

"Yes. Are you ready, gentlemen?"

Jacob Jackson had the face of a prize fighter, broad, blunt and serious. "We are, Miss Kennedy. Shall we follow you?"

As they strolled down the corridor toward Patrick's room, Eve prayed she didn't run into Dr. Long. Eve had already written a long letter to her, explaining that she had to return home. Eve thanked her for her many kindnesses and told her how much she had learned and how rewarding the experience had been. She closed with the sentence, "I shall always remember you fondly and with great affection."

Inside Patrick's room, the men worked slowly and carefully, wrapping him in woolen blankets and lifting him from his bed onto the wheeled stretcher. The corridor lights were low as they traveled quietly toward the side entrance, the men on either side of the stretcher, both looking grim, but determined. Eve gripped the lantern tightly in her right hand, surprised again by the weight of it, and by the potential power of it to change the course of history. She was a mass of nerves and, despite the cold, she felt perspiration pop out on her forehead and run down her back.

They were almost at the side entrance, almost there, when Eve heard a door creak open. She heard footsteps in the hall behind her. Eve did not stop or turn around. She kept walking, her head inclined forward, eyes fixed on the looming door, her stride lengthening, as if her very life depended on it, which, in many ways, it did.

Outside, the air was crisp and cold. Feathery snowflakes fell across the glow of gas lights. A lamplighter had just finished lighting a lamp off to their right, his long wooden pole extended over the gaslight. Daniel and Jacob tugged the two rear ambulance doors open, lifted Patrick from the stretcher onto a waiting gurney, and slid him gently inside the enclosed space.

Eve's impatient gaze surveyed the area, as she wondered if Albert Harringshaw was still having her watched. She didn't see anyone. The night was eerily quiet and, as she turned back to the hospital for a last look, the building was dark and heavy with shadows. Just a few lights flickered in the windows.

Jacob turned to her. "We're ready, Miss Kennedy. Will you be riding in the back?"

"Yes, Jacob."

He held the doors open for her and Daniel took her hand and lifted her up into the cab where she sat on a wooden bench, looking down at Patrick. He shivered and mumbled in misery, but Eve didn't understand a word.

Eve shuddered when Jacob slammed the two doors shut. It was cold. Her teeth began to chatter, and her breath puffed white clouds of vapor.

Both men sat up front, two hunched figures with cigars clenched in their teeth, Jacob shaking the reins. As the ambulance trotted off into the night across the damp and shimmering cobblestones, Eve felt the old loneliness return, as if she were one of the last people on Earth, again wandering off toward an unknown fate. What in the world would she do if the lantern's light failed to return her and Patrick home to safety? Patrick would die, and she would have to flee somewhere, away from Albert Harringshaw's and Inspector Byrnes' trap. San Francisco? Ohio?

She sat heavily on the bench, staring blindly in the dim light, praying for Patrick, praying for help, praying for release and praying for a new life with Patrick in the twenty-first century. That was the thought that quickened her heart and gave her hope. A new life in her own time. How delightful and fun it would be to show Patrick all the wonders of the twenty-first century. She was sure he'd be excited by the technology, the many freedoms, the cars, the airplanes and the food.

When he was fully recovered, their relationship could pick up where they'd left off and they would fall in love again and, this time, they'd be free to play, explore and express all the emotions and desires denied them in 1885. They could get to know each other, like true lovers, and they would fall in love again, just as they had fallen in love before.

Eve's concerned eyes lowered on him. "Hang on, Patrick. Just hang on a little while longer, my love. We're almost there."

CHAPTER 33

In Central Park, the ambulance angled left, progressing at a slow, steady pace through circles of lamplight and falling snow, looking like a dark apparition. It approached The Poet's Walk at the southern end of The Mall, and Eve felt an eager restlessness. They were almost there. She touched the lantern and checked her coat pocket to make sure she had matches.

When the ambulance carriage stopped, Eve took a quick breath to fortify her beating nerves. The double doors swung open and Jacob and Daniel stood at the ready, cigars sticking from the sides of their mouths.

"Ready, Miss Kennedy?"

"Yes."

Daniel helped her down, and she stood aside, holding the lantern with a woolen blanket over her arm. They stood on either side and reached for the gurney. Before hefting it, they turned to Eve for further instructions.

Eve glanced about. Fortunately, it was relatively quiet, with just a few strollers out enjoying the magic of the snowfall. A carriage passed and faded.

Eve pointed left. "Take him to that park bench over there."

Jacob and Daniel exchanged uncertain glances.

"To the bench, Miss Kennedy?" Daniel clarified.

"Yes. Please hurry."

Jacob shrugged and the two men retrieved the stretcher and followed Eve across the broad dirt and snow-covered path toward the empty park bench that was situated about ten feet from the nearest park lamp. The bench was silhouetted and covered by a thin layer of new snow.

Eve stopped by the bench, brushed away the snow and spread out the blanket.

"Sit Detective Gantly here, please."

Again the men exchanged glances.

"Please, gentlemen."

They first lowered the gurney onto the ground. The men stood on either side of Patrick's shoulders and then gingerly lifted him, while Eve reached and secured the woolen blanket he was wrapped in. Patrick was lowered down onto the blanket in a sitting position. Already his lips were turning blue. Both men stared at him with some compassion and, inevitably, both their gazes turned to Eve. Their expressions were bleak and confused.

"I know how this looks, gentlemen, but it isn't what you think. Could you please drive the ambulance a short distance away and wait for me? If I don't come for you within fifteen minutes, please return to the hospital."

Daniel looked about into the cold, snowy night. Jacob shoved his hands into his pockets and stamped his feet for warmth.

Jacob spoke up. "Miss Kennedy, are you sure you want to stay out here like this? Mr. Gantly looks poorly and you could catch your death."

"It's okay. You can go now. Like I said, if you don't see me in fifteen minutes, leave for the hospital."

She opened her purse to take out two ten dollar coins.

Both men held up their hands in refusal.

Daniel said, "No thank you, Miss Kennedy. You've already paid us handsomely. God's speed and Merry Christmas."

Both men tipped their hats, paused a few seconds, then turned and returned to the carriage.

She watched as it lurched ahead and gathered speed. It stopped about ten yards away, but it was only a shadow in the distance, blurred by the scrim of falling snow.

Now that it was time to light the lantern, Eve didn't move. She was suddenly paralyzed with terror and doubt. She looked down at Patrick in a pleading way, feeling foolish, feeling trapped, feeling such raw emotion that it sickened her.

Then she heard bells—the shaking of little crystal bells—the persistent rhythm of bells. She heard a high peel of laughter and when she saw the one-horse sleigh approach, she could scarcely believe it. In awe—with the wondrous eyes of a child—she watched as a sleek, silver, one-horse open sleigh, whose runners were curved up artfully, slid by. A woman dressed in a red cap, her hands tucked in a white muff, had thrown her head back and was laughing gleefully. A bearded man was at the reins, dressed in a fur-lined coat and hat, sitting tall and happy. It jingle-belled off into the night, like a positive Christmas omen.

The festive spectacle helped to break Eve's troubled mood. Alive with a new purpose, she reached into her pocket for the matches. She pulled one out. It was about two inches long. Very carefully, Eve lifted a glass panel on the lantern, took a breath and struck the match on the rough wooden surface of the park bench. It caught, flared and fizzled. Eve swallowed and reached for another. She struck it and cupped her head over the flame to protect it from the wind and snow. But before she could insert it into the lamp, it vanished in a string of smoke shredded by the wind.

Eve cursed and reached for another. She only had three more. This time she struck the match closer to the lantern, but the match didn't catch. After striking the match for the third time, she gave up.

Patrick's face was now the color of snow. His lips were a pale blue, and he was calling out incoherently.

With her breath smoking rapidly, Eve reached for the second-to-last match. She leaned her body close to the bench and to the lantern to protect the flame. In an aggressive motion, she swiped the match lightly against the surface. A spark ignited. The match flashed and burned. Nearly frantic, Eve cupped the flame and slowly guided it through the open glass panel toward the wick. She held her breath as the wick and the light met. Another sharp wind blew, and the flame flickered and danced. Eve held the match steady, her hand trembling, her eyes fixed and wide.

Suddenly, the wick caught—a feeble light, struggling for life. Eve's breath caught as she willed the little light to grow, and she watched and prayed and coaxed it on.

A glorious buttery glow grew and expanded, and the light spilled out into the hectic night, illuminating Patrick's face like a blessing. Eve nearly fell into grateful tears, clasping her hands together in a thankful answer to prayer. Then she quickly wrapped both arms about Patrick's shoulders and pulled him into her, pressing him as close as her strength would allow.

Snow fell, whipped by an erratic wind. Eve stared at the lantern, holding Patrick tight, her eyes expectant. She waited and waited. Nothing happened. How long had it been? Seconds? Minutes?

And then Eve was aware that someone was approaching. She snapped her head left. It was Jacob Jackson. He was twenty feet away. Eve turned desperately to the lantern. She spoke to it, pleading with it.

When she turned again to Jacob, something had happened to her vision. He seemed to be walking in slow motion. He lifted his right arm as if to wave, but it was sluggish, vague and out of focus.

And then the ground fell away and swallowed her. She was tossed into an unraveling silky black hole where there was no high or low, no left or right. She called out for Patrick, and when she saw him, his face was bobbing in and out of yellow light, making him look grotesque, like something from a horror movie. Then he disappeared. She saw spinning lights, like millions of lightning bugs, blinking on and off, circling her, boosting her up and then slinging her off into what felt like vast distances. She heard wind chimes and soft distant music, and there was a dog barking somewhere far below, and then it was gone in a fading echo.

She was riding a turgid, charging wave—wave after thundering wave—sailing, flying, reaching out for anything to grab onto as she was propelled through currents of cold and hot winds, through sounds of battle, through narrow, inky caves.

She called again to Patrick, but her thin voice only came back to her in cries of anguish, then faded into bird song, the sound of the sea, the sound of thunder. Eve strained her eyes to see but saw only blackness and flickering light miles off in the distance, spinning, whirling, spheres of light whizzing by.

And then her nose was assaulted by sweet-smelling flowers, the rich pungent smells of earth and the stinging taste of mint.

Then everything stopped. Motionless. Black. Coldness. Dead silence. Eve felt for balance, but there was nothing to grab or hold on to.

Through a blinding blue light, Eve became aware of the vague outline of a shape advancing toward her. She heard a voice—high and reedy—like a clarinet. It came closer, its sound growing more pleading and urgent.

Eve was cold—cold to the bone. Trembling. Shivering. Teeth chattering.

In her narcotic consciousness, she forced her eyes wide open, struggling to focus on the shape before her, struggling to find an anchor, a solid reality.

"You need help?" a voice said.

Eve looked up as the form slowly began to take on a definite shape. It was a man or a boy. He was squinting down at her.

"Whaaa?" was all she could manage to say. Her tongue seemed twice its size and her lips felt like they'd been shot with Novocain.

"Do you need help or somethin'? That dude next to you don't look so good. He's like all shiverin' and stuff."

"Dude?" Eve asked.

"Yeah… He's like all messed up on something. You both drunk or somethin'?"

Eve blinked away her blurry vision and suddenly everything cleared. She jolted awake with surprise, looking around, dazed but present. It was dark and snowing, and it was cold. People were streaming by, a kid on a skateboard, a couple playfully having a snow-ball fight.

Standing before her was a concerned young black man in his twenties. He wore a Yankee's baseball cap, a bright red parka, jeans, and blue Keds sneakers. He was holding a cell phone with headphones around his neck.

Eve's attention shifted to her right. It was Patrick! He was there. She looked left. The lantern was gone.

"Do you need some help, girl? I'm tellin' you, he don't look good to me at all. If I was you, I'd get him to a hospital. He shouldn't be out here in this cold."

Eve shot up, then wobbled on shaky legs. She was still dizzy. She dropped back down hard on the bench. She touched her head, as if to keep it from falling from her shoulders. "Yes, yes! Thank you. Yes, please. Call 911."

CHAPTER 34

In the ambulance, Eve sat nervously watching while two paramedics prepared Patrick for the Emergency Room. As the siren wailed and the snow flew past the windows, the paramedics placed Patrick on oxygen and began IV therapy, already better medicine than he could have ever received in 1885. Next she asked them the question that had been burning in her ever since she had awakened on the park bench. What day and year was it? Had she lived in 1885 in parallel time to 2016, day-to-day and week-to-week?

When Eve tentatively asked them about the day and year, they looked up briefly, their expressions contorted in concentration. They saw her still startled eyes and wondered if she was in shock.

The taller Hispanic man answered. "It's Monday, December 14th."

"And it's two thousand sixteen?" Eve asked.

Both paramedics gave her another once over and spoke at the same time. "Yes."

The younger one asked, "Are you all right?"

"Yes," Eve said, almost at a whisper.

Eve then informed them that she was a nurse and clearly communicated Patrick's history: an accidental gunshot wound that had turned into blood poisoning. He'd taken no antibiotics. He was trying to heal himself homeopathically. They looked at her sympathetically and doubtfully, but promptly conveyed all the information to the awaiting ER.

Next, Eve borrowed a paramedic's cell phone and called a doctor friend, Dr. Simon Wallister, who had privileges at Mt. Sinai Hospital, where the ambulance was headed. She asked him to call the hospital to help bypass the usual entry/insurance forms and fast-track Patrick to emergency treatment.

Eve was aware that she would have to file a police report, since, by law, every gunshot wound had to be reported. She quickly worked to come up with a plausible story to tell them.

Then there would be a flurry of questions by doctors, and insurance forms to fill out, and friends to call, and family to call, and colleagues to call, and more explanations and more forms to be filled out, and even more questions about Patrick Gantly. After all, he didn't exist anywhere; he was not in any database anywhere on the entire planet. He didn't have a social security number; he'd never worked, never owned property, never had a credit card and never had any identification of any kind. He'd never attended any school, college or university. He didn't have any family or friends— except Eve—and there was no record of his birth. According to the twenty-first century, Detective Sergeant Patrick Gantly simply didn't exist. He had, for all intents and purposes, just been born, except that he had no parents.

How would she explain this to the police, her friends and her family? Welcome back to the twenty-first century, Eve thought. She'd just jumped out of one hot frying pan into another.

Eve decided to call Joni, her perky, red-headed dancer friend and dog walker, but as she entered the number, she felt a fluttering unease and anticipation building in her stomach. Had Joni taken Georgy Boy and cared for him all these weeks? Eve had been worried sick about her dog ever since she'd vanished. She'd managed to push Georgy Boy mostly out of her mind for days, but now the full force of angst hit her.

Joni picked up on the third ring. The paramedic's number wasn't on Joni's contact list, and when she answered, her voice was low and wary.

"Hello? Who is this?"

Eve steadied herself.

"Hello? Who's calling? Who is this?" she said, more forcefully.

"Joni… it's Eve."

Dead silence.

"It's Eve, Joni. It is."

"Eve?!" Joni said, her voice filled with shock. "Eve? What the hell? Where the hell?"

"Joni," Eve said, calmly. "I'm okay. I'm fine."

"Where are you?" Joni demanded. "What the hell happened to you? We've been worried sick!"

"Look, I'll explain everything later. Right now, I need you to listen to me."

"We thought you were dead, for God's sake. Everybody was looking for you: the police, the…"

Eve cut her off. "Joni, please just listen. Do you have Georgy Boy?"

"Yes. Yes, of course. He's fine. He misses you, but he's fine."

Eve sighed out relief. "Okay, good. And my parents? Are they all right?"

"Yes, worried sick, of course, but they're good."

"Okay, now listen. I need you to meet me at Mt. Sinai Hospital."

"Oh God, are you okay? Are you sick? Hurt?"

"No, no. I'm fine. Joni, I need money, credit cards and a phone."

"I've got them. I've got your wallet and your phone. The police sent them to your parents, but they sent them back to me, thinking you might show up and need them. Your father said that. I just can't believe all this. I can't believe it's really you."

"Who found my wallet and my phone, Joni?"

"Some man found them on a park bench in Central Park when you disappeared back in late October, and he called the police. Long story short, I've got them."

"Okay, great. Bring them and meet me as fast as you can. I'll explain everything then."

Eve handed the phone back to the preoccupied paramedic and settled back into her seat, gazing down at Patrick, worried, her arms folded. After all, they'd been through, would he survive? Would the antibiotics save him or was it too late?

Eve felt utterly and completely exhausted. She needed rest and a good week's sleep, away from the stress of the last few weeks. She hadn't had one really good night's sleep since her journey to 1885. As her eyes slowly closed, she saw an image of Patrick standing next to her in that dark hospital room. What had he said?

"We know all we need to know, Eve Kennedy. We will touch, and I promise you we will certainly kiss... and we will love. I will never stop loving you, whether you agree to marry me or not."

Eve shut her eyes and tried to shut off her mind. Yes, what she needed most now was rest. But she couldn't rest, not until Patrick was stabilized and out of danger.

INSIDE THE EMERGENCY ROOM, Patrick was swiftly wheeled into a private room, as per Dr. Wallister's orders, given a thorough examination, and then immediately placed on IV antibiotics.

Eve lingered by his bedside for a time, waiting for Joni. Fortunately, Eve was acquainted with one of the attending nurses, who helped delay the inevitable paperwork and registration until Joni arrived with Eve's wallet and credit cards.

The two friends met in the hallway, just outside Patrick's room. Joni fell into Eve's arms, tears streaming down her face. They hugged and cried and stepped out of the way of rolling stretchers and busy nurses.

They found a waiting room with orange and blue chairs and collapsed into them. Eve studied her friend, her coppery page boy cut, the heavy makeup and the ruby red lips.

"I had an audition just before you called," Joni said, wiping tears and mascara from her eyes. "I rushed right over."

Joni leaned back, taking Eve in, looking her up and down and shaking her head in astonishment. "Look at you. Where did you come from? Where did you get that dress? It's a beauty. It's a better costume than I've seen in some Broadway shows."

In all the chaos, Eve had forgotten she was still wearing her 1885 bustle dress. It was bottle green velvet, with the skirt gathered up in the front with a series of scallops, and the front trimmed with a maroon bow.

Eve looked down at it. "Oh God, I forgot."

"Have you been in a play or making a movie or something?" Joni asked, completely baffled.

"No, no. I'll tell you the whole story someday. Right now I need to call my parents, meet with the police... and..."

Joni's eyes opened wide. "The police? What the hell happened, Eve?" Joni said, holding up the flat of her hand, like a stop sign, her face set in serious anticipation. "And don't tell me you'll tell me later. What happened to you? The whole thing is just weird. Tell me. Now."

But just then, two NYPD detectives started over, wearing unbuttoned topcoats, dark suits and dark ties. The hospital had already contacted them. Eve knew they were detectives; they had that stony, world-weary look about them. She quickly flashed back to the visit with Inspector Byrnes and Detective Sergeant Doyle, when they burst into Patrick's room and threatened her. Was it only the night before? Yes. It seemed like weeks ago, and now that she was back in her world, it seemed like nothing more than a very bad nightmare. But seeing the two detectives approach brought some fear of that nightmare back.

Both girls stood, and Eve tried to appear calm and brave, despite feeling dizzy and disoriented. The two officers gave Eve a puzzled look as they viewed her dress and her hairstyle. Then their eyes cleared as they turned to business.

They'd seen it all and heard it all. Eve's 1880s bustle dress, by comparison to what they had seen and experienced just in the last twenty-four hours, made them only mildly curious.

"It's going to have to wait," Eve told Joni.

Joni swallowed as she timidly faced the detectives. She then turned to Eve. "What have you been doing, Eve?" Joni said, with a fretful shake of her head.

The detectives introduced themselves and presented their badges.

"Hello, detectives," Eve said softly, as she thought about Patrick fighting for his life in the ER. He'd been a policeman, too, and a damn good one at a time when many had been corrupt.

These detectives gave her half smiles and spoke crisply, but respectively.

"Miss Sharland?"

"Yes."

"We have some questions for you regarding the man, a Patrick Gantly, you brought to the hospital. We understand he suffered a gunshot wound?"

"Yes."

Speechless, Joni eased back down in her chair, shaking her head, mumbling to herself, while Eve and the detectives went to a private corner of the waiting lounge.

Eve had known this interview was coming, and she had fabricated a story. Patrick had been cleaning his gun when it accidently went off.

"Were you present at the time the incident happened?"

"No."

"Are you in possession of the gun?"

"No."

She told them she'd angrily thrown it into the Hudson River. She'd never wanted Patrick to own a gun. She'd told him this kind of thing could happen. Eve babbled on, explaining how Patrick had thought natural remedies would heal the wound even though she, as a nurse, had been strongly against it. He ignored her. What could she do?

"What were you both doing in Central Park when he was obviously so sick?" a detective asked.

Eve said they were going to a Christmas party, an 1880s style Christmas party, when he fainted. A man nearby called 911.

Eve knew the detectives didn't entirely believe her, but they had all they needed for the time being. They said they'd follow up. Finally, they asked her for Patrick's entire name and date of birth. Eve had them ready. They nodded and left, one shaking his head and the other chuckling. This would be a good story to tell the guys back at the precinct.

Before leaving the hospital for home, Eve spoke to Patrick's doctor. It was too early for any positive change, of course, but that didn't stop her from asking, anyway.

Eve stood by Patrick's bedside, with Joni beside her.

"Who is he?" Joni whispered.

A frown consumed Eve's lower face. "Just a guy... Just a guy I met a very long time ago and fell in love with."

THEY STOPPED BY JONI'S APARTMENT to retrieve Georgy Boy. When he saw Eve, he barked, jumped and charged for her. Eve froze, startled by his appearance. This wasn't her Georgy Boy! Hers was white with black spots. This dog had large brown spots on his back, and his ears were completely brown. This was not Georgy Boy!

But the dog burst forward and came to her in a rush. Eve dropped to her knees, took him up in her arms and embraced him, burying her face in his soft fur, while he licked and whined with happiness. His scent was the same, his body the same; his spirit was the same, joyful and playful. He rolled over and let her rub his belly, just as her Georgy Boy had always done.

Eve looked up at Joni, her eyes filled with questions. "When did Georgy Boy's ears turn brown?"

"What do you mean? They've always been brown."

"Are you sure this is Georgy Boy?"

Joni stared with concern. "Eve... are you sure you're all right? You're acting a whole lot weird here. Of course it's Georgy Boy."

Eve rubbed the dog's belly as his tail flopped about in happiness, his eyes filled with bliss.

"Look at him, Eve, he's in heaven. His mom and best friend are back."

Eve felt wedged between worlds, half in this one and still half in the other, not fully present in either, each thought suspect, each footstep testing the new earth. She smiled down at Georgy Boy, as he rolled and whimpered with delight.

Eve looked at Joni, long and steadily. Could it be that Eve had changed something in the past that had somehow changed the present?

Yes, Eve thought, I did something—something so small, so seemingly insignificant and undetectable that it changed Georgy Boy's color. How utterly strange. She stared with cold speculation, feeling a shiver of dread. What else had she changed? What else would she discover had changed in the days to come?

Joni's voice was soft with unease. "Eve, you look tired. You need to sleep. Do you want me to go back to your apartment with you?"

Eve felt comforted by Joni's presence, always a sure thing from her pre-time travel days. "Yes," she said. "I'd appreciate that."

Joni gathered Georgy Boy's bowls and leash and food and checkered bed, while Eve and Georgy Boy sat together on the floor getting reacquainted.

IN THE CAB, JONI TOLD the driver the destination. "West 107th between Broadway and Riverside."

They rode in silence, Eve relaxed a little, smiling gently as she watched her world go by, her New York of 2016, the one she loved and was so glad to have returned to.

Half way down the block, Joni spoke to the driver. "The next building on the left," she told him.

The cab drew up to the curb—Eve's brownstone loomed outside. Eve ventured a look and goose bumps popped out on her arms. God, no. It was different. The building was changed. The number was the same, but the building itself was now a rosy brownstone and it stood next to a set of quaint row houses that had not been there seven weeks ago. Eve was certain, positive. It *was* different.

Eve sat back, blinking. She had to accept that the world she'd once lived in had changed, and she was the one who had somehow changed it. She swallowed away a lump and straightened. What else had she changed? What world had she returned to?

Joni paid the driver, pushed open the door and Georgy Boy piled out of the cab, running to the entrance of the brownstone. Joni and a reluctant Eve followed. As Joni unlocked the front door, Eve glanced up and down the street, wondering which of her neighbors she would still know.

She haltingly followed Joni and Georgy Boy up the winding stairs, startled again when they didn't stop on the second floor, but ascended another flight. Evidently, she now lived on the third floor.

After Joni opened the door to her third-floor apartment, Eve nearly shouted out when she realized the layout of the apartment was the same—exactly the same as when she'd left it. All her things were there: the blue throw rug in the hallway; the green tea kettle in the kitchen; the fireplace and chair and end table in the living room; the picture of her parents on the wall and—thankfully—they did indeed look like her parents. Eve rushed into the bedroom: those were *her* clothes in the closet, *her* shoes near the chest of drawers, *her* bedspread and pillows on the bed.

She dropped down on her bed and bounced, sighing out relief. She wanted to cry and laugh all at once. Instead, she teetered over on the bed and shut her eyes, exhausted, but grateful to finally be home.

Joni ordered pizza while Eve showered, letting the deliciously hot water flow freely over her head and down her back, scrubbing herself vigorously, trying to wash off weeks of pent-up frustration and anxiety. She still felt caught between worlds, between thought and emotion, between her love for Patrick and her fear of losing him. She felt edgy and scared, wondering what stark and dramatic changes were waiting for her in the future.

Eve and Joni drank red wine, ate pizza, and talked—but not about Eve's experiences. Every time Joni probed, Eve would say she'd been lost in some weird dream and couldn't talk about it yet. Joni looked skeptical. Eve knew she was disappointed to be kept in the dark, but Eve was too tired, unsteady and preoccupied to come up with anything better. She was grateful when Joni left.

Although she was utterly exhausted, Eve made the call to her parents—a call she'd been dreading. She'd thought long and hard about what she was going to say. She would be waking them up, since it was now almost 2 a.m., but she didn't want to wait until morning. And besides, she had something important to talk to her father about.

Eve sat up in bed, with Georgy Boy lying beside her, his chocolate brown eyes staring up at her worshipfully, his tail sporadically flicking from side to side.

"You're my same little boy, aren't you?" she whispered. His spirit was definitely the same inside that differently colored body.

Eve tapped her parents' number and waited. Her mother's sleepy voice answered.

Eve quickly told her that she was home and that she was fine. As expected, Mrs. Sharland was all emotion, tears and blame. Eve calmed her down the best she could, telling her that for the past seven weeks, she'd been involved in a top secret medical experiment.

Her mother lashed out again and Eve waited with weary patience until her mother's emotion finally ran out and Eve could apologize for not getting in touch.

And then Eve's father came on the line and it all started again. He demanded to know the how, who, what, where and when of this *so-called* medical experiment. He growled and shouted about how he and other FBI field investigators, and not a few policemen, had been out searching for Eve for weeks, and they had come up with nothing. How was that possible? They were seasoned professionals.

Eve's preparation helped. Her father was an FBI man and he knew about secret projects.

"I'll be able to tell you all about it someday, Dad, but not right now. All I can say is that it was top secret and it was for a good cause."

Still, he rumbled on until finally Eve stopped him with the phrase she knew would work. Eve's father had always loved and worshipped her, and she knew he would do anything for her.

"Dad, I need your help."

He abruptly stopped talking. When he spoke again, his voice was filled with sudden urgency. "Help? What's the matter? Are you in some kind of trouble? What kind of help?"

Eve had been carefully composing what she was about to say for many hours.

"I'm fine. Everything's fine. Dad… Listen, I need you to do me a big favor. I need you to create an identity for someone."

There was a long, cold silence.

When her father spoke, his voice was flat and filled with worry. "Evelyn Aleta Sharland, what have you done?"

Wow! Her full name. Now she was in *big* trouble. Her father hadn't used her full name in years.

"Have you had some wild affair with a diplomat's son off in some other part of the world?"

"No, Dad... Nothing like that. Look, I can't you tell right now, but I promise I will tell you someday. But for now, please trust me and please help me do this. It is extremely important. Will you help me?"

AFTER EVE HUNG UP, waves of fatigue rolled over her. She switched off the electric light—yes, the wonderful electric bedside light—tugged the creamy down quilt up to her neck and was soon drifting off into a deep, silky sleep. She felt Georgy Boy nuzzle his cold nose into her right ear, just like he always had. Then he let out a long, ragged sigh. Eve smiled, her hand lazily stroking Georgy Boy's head, and then she floated off to sleep and dreamed that Patrick was sitting at the foot of the bed, smiling.

"Don't worry, Miss Kennedy. I'm here. I'll protect you. By the way, will you marry me?"

CHAPTER 35

Patrick blinked around his hospital room in blank astonishment. His eyes cleared and sharpened as he took in the beeping monitors with their bright flashing numbers and squiggly lines of peaks and valleys. The IV drip was still in his arm. He stared at it, alarmed and baffled.

Where was he? What had happened? Was he dead? Then he saw her enter his room. Eve!

Eve smiled at him, her eyes lighting up with joy when she saw he was awake.

"Hey there, Patrick. Wassup?"

He squinted at her. What did she say? Was it really Eve? It was her hair that first startled him. Her glossy blonde locks were styled in a chic messy bob, parted at the side. She wore tight designer jeans, a tight-fitting red sweater, long hoop earrings and two-inch heels.

Eve sashayed toward him, her face glowing with happiness. Patrick tried to speak, but nothing came out.

She drew up to his bedside, looking down at him with warm blue eyes.

"Feeling more like yourself?" she asked.

He tried to speak again and failed. He just kept staring up at her. Her presence surrounded him like some feverish dream.

"Myself? Where am I?" he finally said.

"Mt. Sinai Hospital in New York City."

He looked her over again, his drowsy eyes still trying to take it all in. "I don't understand... Your clothes, Miss Kennedy. Your hair. What has happened to you?"

Eve posed, with a hand on her hip. "Do you like my new look? I did it all for you, so you could see me as I really am."

He stared, straining to understand. "I don't know you, Miss Kennedy."

She reached and touched his hair. "Yes, you do, Patrick. It's the same ole me, just packaged a little differently."

He held her eyes for a time. "Yes, yes... your eyes are the same."

"I *am* the same, Patrick. Just the same. You've been sick for a long time."

He quietly, politely studied her. "You are quite attractive, Miss Kennedy."

"And you look better today than you have for a very long time."

Eve turned serious. "Do you remember anything, Patrick, about what happened?"

"Just pieces of dreams. Odd dreams," he said, inspecting his room. "What is all this? All these things? I don't understand all this."

"Just relax, Patrick. I'll tell you everything when you're better."

"What day is it?"

"Saturday, December 19th."

He lowered his gaze. "So much time has passed."

Eve thought, *You have no idea.*

He looked at her, expectant. "When can I leave and return home?"

"Tomorrow morning you will be discharged to my care."

His eyes were vague and large. "Your care?"

He thought about it. "Well, there is something intimately pleasant about that, Miss Kennedy."

Eve found a chair, tugged it to his beside and sat down. She looked at him earnestly.

"Patrick, I think the time is finally right for me to tell you the truth about myself: where I came from and who I truly am. It is a bizarre story—even an unbelievable story—but while I'm telling you, I want you to look deeply into my eyes. You know me well now. We have been through a lot together. You will know from my eyes that what I'm going to tell you is the truth. The absolute truth."

Eve's heart was already beating rapidly. After Patrick heard the truth, would he still be in love with her? Would he feel trapped, as she had felt in 1885?

"You sound quite melodramatic, Miss Kennedy. Please tell your story. I have been waiting for this for a very long time."

And so Eve told him everything, leaving out nothing, including the fact that Patrick Gantly was now living in the year 2016.

Patrick did gaze into Eve's beautiful blue eyes as she told her story, honestly and methodically. He saw a clear, strong force in her eyes and, whenever she mentioned him by name, he saw warmth and tenderness. He saw desire. These are what moved him most about Eve Kennedy's outlandish and ridiculous tale of time travel, and how he was now living in the twenty-first century, in the year 2016.

Patrick didn't know why Eve felt it necessary to fabricate such a story, but most of him didn't care, and a lot of him still felt weak and confused and, frankly, uninterested.

It was Eve who enthralled him—richly captivated him—by her graceful gestures, her contralto voice that seemed to vibrate deep into his chest, and her lovely, animated face that was at times serious, at times eager, but always so very pretty, with those glistening, tender red lips that he longed to kiss.

When Eve finished, she sat back, waiting for his response, trying to read his impassive face. Patrick gave her that devastating, lopsided, cocky grin that she had always found irresistible. How she wanted to climb on top of him and kiss it until it vanished.

"So?" Eve asked. "So now that you know everything, what do you think?"

He shrugged his left shoulder. "To be honest, Miss Kennedy, I..."

She cut him off. "Stop calling me Miss Kennedy. My name is Evelyn Aleta Sharland."

He raised an eyebrow. "As you say, then, Miss Sharland."

Eve sighed, shaking her head in frustration. "Whatever. What do you think? What do you think about my story, Patrick?"

"Miss Sharland," Patrick continued. "It was a lovely and entertaining story, but we still have to leave New York. Inspector Byrnes and Albert Harringshaw will not rest until we are under lock and key, or dead. I suggest that you manage my immediate release so that we can book passages on the first ship to San Francisco."

Eve stared at him intensely, her eyes blinking fast. "You don't believe me? I mean, you didn't believe a word I said, did you?"

"Miss Sharland, Eve, it was a highly imaginative story, but stories will not help us escape to San Francisco."

Eve stood up and began pacing the room, thinking. She stopped and turned, suddenly, facing him.

"Detective Sergeant Gantly, I will be back tomorrow morning and you will be discharged. In the meantime, think about everything I've told you, because unless you believe me, tomorrow you're going to have quite a shock."

THE NEXT MORNING, Eve brought Patrick new underwear, a T-shirt, khaki pants, a red and green flannel shirt, blue and white sneakers, and a brown leather jacket, all purchased the day before at Bloomingdale's. He'd stared at them apprehensively, but he put them on, carefully, silent and watchful, still feeling shaky and dazed. He gazed at himself in the mirror for a long time, his face passing from confusion to curiosity.

He sat in a wheelchair and was rolled down the hall by a tall, pleasant black man, whose speech Patrick was fascinated by, as he kept cocking his ear whenever the man used his colorful slang. Eve accompanied Patrick down the corridor, into the elevator, and out into the wide, lower lobby that led to Fifth Avenue. Eve watched Patrick closely, as tension, surprise and fear began to grip him. His body tightened as he became absorbed and worried.

He saw all ethnic types pass, people with cell phones pressed to their ears, dressed casually, young women in tight jeans, low blouses and high skirts. Christmas music was everywhere, emanating from some upper distant heavenly realm, and Patrick kept tilting back his head, trying to locate the source.

Christmas lights blinked, children were loud, no one was smoking in the building and the modern architecture was distracting and disorienting. He saw open laptops, eReaders and women in bright orange and blue hair. He glanced up at Eve with wide, troubled eyes, seeking any explanation. She ignored him, a slight smile pasted on her lips.

And then they passed through the wide glass automatic door to the street—Fifth Avenue and 98th Street. It was boiling with activity, and the cacophony of sound assaulted his ears, agitating his nerves.

And what were those? Those great moving vehicles shooting past, and two kids on skateboards sailing by? A giant enclosed omnibus was blocked by a man, bald as a cue ball, dressed in black leather, astride a shiny machine. The omnibus driver blasted his horn, glowered at the bald man and made a violent gesture for him to move. The insulted bald man stuck a finger up and shouted curses. He then kick-started his machine, and it growled to life, with steam exploding from rear pipes, in jets of gray smoke. The machine roared away in an angry retreat and disappeared into a snarl of weaving, chaotic traffic.

There was speed and noise and the chopping sound of something high over his head. Patrick ducked away, shaded his eyes and looked up to see a helicopter beating its way across the sky, like some whirling metallic monster.

In fear and overload, Patrick threw his hands over his ears and clamped his eyes shut. "Stop!" Patrick demanded. "Just stop! Get me out! Out!"

He was flushed and sweating. "Where am I? What's going on, Eve?"

Eve leaned over and calmly whispered in his ear. "Just take it easy. Relax. I tried to tell you. I tried to tell you that you're living in the twenty-first century. I'll get you home."

With spooked eyes and on shaky legs, he let Eve help him into a yellow taxi. He sank into himself, sitting silent and watchful, his hands balled into fists, his eyes fixed ahead, refusing to look to either side as they traveled home.

Had he died and gone to some sort of hell, where noise and movement assailed every sense and bludgeoned every emotion? Was he lost in some perpetual nightmare from which he couldn't wake himself up?

Eve knew what Patrick was going through. It had been the same for her when she had first landed in 1885.

Inside Eve's apartment, Patrick stood trembling by the empty fireplace, staring bleakly. Eve stood next to him, while Georgy Boy sniffed at Patrick's new sneakers.

"I tried to tell you, Patrick," she said gently. "I wanted to make it easier for you."

He was quiet for a long time before he finally spoke. "I don't feel so well. I need to sleep. I have to sleep."

PATRICK SLEPT SOUNDLY until the next morning, Sunday, December 20th. Eve had insisted that he sleep in her queen-sized bed, and he was too weak and beaten by his experience to argue. Eve had slept on the sofa bed.

She was sitting in her small kitchen at the counter when Patrick wandered in, dressed in the light blue pajamas she'd bought for him.

She examined his face. The color had returned to his cheeks and his eyes were clear. The day-old shadow of beard suited him, and his curly, black hair had grown long, thick and sexy.

Eve felt instant desire, but she masked it. "How are you?" she asked, softly. "How do you feel?"

He ran a hand through his hair. "Physically, fine, I think. The other aspect... Well, I don't know, really. I've been staring out your bedroom window at the cars, as you call them. I've been watching the people stroll by and I feel lost in some kind of crazy dream. I am still trying to figure all this out. I just feel..." He lifted a helpless hand. "... lost."

Eve stood up. "It will take time, Patrick. It took me time."

"Time?" he said, quietly, thoughtfully. "Yes, time. I see now, why you couldn't tell me the truth. Yes, I see that now. Who would ever believe... How could you tell anyone about this? I still do not believe it and I see it with my own eyes."

His eyes explored her. She wore jeans, a white sweater and delicate snowflake earrings. Her hair was piled up and pinned on top of her head.

And then, there it was again—that unimaginable, indescribable attraction to her. She was a magnetic miracle to him. A gift of fascination and allure, in any time or in every time. They stayed silent and motionless, just taking in the joy of looking at each other. Their absolute isolation, the truth, and this new intimacy made them both feel excited, yet shy and unsure.

"Are you hungry?" Eve asked.

"Like a big bear."

"Sit down. I'll fix you some eggs. An omelet. I'm a good omelet maker. Meanwhile, I just made fresh coffee."

While he ate, they talked little, mostly about her apartment and Georgy Boy, who lingered near Eve, not letting her out of his sight.

After Patrick had dressed in his previous day's clothes, they sat in the living room, him on the chair by the fireplace with lighted candles, and she on the couch. She explained the TV and her cell phone and showed him her laptop computer. He was afraid to touch it; afraid it might explode.

"How can it give such vast, precise and rapid information? Where does it come from?" he said, glancing about the apartment. "I just don't understand it, Eve."

Eve thought. "Think of it like this. Picture a gigantic library and all the books. Now imagine that this little box, computer, can access anything in the library almost instantaneously."

Patrick's forehead knotted up in thought. "Yes, but how?"

"Kind of like through invisible telegraph wires."

He nodded, pondering it. "Can you communicate with people from other times? Other worlds?"

"Wow, aren't you a forward thinker."

"Wow?" Patrick said playfully. "As in the Bow Wow verse?"

Their eyes met, as they both recalled their conversation in the tea shop in 1885.

"No, we can't communicate with people in other worlds and other times," Eve said thoughtfully. "At least not yet."

As they drank coffee, Eve covered some world history between 1885 and 2016, showing him photos on her laptop, including the Harringshaws. Eve was delighted to see a beautiful shot of John Allister and Evelyn on their wedding day, a photo which had not been there in October when she first researched the family. The newlyweds were shining with happiness.

She watched Patrick's eyes fill with wonder, bright interest and then disappointment.

"I would have thought the wars would have stopped; the killing; the poverty. It's all still here in this time?"

Eve took his hand. "It's better, Patrick. In this time, it's better than it was in 1885. We *are* making progress, even if it's slow. I'm sure there are people who would disagree with me, but I'm an optimist. I believe things are better, and in another 130 or so years, the world will be better still. I'm sure of it."

Patrick stood and paced the room for a while. Then he stopped, tugged on an ear, and stared into space.

"What will I do here, Eve? What can I do in this time? I don't know anything about this time and place. I'm a total stranger. I'm a baby."

Eve got up, went to him, and took his hand. "Anything you want to do, Patrick, you can do. You're smart, young and wildly handsome—my friend Joni says you'd make a great James Bond."

"James Bond?"

"I'll show you all his movies. You'll love them."

"What are movies?"

"Never mind. Anyway, once we get you an identity, you can explore and do whatever appeals to you. There are so many opportunities for a man like you. You'll find something. I know you will."

Georgy Boy nudged Patrick's leg, so he crouched down and scratched him under his chin.

Patrick looked up at Eve. "And what about us, Eve?"

"Us?" she said, swallowing away a flutter.

Patrick straightened and inched close to her. "My feelings for you have not changed. Have yours for me?"

Eve felt the power of the moment—that easy, sexy play of energy—that wonderful connection they'd always had.

"No, Patrick. They have not changed. They've grown. I want us. I want us very much."

"Want us?"

"Yes… I want us to be together, to grow together. I want us to love together."

He reached for her hand. "Oh yes, my lovely Eve. We will definitely love together."

He kissed her, exploring the mouth he'd grown to love, as she moved easily into the wall of his chest, feeling herself melt away into love. Feeling herself in love, consumed by love and blazing with love for the first time in her life. It had all been worth it—her difficult journey into the past. Finding Patrick's love had made everything worthwhile.

"You will marry me then, Miss Kennedy?" Patrick asked, kissing her nose.

"Yes, I will, Detective Sergeant Gantly. But only if you agree to wear a bowler hat every once in a while when you come to bed."

And then in her formal speech Eve said, "I think I shall like that, Detective Sergeant Gantly. Yes, sir, I think I shall like that very much. That hat on your very sexy head always did turn me on."

EPILOGUE

In their 1880s-style antique, one-horse open sleigh, Eve and Patrick swept across a bridge that spanned a wide lake with sunset-painted water. Their bay-colored horse advanced at an easy trot, down winding snowy trails, under snow-heavy trees, breaking out into the glowing white panorama of Central Park.

Eve laughed wildly as Patrick, at the reins and wearing a fur-lined hat, guided the horse easily, the harness bells jingling. Eve broke into a chorus of *Jingle Bells* and Patrick joined in, although he was way off key and didn't know the words. Eve sang and laughed, struggling to harmonize with him, as the sleigh went gliding away along the Bridal Path and a lowering silver sky.

It was Christmas Eve, snow was falling and five inches were already on the ground. They raced on, their faces stinging from the cold, their feet like ice, and their spirits high.

They arrived back home in time to rest, shower and dress for dinner at a nearby restaurant with Joni, her boyfriend and a few other friends. Afterwards, they all planned to attend a Christmas Eve service.

Eve's parents were arriving on Christmas Day morning, staying at a hotel in midtown. Eve and Patrick anticipated the meeting with apprehension and concern, but they didn't let it dampen their mood. Eve's father had already begun working on Patrick's new identity, but he wanted to meet the man and ask him "a thousand questions," something Patrick was not looking forward to. Mr. Sharland had demanded that Eve tell him the entire story—the unvarnished truth—about what had happened to her, how she had met Patrick, and why she was going to marry him.

Patrick was resting in the bedroom. Eve had just dressed in her new red dress and was brushing her hair when the doorbell rang. She hurried to the hallway, thinking it was a package delivery. She pressed the speaker button.

"Who is it?" she asked.

A scratchy male voice responded. "Miss Evelyn Sharland?"

"Yes. Who is it?"

"Mark Wallingford. I'm an attorney."

Eve stared at the speaker in mild surprise. "What's this about?"

"May I come in, Miss Sharland?"

"It's Christmas Eve," Eve said.

"Yes, Miss Sharland. I won't take up much of your time. It is rather important."

Patrick appeared in the living room, sleepy-eyed, putting a fist to a yawn. "Who is it?"

"An attorney."

"On Christmas Eve?"

Eve shrugged.

Patrick left to put on a fresh shirt.

The doorbell rang and Eve smoothed out her dress before opening the door. A small, officious looking man, with closely cropped gray hair and black-rimmed spectacles, stared at her with cool, business-like eyes. He was dressed in a topcoat that had a dusting of snow on the shoulders, and he was carrying a worn leather briefcase.

"Miss Sharland, I presume?"

"Yes, come in," Eve said, stepping aside.

The man entered, and Eve took his cashmere topcoat and hung it up in the hall closet.

She offered him the chair by the fireplace, and he sat down.

After Patrick entered and introduced himself, he sat on the couch next to Eve.

"Would you like a drink, Mr. Wallingford?" Eve asked.

"No, thank you."

Mr. Wallingford then snapped open his briefcase and drew out a powder-blue envelope. He stood up, stepped over and handed it to Eve. She stood and took it, questioningly.

Mr. Wallingford returned to his chair, his expression affably somber.

"Please open it and read the enclosed letter, Miss Sharland. I will wait as you do so."

"What is it?" Eve asked. "Can you at least explain what all this is about?"

Mr. Wallingford licked his lips and adjusted his glasses. "Miss Sharland, I represent the Harringshaw family."

Eve eased back down, unsteadily, and then she and Patrick exchanged stunned glances.

"The Harringshaw family? What's this about?" Eve said, feeling sudden unease.

Mr. Wallingford indicated to the letter. "I do not know the contents of the letter, Miss Sharland, nor does anyone else. It was addressed to you and only to you— For Your Eyes Only. I was instructed to deliver the letter and then have you sign a consent form, indicating that you have read said letter, and that you agree to its contents."

Eve looked at Patrick again, and her eyes widened a bit. He nodded. Eve inserted her thumb under the sealed flap and opened it. Hesitating, she slowly drew out the cream-colored bond letter that had been folded twice. She smoothed out the two creases, took in a little breath and began to read.

Dear Miss Kennedy, or should I say Miss Evelyn Sharland:

If you are reading this letter, then my suspicions, no matter how strange, melodramatic and surprising even to me, are quite correct. At any rate, forgive an old man who is in the last weeks of his life and whose lovely wife, Evelyn, has gone to heaven already five years before, to wait on him.

Perhaps, Miss Sharland, you will recall our last conversation in my dear wife's hospital room at the Gouverneur Hospital back in December 1885. I certainly do, although forty-five years have passed.

Evelyn related your incredible and imaginative time travel story to me in the greatest of detail, as I'm certain you will recall my telling you so. Perhaps you will recall I queried you about the story, because you had been quite specific as to your home address and the year you had said you had traveled from. Your story was precise and rich in every detail, which raised my interest to a keen level.

In any event, neither Evelyn nor I thought much more about it until you simply vanished. You and Detective Sergeant Gantly, that is, the brave detective who saved my brother, Albert, from certain death.

Perhaps, then, you can imagine the confusion and astonishment caused by your sudden disappearance. My brother and Inspector Byrnes spent much time and money searching for you both, but to no avail, for which they were quite vexed and bewildered. I conjecture that losing a suspect had never happened to the great Inspector Byrnes before. He was quite beside himself. Very miffed and agitated.

All that was ever found was a lantern on a park bench in Central Park, but then even that promptly disappeared and it has never been found or accounted for. As I recall, one of the ambulance drivers who worked at the hospital admitted that he and another employee had driven you out to the park and deposited you and Detective Sergeant Gantly on a park bench. This ambulance driver was questioned relentlessly, but nothing ever came of it. He simply stated that you and Detective Sergeant Gantly vanished into the night.

With regard to the lantern, after your disappearance, I spoke to Mr. Clayton Sharland, and he confirmed that, despite your declaration to me that you did not find Evelyn's lantern, he was witness to your purchasing the same lantern from a little girl the very

*morning of your disappearance. I found the whole af-
fair rather mysterious and quite unbelievable at the
time. But since then, I have had time to recollect those
days, especially since the death of dear Evelyn. My
mind has been changed, Miss Sharland, and perhaps
that is due to age and coming to the end of my life; a
long but a very good life, thanks in no small measure to
you.*

*You may be interested to know what became of Miss
Helen Price. Your friend, Dr. Eckland, generously tes-
tified in her defense at her trial, claiming that she had
been a virtuous woman who had indeed been deprived
of her virtue. He also helped the defense, claiming that
Helen Price was under the influence of "female hyste-
ria" at the time she fired the shot that was meant for my
brother. Perhaps you may recall that at that time, medical theories held that women could be driven crazy because of their reproductive system.*

*In any event, Miss Price was acquitted, to my broth-
er's infinite disappointment and indignation. Miss
Price fled to Europe—Italy, I believe—where she married and had children, although the number is unclear.
According to my sources, Miss Price passed from this
world in 1919, during the world-wide influenza epidem-
ic.*

*As to Dr. Eckland, in retaliation for his defense of
Miss Price, my brother tarnished the good doctor's
reputation and sought to ruin his career, which, I am
sad to say, he accomplished. After all, the good doctor
did turn against his class, or so the papers of the day
stated.*

Dr. Eckland was made a social outcast. His remaining years were spent with Dr. Long at the Gouverneur Hospital. They became good friends and valued colleagues. My last conversation with the doctor found him in high spirits and good humor. For his part, and to his enduring credit, he told me that he never regretted what he had done for Miss Helen Price. He said he loved his work at the hospital and that he had learned much from Dr. Long.

He spoke kindly of you, Miss Sharland, relating that it was you who first brought him to the hospital, the same night that Detective Sergeant Gantly so gallantly took the shot meant for my brother (who, incidentally, perished on the Lusitania in 1915, along with 1,197 other poor souls).

Dr. Eckland said how thankful and delighted he was to be working alongside Dr. Long, helping the distressed women, the ragged children and the poor, who had no other refuge—nowhere else to go.

Dr. Eckland died a peaceful and a happy man in 1891. His funeral was attended by crowds of the poor and the rich alike, and I believe he would have smiled with humble satisfaction to have witnessed it. Dr. Long spoke eloquently at his funeral, saying 'Dr. Eckland was a good and a kind man, and a dedicated doctor, who possessed a generous spirit and an even larger heart.'

Miss Sharland, I have never forgotten your kind and generous nature as it was directed toward my dear Evelyn. Quite simply put, you saved her life and, in thus doing so, you also saved mine. We had thirty-nine wonderful years together, before Evelyn passed away in May 1925. I will always be eternally grateful to you.

Accordingly, I have placed a sum of money into a trust in your name, with clear and definite instructions to my attorneys that the letter you are now reading not be opened by anyone except yourself at the right and proper time. It will be delivered to you at your address on West 107th Street, on Christmas Eve, December 24th, in the year 2016.

I visited that brownstone only the week before this writing, and I have fondly speculated about your receiving this letter, Miss Sharland. I have dreamed about your time and sorely wish there were some way that I could witness the day you receive this letter. The street is a quiet one, and the brownstone that you will one day occupy is most attractive. As you are aware, back in 1885, West 107th Street did not exist, so this was a particularly special treat for me. And to think, you have not yet been born, although I have met you and you have changed my life in inconceivable ways. The world is indeed a mysterious place filled with many wonders.

I believe you will receive this letter, Miss Sharland, so please accept the trust as a small token of my gratitude and my good wishes for you. May you live the happiest of lives as mine has been, but would not have been, had you not come to rescue my beloved Evelyn, and the man who loved her with all his heart until the instant she took her last breath. Shall I say it, Miss Sharland, as I write this with wet eyes on Christmas Eve? Shall this old and dying Gilded Age romantic say that I love Evelyn still and will love her for all time, and

*in whatever time we may or may not find ourselves?
After all, love is the greatest mystery of all, is it not,
Miss Sharland? For true love uplifts, it bears all
things, it lightens our hearts, and it brings inexpressible
happiness—and it is eternal, so I believe.*

*Merry Christmas, Miss Sharland.
With gratitude and with warm affection,
Yours,
John Allister Harringshaw
Newport, Rhode Island, December 24, 1930*

Eve reached for a tissue and blotted her eyes. She
handed the letter to Patrick, and he read it quietly, while
Mr. Wallingford patiently waited, reaching over several
times to rub Georgy Boy's head, who lay contentedly at
the man's feet.

Eve and Patrick sat erect and still, as Mr. Wallingford read the total amount of the trust.

"After taxes, and with interest accrued over a period
of eighty-six years, the total amount which will be deposited into your account, comes to five million, six
hundred and fifty-four thousand, two hundred and
twenty-one dollars."

Mr. Wallingford looked up into Eve's and Patrick's
faces, which were blank with shock.

AFTER MR. WALLINGFORD LEFT, Eve called
Joni and told her that she and Patrick might be late for
dinner. They wanted to play in the snow with Georgy
Boy. She didn't tell Joni about the sudden windfall.
Eve and Patrick needed time alone together to regain
their composure and to discuss their future plans now
that everything had changed yet again.

413

And then Joni said something that froze Eve in place.

"Oh, by the way, Eve. I forgot to tell you that I have the lantern you bought at that antique shop. It was on the park bench next to your purse and cell phone. I thought you might want it back. Should I bring it over tonight?"

Eve had pushed the lantern completely from her mind. She'd thought about it, for sure, but she'd assumed it had vanished. She hadn't asked Joni about it because she didn't want to know. Out of sight, out of mind. The idea of it made her jumpy and confused.

"Joni, you said the police called you because you were on my cell phone contact list."

"Yes."

"And when you met with the police, you showed them my last text to you, and you told them that, most likely, you were the last person I'd contacted before I disappeared? And you told them you had Georgy Boy?"

"Yes. All of that. I told you that."

Eve's jaw clenched and then released. "Joni, the man who found my purse, my cell phone and the lantern, did he report finding anything else?"

"No. Nothing else."

"He didn't report finding an old letter?"

"No. There was no letter."

"Okay, Joni, thanks," Eve said, uneasily.

"You sound funny," Joni said.

"It's nothing. Yes, bring the lantern tonight. Yes, I'd like to have it." And then as an afterthought. "At least, I think I'd like to have it."

After hanging up, Eve stood, lost in thought. Of course there was no original Christmas Eve letter, because John Allister had never written it. The letter never existed, so it was never placed in the lantern. The letter wasn't written because Eve had gone back in time and changed history. Evelyn Sharland had survived. John Allister and Evelyn Sharland were surely together on Christmas Eve 1885. There was no need to write that sad Christmas Eve letter.

Eve stood mystified. But *she* had the memory of finding the letter and the memory of reading it. What did that mean? The letter is what had originally touched her and helped to send her back in time. If there was no original letter, then was Eve now living in an altered world, remembering yet another?

The Christmas Eve Letter was now the letter John Harringshaw had written to her in 1930. So what was this world Eve was living in now? Georgy Boy was a different color. She was living in a different apartment. As the days went by, would Eve become aware of other differences and subtle events that were not part of her original life before she embarked on her journey to 1885?

Eve felt a jab of fear. In her own small way, she had changed the course of history. In this world—the world she was now living—Eve had never found John Allister's letter in Granny Gilbert's antique store, because it didn't exist.

So then what about the lantern? Did it hold any power in this time? Was it still a beacon—a conduit that could somehow connect the old world with the new world? Okay. Then which old world? Which the new world? More importantly, should she destroy the lantern or should she take it back to Central Park, light it and see what happens?

Patrick came in from the kitchen. "Everything okay?"

Eve nodded, lost in her own stare. "Yeah, yes, I think so."

"Ready for our Christmas Eve walk, Miss Kennedy/Sharland?" he asked, coming up to her with a playful grin. He leaned down and kissed her longingly.

Eve kissed him back, pressing herself into him and whispering her love for him. She stroked his cheek, feeling the day-old beard. "Yes, Mr. Detective, let's go."

Patrick struggled into his black overcoat, hat and gloves, and then fastened Georgy Boy's leash, while Eve swung into her black wool coat, red woolen cap and gloves. Eve switched off the Christmas tree lights and, before she left the apartment, she paused a moment to glance around, to remember the first night she'd read John Allister's letter; the night she had been so touched by it; the night she had felt so terribly lonely.

She smiled with calm satisfaction. What did it matter what world or what time it was? What did any of it matter? She loved her new world. She loved Patrick Gantly, with all her heart, and whatever the challenges—whatever the surprises or the hardships—they'd face them all together, as husband and wife. That's all that mattered now.

"Coming, Eve?" Patrick called from downstairs.

Outside, Eve paused to look up at her brownstone, as large lacy snowflakes drifted down. She thought of John Allister and she stamped about in the snow until she figured she was standing on the same spot he had stood in 1930, just before he'd written the Christmas Eve letter to her. She smiled at the thought, and she wished Mr. and Mrs. John Allister Harringshaw a Merry Christmas, wherever they were.

Eve, Patrick and Georgy Boy ambled over to Riverside Park. It was a magical snowy night, with a soft wind and heavy gray moving clouds. In the distance they heard carolers singing *Silent Night*, and the sound of it warmed them and brought them closer.

Kids pulling sleds and red plastic toboggans hurried by, pointing to a far hill where the best sledding was. Eve heard the children's shouts and high laughter. Maybe later, she and Patrick would swing by and watch them or, better yet, maybe they'd join in and make some runs down the snowy slopes in an old wooden sled.

Georgy Boy sniffed at the ground and then snorted, picking up a scent even in the snow. Eve and Patrick took hands and roamed aimlessly along the snowy carriage path, their breath puffing out white clouds. They stopped once, looked at each other lovingly, and then kissed under an amber park lamp.

And then Patrick said something, but the whistling wind covered his voice.

When he leaned toward her and repeated it, Eve laughed, went to tip toes and kissed him. She grabbed his hand and tugged him and Georgy Boy off into a hazy curtain of falling snow

Thank you for taking the time to read *The Christmas Eve Letter*. If you enjoyed it, please consider telling your friends or posting a short review. Word of mouth is an author's best friend and it is much appreciated.

Thank you,
Elyse Douglas

Other novels by Elyse Douglas that you might enjoy:

The Christmas Diary Book 1
The Christmas Diary Lost and Found Book 2
The Lost Mata Hari Ring – A Time Travel Novel
Time Stranger – A Time Travel Novel

Book 2 The Christmas Eve Daughter – A Time Travel Novel
Book 3 The Christmas Eve Secret – A Time Travel Novel
Book 4 The Christmas Eve Promise – A Time Travel Novel
Book 5 The Christmas Eve Journey– A Time Travel Novel

The Christmas Women
Christmas for Juliet
Christmas Ever After
The Summer Diary

The Other Side of Summer
The Summer Letters
The Summer Diary
Daring Summer

The Christmas Town – A Time Travel Novel
Time Stranger– A Time Travel Novel
Time Sensitive – A Time Travel Novel
Time Change – A Time Travel Novel

www.elysedouglas.com

Made in the USA
Las Vegas, NV
01 December 2021

35804075R00236